Praise for Paige

'Another perfect summer page-turner from Paige Toon'

Mirror

'I loved it – I couldn't put it down!'

Marian Keyes

'Wonderful, addictive, sharp and sexy'

Cosmopolitan

'Brilliant . . . one of the rising stars of chick-lit'

Heat

'Laugh-out-loud funny and touchingly honest. This is summer's poolside reading sorted!'

Company

'Charming and romantic. Real old-school chick-lit, like they used to make in the old days'

Lisa Jewell

'Witty and sexy – perfect holiday reading material'

Closer

'A fast-paced and funny read . . . Superior chick-lit with great jokes and a thoughtful heart'

Daily Express

Also by Paige Toon

Lucy in the Sky

Johnny Be Good

Chasing Daisy

Pictures of Lily

Baby Be Mine

Paige Toon

One Perfect Summer

SIMON & SCHUSTER

London · New York · Sydney · Toronto · New Delhi

First published in Great Britain by Simon & Schuster UK Ltd, 2012
A CBS COMPANY

1 3 5 7 9 10 8 6 4 2

Simon & Schuster UK Ltd
1st Floor
222 Gray's Inn Road
London WC1X 8HB

Simon & Schuster Australia, Sydney
Simon & Schuster India, New Delhi

www.simonandschuster.co.uk

A CIP catalogue record for this book
is available from the British Library

B Format ISBN 978-1-84983-128-4
EBook ISBN 978-1-84983-129-1

Typeset by M Rules
Printed and bound by CPI Group (UK) Ltd, Croydon, CR0 4YY

For Nigel Stoneman
who, with five little words, helped
make my dreams come true

ONE PERFECT SUMMER

When I Was Eighteen . . .

Chapter 1

'There'll be bluebirds over . . .'

'We're going to Dorset, not Dover, Mum.' I interrupt as she launches into another rendition of 'The White Cliffs Of Dover.'

'I know, but I can sing, can't I?' She pretends to be wounded.

'It would be better if you stuck to painting,' I tease.

She flashes me a grin and I smile back at her from the front passenger seat.

'This is going to be fun!' she exclaims, reaching for the knob on the car's radio. She's about to settle for Heart so I quickly intervene. Dammit, there's no XFM this far out of London!

'iPod?' I suggest hopefully.

'Go on, then,' she concedes. 'Anything to get you in the holiday mood.'

'I am in the holiday mood,' I try to convince her as I plug in my brand-new white MP3 player – a present from my parents for my recent birthday. Mum gives me a discerning look before returning her eyes to the road.

'I know you're disappointed Lizzy can't come, but you'll still have a good time. Plus, you'll be able to get started on all your university reading.'

'Mmm.'

'Over' by Portishead begins to play.

'For goodness sake, Alice, this is making me want to slit my wrists!' protests Mum after a while. 'I mean it,' she continues when I ignore her. 'Something more upbeat. *Please!*'

I sigh, but comply. Madonna's 'Holiday' starts belting out from the speakers.

'This is more like it!' She starts to sing again.

'*Mu-um*,' I moan. 'Remember your vocation.'

She laughs. 'That's a big word for a teenager. Aah, but you *are* going to Cambridge University.'

'University *in* Cambridge, not the University *of* Cambridge,' I correct her for what feels like the umpteenth time. I'm actually going to Anglia Ruskin, but she seems to forget the details when relaying this fact to her friends.

'It's still a big deal,' she says and I don't disagree because it's nice to have proud parents. Then she's off again: '*Holiday!*'

And like they say, if you can't beat 'em, join 'em, so I do.

My mum is an artist. She specialises in painting abstract landscapes using oils, and incorporating other materials like metal, sand and stone. She's struggled for years to make decent money, so although her last collection sold well, my dad is still the main breadwinner. He's working at his accounting job in London during the week and will be joining us in Dorset at the weekends. It's the middle of July now and we'll be here until the end of August. Mum plans on spending these six weeks working on her new collection which, to her delight, is being exhibited at a super-cool East London gallery in September.

As for me, initially I agreed to this long summer break because my best friend, Lizzy, was going to come too. She's heading off to university in Edinburgh and we're both sad at the idea of leaving each other. We've spent the last few years living practically in each other's pockets, so this will be the end of an era. The pair of us envisaged long, lazy summer days sunbathing in the garden or borrowing Mum's car to go to the beach. But Lizzy's mum, Susan, recently discovered she had a lump in one of her breasts, which turned out to be malignant. The shock was immense and I still feel absolutely sick at the thought of what my friend and her family are going through. Susan is having an operation this week to remove the lump and then will have to undergo chemotherapy; so, needless to say, Lizzy needs to be with her right now.

'Isn't this pretty?' Mum says. I look out of the window at the rolling green hills. 'Look! Are those wild horses?' She doesn't wait for me to answer, not that I'd know. 'You could have riding lessons while you're here. And there's a castle not too far from where we're staying. You can catch a steam train from Swanage that takes you all the way there.'

'I know, you've told me already.'

'Well, that will be fun, won't it?'

'Sure,' I reply non-committally. It *would* have been fun. If Lizzy were here. Oh, I hope her mum is going to be okay . . .

'You might make some new friends,' Mum suggests hopefully, oblivious to my inner turmoil.

'I'm not eight anymore,' I reply with a wry smile.

'I know, but you'll have a good time,' she says again.

I think she's trying to convince herself of that as much as she's trying to convince me.

The cottage where we're staying is off the beaten track. It's built out of cream stone, and a dry stone wall encloses a small, grassy garden at the back. There's a bench seat out at the front in full sunshine and I can already picture myself sitting there and tackling some of my English Lit books.

The place has been recently renovated, and it feels cosy and clean. Mum puts the kettle on and unpacks milk from the cool-box while I sit at the kitchen table and look over the manual left by the owners.

My mum is tall and slim with shoulder-length blonde hair and green eyes. I take after my dad's side of the family. I'm shorter at five foot five inches tall and I have long, very-dark-brown-almost-black hair. My eyes, although green like my mother's, have a slightly Oriental look about them. My paternal grandmother was Chinese, but she died before I was born.

'What does it say about things to do around here?' Mum asks as she puts a cup of tea down in front of me.

'Pretty much everything you've already told me,' I reply. 'Apparently there are some nice walks along the cliff if you go up there.' I point in the opposite direction to the way we came in. 'There's also a pub within walking distance if you head that way.' More pointing.

'That sounds promising. Maybe we could go there for an early dinner and then relax in front of the telly for the night?'

We drive to the pub because, despite having sat in a car for almost three hours, neither of us has the energy to walk.

Our nearest village is lovely. Limestone cottages with painted window frames in shades of blue and green line the streets, and the sea is visible across the rolling hills. We walk up the steps to the pub. There are grey stone tables and bench seats outside with views towards the sea and we decide to come out here to sit down, but first we head inside to have a nose around, and to order.

I see him almost immediately, the guy working behind the bar. He's tall – about six foot one or two – has chin-length, dead-straight black hair and his right eyebrow is pierced with a silver ring. He's pulling a pint and looking down, but as he glances up his dark eyes momentarily meet mine. POW! I know how crazy this sounds, but it feels like my heart has just leapt out of my chest and slammed into him.

Then he's looking down again, filling the pint glass to the brim and carrying it, somehow without spilling a drop, to a middle-aged man at the other end of the bar. The hairs on the back of my neck are standing up. Mum snaps me out of it.

'He looks to be about your age,' she says, gleefully nudging me as she nods in the direction of the unsettlingly attractive bartender.

'Shh!' I warn, inwardly cringing and trying, but failing, to tear my eyes away from him as he takes money from the man and goes to the till. He comes our way and my pulse quickens.

'What can I get you?'

A big, burly man with short, gelled black hair and enormous tattoos on his arms has materialised in front of us. The disappointment is intense.

'A glass of white wine, please,' Mum asks pleasantly. 'Alice?'

'Um . . .' My eyes dart towards the guy, but he's already taking another order. 'Half a cider, please.' The man gets on with the job without another word. He's wearing a white vest and his dark chest hairs are visible beneath the fabric. I wonder if he's the gorgeous boy's father. He plonks a half-pint glass full of honey-coloured liquid in front of me. Some of it sloshes over the brim, but he makes no apologies, nor does he smile as he requests money or when he returns Mum's change. I feel oddly uneasy about him.

'Do you have any menus?' Mum asks him.

'We don't do food,' comes his gruff reply.

I glance over my shoulder as I follow Mum through the door, and then I'm outside in the late-afternoon sunshine.

'This is nice,' Mum says when we sit down. 'He was a bit tasty.' She nudges me again, once more snapping me out of my reverie.

'Mum, no one says "tasty" anymore.' I sound unbothered, even though I'm not.

I try to concentrate while she engages in conversation, but soon the gentle sound of clinking glass from behind us makes me turn around. I realise with a flurry of nerves that he's there, collecting empties from recently vacated tables.

'Hello!' my mum calls cheerfully.

Oh, Christ, Mum, *shut up*!

'Alright?' He gives her a vague smile and his eyes flicker towards mine. POW! That feeling again. It's like I'm made of metal and he's a powerful magnet. What on earth has got into me?

'We're on holiday,' Mum tells him. 'Can you recommend anything nice to do around here?'

'Um . . .' He stands upright and thinks for a moment, holding the glasses he's collected between his fingers. 'Have you been to Corfe Castle yet?'

'We've only just arrived.' She shrugs and smiles.

He's wearing black jeans and a black indie-rock T-shirt. My kind of guy.

'Where are you staying?' he asks, glancing at me. I'm unable to speak so, thankfully, Mum does.

'In a little cottage over those fields. We're here for six weeks, so if you've got any ideas . . .'

A dog starts to bark and his head shoots around towards the pub. Almost on cue, the big, burly man storms out.

'JOE! Sort it out,' he shouts angrily.

Joe . . . The gorgeous boy has a name . . . Well, of course he has a name, Alice.

'Coming,' Joe shouts back wearily. 'Gotta take my dog for a walk,' he says to us as he turns away.

'Do you want some company?' Mum calls after him hopefully, as the annoying nudging arm comes out to play once more. 'Alice is desperate to meet people her own age.'

'Mum, no!' I hiss, mortified.

He looks at me as my face turns bright red and I would give anything – *anything* – for the ground to open up and swallow me, or for an enormous Pterodactyl to swoop down from the sky and gobble me up. I really don't care, I'm not fussy, I just DO NOT want to be here right now.

'JOE!' the man shouts again, interrupting any reply.

'No, no, it's okay, you go ahead,' I manage to splutter.

'Okay. See you around.' He quickly makes an exit. My face continues to burn as I bury it in my hands.

'That was so embarrassing!' I screech under my breath.

'Why?' Mum asks.

'I cannot believe you just did that,' I moan.

'Goodness sake, Alice, he's just a boy,' she replies, sounding all uppity.

But he's not. He's not 'just a boy'. Do not ask me how I know this, but somewhere, deep inside, my heart has already started to fracture and I know that Joe has everything to do with it.

Chapter 2

Back at the cottage, I found myself lying on my bed and staring up at the ceiling thinking about You Know Who. And then it occurs to me that I might bump into him if he's walking his dog . . . I hurry downstairs.

'I'm going to go for a walk.'

Mum tears her eyes away from her sketchpad and looks up at me. 'We can watch telly together, if you like?'

'No, don't worry. I need some fresh air.'

The wind has picked up so I tie my hair into a loose bun and slip on my waterproof and wellies, in case it's muddy. I turn left onto the track and follow a sign for Priest's Way. After a while I see another sign for something called Dancing Ledge. That sounds pretty. I carry on walking. There are a few people out and about, and every time I see a dog before its owner I jolt with anticipation. I know I'm being an idiot, but I'm bored; I can daydream.

I turn right into a grassy field and make my way along a stone track lined with wild flowers. The sea is visible up ahead –

shimmering dark blue in the hazy evening sunlight – and I pause for a moment to breathe in the fresh air.

God, he was gorgeous. I feel nervous at the thought of seeing him again, but I'll be dragging Mum to that pub tomorrow, whether she likes it or not.

I remember with sudden mortification how she told Joe I was 'desperate' – and how I blushed! He couldn't escape fast enough. I instantly feel deflated and I almost decide to return to the cottage, but I've come so far, I may as well see this Dancing Ledge, whatever that may be. I pass through a gate and then the path narrows and becomes rockier and steeper, leading me downwards between tall gorse hedges. It's sheltered from the wind here, and then suddenly . . . well, I have never been a nature freak, but the view as I come out of the gorse nearly takes my breath away. In front of me is a grassy slope which seems to roll away to a sudden stop. To my left, more rolling hills jut away at the cliff edge. It's breathtaking, and slightly scary, but I wander a little way down the slope and sit on the grass. No wonder Mum chose Dorset as a destination – she should come here to paint.

A big, black, shaggy-haired dog bounds past me, coming from the direction of the gorse walkway. He runs towards the cliff edge and I tense up, but then he turns around and comes my way. I hold out my hand to him and smile – I like dogs – and he rewards me by manically wagging his tail and panting the biggest doggy smile I've ever seen.

'Hello!' I say as I pat him vigorously. Out of curiosity I glance behind to look for his owner and then . . . *no way*! I must be psychic or something, because there he is! JOE! It's bloody Joe! My stomach swirls with Amazonian-sized butterflies as he approaches.

'DYSON!' he shouts with a furious wave of his hand. 'AWAY!'

Dyson, who I'm assuming is the dog, starts to bark like a nutcase before chasing his own tail. Joe shakes his head with amusement and then Dyson launches himself at me and knocks me backwards.

'Oh, shit! Sorry!' Joe exclaims, rushing over and dragging his dog off me. 'DOWN, BOY!' he shouts at his dog. 'Are you okay?' he asks with concern.

'I'm fine,' I manage to splutter.

His face breaks into a grin as he looks at me directly. 'It's you.'

'Yep, it's me.'

My nerves – strangely – have dissipated. Then he collapses down on the grass next to me and I nearly have a heart attack.

'Alice, right?'

'Yeah.'

'I'm Joe.'

'Hi.' My face heats up so I look at Dyson. 'I thought he was going to fall off the cliff.'

'It's a steep slope all the way down. There's a fence at the bottom.'

'Aah, okay. Dyson is a funny name for a dog.' Said dog is now sprawled out in a coma-like position next to him.

'I named him after the vacuum cleaner.' Joe reaches across and pats him. Dyson's tail pounds the grass as it wags.

'What do you mean?'

'He snaffles up rubbish on the pavement like it's steak.'

'Yuck!' I pull a face and laugh.

'He's one gross dog,' he says affectionately. 'So you're here for six weeks?'

'Yeah.' I focus on his chunky black boots. I feel tongue-tied.

Come on, Alice, talk or he'll walk! 'My mum's a painter,' I explain quickly.

'Oh, right. That's cool.'

'Was that your dad working at the pub?'

He rolls his eyes and pulls up a handful of grass. 'Yeah.'

'Don't you get on?'

He looks across at me. His eyes are so dark. 'Not particularly,' he replies.

And then there's that feeling again, that magnet, pulling me in. For pity's sake, I said I was psychic, but at this rate psycho would be more apt.

'Have you lived here for long?' I ask, trying not to act like a crazy person.

'Only since May.' He breaks eye contact and I feel an immediate sense of relief. He rests back on his elbows.

'Where were you before?'

'Somerset, then Cornwall. We've lived in Dorset before, though. We used to have a pub in Lyme Regis.'

'Wow. You move around a lot.'

'Not by choice,' he admits, turning the tables before I can press him further. 'Where do you live?'

'London.'

'Which part?'

'North London. East Finchley. Do you know it?'

'No. I don't know London very well. But I'm going to move there soon.'

'Really?' My heart leaps and then crashes when I remember I'm off to Cambridge in September. I tell him this.

'Are you? Why?'

'I'm going to university.' His eyes widen. 'The former

polytechnic,' I hurriedly explain. 'I'm not smart enough for the actual university.'

'I'm not smart enough for *any* university,' he replies.

'I'm sure that's not true,' I feel compelled to say.

'It is.' He shrugs and stares ahead. 'But I'm getting out of here, anyway.' He stands up. 'I've gotta get back. Tomorrow night is *Quiz Night*,' he says with derision. 'And I've got to write the questions. Which way are you going?'

'Back up there.' I scramble to my feet and point to the gorse walkway.

'I'll walk you.' Re-*sult*! 'You know, seeing as you're desperate for company, and all that,' he adds. I blush, but he elbows me jokily.

'Bugger off,' I reply and his corresponding laugh fills me with warmth.

He has a grey hoodie tied around his waist and his bare arms are tanned from the rare heatwave we've been enjoying this summer. I unzip my waterproof to let some air in – the exercise has warmed me up, too. We walk side by side as we navigate the rocky path.

I return to our conversation. 'This place is so beautiful. Why would you want to leave?'

'Yeah, it's pretty nice, but . . . I don't know. Im leaving as soon as I get a car, I'm out of here.'

'Are you taking Dyson with you?'

'Of course.' He frowns. 'I wouldn't leave him with my parents.'

'Why do you work for them?' I ask, seeing as they clearly don't get on.

'I can't afford to move out yet, but working pays my rent.'

'They make you pay *rent*?'

'Well, I *am* eighteen. Just.' He snorts. 'Not that they didn't have me working behind a bar for a few years before that . . .'

'Isn't that illegal?'

'Yep,' he replies bluntly.

I can't imagine my parents ever charging me to live at home with them, or putting me to work behind a bar when I was just a kid. Maybe I'm naive.

Dyson runs ahead and we soon catch up to see him trying to drag an impossibly large stick out from underneath a tree. He drops it and growls at it before barking at Joe and wagging his tail.

'You daft dog,' Joe says, shaking his head. 'You can't play fetch with that.' Dyson barks again. 'Find a smaller one. Go on!'

Nope. Dyson wants that one.

'I'm not throwing it,' Joe says adamantly, and there's something endearing about the way he speaks to his dog.

Woof!

'No.'

Woof, woof, woof!

'Bloody hell,' Joe mutters, grabbing one end of the stick while stamping hard on it somewhere in the middle. With a crack, the wood snaps in half. I watch, smiling, as he throws it a hefty distance into the field and a deliriously delighted Dyson bounds after it.

'You softy,' I say.

'Too soft.' He glances sideways at me.

'How long have you had him?' I ask.

'About two years. I found him roaming the beach when we lived in Cornwall. He followed me home and I made the mistake of feeding him. He wouldn't leave me alone after that.'

'I wonder who he belonged to.'

Dyson returns with the stick so Joe throws it again. 'Who knows? He didn't have a collar. He was really scrawny, so either he was treated badly or he'd been homeless for a while. My dad nearly kicked off when he found out I was giving him leftovers from the pub kitchen.'

'Why should he care? Waste not, want not, right?'

'He can't stand dogs.'

'Why did he let you keep him, then?'

'He was pretty distracted at the time.'

'What with?'

'You're going to know my whole life story at this rate.' He grins at me and changes the subject. 'Alright, then, Brainiac, help me come up with some questions for this stupid quiz.'

By the time we reach the cottage, I've found out that Joe has the same taste as me in music, TV and film, so it's been an amusing walk back trying to outdo each other with our knowledge of indie rock, British comedy classics and sci-fi flicks.

'I'm going to have to come to this quiz now, just so I can win,' I say.

He laughs and leans back against the cream-painted wooden gate. My nerves swiftly return. 'I haven't finished with the questions yet. I might put in something about *Big Brother*, just to trick you.'

'That would mean watching it. Are you sure you've got the stomach for that sort of research?' I ask drily.

'Actually, no.' He stares at me and the butterflies go berserk. 'So you're coming, then? To the pub tomorrow night?'

'Is that okay?'

He smiles. 'Definitely.'

I smile back at him. 'Cool.'

'Right, then. See you tomorrow.'

'See you tomorrow.'

We stand awkwardly for a brief moment until he realises he's blocking my way. He leaps away from the gate and then recovers by reaching over and undoing the latch.

'Thanks.' I'm still beaming as I pass. 'See you tomorrow,' I say again as he closes the gate after me.

'See ya.' He turns away and clicks his fingers at Dyson. 'Come on, boy.'

I stand and watch them until they're out of sight.

Chapter 3

'Name the vessel aboard which Luke Skywalker meets Princess Leia for the first time.'

I hastily scribble down an answer on my sheet of paper.

'Alice . . .'

I glance up at my mum's disapproving face. 'What?'

'Do you really think you should be participating in this quiz if you helped with all the questions?'

'I didn't help with all the questions!' I snap. 'He came up with these ones on his own. It's not my fault we've got the same taste.'

I look over at Joe behind the bar. He looks amused as his mother – a heavy-set woman with frizzy, dyed-blonde hair, heavy eye make-up and an orange tan – reads the next question.

'Who walked out of the *Big Brother* house on Day 20 of this year's series?'

'You bastard,' I mouth at Joe. He laughs and carries on pulling a pint.

'What? Don't you know that one?' Mum asks me wryly.

'No. Happy now?'

She raises her eyebrows. 'I suppose so.'

Today felt like one of the longest days of my life. Mum worked and I sat around trying, but failing, to get into my university reading. All I could think about was seeing Joe again. I would have gone to the pub at lunchtime if I hadn't thought I'd look desperate.

'Ladies and gents, we're just going to take a short break and we'll resume in a minute,' Joe's mum tells us in a thick West Country accent. Strangely, Joe may have been brought up around here, but his accent isn't nearly as broad as his parents'.

'I'm going to nip to the loo. Do you want another on my way back?' Mum indicates my drink.

'Sure.'

I scan my quiz sheet to check my answers.

'Alright?'

With a start, I look up to see Joe standing there.

'Budge up.' He nudges me so I shift along the bench seat.

'*Big Brother*?' I ask him with a raised eyebrow.

'I had to resort to internet research. Wait until you get to the question about *Pop Idol*.'

I groan comically and he laughs. 'What are you doing tomorrow?'

'Nothing,' I reply hopefully.

'Want to go to Corfe Castle with me?'

Is this a *date*?

'Sure!'

'There's a bus stop at the end of the road. We can catch the bus to Swanage and then take the train to Corfe Castle.'

'Is this the steam train?'

'Yeah.'

'I could drive us to Swanage, if you like? I could borrow Mum's car.'

'In that case, you could drive us to Corfe Castle.'

'Where's the fun in that? I want to take the train . . .'

'Actually, me too.'

'JOE!' his mum barks from the bar.

'Coming,' Joe replies wearily. 'Catch you later.' He's about to walk off, but then he stops suddenly and bends down to whisper in my ear: 'The answer is Darius Danesh.'

He gives me a meaningful look, his dark eyes still managing to sparkle in the dim lighting. Then he's gone.

Mum returns with a fresh round.

'Thanks,' I say, taking a sip of my drink.

'What are you smiling about?' she asks with a knowing look.

'Nothing,' I reply breezily.

'Wouldn't have anything to do with a certain someone behind the bar, would it?'

'Cut it out, Mum.'

She giggles, annoyingly, then her brow furrows with curiosity. 'Looks like his mother is giving him a bit of a talking-to.'

My eyes dart towards the bar and at that moment both Joe and his mum look at me. Joe quickly averts his gaze, but his mother gives me a cold, hard stare. A bad feeling washes over me, and before I know it she's storming over to our table.

'You're cheating!' she accuses me.

'No, she's not!' Mum scoffs on my behalf.

'My son says she helped him come up with the questions!'

I realise with horror that the bar has fallen silent and everyone is watching this exchange. It's at times like these that I could do with my old friend the Pterodactyl. Joe rushes over to join us.

'She didn't help me with the questions,' he says. 'She just knows a lot of the same stuff as me. And look . . .' He grabs my quiz sheet. 'See? She didn't know the *Big Brother* one.'

'Sandy! Even *I* know that!' a drunken man shouts out from the table next to us. His laughs are silenced by the look Joe's mum gives him. She snatches my sheet from Joe and then challenges me with a new question:

'Which band plays the song over the opening credits of *The Royle Family*?'

I grimace before answering truthfully: 'Oasis. "Half the World Away".'

'See? She even got the extra point by knowing the title! She's a cheat!'

'No!' I shout. 'I just know that one! He's right, we have the same taste.'

'Well, if you've got the same taste, you won't know this; Joe can't stand the bleedin' show.' She takes a deep breath and then speaks loudly so the whole pub can hear. 'Who came third in the first series of *Pop Idol*?'

'Um . . .' My eyes dart towards Joe. He looks panicked. 'I don't know,' I reply.

'You're lying,' she sneers, drawing her lips, plastered with salmon-coloured lipstick, into a thin line. 'You're out of the quiz.'

'That's not fair!' Mum exclaims.

'No, it's fine,' I reply tersely. 'I'll sit the rest out.'

'She's not cheating!' Joe defends me, but I can see he's not going to convince this woman – his mother, of all people.

We still have quite an audience and she turns around and addresses everyone in a booming voice. 'We'll continue. For those of you who didn't hear those last two questions, I'll read them again: Which band plays the song over the opening credits of *The Royle Family*?'

I look at Joe, my face still flushed with embarrassment. He stares back at me, mortified.

'Joe! Get back to work.'

This time it's his dad doing the barking. Joe turns away, but not before I see the apology in his eyes.

'Let's get out of here,' Mum snaps, collecting her things.

'No,' I put my hand on her arm.

'Why not?' she asks in disbelief.

'I don't want to look like I'm running away.'

She regards me for a long moment before grudgingly picking up her wine glass and taking a sip. 'Alright, we'll finish our drinks first.'

In all honesty, I do want to leave. Even Joe, with all his gorgeousness, isn't enough of a reason to keep me here. Surely if anything can put a girl off a guy, it's his family.

I'm too embarrassed to walk out of the pub while the quiz is in full swing, but as soon as it's over and the background noise pipes up again, we make an exit. I daren't say goodbye to Joe with his parents around, but luckily he's serving a customer at our end of the bar and he glances up and makes eye contact as we start to walk past.

'We're off,' I say.

He indicates the outside door and gives me a meaningful look before mouthing: 'Wait.'

I nod and go to the door.

'I'll be with you in a minute,' I say to Mum as she heads for the car.

She raises her eyebrows, but doesn't comment as she walks off.

I shift from foot to foot for a moment, and then Joe appears. He gently takes my arm and guides me around to the side of the building, and even with all the embarrassment I've endured over the last half an hour, my heart pounds at the unexpectedness of his touch.

He turns to face me in the darkness. 'I'm sorry about that. They're a nightmare!'

'Don't worry about it,' I mumble.

'I wouldn't blame you if you wanted to give Corfe Castle a miss.'

'No,' I say quickly. 'I still want to go.' Awkward pause. 'If you do . . .'

'Of course I do!' He stares at me directly. 'Fuck this,' he says suddenly, roughly shoving his hair away from his face. 'I can't stand this for much longer.' He looks off to the dark hills and the sea in the distance. 'Anyway,' he says abruptly, briefly touching his fingers to my arm. 'What time shall we go? Eleven?'

'Sure,' I reply.

'I'll see you then.' He backs away. 'Meet me up the hill.'

'Okay.'

After he's gone I check my feelings. Crush back in force. Even his freakishly evil parents haven't put me off him.

Chapter 4

'I'll get these,' Joe says as we approach the ticket booth at Swanage station.

'No, I've got money.'

'Forget it, I'm paying.'

So this *is* a date!

'You'll never be able to afford to buy a car at this rate,' I tell him with a smile that fades when I realise he may well have done this trip with other girls.

'It's the least I can do after last night,' he replies, moving forward.

'Have you done this trip much before?' I ask awkwardly.

'No, first time.'

I don't know why I should be relieved – even if he hasn't taken another girl on this train, he will have had girlfriends in the past. Lots of them, if his looks are anything to go by.

The steam train is already waiting at the station and Dyson bounds forward, pulling hard against the leash in Joe's hand.

'Steady, boy,' Joe says to him in a low voice. 'He hates being on this thing.' He indicates the leash.

I was a bit surprised when I turned up this morning to see Joe waiting on the hill with Dyson in tow. I wasn't expecting we'd have company of the canine kind. Not that I mind. I get the feeling Joe is a 'love me, love my dog' kind of guy. I don't think I'd stand a chance with him if I couldn't bear his pooch.

I look up at the rusty beams overhead and the old-fashioned signage flanking the platform. I feel like I've been transported to another era as we board the train and sit opposite each other, a wooden table separating us.

I've tied my hair into a loose ponytail as it's quite hot today, and I'm wearing cream shorts and a pale pink T-shirt. I may like indie and Emo boys, but I wouldn't choose their style of dress for myself.

'Did you tell your parents you were seeing me today?' I dare to ask.

'Did I bollocks.'

'What do they think you're doing?'

'Who knows? They don't give a toss what I do, as long as Dyson's out of the way.'

The train chuffs out of the station with a whistle and a hiss. Joe casually puts his foot up on my seat. 'So what are you doing, going on holiday with your parents at your age?'

I tell him about Lizzy and his amusement dies.

'That sucks.'

I called Lizzy last night. It was a sombre conversation. Her mum is having the operation to remove the lump in her breast this afternoon, so she's nervous. I'll call her later to find out how the op went.

'Do you have many friends around here?' I ask Joe.

'Nah. We moved only a couple of months ago and I don't go

to school anymore, so . . .' His voice trails off. 'It's not really worth making friends if I'm going to be leaving.'

'That's right, you're off to London,' I say with a teasing smile. 'What are you going to do there?'

He shrugs. 'I don't know yet. Get a job. See what comes up, where life takes me . . .'

'That's very carefree of you. I couldn't stand that. I'm a planner.'

'I can tell.'

'How can you tell?' I feel slightly affronted.

He smiles playfully. 'Just can.'

'Well, maybe I'll surprise you one of these days.'

'Maybe you will.' He holds my gaze and my stomach goes all jittery. The feeling intensifies tenfold as the seconds tick by and neither of us looks away, then Dyson shifts position at our feet, distracting us both. I really need to get a grip.

We pass through Herston Halt station and Harman's Cross with its pretty flowers planted on the banks, and then it's green fields galore until we reach Corfe Castle.

'What do you want to do?' Joe asks me as we wander up the street towards the town's small centre. 'Are you hungry?'

My stomach rumbles its own reply, but he doesn't hear, thankfully. 'I am a bit. Where shall we go?'

'I don't know. It's my first time here too, remember.'

'That's right. I can't believe you haven't brought other girls before now.'

He cracks up laughing. 'I haven't met any other girls!'

'Sure you haven't. You met me pretty quickly.'

'Your *mum* made that introduction. And then Dyson followed up on it. I haven't lived here long enough to know anyone else.'

'What about girls on holiday?' I don't know where my confidence is coming from to ask him these questions, but talking to him is amazingly easy.

'Summer holidays have only just started.'

I instantly feel crushed.

'I don't mean . . .' He quickly corrects himself. 'I mean no one my age has been around, girls *or* guys. Anyway, now you're here you can keep me company.' Pause. 'If you want to.'

He blushes! He actually blushes!

'Of course I do,' I say, happily. So it's not just me. 'Oh, look! There's the castle.'

We continue in the direction of the ruined castle sitting on top of a steep hill. Ivy clings to its crumbling walls, and people wander along the grassy slopes beside it.

'What about that café for lunch?' I point up ahead.

We enter the café and go through to the other side, into the garden. Corfe Castle towers right there above us and it's quite something to be able to sit at a table with this view and not even have to pay an entry fee to walk through the nearby gates.

Joe is wearing a faded yellow Kingmaker T-shirt today and black jeans. I nod at his top.

'I love Kingmaker.'

'What's your favourite song?'

'"Really Scrape the Sky" is brilliant, but my favourite has got to be "You and I Will Never See Things Eye to Eye".'

He smiles. 'Me too. I always imagine that playing at the beginning of a film.'

'Yeah! That would be so cool. The way the bass kicks in just before the vocals . . .'

'Exactly.'

I laugh. 'I'll think of you if I ever see a film that has that on its soundtrack.'

'Maybe I'll put a Kingmaker question in next week's quiz,' he jokes.

'Oh, God, don't.' I bury my head in my hands. 'Last night was mortifying.' I peek through my fingers at him, but he's not smiling.

'I'm sorry. My parents hate me.'

'That's a crazy thing to say.'

He shakes his head, his expression bitter, then stares down at his hands.

'Do you have any brothers or sisters?' I ask tentatively.

He glances at me before looking away, but he doesn't answer.

'Did you hear—'

'Yeah,' he cuts me off. He sighs. 'I have a brother, an older brother.'

'Where is he?'

'Jail.'

'Oh.'

'Yep. I probably should have told you this before the train left to go back to Swanage.'

'Why?' I'm confused.

'In case you wanted to get back on it.'

'Don't be ridiculous,' I brush him off. 'Why's he in jail?'

'Because he's a dickhead.'

'I mean, what did he do?'

'I know that's what you meant. Sorry. He's been in and out of detention centres ever since I can remember – joy riding, drug dealing, you name it. The last thing that landed him in jail was armed robbery.'

'Jesus.'

'My family is *great*!' he says sarcastically. 'And the best thing about all of this? Mum and Dad still think the sun shines out of Ryan's arse.'

Ryan, I'm assuming, is his brother.

'Do you have any siblings?' he asks me.

'No.'

'You're lucky.'

'I never thought that when I was growing up. I was lonely.'

'Better to be lonely than black and blue.'

'He beats you up?' I exclaim, and from the look on his face I know instantly that he didn't mean to reveal this information.

'Here comes our food,' he says abruptly. He doesn't want to talk about this anymore – and who could blame him?

'That was such a fun day,' I say later in the car as I pull over near the pub.

He smiles across at me. 'It was, wasn't it?'

'Are you working tonight?'

'Afraid so. What are you up to tomorrow?'

I'm so relieved he asked me that question first. 'Nothing. What about you?'

'I'm coming your way if you want to join us for a walk?'

'Us' meaning him and Dyson.

'I'd love that.'

'Okay. I'll see you at around ten thirty.'

'Great.'

Awkward pause. We both jump as Dyson starts to bark furiously at a dog walking past with its owner.

'I'd better put him out at the back. I'm late for work.'

'Will your parents kill you?'

He cocks his head to one side. 'Let's hope not.' He climbs out of the car. 'See you tomorrow.'

I let out a deep breath and some of the tension that's been inside me all day slowly evaporates. Good tension, not bad tension, but tension nonetheless. And then I check my watch as a feeling of melancholy settles over me. It's just after six o'clock. That's one, two, three . . . I silently count the hours in my head until I come to ten thirty in the morning. *Sixteen and a half hours* until I see him again. How am I going to pass the time?

If Lizzy could see me now she'd think I'd lost my head. Lizzy! I need to call her. Damn – I said I'd call her at five. I make a plan to ring as soon as I get back to the cottage.

Chapter 5

'She's trying to be brave, but she's in a lot of pain.'

'I'm so sorry,' I murmur.

I'm on the phone to Lizzy. She's at the hospital.

'How's your sister?' I ask. Lizzy has just the one: Tessa. She's younger than us by three years.

'I don't know. She doesn't talk about it, and she barely comes out of her room when we're at home.'

'She must be worried.'

'We all are.'

'I wish I could give you a big hug,' I say sadly.

'I wish you could too,' she replies and I know she has tears in her eyes. She's not the only one.

'How's Dorset?' she asks.

'It's okay,' I reply.

My heart aches to tell her about Joe, but I don't feel that I can.

'How is she?' Mum asks when I return downstairs. I fill her in. 'Poor thing,' she empathises. 'Did you have a good day?'

'Yeah.' I nod, unable to keep the corners of my lips from turning upwards.

'You like him, don't you?'

'Might do,' I reply, looking down.

'Shame about his mother,' she comments.

'Mmm. I wasn't too keen on her, either. Neither is Joe, for that matter.'

'Oh, well,' Mum says, 'at least we're only here for six weeks.'

My heart plummets. Six weeks felt like an age on the car journey down here – now it's nowhere near long enough. 'What do you mean, "at least"?' I ask her.

'Well, it's not like you're going to fall for him, is it? He's hardly going to be a permanent part of your life. Imagine dealing with his mother! And his father ... From the look on his face when he gave me my change it's like he thought he'd burst an artery just by cracking a smile ...'

But I'm not really listening to her rant, because I'm still thinking about the falling-for part. It doesn't seem like such a slim possibility to me.

By 10.15 the next morning, I'm sitting out on the bench trying to read *Titus Andronicus*. Mum was a bit disturbed when she discovered I was seeing Joe again so soon, so I promised to take a couple of books with me on our walk. I may stay at the cliffs and do some reading if Joe has to get back to the pub.

Dyson appears at the gate before Joe does, but I force myself to calmly pack my book into my bag before going to meet him.

'Thought I'd do some reading at the cliffs,' I explain, slinging my bag over my shoulder.

'What are you going to be studying?' he asks as we set off down the track towards Dancing Ledge.

'English Lit. It'll probably be dead boring if Shakespeare is anything to go by.'

'I'm sure you'll have a laugh no matter what.'

'I hope so.'

'Are you excited?' he asks.

'Yes, I am, kind of. And a bit nervous. I haven't spent much time away from home before.'

'Where's your dad?' he asks.

'He's in London. He's coming down tomorrow night for the weekend.'

'Have you got lots of family things planned?'

I shrug. 'No, not really. You?' I try to sound casual, but inside I'm desperately hoping we can see each other.

'I have to work. Weekends are really busy at the pub.'

'Oh, I see.' Much as I want to, I can't mask my disappointment.

'You should stop by.'

'I'm not sure that would go down too well with your parents.'

'Nothing goes down well with my parents. You just have to learn to ignore them like I do.' That's bravado talking. It's obvious their behaviour upsets him.

We leave the track and enter the meadow, and soon we're face to face with that spectacular view.

Today the sea is sparkling like billions of diamonds. Butterflies flit around the wildflowers and a few boats with white sails glide through the water. I can hear the cry of gulls from the cliffs below.

'Do you want something to eat?' I ask, turning to Joe. 'I brought some snacks.'

'Good one,' he says, so I open up my bag and pull out a picnic blanket. 'A rug too? So organised,' he teases.

'That's me,' I reply.

'That's right,' he says as he helps me lay out the rug, 'you're a planner.'

'Bugger off,' I joke.

'Hey, nothing wrong with that.'

He collapses down on the rug while I get out some crisps and drinks. I also brought a little plastic bowl for Dyson and I pour some water from a bottle into it.

Joe laughs. 'Okay, now you're making me look bad.'

'Do you have to work today?' I ask.

'Not till this afternoon. That's one good thing about the pub – it doesn't do lunch, so I'm not drafted in to work in the kitchen like I have been in the past.'

'Does that mean you can cook?'

'If shaking frozen scampi and chips into a sizzling pan of oil can be called cooking, then yes, I can cook. Otherwise, no.'

He pulls over my bag and takes out a book. 'So what are you supposed to be reading?'

'Shakespeare and the Greek Tragedies.'

He flicks through *Titus*. 'What the hell? It looks like it's written in a foreign language!'

I laugh.

'I can't understand a bloody word.'

'Neither can I, half the time.'

He throws the book back down.

'Did you really never want to go to university?' I ask.

He thinks for a moment. 'I guess I didn't see it as an option. My parents are *not* academically minded,' he says with a raised eyebrow. 'So they didn't exactly encourage me, and with all the shit going on with my brother ... Well, let's just say school wasn't my number one priority.'

'When is your brother getting out of jail?' I ask quietly.

His face hardens. 'He's coming up for parole soon. I hope I'll be out of here before that happens.'

'Will he come back to live with your parents?'

'Yep.' His reply is curt. 'I'll take Dyson down the hill to give you some peace.'

'You don't have to,' I say quickly. Studying is far from my mind at the moment – I'd rather spend time with Joe. But he and Dyson are already on their feet.

'See you in a bit,' he says.

'Okay. Thanks,' I reply.

I watch him as he sets off down the steep grassy path. When he is finally out of sight I pick up a book. I sigh. I really can't be bothered to read Shakespeare right now, but I suppose I should. I turn around and lie on my stomach, facing up the hill. There's something deliriously comfortable about it. A seagull flies over my head, high above the ocean, but low against the land. It's so close I can hear its wings flapping. I try to read. The tall grass around me sways in the breeze. It's so peaceful and quiet. My whole body feels relaxed. The words are in front of my eyes, but they're not going in. I close my eyes for a moment and feel the warm sun on my back.

The next thing I know, Dyson is licking my face.

'Argh!'

'DYSON!' Joe shouts.

I push the dog away, but I'm in hysterics. Joe is halfway up the steep incline, trying to run.

'Sorry!' He's panting when he reaches me. He stretches out the bottom of his T-shirt and uses it to wipe Dyson's slobber from my cheeks. I can't stop laughing. 'Gross dog strikes again,' he says.

He checks my face with his fingertips to make sure I'm free of slobber. His hands seem to linger. My giggles dissolve and I steadily meet his eyes as butterflies swarm into my stomach.

'God, I fancy you,' he says suddenly, and I know in that moment that he's going to kiss me. My heart starts pounding ten to the dozen. I tilt my face up towards him and his lips touch mine, gently at first, then deepening to become more passionate. I know it's a cliché, but it's as if fireworks are going off inside my head. My whole body tingles like nothing before.

He pulls away, but stays close. And then an enormous slobbery dog tongue comes out of nowhere to lick my cheek.

'Argh!' I scream again.

'Dyson, get off!' Joe shouts, shoving him away. We look at each other and crack up laughing. 'Next time I kiss you, I'll make sure he's not around.'

'I don't want to wait that long,' I say, drawing him near. He's still smiling when his lips touch mine.

We wander, hand in hand, back to the cottage. The jittery feeling doesn't leave me and it's blissful. We take our time, but we're home far too quickly. My mum's car isn't in the driveway.

'Do you want to come in for some lunch?' I ask hopefully.

'Um . . .' He checks his watch.

'My mum is out,' I add.

'Yeah, go on, then.'

I beam from ear to ear as I lead him to the front door.

'Where do you think she's gone?' he asks, following me inside but leaving Dyson on the driveway. We've closed the gate to make sure he can't escape.

'Probably sitting on a beach somewhere, sketching.'

'Have you got any of her work, here?'

'In the conservatory. I'll show you in a bit. Shall I make some sandwiches?'

'Sounds good.'

'Ham and cheese? Peanut butter? What do you fancy?'

'You,' he says with a smile, pulling me in for another kiss. He presses me up against the counter and I wrap my arms around his neck. The kiss is over far too quickly. 'But I've already told you that,' he adds. 'Ham and cheese. Let me help you.'

We work side by side and, before taking our food out to the garden we pause in the conservatory to have a quick look at Mum's paintings.

'I don't know anything about art, but I like them,' Joe says.

'That's all you need to know, in my opinion. That's what it's about, right? What you like and what you don't like?'

'I guess so. Smartarse.'

'I prefer Brainiac.'

He chuckles and follows me outside to the sunny garden. We sit on the soft, spongy grass and Joe tucks into his sandwich. I take a bite of mine, but I'm not very hungry. The winged caterpillars are taking up all the room in my stomach.

'I like this cottage,' he says.

'It's nice, isn't it? But your pub is in a great location. Do you live upstairs?'

'Yeah.'

'You must have an amazing view.'

He nods. 'My bedroom is the best thing about living there

because it faces the fields instead of the car park at the back. I'd probably appreciate it more if my parents weren't always knocking about.'

'Is it noisy?'

'I don't mean knocking about in that way.'

'No, I know.' I smile and he touches my face fondly.

'It would be noisy if I ever spent any time in my bedroom,' he explains. 'But I'd rather get outside with Dyson. Anyway, I work most nights, so I'm usually the last one upstairs.'

'You work a lot.'

'I have to.'

'Have you saved up much money towards a car?'

'It's going alright. They pay me as little as possible and then I still have to shell out for rent, so it's taken longer than I wanted it to.'

'Couldn't you work somewhere else that pays better?'

'Not without moving out and then I'd still have the rent problem. I'll be doing that soon enough. I just have to stick it out for a couple more months.'

A feeling of melancholy engulfs me. I've known Joe for only a few days, but the thought of losing him in under six weeks already feels unbearable.

'You not hungry?' He nods at the sandwich that I've barely touched.

'No.' I shake my head.

He lies down and pulls me to him for a kiss. The sound of a car in the driveway makes us both jump away from each other.

'My mum must be back.'

'I'd better get going.' He stands up.

'You don't have to rush off . . .'

'I should get back, anyway. My shift starts in an hour.'

'Okay.' I'm disappointed.

He goes out through the back garden gate to the driveway. I follow him to see my mum trying to open the car door without hitting Dyson. The dog starts to bark with excitement.

'Sorry!' Joe shouts. He seems to do a lot of apologising for his pooch. He hurries to the car and grabs Dyson's collar, dragging him away so Mum can get out.

'Hello, there,' she says, and there's an undercurrent to her tone which is not as pleasant as it usually is when speaking to my friends. It makes me feel nervous. I suppose she's still smarting about Joe's mum the other night.

'Hi, Mrs . . . Sorry, I don't know Alice's last name.'

'Simmons,' Mum and I answer simultaneously. 'But you can call me Marie. Did you have a nice walk?' she asks.

'Yeah, it was nice.'

I realise that Joe is nervous, although for different reasons to me. It endears me to him even more, if that's possible.

'I was just leaving,' he says, struggling to hold Dyson back.

'I'll see you out,' I say, indicating the front gate. He goes through and lets go of Dyson's collar. The dog shoots off down the track.

Joe turns back to close the gate, leaving me on the other side. 'Are you around tomorrow?' he asks.

'Tomorrow and for the next six weeks,' I reply with a smile.

'Five and a half,' he corrects and my heart sinks. 'Shall I swing by in the morning?' he asks, oblivious.

'Sounds good.' That's a lie. Tomorrow is too bloody far away.

'Okay. Is nine too early?'

'Nope.' Six a.m. would be better. I'd even be happy with five.

This evening would be ideal. Actually, if you could just not leave at all, that would be pretty much perfect.

'See you.' He glances over my shoulder at Mum, who is unpacking the last of her things from the car. He starts to walk away as she heads inside to the kitchen.

'Joe!' I call and he spins around. I beckon for him to come back and then I lean over the gate. 'You forgot something.'

He grins and kisses me quickly, then turns to leave.

'Hang on.' I grab his arm. 'What's *your* surname?'

'Strickwold.'

'Joe Strickwold,' I repeat.

'It's a bit of a tongue-twister.' My fingers fall away from his bicep into his warm hand as he steps away. 'Till tomorrow?'

'Yes.' I nod, giving his hand a quick squeeze. Then he's off.

Chapter 6

'You've moved your relationship onto the next level already,' Mum teases when I walk back into the kitchen with a spring in my step.

'You saw that, did you?' I feel my face heat up.

'A bit hard not to. The window is right there.'

'How was your day?' I change the subject. Thankfully, she lets me.

'Very good. I went to Lulworth Cove and picked up a few bits and bobs. I found a fossil of a sea snail or something like that. I want to go back in the morning. You should come with me. It's very pretty.'

'Um, no, I can't,' I reply. 'Joe's coming to get me at nine.'

'Joe again?' Uh-oh. I know that tone. 'Aren't you seeing a bit too much of him?'

'God, Mum, it's only been a few days,' I reply huffily. I hate it when she questions me like this. I'm eighteen, for pity's sake. 'I thought you wanted me to make friends?'

'Friends? Is that what you are?' Her tone is wry.

'Well, you know . . .'

'I just don't want you to let your work suffer.'

'I won't. I've got weeks of summer sprawled out before me. I'll get it done,' I say, forcing breeziness into my tone.

She smiles at me. 'I guess you know what you're doing.'

'I do. Show me the fossil, then?'

The next morning Joe and I return to Dancing Ledge. The jittery feeling has been in my stomach all night and it's even more intense now. I don't want to keep my hands off him. He's so warm and perfect. To my amazement, he seems to feel the same.

'I could kiss you all day,' he says.

'Don't you need to eat?'

'Nope.'

'Drink?'

'Nope.'

'Me neither,' I say.

'I really can't get over your eyes,' he says, staring into them, almost searchingly. 'They're the greenest green.'

'I like yours too,' I admit.

'Boring brown.'

'They could never be boring. No, it's like they have an inner light or something. They're dark, but they still seem to sparkle.'

He starts to laugh at me.

'Don't be mean!' I cry, whacking him on his arm. 'Maybe that did sound a little corny, but it's true.'

'Where are your parents from?' he asks suddenly.

'They're both British, but my grandmother on my father's side was Chinese.'

'Where was she from?'

'Beijing originally, but her parents took her to Britain when she was young. My grandfather was British.'

'I didn't think Alice Simmons sounded very Chinese.'

'No.'

'Do you speak it?'

'Mandarin? No. I wish I could, but my dad always speaks English.'

'Maybe you could take it as a subject at university.'

I look ahead, thoughtfully. 'That's a really good idea. They do have an option to take a language module. I'll check it out when I get there.' I gaze across at him. '*Xie_xie*.'

'What does that mean?'

'Thank you.' I smile. 'For the idea.'

He shakes his head with amusement. 'You are *such* a brainiac!'

'So, Joe Strickwold,' I say. 'When are you coming to visit me in Cambridge?'

'Joe Strickwold – you even said it without tripping over it.'

'I've been practising: Joe Strickwold, Joe Strickwold, Joe Strickwold.'

'Impressive. Alice Simmons, Alice Simmons, Alice Simmons – actually, yours is a bit of a tongue-twister too.'

'Alice Strickwold. Jesus, that's even worse.'

'I'll have to change my name to something simpler before you marry me,' he jokes.

A thrill goes through me. I know, I'm getting way ahead of myself.

'Oi, you haven't answered my question.'

'About coming to visit you in Cambridge?' he checks. 'You might be sick of me by then.'

'I doubt it.'

'You won't want me cramping your style when you're meeting all these smart know-it-alls.'

'I'm absolutely certain that's not going to happen.'

'You can't be certain.'

'Yes, I can. I don't want to go out with some ponce from Cambridge University. They wouldn't want to go out with me, anyway.'

'No guy would ever turn you down.'

'Stop it!' I laugh. 'How can you say that?'

'You're beautiful.' He shrugs as if it were obvious, even though no one has ever said that to me before.

'I think you're gorgeous too.'

'Come here and kiss me.'

I do as I'm told.

I can't bear it when he leaves me that afternoon. The hours without him drag by like nothing I've ever known. I've never had a crush like this before. And yes, I *am* calling it a crush, even though the L word has popped into my mind on more than one occasion. My head tells me it's far too soon to be using words like that, but, God, I like him so much. 'Like' really doesn't cut it. I adore him . . . I fancy him . . . None of those phrases do it justice, either. I *need* him. I'm *obsessed* by him. That's more like it. I'm not going to tell him this, though, for crying out loud. I sound like a nutcase and he'd run a bloody mile. I suppose I'm still in the honeymoon period.

My dad arrives on Friday afternoon and it's damn near impossible to concentrate during dinnertime when he's talking about his week at work. My mum knows what's up with me, I'm sure of it.

She's planned a jam-packed weekend for the three of us and I swear that she's trying to keep me from Joe, unaware that he's busy at the pub. After dinner, I try to watch telly because reading is futile, but even that won't take my mind off him. I keep thinking about walking across the field to the pub so I can see him, but I'm too wary of facing his parents when I get there.

When Mum and Dad go upstairs to bed I go outside to the gate and stand there, looking out into the blackness. In some small and silly way I feel like it's bringing me closer to him.

I wish he had a mobile phone so I could call him, but he's putting all of his money towards a car.

I turn and sit on the bench. It's a clear night and the stars above are bright. Unlike in London, there is no orange haze here from streetlights. It's beautiful.

I finally cracked yesterday and told Lizzy about Joe. Her mum is recovering from the operation quite well, although they won't know yet if they've removed all of the cancer. Susan starts chemo next week; it will be horrendous for her, let alone for my friend, who will have to watch her mother go through hell.

Lizzy was surprised that I had met a boy – and even more surprised that I'd kissed him. We had both thought we'd be in a bit of a backwater here. She tried to sound excited for me, but I know she just wishes she were here having fun and that all this awful stuff wasn't happening to her family.

I suppose I should go to bed. I'm about to stand up, but freeze. Is that . . . a *dog* panting?

'Joe?' I ask quietly.

'Alice?'

I get up and run to the gate.

'Where are you?' I whisper into the darkness, and then I see him, stepping onto the track from the field. Dyson is already at the gate, wagging his tail. He crouches, ready to bark, and my reflexes work quicker than I would have ever given them credit for because I rush out of the gate and bend down to pat him rigorously before he can utter a sound. I don't want him to rouse my parents. Their bedroom overlooks the garden at the back, but I don't want to take any risks.

Joe reaches me and I stand up and throw my arms around his neck.

'What are you doing here?' I ask, beyond delighted.

'I took Dyson for a walk and my feet just kind of took me this way. I'm not stalking you,' he adds.

'I wouldn't mind if you were.'

He grins. 'What are you doing outside?'

'Waiting for you,' I reply with a smile. His kisses are tender, more tender than they have been. Out of the blue I feel like I'm going to cry. It's the weirdest feeling.

Dyson whimpers and collapses in the dirt at our feet. Joe glances down at him and then back at me. The bizarre urge to cry vanishes.

'Did your dad arrive today?' he asks.

'Yes.'

'Are they asleep?' He nods towards the house.

'I think so.'

'He'd kill me if he knew I was out here with his daughter.'

I giggle. 'I am eighteen, you know.'

'It wouldn't make a difference. If you were *my* daughter . . .'

'What a gross thought!'

'Urgh!' He grimaces and gently punches my arm. 'What are you doing tomorrow?'

'You're working, aren't you?' I check before answering.

'Yeah.'

In that case . . . 'We're going to visit some castle by the sea.'

'Portland?'

'That sounds familiar. Have you been?'

'No. I'd like to go, though.'

'Come with us?'

'I have to work, remember.'

'Pull a sickie!'

'What, with my parents right there to check up on me? And they *would*,' he adds. 'No. Anyway, you'd better spend some time with your dad. I don't want to gatecrash.'

'You wouldn't!' I am desperate for him to come, even though I know that he won't.

He smiles and kisses me. Again.

'You should go inside,' he says, pulling away and rubbing my arms with his perpetually warm hands. 'You're cold.'

'Come and sit on the bench with me for a bit,' I plead.

He hesitates and then nods. 'Stay.'

'Bring him in, just in case he barks,' I suggest.

'Okay.' The delighted dog squeezes through the barely-open gate and I breathe in sharply as he runs down the driveway, but I know that the garden gate is locked so he won't have a chance to bark up at my parents' window. I'm past caring, anyway. I'd keep Joe here at all costs.

We sit down on the bench and snuggle into each other. He wraps his arms around me and drapes his coat over my shoulders. I nuzzle my face into his neck.

'That tickles.' He chuckles, so I kiss him there. 'Stop,' he says, laughing quietly. Then he bends down to kiss *my* neck.

'Argh!' I whisper, trying not to squeal. It does tickle.

'See?' He raises one eyebrow at me in the darkness. I put my fingers up to touch the silver ring that is pierced there.

'Did it hurt?'

'Not much.'

'Have you had many girlfriends?' That question came out of nowhere.

'Not really,' he replies. What does 'not really' mean?

'What does "not really" mean?' If he thinks I'm a saddo, so be it.

'I haven't been serious with anyone.'

'What does "serious" mean?'

'Alice!' he exclaims, laughing. Is he embarrassed?

'Have you had many boyfriends?' He turns the question around before I can pry further, but I *will* get to the bottom of this discussion; he just doesn't know it.

'No,' I reply, then, with a smile: 'Not really.'

'What does "not really" mean?'

'I haven't been "serious" with anyone, either.'

He's no longer smiling, and nor am I. He kisses me gently.

'I can't go a whole weekend without seeing you,' he murmurs.

'Me neither.'

'Shall I come by tomorrow night after closing?'

I nod, and then we're kissing again.

Chapter 7

I'm in a daze the next day as I wander around Portland Castle checking out Henry VIII's handiwork. He had the castle built in the 1540s to protect against French and Spanish invasion, but that's all I can tell you about it, other than the fact that it is very big and very grey. The rest of the time I'm in another world. I'm not entirely oblivious to the looks my parents keep giving each other, though. My dad attempts to broach the subject when we find ourselves on our own.

'Mum says you've met a boy.' My dad has short, brown hair like his father, and a brushstroke of his mother's eyes.

'Mmmhmm,' I reply non-committally.

'I hope you're still making time—'

'. . . to do some work, yes, Dad,' I interrupt him with a yawn. 'What you and Mum seem to forget is that I was planning to come on this holiday with Lizzy, so I wouldn't exactly have been holed up in my bedroom reading if she were here. What's the difference?'

'Well . . .' he splutters. 'Lizzy's Lizzy.'

'And Joe's Joe. He's not taking up any more of my time

than Lizzy would have been. Less, in fact, because he has to work.'

'Yes, I heard about that.'

'About the pub?'

'His parents.'

I sigh. 'He's nothing like them.'

'You say that, Alice, but it's impossible to avoid one's genes entirely.'

'Well, Joe has,' I snap.

I don't want to remind him of my age, but I will if he keeps pushing me.

'Look,' I say in a gentler tone, 'this is my last summer before I leave home. Please let me enjoy it.'

He wraps his arm around my neck. 'Okay, sweetie. I've said enough.'

I suddenly feel gracious. 'You should meet him. I'll introduce him to you before the weekend is over.'

He nods. And then we're back to our history lesson.

My promise to my dad has to wait, because Joe comes to see me again just before midnight, when my parents have already turned in for the night. We sit out on the bench for almost two hours. I'm absolutely shattered by the time he leaves, and I fall into bed without brushing my hair or taking off my make-up. I don't tend to wear much – only mascara and a little eye-liner – but my lashes will certainly be stuck together in the morning.

My alarm rouses me from a deep, deep sleep at seven. I press Snooze without even thinking and then abruptly come to, leaping out of bed and rushing to the shower. He'll be here for a quick walk with Dyson at eight o'clock, and I'm supposed to be leaving with Mum and Dad at nine to go and see the Cerne Giant – a 180-foot-tall chalk figure carved out of the hill – before going for a drive all the way to Exmoor National Park. I wasn't kidding when I said my mum had a jam-packed weekend planned.

By eight o'clock, though, Joe hasn't arrived. At eight twenty-five, I go back inside because it has started to rain. By eight forty, I'm climbing the walls, and by five to nine, I'm seriously worried.

'He's probably just slept in,' Mum assures me. 'Come on, darling, we need to get going. There's no time for your walk with him now, anyway.'

Much as I don't want to, I agree on the premise that we drive via the pub.

We're in Dad's car and starting off down the dirt track to the main road when I see him, jogging across the field towards the cottage.

'STOP!' I shout. Dad brakes. I climb out of the car and run. 'JOE!'

The relief he feels when he sees me is palpable.

'I'm sorry!' He bends over, panting and out of breath. 'I ran the whole way here.'

'Where were you? I was worried!' I exclaim.

'I'm so sorry.' He looks apologetic. 'I just slept in.'

'You *slept in*?' I whack him on his arm and my face breaks into a grin. 'I thought something had happened to you! I was about to go to the pub to make sure you were okay!'

'Really?' He grins back at me, still out of breath. 'You were going to risk facing my parents to check up on me?'

'Of course!'

He glances over my shoulder. 'Is that your dad?'

'Yes.' I pull a face at him. 'I meant to tell you last night that he wants to meet you.'

He looks worried. 'Okay.' He stands up straight.

We walk with trepidation towards the car. My dad puts down his electric window.

'Hello,' he calls as we get nearer.

'Dad, this is Joe. Joe, Dad.'

'Hello, Mr Simmons. Mrs Simmons.' He nods at Mum in the front passenger seat while shaking Dad's hand, extended through the window. I'm glad Dad doesn't get out. This feels formal enough as it is.

'Jim and Marie,' Dad says good-naturedly, jabbing his thumb towards himself and Mum. 'Alice says you live nearby?'

Joe points across the field. 'At the pub in the next village.'

'Maybe we'll stop there on the return journey.'

That's my cue to get back in the car.

'That'd be great,' Joe replies as I grimace inwardly. I have no intention of returning to the pub anytime soon.

'I'll just be a minute,' I say to Dad, so he puts his window up. I lead Joe to the back of the car, out of view.

'Will you come and see me again tonight?' I ask.

'It sounds like you're coming to see me this afternoon,' he replies.

'If we don't . . .' I say awkwardly.

'My parents will be okay,' he tries to convince me. 'I won't let them bother you. Sit outside!' he suggests brightly.

'Okay,' I reply with reluctance. 'But if I don't . . .'

'I'll be here at eleven thirty. Earlier closing time on Sundays.'

'You're knackered, though.' I remember his reason for oversleeping. He's had to walk all this extra distance to and from me for the last few days.

'I'll still come,' he promises, cupping my face. I tilt my head up to kiss him. 'You'd better go.'

'I'll see you later.'

'At the pub,' he urges.

I nod and climb back in the car. He stands and watches until we're out of sight. Dad waits until then to speak.

'He seems nice.'

'He is, isn't he?' I beam.

'Don't think much of the ring in his eyebrow, though.'

I roll my eyes and smile. Nothing can dampen my mood today.

I follow Joe's advice early that evening and sit outside the pub when we arrive. Dad goes in to order, returning to the table with our drinks and a couple of packets of salted peanuts.

Joe appears at the doorway and my heart flips. He sees me immediately and comes over.

'Hello!' I sit up straighter.

'Hi.' He looks delighted to see me, but he doesn't kiss me in front of my parents. 'How was the giant?' he asks them.

'Big!' Mum exclaims.

'Not what I was expecting,' Dad replies huffily and Mum and I both giggle. The size of the giant's enormous erect penis was what really put him off. Those Iron Agers were *rude*! ... *If* the chalk giant dates back to the Iron Age – no one is really sure.

Joe sits down beside me, close, so our arms are touching. My hairs immediately stand on end and I wish the world around us would disappear so I could kiss him. I put my hand on his knee, under the table.

'Have you had a busy day?' Dad asks Joe.

'It's been pretty hectic, yeah.'

'This is a stunning setting,' Dad adds.

'We're lucky,' Joe replies.

We make chit-chat for a couple of minutes until Joe turns to me, regretfully. 'I'd better get back to work before anyone notices I'm missing.'

I nod, sadly.

'It was nice to meet you,' he says to my dad.

'See you again soon, I imagine,' Dad replies.

Joe puts his hand on my hand, still resting on his knee under the table. He squeezes it. Mum and Dad turn to each other and pretend to be otherwise engaged.

'Are you still coming tonight?' I ask quietly.

'Yes, if you want me to.'

I nod swiftly and he smiles, kissing me quickly on the lips before standing up.

'See you soon!' he says cheerfully to my parents.

I'm on edge until he's safely back inside, then let out a deep breath.

'I guess we should get going,' Mum says.

'I'm starving,' Dad responds, knocking back the last of his half-pint of shandy. 'And I'd better set off to London in an hour.'

I hear Dyson whimpering as we pass the pub's outside courtyard, and it pains me not to be able to go and pat him. He must hate it, being tied up out at the back. I feel a wave of affection for him and silently promise to have some treats ready when Joe comes to see me later tonight.

Chapter 8

About halfway through my holiday, Joe takes a day off so we can go together to Brownsea Island. The island belongs to the National Trust and it's supposed to be breathtakingly beautiful. No dogs are allowed, though, and Joe was feeling guilty about leaving Dyson all day with his parents, but in the end it was my mum who came through.

'Leave him with me. He can keep me company in the garden.'

'No, he'll be a nightmare,' Joe responded. 'He'll probably knock over your easel or eat your paint or something.'

'He'll be *fine*. He's a good dog.' Mum patted him affectionately. 'If he's a problem I'll stick him out on the driveway.'

Joe hesitated.

'He'll be fine, I promise!' she insisted.

'Are you sure?'

'Absolutely.'

I think she was worried about leaving Dyson all day with Joe's terrible parents as we are. In the end, Joe conceded.

*

The boat for the island arrives and we climb aboard. We sit near the front on the left. Joe wraps his arm around me and pulls me close. I rest my head on his shoulder as we wait for the boat to start. Soon we're zooming past white cliffs towering overhead and staring in at smugglers' caves.

Over the Tannoy, the tour guide tells us that this area was the inspiration behind many of Enid Blyton's books.

'Did you read Enid Blyton when you were a kid?' I ask Joe.

'Yeah, *The Famous Five* books were awesome.'

'I loved those too. And *The Magic Faraway Tree*.'

'Yeah!' he enthuses. 'The lands at the top of the tree that kept changing . . .'

'And the different fruits that grew on the tree as you climbed up!'

We pass Old Harry's Rocks, tall free-standing chalk stacks projecting out of the ocean and named, allegedly, after Harry Paye, the infamous pirate, who used to store his contraband nearby. The man sitting in front of us tells this story to his two excited young boys while their mother looks on fondly.

'It's really interesting, all this history,' Joe comments.

My brow furrows. *He's* so interesting – *and* interested – that I don't understand why he doesn't want to go to university. Is that really snobby of me?

I cuddle in close and press my cheek against his chest. He holds me even tighter.

Soon Brownsea Island and its pretty castle appear before us. We dock at the pier and walk through to the entrance to pay our fee. We've brought a picnic, so we wander until we come to a meadow. There are a couple of peacocks ambling about, and some geese, ducks and chickens too. I throw a mother duck and her babies some bread.

'Now you've done it,' Joe teases, as the chickens come running and clucking. Soon a whole host of wildlife is right on our doorstep. A chicken hops onto our picnic rug.

'That's one step too far, matey,' Joe says, pushing it away with his foot. It comes straight back again. 'Fuck me, these birds are persistent.'

I start laughing as a peacock shakes his tail-feathers in our direction.

'Steady, boy,' Joe warns.

'Hey, look!' I exclaim, looking behind the peacock. 'That's a baby peacock! I've never seen a baby peacock before. What do you call female peacocks, again?' I ask, looking at its brown – and far less interesting – mother.

'Peahens?' Joe says.

'Yeah, something like that.'

'If a peacock is a male and a peahen is a female, what's the generic term for them?' Joe asks. 'Pea?'

I start to giggle. 'I have no idea.'

'I'm going to look that up one day,' he says.

'I thought I was the brainiac?' I tease.

'I can't stand this for much longer,' he says, pushing away another chicken.

'You've got to admit, though, they are quite attractive hens. If I was going to own a hen, I'd want it to look like that.'

'If I still know you in ten years' time, I'll buy you one.'

I smile. 'Why ten years? Why not two years?'

'You'll still be at university in two years' time. I'm not sure your room-mates would appreciate the gesture.'

'True. Anyway, I like the sound of ten years.' My heart clenches. 'We will still know each other in ten years' time, won't we?'

'We'd better,' he replies. His smile fades and he kisses me. 'Come on, let's go for a walk before the birds try to eat us too.'

We make our way through pine trees and come to the cliff edge.

'Don't stand too close!' I pull him backwards in alarm.

'It's fine!' he insists with a grin.

'Just come away from the edge.' I'm terrified.

'I am away from the edge, Alice.'

'Further away!' I feel like I'm having a panic attack.

He does as he's told, regarding me with apprehension.

'I don't want to lose you,' I say. 'I *can't* lose you.'

'You're not going to lose me,' he says quietly, full of concern. 'I'm not near the edge.'

I feel bizarrely like I'm going to cry again. It makes me feel so out of control.

But call me psychic, psycho, or whatever you like, suddenly I just *know* he's going to hurt me, and I won't be able to stop it from happening.

He takes my hands and squeezes them.

'Sorry,' I say, forcing a shaky laugh.

'Let's go down to the beach.' He tries to coerce me out of my odd mood.

'Sure.' I nod quickly. He leads the way and I hope to God I'm not scaring him off with my behaviour.

I've calmed down by the time we reach the steep steps to the beach. We've only got a couple of hours before our return boat journey. We sit against a crumbling brick wall built into the cliff.

'I love it here,' Joe says. 'It's magical.'

'My mum should come,' I reply. 'She'd adore it.'

'Tell her to bring your dad one weekend.'

'Only if you take a sickie so we can have the house to ourselves.'

He glances at me and abruptly looks away. A shiver goes through me and I wonder if he's also thinking the same thing. I want to be close to him. *Closer* to him. As close as it is possible to get to another human being.

My thoughts dart towards Lizzy and I feel a little sick . . .

Lizzy and I went to an all-girls' school and we both had this bugbear about some of the girls in our class. There was this one small group in particular – led by a girl called Pippa – who were obsessed about losing their virginity before they went to university. Pippa turned eighteen earlier this year and you should have heard her moan: 'I can't believe I'm eighteen and still a virgin . . .'

Of course, Lizzy and I were – *are* – virgins too, so we didn't really want to hear someone going on about how this is a bad thing. We both want to wait for someone special – and it certainly didn't matter to us that we were going off to university without having 'done it'. But Pippa was obsessed. She went on holiday to Ibiza at Easter and shagged some random guy. She was adamant it was special; she said she fancied the guy like mad and they'd vowed to stay in touch. But they haven't. And it's hard to believe that somewhere, deep inside, Pippa doesn't regret her actions.

I know – I just *know* – that Lizzy wouldn't understand about Joe. She wouldn't understand if I lost my virginity to him weeks before going away to supposedly start a brand-new, free and single, *adult* life. She'd think it was a waste. She'd think I was just like Pippa.

I try to put my friend out of my mind.

'Wouldn't it be cool if we could stay here tonight? Not catch the boat back,' Joe says with a smile. 'I'd build a fire here on these rocks and we could sleep under the shelter of those ferns up the hill.'

'What would you cook for dinner?' I ask, getting into this idea.

'Chicken?' he suggests and we both laugh.

'I would *love* to stay here with you,' I say quietly after a while. He puts his hand on my waist. My body tingles with anticipation as he slides it upwards. I put my hand inside his T-shirt and he draws a sharp intake of breath. I pull him closer, wanting him to be so *much* closer.

The sound of a squealing child makes us break apart. The family from the boat are walking along the sand nearby. The mother gives us a disapproving look and I feel my face heat up as I take my hand away from Joe's chest. He smiles at me, awkwardly.

'Shall we go?'

I nod, still blushing.

'Let's see if we can find a red squirrel.' He tries to project some enthusiasm into his voice, but it does little to alleviate my embarrassment. I get up and he helps me across the rocks to the steps.

We get back early that evening after a blissful whole day together. Dyson is deliriously excited to see Joe.

'Was he okay?' he asks my mum.

'Good as gold,' she replies. 'I haven't fed him any dinner yet, so he might be hungry.'

'Cool. I'll feed him when I get back to the pub.'

'Lizzy called for you,' Mum says to me. 'You forgot to take your phone with you.'

'Oh, thanks.' I hadn't even realised it was missing. Too distracted with a certain someone. 'How was she?' I ask.

'Good. In fact, Susan's chemo treatment is going so well that Lizzy said she might be able to come and stay with us this weekend.'

'Really?' I'm delighted to hear about Susan, but my heart inadvertently sinks as I process the second half of my mum's sentence. A funny little part of me is reluctant to introduce Lizzy to Joe. It's strange: she and I have dissected every single crush either one of us has ever had since the age of nine, but for some reason I don't want to share Joe with her. I'm too frightened she might not see in him what I see. I don't want her to taint him in any way.

'That'd be awesome,' Joe enthuses, oblivious to the thoughts racing around my head.

'Wow, yeah.' I try to sound pleased.

Joe turns to me. 'I'd better get back. Thanks again,' he says to Mum.

'You're very welcome.'

I follow him to the gate.

'Walk tomorrow morning?' he asks.

'Sounds good,' I say with a smile as he touches his lips to mine.

'I love you.' He says it out of the blue, almost as though he's already said it to me a million times. He immediately looks shocked, but I have the biggest smile on my face.

'I love you too,' I reply.

'Do you?' His face breaks into an enormous, mirroring grin.

'Isn't it obvious?'

Dyson starts to bark at him.

'I'd better get him back for dinner.'

'Okay. See you in the morning.'

'Or later?' he suggests.

'You really want to walk all the way back here tonight after seeing me all day?'

'You're tired,' he says with sudden realisation.

'No, it's not that,' I answer hurriedly. 'I'm thinking of *you*. I would always rather see you than sleep.'

'I'll be back later, in that case.'

'Wicked.'

Chapter 9

'I'm so pleased you're here!' I squeal. After my initial, wholly selfish reservations, I couldn't wait to see Lizzy. And here she is, on the station platform, on Friday afternoon.

'I'm so pleased I'm here too!' she squeals back.

We hug each other tightly.

She fills me in about her mum on the way back to the cottage. The chemo is awful, but the doctors are encouraging about Susan's recovery, so that's an enormous weight off my friend and her family's minds.

'Now tell me about you!' Lizzy insists. 'Is that boy still on the scene?'

Nerves wash over me for some reason. I so want her to understand about him. 'Joe?' I try to sound breezy. 'Yes.'

'Am I going to meet him?'

'I thought we might go to his pub tonight.'

'Cool. As long as you two don't snog each other's faces off in front of me.'

'Gross!' I try to laugh.

'I don't want to feel like a gooseberry,' she adds, and I can tell the thought has been worrying her. I'd be the same in her situation.

'I promise you I won't, and, anyway,' I say, 'his parents will be there.'

'Well, hopefully there will be some hot boy talent for me.'

'Hopefully!' I reply, even though I haven't seen any other nice guys so far. Then again, I've only had eyes for Joe so I can't say I've been looking.

We go to the pub at six o'clock, after an early dinner with my mum. Dad had an important meeting this afternoon, so he won't be here until nine, which is why Lizzy opted to catch the train rather than hitch a lift with him.

We decide to walk across the field to the pub and I'm surprised and slightly disturbed by how far it actually is. I can't believe poor Joe has walked all this way to and from the cottage twice a day, not to mention the extra further distance to Dancing Ledge which we do together. No wonder he's so fit ... Oh, I so hope Lizzy agrees!

I'm wracked with tension by the time we arrive. We go inside to order, and he's there, pulling a pint, at our end of the bar. He looks up and sees me and – POW! – that feeling again, like the very first time I saw him. Magnet ... Metal ... My heart cartwheels. He grins at me and then at Lizzy.

'Hello,' I say shyly, as we reach the bar.

'Hi,' he replies fondly. 'You must be Lizzy?' He smiles at her and I turn to see her nod. Is she ... *blushing*?

'Nice to meet you,' she says.

I notice Joe's dad at the other end of the bar serving another customer. He has his back to us. His mother is nowhere to be seen.

'What are you drinking?' Joe asks Lizzy, putting down one pint on the counter and pulling another.

'Um . . .'

'Cider?' he asks me while she deliberates.

'Yes, please.'

'I'll have one too,' she says.

'I'll bring them out to you,' he promises.

I reach inside my bag to get my purse.

'Alice,' he tuts, shaking his head.

'Are you sure?' I check, hesitating.

'Of course.' He frowns and hands the two pints to a waiting customer.

I smile and lead Lizzy out.

'Oh. My. God,' she says quietly.

'What?'

'He's flipping *gorgeous*!' she squeals under her breath.

I burst out laughing with delight.

Joe brings our drinks outside a few minutes later.

'Sorry for the wait,' he says, sitting down beside me. 'It's really busy tonight.' He crosses his tanned arms on the table in front of him. He's looking even more sexy than usual tonight, in black jeans and a grey T-shirt with a hot-pink surfer-style graphic on the front. He's wearing a chunky watch with a worn brown leather strap on his wrist.

Lizzy was insistent that we make a bit of an effort with our own outfits tonight, even though I told her this is just a small village pub. We've both got dark-blue jeans on, and Lizzy is wearing a black chiffon top, while I'm wearing a red and pink one. We changed into our heels from our trainers once we reached the road. Lizzy has blue eyes and shoulder-length brown hair, and tonight she's ironed her slight curl out of it so it's dead straight. I wanted to keep the tousled look to my long, dark hair because Joe told me the other day how much he likes it. But she insisted on putting eye-shadow on me – a smidgen of greeny-gold.

'How's your mum feeling?' Joe asks Lizzy, who, to my glee, is blushing again.

'She's a lot better, thank you,' Lizzy replies.

'Did you come into Wareham Station?' he checks.

'That's right.'

He tries to make chit-chat with her, but she's strangely lost for words.

'I'd better get back to work,' he says after a while.

He kisses me quickly before standing up. 'I'll come and see you again in a bit,' he tells us both. 'I'll bring out some more drinks for you. Same again?'

'Sure.' We both nod. We haven't even started on these ones yet.

He gets up and starts collecting empties.

Lizzy looks across the table at me and grins. I know she wants to talk to me about Joe, but she can't until he's back inside. I'm acutely aware of his presence around us – I can hear him clinking glasses together from the other side of the beer garden, and when my ears fail me I seem to have an innate sense of his whereabouts, even when he's behind me. Finally Lizzy raises her eyebrows and leans in for the kill.

'Is he a good kisser?'

'Mmm.' I try to keep a straight face.

'On a scale of one to ten?' she asks.

'Off the scale.'

'No!'

'Yes.'

'Have you . . .'

I know what's coming.

'No.' I shake my head abruptly.

'Okay.' She seems to relax a bit. 'But you really, really fancy him?'

'Can't you tell?'

'Does he have a brother?'

I start to laugh, then remember that it's not funny. 'He does, actually.'

Her eyes light up.

'But you'd never go there.'

'Why not?' she asks with a mixture of disappointment and curiosity.

'He's in jail.'

I explain to her about Ryan – what I know of him, anyway.

'Joe doesn't talk about him much.'

'Too busy kissing you,' Lizzy teases. I don't deny it. 'I hope you're not going to do a Pippa on me,' she adds jokily.

I try to laugh off her comment with a roll of my eyes. 'Not likely,' I reply.

'Good,' she says, laughing. But I know she's worried. She's worried about losing me, about us drifting apart, going in opposite directions . . . This is one relationship which she has no part of, and that's unsettling.

We move onto the subject of Joe's parents.

'Is that his dad behind the bar?' she asks.

'Yes. I don't know where his mum is – with a bit of luck, she's upstairs for the night.'

'I can't believe she called you a cheat in front of everyone!

Still, he's worth it, right?' Another grin, another raised eyebrow.

'I bloody hope so.'

By ten thirty, my friend is fading, and we still have to walk home.

'I'm sorry,' she says. 'These last few weeks have been exhausting.'

'I know,' I murmur with sympathy. 'I feel so bad that you've had to go through all that.'

'Fingers crossed the worst is over.'

'I'm sure it is,' I say, although I have no idea. 'I'll let Joe know we're leaving.'

He's popped out to see us every so often with drink refills, when he's been able to escape unnoticed. I haven't dared to go into the bar, even for a loo break, but now the alcohol is giving me some much-needed courage.

'I'll come with you,' Lizzy decides, grabbing her bag.

We walk inside. To my dismay, Joe's mother is now serving. Thankfully Joe sees us before she does. His wary look in her direction, however, doesn't go unnoticed.

'We've got to head off,' I say.

'I'll walk you out.' He motions to the door.

I turn and glance in his mum's direction, and at that same moment she looks up and sees me. Her mouth is set in a hard, thin line. Permanently? Perhaps.

'Can't you stay a bit longer?' Joe asks us when we get outside. 'Then I could walk you back.'

'Sorry,' Lizzy interjects. 'It's my fault. I'm really tired, with everything that's been going on recently . . .'

'Of course, of course,' Joe says quickly.

'We'll see you tomorrow?' I ask hopefully. We agreed yesterday that he shouldn't come to the cottage while Lizzy is there – three's a crowd, and all that.

'Definitely. Come over as early as you can.'

'JOE!'

We turn to see his mum come around the corner of the pub.

'I'll be there in a minute,' he says wearily.

'You'll be there right bloody now!' she snaps.

'I'll be there in a minute,' he says firmly.

The look on her face . . . Uh-oh.

She storms towards us. Joe steps in front of Lizzy and me, protectively. What the hell does he think she's going to do?

'Get your arse inside right this second!' she hisses. She jabs her finger at Lizzy and me. 'These two slags have taken up enough of your time tonight!'

Lizzy and I nearly fall over at her words.

'MUM! I cannot *believe* you just said that!' Joe shouts.

'GET INSIDE!' she bellows.

'Go,' I urge him, my hand on his arm. I don't want him to lose his job – his only way out of here.

'I'll be there *in a minute*,' he repeats through clenched teeth.

She backs away. 'Just you wait until your father hears about this . . .' Her tone sends a chill through me.

It's only when she disappears around the corner that Joe turns to face us. I've never witnessed such a mixture of emotions on anyone's face before. Anger, fear, anxiety, remorse . . .

'You should have just gone,' I say worriedly, sensing Lizzy's shock beside me. I know she wants to be out of here, pronto, and to my utter dismay I know that neither of us will be coming back tomorrow.

'I'm going to walk you home,' Joe says suddenly.

'No,' I urge. 'No. You should go back inside. Don't make it worse!' He hesitates. 'Come and see me later?' I suggest. This wasn't the plan but I know he needs me, and Lizzy will be asleep, anyway. 'Please,' I press. 'As soon as you finish. I'll wait on the bench.'

He looks at me, his eyes glistening. He nods abruptly and squeezes my hand before letting it go.

Chapter 10

'I'm sorry,' I say to Lizzy as soon as we've changed into our trainers and are stomping across the field to get as far away from the pub as possible. We're both worried his lunatic of a mother will follow. Thankfully she doesn't like dogs, otherwise she'd probably set Rottweilers on us.

'I can't believe that! What a bitch!'

'I did warn you . . .'

'Oh, God . . .' Lizzy's still in shock. 'I know he's gorgeous and all that, but *Alice*! His *mother*! How can you bear it?'

'I don't have to see much of her,' I say. 'He wants to get out of there.'

'Where does he want to go?'

'London.'

'Not Cambridge?'

I hesitate. 'No.' At least, not that I know of . . . Although I have found myself dreaming recently.

This seems to pacify her somewhat, and I hate her for it.

Oh, God, I don't hate her. I don't mean it.

'Please don't say anything to my parents about tonight,' I beg.

'I won't,' she says crossly.

I have no fingernails left by the time Joe arrives at close to midnight.

'I came as quickly as I could,' he says reaching the gate, out of breath. I get up to meet him. 'Dyson, stay there,' he commands, coming inside and closing the gate behind him.

He engulfs me in his arms and holds me tight. I can feel his heart hammering hard inside his chest. I've been terrified he wouldn't come.

I try to pull away, but he's reluctant to let me go. I look up at him. 'Are you okay?' I ask, but he won't meet my eyes. 'Joe?'

He looks down at me and his eyes fill with tears. He gulps in a mouthful of air and I can tell he's trying not to sob. He exhales, shakily. 'It's okay,' I murmur, squeezing him tightly.

'It's not,' he whispers. He pulls away. The look on his face is scaring me. 'My brother gets out tomorrow.'

'Out of jail?'

He nods, and then his anguish turns to bitterness. 'My parents couldn't even be bothered to tell me.'

'But they told you tonight? What happened?' I pull him to the bench and he sits down beside me.

It takes a long time for him to answer. 'I was so angry with my mum for speaking to you like that. I told her I'd leave if she ever spoke to you like that again.'

'What did she say?'

Pause. 'She *laughed* at me.'

He's not even angry about it. He's just so hurt. I can feel his pain, because it's mine too.

'Then she told me Ryan would prefer my room to his, anyway.'

'I don't understand,' I say after a while. 'How could you not know this was going on?'

'I hardly speak to them. I hardly ever see them,' he admits. 'We don't talk when we're working, and I'm out of the pub the second I can get away.'

It's true, I've seen him practically every minute that he's not working.

'Is your dad here?' he asks suddenly, looking back up at the dark cottage.

'Yes,' I reply. 'He and Mum were already in bed by the time we got back. Lizzy's asleep,' I add, although I'm not sure if that's true. I hope she can't hear us. Our bedroom overlooks the front garden and is just metres away above our heads. 'Shall we go for a walk?'

'I don't want to keep you up.'

'Joe . . .' I say tenderly.

We walk down the lane, passing the last few cottages. Dyson runs ahead of us and we can hear his nose sniffing and his paws padding further along the dirt track. There's a full moon tonight, and the air is unnervingly still. We go through a gate into a field and sit down on the grass up against a dry stone wall. It feels better to be out here alone. Well, alone except for Dyson. But his presence is comforting. Joe looks past me, deep in thought.

'What are you thinking about?'

He shakes his head abruptly. 'Nothing.'

'Tell me.'

Finally he answers. 'I don't want to go back.' Pause. 'But I have to.'

'Do you really have to?'

'My money is hidden under my mattress, for one.'

'Don't you have a bank account?' I ask with a frown.

'My parents don't exactly do things by the book,' he says with a wry smile. 'They pay me in cash.' His face hardens. 'I can't believe he's coming back tomorrow. It's been four years since I've seen him.'

'How old is he?'

'Twenty-six.'

'Maybe he's changed?'

'No. No. He hasn't changed.'

'But you have.'

'What do you mean?' he asks.

'You were only fourteen when you last saw him. You've grown a lot since then.'

'He'll still be bigger – and stronger – than me.'

'Bloody hell, Joe, I don't mean I want you to fight him!'

'I'd kill him if he ever touched you.'

'Stop it! Why would he touch me, anyway?'

'To get at me.'

He pulls away roughly, as though the thought angers him too much to be near me.

'What did he do to you?' I ask carefully. 'Did he used to beat you up?'

Nothing, and then he nods.

'Often?' I ask.

'Once I ended up in hospital.' I have to strain to hear him. 'My parents told the police that I'd fallen downstairs. They threatened to leave me on the streets if I ever told anyone the truth.'

I gasp. 'How old were you?'

'Six.'

'Six!' My eyes widen with horror. 'Six?'

He nods.

'Oh, my God, Joe, that is awful.'

'That wasn't the first time he hurt me and my parents did nothing about it. Or the last,' he says bitterly. 'They don't care about me.'

He's said this once before, but I didn't believe it then.

'No wonder you want to get away . . .'

He turns to look at me. 'The only thing keeping me here now is you,' he says simply.

We kiss, gently at first, then more passionately as we fall back onto the grass. He hovers above me, supporting his own weight so he doesn't crush me. His tongue explores my mouth and I wrap my legs around him, pulling him closer, wanting him to be closer. I slide my hands up inside his T-shirt and drag my fingernails down his back. He gasps into my mouth and I feel him down there, hard and pressing into me.

I pull him in tighter. I want him so much . . .

His lips trail to my neck and his hand slides up my shirt to my breast.

'I want you,' I whisper urgently.

He moves away from my neck and kisses my lips again, gently.

'I love you,' I add, wondering if he heard me the first time.

'I love you too.'

'Did you hear me?' I ask, unable to keep the worry from my voice.

He laughs quietly.

I release my grip on his legs.

'I want you too, but Dyson is putting me off a bit.'

I glance to his left at Dyson, who is panting and watching us both intently while his tail thumps against the ground. I start to laugh too.

'Plus, I don't have anything.'

'Anything?'

'A condom.'

'Oh.' I instantly feel silly. I hadn't thought about that. I know I should have, but in the heat of the moment it hadn't even occurred to me.

We sit back up and he takes my hand. We both stare ahead at the moonlit field.

'I'm a virgin,' I blurt out.

He looks across at me and squeezes my hand. 'Me too.'

'You're not,' I say with widened eyes.

He nods. 'I am.'

'But . . . *How?*'

He laughs. 'What do you mean, "how"?'

'You're so . . . good-looking! How can you have not shagged girls before?'

He shrugs. 'The same question could be directed at you.'

'I haven't found anyone I've liked enough.'

'Me neither.'

'But boys don't . . . Boys aren't like that.'

'Like what?' he presses. 'You don't think it matters to us whether or not it's special?'

'I don't know . . .'

'Okay, maybe not to some guys, but it matters to me.'

'Haven't you ever got close to anyone else?'

'There was a girl once.'

I instantly feel jealous.

'I thought I loved her.'

'How old were you?'

'Fifteen. It was when we were in Devon, before we moved to Cornwall.'

'Why did you move?'

'We couldn't really stay after what Ryan had done,' he says unhappily. 'Business went tits up. And my parents had never exactly been popular with the locals, in any case.'

'*Did* you love her?' I ask, still feeling sick.

He looks at me directly. 'No. I love *you*. What I felt for her was not even on the same page.' He smiles. 'Not even in the same book. Not even in the same library.'

I smile back at him. 'I've never been in love before, either,' I tell him. 'I can't imagine ever feeling this way about anyone ever again.'

Was that too honest?

'Me neither.' He doesn't take his eyes from mine and I draw him close.

'Fuck off!' Joe hisses after a while and I look past him to see Dyson right there, peering at us. I burst out laughing. He looks back at me. 'God, Alice, I want you so much.'

'I want you too.'

Lizzy . . . Pippa . . . Out, thoughts, out!

As if reading my mind, he speaks. 'I guess I should take you home before Lizzy starts to fret.'

I nod reluctantly and he stands up, holding his hands down to pull me to my feet. 'What are you two doing tomorrow?'

'I was going to show her Corfe Castle,' I reply. 'I think she'd like that.'

'It's good you're taking her mind off her mum. I'm sorry about tonight.'

'It's not your fault. She'll understand.' But in truth, I'm not sure that she will.

Chapter 11

'Are you alright?' Lizzy asks me for the umpteenth time the next day.

'I'm fine,' I reply.

'I've never seen you like this before,' she adds and I don't know how to respond.

It's true. I've been on another planet all day. I keep staring ahead, lost in my thoughts, wondering if Joe is okay.

'Does he have a phone?' she asks. 'Couldn't you call him?'

'No, he doesn't. Only the pub's public phone. I don't know the number, and his parents would probably answer it, anyway.'

'What time does his brother get here?'

'I'm not sure.' I look at her and smile. 'Thank you. You're being so nice. I'm sorry about all of this. I'm supposed to be the one cheering *you* up, not the other way around.'

'This is taking my mind off things.' Lizzy shrugs and pulls her cardigan across her chest.

After last night's hazy heat, today is cool and cloudy. We're at the Corfe Castle miniature village. It's so sweet, but I can't appreciate any of it.

'Shall we get some afternoon tea?' Lizzy suggests.

'Yes, of course.'

We eat in the adjoining café, overlooking the gardens. It's not so cold that we have to sit inside.

'You really like him, don't you?' she says, interrupting another one of my dazed stares.

'I love him.' It comes out of my mouth automatically, before I'm sure if it's a good idea or not.

'Do you really?' she asks with widened eyes.

I nod.

'I can't say I'm that amazed, actually,' she goes on. 'The way you were looking at him last night . . .'

'He loves me too.' I try not to sound defensive.

'Has he told you that?'

'He said it first.'

'Oh,' she replies. 'Wow.'

I don't want to let her surprise bother me, but I can't help it.

'Where did you go last night?' she asks. She appeared to be asleep when I finally got to bed.

'We went for a walk. Could you hear us?'

'Not what you were saying.' Aah. So she *was* awake, then. The walk was a good move.

I remember with a sudden shiver how heated things got last night.

'You've gone red!' she exclaims. 'Did you . . .'

'No!' I respond hotly. 'I told you, we haven't done anything like that!'

She falls silent, and it's not a pleasant silence. But I don't want to talk about last night to her. It felt special. Just between Joe and me.

And Dyson. Ahem.

Feeling awkward, I slice one of my scones in half and proceed to carefully smear it with strawberry jam and clotted cream. She does the same. After that, we manage to strike up a conversation that doesn't involve Joe.

'So what are we going to do tonight?' Lizzy asks in the car on the way back to the cottage. 'Do you want to try going back to the pub?'

'Would you do that for me?' I ask with amazement.

'Of course I would. You and me, we can take on that silly wench,' she says buoyantly.

I smile. 'There're also his dad and his jailbird brother to consider.'

'Easy-peasy.'

I think for a moment. 'Maybe we could drive over there now and I'll see if I can get Joe's attention?'

'That's an idea.'

'You can stay in the car and keep the engine running in case I have to make a mad dash for it.'

'We're not robbing a bank,' she teases.

'Unlike his brother,' I add. I can't actually believe I'm joking about it.

Dyson is nowhere to be seen. Heart pounding, I scan the packed beer garden for any sign of Joe, and then wait off to the side for a while in case he comes out. After ten very long minutes my pulse still hasn't settled and I'm wondering if I dare venture inside. A middle-aged man seated at the table near me stands up and asks his wife, I presume, if she'd like another Chardonnay. I grab my chance.

'Excuse me!' I say urgently. He looks over at me. 'Would you mind . . .' This doesn't sound very good. 'Would you mind looking to see if a young man is behind the bar? Dark hair, eyebrow pierced . . .'

He gives his wife a knowing look and I inwardly squirm. 'No problem, love.'

I relax slightly now that things are in hand, but I'm still unbearably tense by the time he returns.

'There was a young man there, yes.' My heart lifts. 'But he had blond hair and tattoos. I didn't see an eyebrow piercing.'

That must be Ryan. Where's Joe?

'Sorry,' he says, seeing my face.

I back away, mumbling my thanks, and return to the car.

'Was he there?' Lizzy asks.

'No, I don't think so.' I put my seatbelt on.

I'm on full alert the whole way back, peering across the field to see if I can spot him wandering.

'You watch the road,' Lizzy insists. '*I'll* look.'

'Have you seen Joe, by any chance?' I ask my mum the moment we're through the door.

'No,' she replies, frowning. 'Isn't he at the pub?'

My dad comes into the kitchen. 'Hello, you two!' he says brightly, then, when he sees our faces: 'What's up?'

Lizzy looks away, bound by her promise to me to not breathe a word, but here and now I'm so concerned that I don't know how I can keep this from them.

'Joe's brother has come out of jail,' I blurt out. 'He hurt Joe really badly when he was a kid, and I'm worried he's done something to him now.'

'I didn't even know he had a brother, let alone was in jail,' Mum says, shocked.

'What do you mean, he hurt Joe?' Dad asks sharply.

'He used to beat him up. He put him in hospital once. Joe's terrified of him. I don't know what to do.'

Dad thinks for a moment. 'Perhaps we could go to the pub? Scout it out?'

Hope fills me. I don't think Joe's parents will link my parents to me.

I nod. 'That could work.' A thought occurs to me. 'Hang on . . . I might know where he is.'

'Where?' they both ask at once.

'Dancing Ledge.'

'The cliffs?'

'Yes.'

'We'll come with you,' Dad says, reaching for his coat.

'No, it's okay!' I reply swiftly. 'I'll go alone.'

Lizzy shifts from foot to foot. 'With Lizzy,' I add, looking at her. 'If you'd like to?'

She nods.

The wind has picked up so I knot my hair into a long plait as we set off down the path, and tuck it into my coat.

'The cliffs are beautiful,' I say determinedly. 'You should see them, anyway.'

I feel bad enough for ruining her weekend, let alone dragging her on a wild-goose chase.

'Okay,' she says.

'I'm so sorry about this,' I add.

'Stop apologising,' she says. 'I'm glad I can be here for you.'

I wrap my arm around her and give her a quick squeeze. I owe her.

We reach the gorse walkway at last. There's been no sign of Joe this entire time and I'm on edge as we stumble down the rocky path. In my mind, I imagine him there on the hill, waiting for me, but it suddenly occurs to me that it's not very likely. He could be *anywhere* . . .

'Wow, that's amazing,' Lizzy says when we emerge from the gorse. I'm not looking at the view – I'm scanning the hills.

'I'm just going to go . . .' My voice trails off and I carry on down the steep slope.

'Is it dangerous?' Lizzy calls after me, raising her voice over the sound of the wind.

'No,' I call back. 'There's a fence at the bottom.'

'Okay.' She follows me reluctantly.

'You can wait here, if you like? If I find him I'll come straight back,' I promise. 'I'll only be fifteen minutes.'

'Okay.' She nods and sits down on the grass. I hurry down the path, the momentum of the slope pushing me forward. I've never run down a hill this steep before. In fact, I haven't run down a hill since I was a child. It's strangely liberating.

I reach the bottom, breathing heavily. I take off my coat as I'm boiling now, and pass through the gate to Dancing Ledge. A dog barks. I know instantly that it's Dyson.

'JOE!' I shout. 'JOE!'

The dog barks again, more excitedly this time.

'JOE!'

'ALICE?'

The relief is immense. He comes around the corner of a rock and sees me, the smile momentarily sweeping the worry from his face.

'ALICE!' He runs to me, and I to him, and then we're in each other's arms with Dyson barking and bounding about at our sides. 'You came,' he breathes into my hair.

'I went to the pub,' I try to tell him, gasping for breath.

'You didn't?' he exclaims, his hands on my face, pushing loose strands of hair away from my eyes while the wind does its utmost to unwind my plait.

'They didn't see me.' I explain how I enlisted a stranger's help.

'Yep, that was Ryan,' Joe says, when I've repeated the man's description of the tattooed blond guy behind the bar.

'Lizzy is waiting up the hill.'

'Cool, okay.'

We start to make our way back up there.

'Did you tell them you're leaving?' I ask.

He shakes his head. 'Not yet.'

'How did you get away from work?'

He sighs. Lizzy appears in view and I wave up at her. She returns my wave with a smile – she'll be pleased for me that I've found him.

'I got back to the pub last night to find my parents had moved most of my stuff out of my bedroom to the one at the back.'

'No! That's so out of order!'

'I wasn't even that bothered about it. I'll be leaving soon, anyway. But I was worried about my money.'

'Had they found it?'

'No, thank God.'

I breathe a sigh of relief for him. 'Where have you hidden it now?'

'I haven't. It's in my pocket.'

I glance down at the bulk there.

'I wondered if you would look after it for me?'

'Of course.' I feel honoured that he trusts me, even though I know that he should.

'Thank you.' He reaches over and strokes my palm. I want him to take my hand, but we've almost reached Lizzy. She stands up as we approach, and then tries to fend off Dyson.

'Hey,' she says to Joe, full of concern. 'Are you okay?'

Joe nods. 'Come here, boy.' He pulls Dyson away from her.

Lizzy brushes him off. 'Did you see your brother?'

I realise that I haven't even asked that question yet.

'Yes,' he replies.

'Shall we stay here for a bit?' I ask. We sit in a line facing the view. Dyson flops down on the grass beside me, while Joe is in the middle. I turn to face him. 'What was he like?'

'The same.' Joe stares ahead at the ocean.

'Did he hurt you?' Lizzy asks with trepidation.

'No.' Pause. 'Not yet.'

A chill goes through me. I take his hand.

'I don't want you to go back there.'

'It's okay,' he says. 'It'll be okay for a bit.'

'Did he threaten you?' Lizzy presses.

'No. It's not that he said or did *anything*,' Joe explains. 'It's just the way he looks at me. It's ... I don't know how to describe it. *Menacing* ... He's such a fucking bully!' he erupts. 'And my parents do nothing to stop it! They never have. He's always been a nasty bastard – evil – but they can't see it. Or maybe they can. Maybe he appeals to them because they're evil too.'

'No wonder you want to get away,' Lizzy murmurs.

'It's amazing you've lasted this long,' I add.

'That's only because he's been in jail for the last four years.'

'That doesn't seem like long enough for armed robbery ...'

'He was an accomplice to a hardened criminal. They've let

him out early for good behaviour.' He snorts. 'So he'll be well and truly ready to let off some steam.'

'I don't want you to go back there,' I say again, more urgently this time.

He looks at me sadly. 'Where else am I supposed to go?'

'Come and stay with me,' I say, even though I know my parents would object.

He smiles and shakes his head. 'It won't be for long, Alice. Just over two weeks.'

'Why two weeks?' Lizzy asks with a frown.

'That's when Alice is leaving,' he says simply.

I squeeze his hand, hard.

Chapter 12

Lizzy leaves on Sunday afternoon after a morning at Lulworth Cove. I think she's secretly pleased to be going home, even though she keeps batting off my apologies with 'this took my mind off things' responses.

I wait on the platform and wave her off. When the train disappears around the corner I'm engulfed with sadness. That was one of the last times I'll spend with my friend before we go off to university and I messed it up. So much for sunny days at the beach checking out boys. I remember the excitement of getting ready to go to the pub on Friday night and her squealing about how gorgeous Joe was, and I am full of regret. I so wish the weekend had continued like that. Even the weather has turned. It's cloudy and very windy today and the air feels damp.

My parents have been wary around me all day. My dad insists on a pep-talk before he sets off back to London.

'Now, Alice,' he says, and I instantly bristle at his tone as he leans over the island counter in the middle of the kitchen. 'You're leaving in two weeks.'

'I know, Dad, everyone keeps reminding me.'

'Who's reminding you?' Is that relevant?

'You, Mum, Lizzy, Joe . . .'

'Ah, Joe too.'

'Yes, Dad, and he's leaving too.'

'Where's he going?' he asks with surprise.

'London,' I reply with a sigh.

'Not Cambridge?'

Here we go again . . .

'No, Dad.'

He breathes an actual sigh of relief. I sigh too, but it's with unhappiness.

He senses my disheartenment. 'You might be able to see him when you come home during the holidays.'

'I guess so.' That seems like an unbearably long time to be apart. 'Anyway, don't worry. I'll get on with some work this week.'

'That would be a good idea. Take your mind off things,' he says perkily, standing up straight.

As if . . .

Mum and I come out onto the driveway to wave him off.

'Bye, love,' Mum says, giving him a kiss.

'Have a good week,' he says to her fondly. 'You're doing great, Marie. This collection is going to fly.'

She puts her arms around his neck and they hug. I'm seeing their relationship in a new light. What it must be like to have someone by your side, looking after you and caring for you, forever . . . Joe is always at the forefront of my mind, but now the ache for him intensifies.

'What time is Joe coming over?' Mum asks when my father has gone, reading my thoughts.

'After closing time,' I reply, 'which is earlier on Sundays.'

'Eleven o'clock?'

'More likely to be eleven thirty once he's cleaned up.'

'Gosh, Alice, that's late.'

She doesn't even know that he's been coming here after work every night. She's always asleep by then. I wonder if I should have kept this information to myself, but I guess it's futile.

It's cold out on the bench that night as I wait. To my surprise, the kitchen door opens and Mum appears.

'Alice!' she exclaims. 'What are you doing out here?'

'Waiting for Joe,' I tell her.

'Come inside. You'll catch your death!' she cries. 'I'm going up to bed, anyway,' she adds knowingly.

I shiver and stand up, but return to tape a note to the bench telling Joe to come inside.

I wait in the kitchen. When I hear the gate latch I run to the door.

'Joe?' I whisper into the darkness.

'Hey,' he says, coming around the corner.

'Mum's asleep,' I tell him. 'She said to come inside.' He looks wary. 'Leave Dyson on the driveway,' I suggest.

I take his cold hand and lead him into the living room, acutely aware that my mum's bedroom is directly overhead.

We sit on the sofa together and I cuddle in close. He looks shattered.

'You're so tired.' I reach up and stroke his face, compassion washing over me. 'Lie next to me.'

I shift to the edge of the sofa and he slides down, wrapping his arm around my shoulders to keep me from falling off. He turns his body in towards mine and holds me close. I shut my eyes. It's blissful in his arms.

'I wish we had this place to ourselves,' I whisper after a while, the slow steady sound of his breathing making me feel dozy. He doesn't reply. 'Maybe we should run off together.'

Again, no answer. I pull away and look up at him. He's fast asleep. He looks so peaceful. I push his hair away from his face. His eyelashes are long and dark, and there are the beginnings of stubble on his jaw. His skin is perfectly smooth and tanned. I study the silver ring through his brow. I gently kiss his lips. He's out cold. I smile at him as love floods me. And then the ache returns. I know it's a dull and distant replica of what's to come.

Chapter 13

I stay with Joe on the sofa that night until almost four o'clock in the morning, when he jolts awake. I put my hand on his chest to calm him.

'It's okay,' I whisper. 'You fell asleep.'

He sits up abruptly and I do the same. My eyes are stinging painfully. I've dozed in and out of sleep for the last three hours, but haven't been able to nod off properly.

'I'd better get back,' he mumbles groggily.

'Stay until the morning,' I plead.

He looks around at the dark living room. 'Where's Dyson?'

'I brought him into the kitchen.'

He nods and goes to stand up. I pull him back onto the sofa. 'Stay until the morning,' I persist.

He shakes his head and his eyes dart up at the ceiling.

'Mum won't mind,' I assure him.

'No. I'd better get back.'

I sigh heavily as he stands up. I follow him into the kitchen, where an unusually tired Dyson slowly rises to his feet.

'I'll see you later?' he says at the door.

'Are you working all day?'

'Only the evening.'

'So come at lunchtime. Maybe we can take a picnic to the ledge.'

He nods and bends down to kiss me, then opens the door and ushers Dyson out.

'I love you,' I call quietly after him.

'I love you more.'

'No, you don't.'

'Yes, I do.'

He smiles back at me, some of the worry gone from his face. I stand in the doorway for a moment before going upstairs to bed.

The cold, windy weather holds through to the next day. Mum is working in the conservatory when I wake up and the smell of her oils permeates the house.

'I'm going for a picnic with Joe,' I tell her after finding myself sleeping in until almost eleven o'clock.

'A picnic!' she exclaims. 'In this weather? Why don't you just stay here?' I hesitate. 'Am I cramping your style?' she asks with a raised eyebrow.

'Your paints stink,' I joke, walking through to the kitchen to prepare some sandwiches.

Joe comes inside to say hello before we set off. My mum wants the full low-down on his brother. Joe is surprisingly perky.

'It's been alright, actually,' he says.

'Are they talking to you now?' I ask.

'No,' he concedes, laughing a little. 'But it's better than the alternative.'

'We'd better get going,' I say. 'I'm starving.'

'You should have had breakfast,' Mum says wryly.

'I slept in,' I tell Joe.

'I didn't get back to sleep,' he replies.

'Joe and I fell asleep on the sofa last night,' I admit to Mum.

Both eyebrows go up. 'Oh, *really*?' she says.

Joe shifts awkwardly at my side. 'Let's go!' I say merrily, hoping to put an end to his embarrassment. Although *why* he is embarrassed is beyond me. It's not like we did anything.

'Did you have to tell her that?' he mutters under his breath when we're out of the door.

'Why not?' I reply. 'We're both eighteen, what's the big deal?'

He shrugs. I put my arm around his waist and smile up at him, but he stares ahead at the path. I release my grip, a little put out. If he notices, he doesn't comment on it.

We pass a couple of dog walkers on the way, but apart from them the cliffs are practically deserted.

'Let's walk down to the ledge,' Joe suggests.

The grass is slippery underfoot, but his hand holds me steady. There are steps cut out of the rock at the bottom of the hill.

'Let's keep going,' I say. We carefully navigate the steps and come to a chalky slope leading to the cliff. The cliff is only about ten metres high down here, and below is a flat area of rock just above sea level – the actual Dancing Ledge. My dad was reading aloud about this place only yesterday, and he told Mum, Lizzy and me that the rock here was blasted away by local quarrymen and used to construct Ramsgate harbour in east Kent. It's called Dancing Ledge because the area of stone cut out of the cliffs is the same size as a ballroom dance floor. And within that 'dance floor' is a man-made swimming pool, created for the use of local schools about a hundred years ago.

'We'll have to come back when it's sunny,' I say, looking at the clear pool of water, grey today, but greeny-blue on a sunny day I imagine. 'Could we climb down?' I ask him.

He glances at Dyson.

'Not to worry,' I say, remembering his fear about Dyson running off.

But he delves into his coat pocket and pulls out a leash. 'He'll be fine.'

'That was well thought out,' I say, impressed.

'Come on, boy,' he says, leading Dyson back up to the fence. The dog barks with annoyance at being tied up, but Joe pulls a plastic bag out of his backpack and unwraps it to produce a very large bone. I can practically see Dyson salivating from here. He flops onto the grass and starts to gnaw. Joe flashes me an amused look as he jogs back down the steps.

'I thought you weren't a planner,' I tease as he gets closer. He shrugs without looking at me and nods at the cliff edge. 'You ready?'

'Let's do it.'

Joe goes first and promises, with a grin, to catch me if I fall. I jump the last metre and land safely on the rock. It's completely deserted down here. No one else wants to brave the weather conditions, but despite the wind, the sea is not rough. The water laps onto the ledge and we can see that the rock comes to a sudden stop just beyond it. The water looks very deep.

'You can dive in,' Joe tells me.

'Have you?' I ask him.

He nods.

I bet he looks hot in his swimming trunks. I see the dark outline of a couple of caves beyond him. 'Have you been inside the caves?' I ask.

'Yeah. Want to have a look?'

'Sure.' He leads the way. We reach the caves and go inside. The sound of the wind whistling through the hollowed-out space is loud, but it's much more sheltered.

'This is cool!' I exclaim. 'Shall we eat in here?'

'Yeah, okay.' He bends down and opens his backpack. Earlier, I gave him the food I'd prepared, along with a picnic rug, which he hands to me. I lay it out on the smooth rock. Joe sits down, but doesn't look at me when I hand him his sandwich. It occurs to me that he's barely looked at me since he went off to tie up Dyson. I instantly feel on edge.

'Are you alright?' I ask nervously.

'Yeah, I'm fine.' He shrugs again, not meeting my eyes.

He stares out of the cave opening while eating his lunch. I take a bite of my sandwich. His arm brushes against mine and it makes my hairs stand up, but I feel strangely separate from him. I don't know what's going through his head.

We eat in silence and after a while he puts his leftover sandwich down and links his arms around his knees.

'What's wrong?' I ask gently, putting my food down too.

He looks at my knees and shakes his head, but doesn't answer.

'Joe, you're starting to worry me.' He still won't look at me. 'What's wrong?' I ask again.

'Nothing,' he says. 'And everything.'

I tilt his chin towards me and force him to look at me. His eyes meet mine, darker in this cave, but still intense. A jolt goes through me, and then we're kissing. We fall back onto the rug and

I pull him on top of me, shivers travelling all the way up my body into my head. They keep coming in waves as he kisses me like never before. His hands slide inside of my top to my breasts and I gasp into his mouth as I reach down to unbutton his jeans.

He looks at me and nods and I know that this time he has come prepared.

Butterflies sweep into my stomach as I realise that this is it: I'm going to lose my virginity to Joe, beautiful, lovely Joe. A boy I love, a boy I will always love. Tears prick my eyes and I feel momentarily overwhelmed at the intensity of this thought, but I keep my lips pressed to his as we ease ourselves out of our jeans. He goes slowly and is worried when I cry out. The pain is acute, yet perfect, and I don't want him to stop. Ever.

Chapter 14

'Wow. You look beautiful.'

It's Friday night and I've made an effort for Joe – an extra effort. I've persuaded my parents to go out for dinner and invited him over to the cottage for the evening. I've put on a little more make-up than usual and am wearing a short cream and red slip dress with my hair tied up into a tousled bun. I feel a bit overdressed for staying in, but I don't care.

'Are you hungry?' I ask.

'Only for you.'

I laugh. 'That's so corny.'

'I know.' He looks at the oven. 'That does smell good. What is it?'

'Chicken wrapped in prosciutto with a white wine and cream sauce.'

His mouth falls open. 'That sounds amazing!'

'It's dead easy,' I say flippantly. 'It's my mum's recipe.'

'Okay, maybe I am a little hungry after all.'

It's still bright and sunny outside by the time we sit down at the table, but I light a couple of candles, anyway.

'What time are your parents back?'

'They promised not until eleven.'

'That was decent of them,' he says. 'I feel bad.'

'Not bad enough to keep your hands off me, I hope.'

He grins. 'No.'

'Then hurry up and eat so we can go upstairs.'

It's so different being with him in a bed. Feeling his naked body connected to mine is blissful in the extreme. On two occasions cars go by outside the cottage and we're both on full alert in case it's my parents returning early, but the rest of the time there's nothing on my mind except Joe.

'If you came to Cambridge with me we could do this every day,' I murmur later.

'Only once a day?'

'I didn't actually specify that.'

He laughs. I climb on top of him and peer down at him. We're both still hot and sweaty from the last time.

'Again?' he asks with a slight look of concern.

I giggle. 'No, don't worry. Twice was enough.' Pause. 'For now.' I peck him on the lips. He stares up at the ceiling.

'What are you thinking about?' I ask.

'Nine days.'

Nine days until I leave.

My smile falls. 'I can't believe I've only known you for just over a month.'

He nods and looks into my eyes. 'It feels like longer.'

'A lifetime.'

'Not yet.'

Happiness bubbles through me. 'Not yet?'

'I love you so much. I can't imagine ever loving anyone more,' he says seriously.

'Me neither.'

Our kiss becomes more passionate and I feel him growing harder beneath me.

'Once more?' I ask.

'Not if you don't want to. I don't want to hurt you.'

'You won't,' I whisper.

At least, not in that way.

I cry after the last time. It feels more intense somehow, like we know our time together is limited.

At ten to eleven, Joe is ready to leave. Neither of us wants to face my parents. Every day we're brought down to earth with a bump, and we don't want that tonight. It's been too special.

'I'll walk you to the gate,' I say, opening the front door.

He steps outside onto the driveway and then freezes.

'What's wrong?' I ask him.

He's tense as he stares into the darkness.

'What?' I ask, full of alarm. I go to peer out of the door, but he puts his hand out to stop me.

'Dyson!' he calls quietly into the darkness.

The dog appears around the corner and Joe visibly relaxes.

'What is it?' I press.

'Nothing. I thought I could smell smoke.'

'Smoke?'

'Cigarette smoke.'

I give him an inquisitive look.

'Ryan,' he says simply.

Now I'm the one who's tense. 'Come back inside.'

'No, no, it's fine. It was probably just someone walking their dog. Dyson doesn't seem worried.'

It's true. Dyson has flopped down at Joe's feet.

'Are you sure?' I ask, feeling anxious.

'Definitely. I'll come by in the morning around ten.'

I nod. 'Okay.'

'I'd better go before your dad gets back and realises I've been shagging his daughter.'

I whack him on his arm.

'Love you.' He kisses me quickly.

'You too.'

And then he's gone.

Chapter 15

At nine forty-five the next morning, I take my usual position outside on the bench. I've brought one of my course books – this time I'm trying to tackles Sophocles' *Oedipus* – but no doubt I'll sit and stare at the words and not take in any of them. I feel nervous when I think of starting university in a few weeks. I'm way behind on my preparation, and I do indeed like to be prepared. Maybe I will be a fly-by-the-seat-of-my-pants kind of girl on this one occasion. The Greek Tragedies can't compete with Joe.

By ten past ten, Joe still hasn't arrived. I try to tell myself he's just slept in, but apart from the last time he did that he's usually very punctual. By ten forty-five, I'm anxious. My dad comes outside.

'Joe still not here?' he asks.

'No.'

'He's probably just slept in again,' he says nonchalantly, but his words do nothing to alleviate my concern. 'He's a big boy, he can look after himself.'

I stand up, full of determination. 'Can I borrow Mum's car to go and check on him?'

He frowns, finally taking me seriously. 'I'll drive you,' he decides. 'I don't want you going there by yourself.'

'Thanks, Dad.' But I'm not ready to breathe a sigh of relief just yet.

I stare out of the car window, but there's no sign of Joe. My dad parks and comes with me, refusing to let me go alone. I check the side of the pub and nearly faint with relief when I see Dyson tied up there.

'Dyson!' I call.

He stands up and starts to bark madly in my direction.

'Shh!' I exclaim, rushing over to him to try to stop him from alerting Joe's parents. He's deliriously happy as he licks my face and hands. 'Where's Joe?' I ask him. He starts barking again and the fear and worry return.

'I'll go and check inside,' my dad says.

I turn back to Dyson. 'Is he asleep?' I ask him. He licks my face with his huge, slobbery tongue.

'Argh!' I bat him off good-naturedly.

'Hello, beautiful.'

The hairs on the back of my neck stand up instantly. Slowly I turn around to see who I can only assume to be Ryan, leaning against the pub's back door. He's taller than Joe – and bigger, much bigger. His arms are decorated with tattoos and his blond hair is shorn. Stubble that is almost a beard, but not quite, graces his jaw. He's wearing a white vest like the one Joe's dad was wearing on the first night we came to this pub.

I stand up. Dyson crouches low and growls at him.

'Fuck off,' he says nastily to the dog. 'Pathetic piece of shit.'

I have an urge to back away, but I keep my feet firmly on the ground.

Ryan takes a cigarette out of a crumpled packet in his pocket and puts it to his lips, lighting it with a match. He starts to walk towards me. Dyson's growls grow louder.

'Fuck off,' he says again. I start to back away. 'Hey, where are you going?' he asks in a silky voice.

My dad appears behind me. 'Alice!' he says.

Understanding registers on Ryan's face. 'Ah,' he says and his tone sends a chill spiralling down my spine. 'So *you're* Alice.'

'Where's Joe?' I demand to know.

'Alice, come,' my dad interrupts. There's urgency to his tone.

'Where's Joe?' I turn this question on my dad. He takes my arm and marches me around the corner. 'Dad?'

I can hear Ryan chuckling darkly behind me.

'He's in hospital,' Dad tells me as we get closer to the car, his lips set in a hard, thin line.

'What?' I exclaim, blood draining from my face.

'Come on,' he says, more gently this time. He opens the car door and pushes me inside. 'We'll go there.'

'What happened?' I ask as he pulls onto the main road.

'His mother said he fell down the stairs last night.'

'That's a lie!'

'I know.'

'She said he was concussed. They've kept him in overnight for observation.'

'Joe!'

He looks up from his hospital bed and sees me and I barely register the bandages wrapped around his head because we're in each other's arms before I know it.

'Alice,' he breathes into my hair. I pull away and touch the bandages, tears in my eyes. I try to keep my anger in check.

'What did he do to you?'

He looks past me to my dad, standing at the foot of the bed.

'Are you okay, son?' Dad asks abruptly.

Joe nods. He's in a ward with seven other people, but the curtain has been partially drawn around his bed so he has some privacy.

'What happened?' I ask, speaking quietly, so as not to disturb the other patients.

'He smashed me on the back of my head with a bottle.'

My dad breathes in sharply. 'Your mother said you'd fallen down the stairs.'

Joe meets his eyes, but doesn't deny it. 'I'll wait outside in the corridor,' Dad says, turning to leave. Joe looks at me once he's gone.

'You went to the pub?'

'Yes. Dad went inside.'

'Did you see Dyson?'

'He was out at the back.'

He looks relieved.

'I met Ryan.'

The look on his face . . . Horror, fear, anger . . . 'What did he say to you?'

'Nothing.'

He pushes me away. 'I'm going to kill him.'

'Stop it!' I snap. 'He didn't say *anything* to me!'

He glares at me, but I know his fury is not directed at me. 'I don't believe you.'

'He called me beautiful . . .'

Joe tenses.

'. . . and then laughed at me when we left to come and find you.'

He regards me. 'That sounds about right.'

'He didn't know who I was at first.'

'But now he does?'

I nod, warily.

He makes to stand up. 'I've got to get out of here.'

'No, Joe.' I try to push him back down. 'Stay here until they say you can go.' A thought occurs to me. 'Wait.' I look at him hopefully. 'Have you told the police what he did?'

He shakes his head. 'No.'

'But you have to! This would land him back in jail!'

'I can't.'

'Yes, you can!' I say fervently. 'You must!'

'I can't!'

'Why not?'

'He said he'd kill Dyson if I breathed a word about it.'

I put my hand over my mouth. Another thought comes to me. 'But he wouldn't have a chance if we went to the police now. They'd go and arrest him.'

'No. My parents would deny it. They'd say I'm delusional. They've done it before.'

I stare at him, lost for words.

He gets up, and this time I don't stop him. 'Will your dad give me a lift to the pub, do you think?'

'You can't go back there!' I exclaim, my speech returning.

'I have to get Dyson.' He's adamant and I know I won't change his mind.

'Okay, but we're staying with you.'

Chapter 16

Joe insisted we drop him off at the pub and not wait for him. My dad wouldn't have wanted Dyson in his car on the return journey anyway, so I agreed to go back to the cottage and wait on the bench. But after a while I think, 'What am I doing?' and set off across the field instead. I don't relax until I see Joe and Dyson – tiny specks in the distance. We run the rest of the way to each other – just like you see in the movies – and then we stand in the middle of that green, green field, breathing hard into one another's shoulders as we clutch each other tightly. Finally we turn and walk back towards the cottage, hand in hand. My parents are standing anxiously outside on the dirt track, looking left and right. Then they spot us and I can see their relief from here. I wave as if to say, 'It's okay,' but they don't wave back.

'We were worried about you!' Dad snaps when we're in earshot.

'I went to meet Joe,' I explain.

'I can see that.'

Joe looks awkward.

'Come inside.' Mum bustles us into the cottage. Joe leaves Dyson on the driveway. 'Let me have a look,' she says, turning to

Joe. He sits on a kitchen chair and she carefully unwinds his bandage. I stand by, watching, and flinch as the deep wound is revealed. The doctors have had to shave off some of his hair.

'Your hair will grow back and cover the scar,' she assures him. 'Go through to the living room and I'll make some tea.'

I take Joe's hand and lead him to the sofa. I automatically snuggle up close, half draping my knees across his lap. He edges away slightly.

'What's wrong?' I ask.

'Your parents,' he mumbles.

I move away so he doesn't feel uncomfortable. Mum brings through a tray laden with tea and biscuits. Dad is still looking disgruntled. Barely two minutes go by before he starts with the questions.

'What are you going to do now?' he asks Joe.

'Dad . . .' I frown. It's too soon to be pressing him to make a decision.

'It's fine,' Joe tells me. 'I don't know,' he replies to my dad.

'Well, you can't go back to the pub,' I interrupt heatedly.

'I can't stay here.' Joe gazes at me calmly.

'Yes, you can! Can't he?' I turn to my parents. They both avert their gaze. 'What, you're going to send him back to that hellhole? He could be beaten to death!'

'Of course you can stay here tonight,' my mum interjects quietly.

'Marie—' Dad starts.

'Thank you,' I say forcefully, looking pointedly at both of them.

'You can sleep on the sofa,' Mum adds.

My dad gets up and walks out. Joe looks after him, warily. We hear the front door slam.

'I'll talk to him,' Mum says. She follows Dad out.

Joe breathes a heavy sigh and looks at me. 'I can't stay here.'

'Of course you can!'

'No, Alice, it's not fair on your parents.'

'Bugger them! They'll deal with it! You're not going back to the pub.'

'I'll be okay,' he says softly.

'No, Joe. No, you won't. You're staying here.' I'm adamant.

'I could stay at a hotel.'

'No, you need your money. Anyway, it's the middle of the holiday season – most places will be booked out and everything else will be overpriced and awful. We've only got to get through the next week and then we'll be out of here.'

'Maybe I should just go now.'

'No!' I exclaim automatically, before asking, 'What do you mean?'

'I could go to London.'

I instantly feel crushed. 'I hoped you'd come to Cambridge,' I say in a small voice.

His face softens as he regards me. 'I'm not sure I could do that to you. I'd cramp your style.'

'What the *hell* are you talking about? I *want* you there! I don't want to go without you!'

He smiles sadly. 'If you want me there I'll be there. But I can't stay with your parents until you leave, Alice. I'll have to meet you there, somewhere down the line.'

'What? No! Come with me! I'm not going alone.'

He sighs and puts his arm around me, pulling me close. He kisses my forehead, but I'm tense and overwrought with anxiety. What does he mean, he'll meet me there, somewhere down the line? I'll talk him into it, I promise myself. I'm not going to Cambridge without him.

My dad hurries into the room and we both jump apart from each other.

'Joe! Your dad's outside.'

Joe leaps to his feet and stumbles in the direction of the kitchen. He winces and puts his hand to his head. I grab his arm to hold him steady.

'Are you okay?' I ask.

'Got up too quickly,' he mutters, pulling away and following my dad to the door. Dad tries to block my exit, but I push his arm away roughly.

'Move!'

'Alice, I do not want you going outside,' he says sharply. Mum pulls me back firmly, then Dad goes out of the door. Mum and I hurry to the kitchen window.

My dad stands protectively on Joe's left, facing his big, beefy father. His hair is still gelled and black, and his tattoos ink out from underneath his tight grey T-shirt. It's not a warm day, but he doesn't look like the type to complain about the cold. He doesn't look angry, or sorry. Considering the events that have led to this point, they have a surprisingly unanimated conversation. Finally they turn away from each other and Joe comes back inside, closely followed by Dad. Joe's dad turns and walks out through the gate.

'Ryan's done a runner,' Joe says miserably. 'He wanted to know if I'd seen him.'

'Oh.' So he wasn't checking up on his younger son, asking him to come home. 'Was he okay with you? Did he seem threatening?'

'No,' Joe replies. I look at my dad for confirmation. Dad shakes his head in response. 'Maybe I should go back home,' Joe says.

'You can't!' I can feel myself getting worked up again.

'Look, stay here tonight,' Mum butts in. 'See how you feel tomorrow.' She glances at Dad, who nods.

'That seems like the best idea,' he replies. I look at Joe and smile. He doesn't smile back.

It's clear that night that Dad is not going to go to bed until I do, so finally I give in and say goodnight. It's ridiculous.

'I'll bring Dyson in,' I say, yawning.

'Bring him where?' Dad halts in his tracks.

'To the kitchen,' I respond.

'No,' Joe quickly cuts in. 'He'll be fine outside.'

I stare at my dad, but know he's not going to give in. Not a dog person. 'Right, that's settled, then,' he says, turning towards the stairs. He pauses at the bottom and looks back at me.

'I'll be up in a minute,' I tell him firmly. His eyes dart between Joe and me and he leaves, realising that, in this small way, he's not going to be the victor.

He creaks his way up the stairs slowly. I wait until he's inside the bathroom before going to Joe, who is still sitting on the sofa.

'Let me help you make up your bed,' I say, lifting up the sheets that Mum brought down. We do the job together, then he glances at me awkwardly.

'Night,' he says.

'Are you sure Dyson will be okay outside?' I check.

Almost in response, Dyson starts to bark manically. Joe and I meet each other's eyes for a split second before rushing to the door.

'DYSON!' he shouts, running out into the darkness. I follow him, and as soon as my feet touch the driveway I hear a loud yelp. Then: silence.

'DYSON!' Joe shouts again.

'DAD!' I scream into the house. 'DAD!'

Joe runs out of the gate.

'JOE!' My voice sounds off into the darkness. 'WAIT!'

My dad bursts out of the kitchen door, then reaches back inside to grab a flashlight.

'JOE!' I scream again.

'DYSON!' I hear him shout.

My dad holds me back behind him as we rush through the gate. Then we hear Joe to our left.

'Dyson . . .'

I will never forget the tone in Joe's voice. My dad points his torch up the track. Joe is crouched down over a hairy lump, tenderly holding his dog's head. 'Dyson . . .' he says again. 'It's okay, it's okay, good boy . . .'

Dad quickly flashes the light around to scan the scene, but there's no one to be seen. He returns the light onto Joe. I break away from my dad and run to him.

'He's still breathing,' Joe says, tears pouring down his distressed face. Dyson judders under his touch and his tail twitches in a feeble attempt to wag. Dad reaches us and shines his light at Dyson. His black scraggy hair looks stark and bright under the flashlight's glare. The light moves to his head and I reel away. There's huge gash to his skull and blood is pouring from it, all over Joe's hands.

'It's okay, good boy,' Joe whispers tearfully, rocking backwards and forwards on his heels.

Dad's light moves to a large, blood-splattered rock nearby.

'We've got to get him to a vet,' Joe says.

'I'll take Mum's car,' I tell Dad.

'I'll drive you,' he says.

Joe gingerly tries to lift Dyson, but he's too heavy to carry alone. Dad takes over from me and I run on ahead to get Mum's car keys and tell her what we're doing.

Joe sits in the boot, tenderly cradling his dog.

'How's he doing?' I ask from the backseat as Dad navigates the bendy country roads.

'He's still breathing,' Joe replies and a tiny spark of hope hits me. Maybe it will be okay . . .

'I'm so sorry,' I say.

He doesn't answer me, instead murmuring, 'It's okay, it's okay,' over and over again as he strokes Dyson's head. Tears continue to pour down his cheeks, but he's keeping his sobs in check.

'Alice!' Dad gets my attention from the front seat. 'You'd better call ahead to warn them.'

He hands me his mobile phone and I ring directory enquiries to locate an emergency number for the vet on night duty.

My dad waits in the waiting room, while I go into the consultation room with Joe. The vet glances with curiosity at the bandage wrapped around Joe's head, but he doesn't comment. He's a tall slim man with short, sandy blond hair and a kind – albeit tired – face. He helps Joe lay Dyson out on the table and quickly checks him over.

'What happened?'

'We found him like this,' Joe replies numbly. 'There was a rock nearby.'

'Did you see who did it?' the vet asks, his eyes once more darting to Joe's bandage.

I'm about to interject, but Joe quickly shakes his head. 'No.' He gives me a direct stare and my mouth closes.

'Can you operate?' Joe asks.

'There's little chance he'll survive,' the vet tells him gently.

Joe looks down at Dyson.

'The kindest thing would be to put him out of his misery.' He gives Joe a sympathetic look.

I gulp back my tears and put my hand on Joe's arm.

'No,' Joe says and it's like his throat is closing up because he can hardly get the word out. 'Try.'

The vet indicates the door.

We wait outside for an hour, me gripping Joe's hand tightly as he stares at the vinyl floor. Finally the door opens and the three of us jump to attention.

'He's alive,' the vet says and Joe's face lights up. 'But it's not good.' Joe's smile freezes on his face and then fades. 'I don't know if he'll make it through the night.'

Joe nods. 'Can I stay with him?'

The vet shakes his head. 'I'm afraid not. He's in safe hands. You can come back in the morning.'

'What time?' Dad asks.

'Call me first thing.' He hands over a card. Joe takes it and stares at it in a daze.

'Come on,' I say gently.

It's a long, long night. Dad trundles upstairs to bed as soon as we get back to the cottage. I can hear him talking to my sleepy mother in the room above our heads. I stay with Joe on the sofa and there are no complaints. I rest my head on his chest and he stares up at the ceiling, too upset to speak or sleep.

'Do you think it was Ryan?' I ask carefully, lifting my head to look at him.

Joe hesitates before nodding.

'Why didn't you tell—'

'I don't know,' he interrupts.

'Why do you feel loyal to him?' I try to keep my frustration under control. 'After everything he's done to you?'

'It's not loyalty,' he says. 'It's like I'm bound by him.' He keeps staring up at the ceiling, deep in thought. 'Silence is almost second nature to me now.'

I press my face to his chest. The next thing I know, Joe is edging himself away from me. I come to, groggily. Dawn is spilling under the curtains.

'I need to call the vet,' he tells me quietly. I sit up and rub the sleep out of my eyes as he delves into his pocket for the vet's card.

I dig out my phone, but I'm out of credit and I forgot to top up. 'I'll see if I can borrow Dad's,' I say.

'No.' He pulls me back. 'Don't wake him. There's a payphone down the road.'

'Don't be ridiculous!' I snap.

He furrows his brow with annoyance at me. It's the first time he's looked at me like this and it makes me feel wretched. 'I'll go to the payphone,' he reiterates firmly.

'Okay. I'll come with you.'

We reach the payphone and Joe goes inside. I stand against the door, holding it open. It's sickening, waiting for someone to answer, but eventually they do.

'I came in last night,' Joe tells the person on the other end of the line. 'With my dog.' Pause. 'Sorry,' he says, and I think he's being chastised for calling too early. 'Please could you check on him now?' he begs. 'Thank you.' He looks across at me. 'She's going to check.'

'Is it not the vet from last night?'

'No.' He shakes his head. 'I think it might be his wife. She said he's still in bed.'

'They must live at the surgery.'

He nods. I notice his knuckles are white from clutching the phone so tightly. Suddenly he perks up.

'Yes?' he asks. My eyes widen with anticipation. 'Oh, no,' he says quietly. Blood rushes into his knuckles as his hand goes limp. I step into the booth and take the phone from him.

'Hello?' I speak into the receiver.

'Hello?' the woman at the other end replies.

'What happened?' I ask.

'He didn't make it, I'm afraid.' She sounds apologetic.

Sobs well up inside me. I turn quickly to look at Joe. He's hunched over at the side of the road.

'What would you like us to do with the body?' she asks.

'I don't know.' I stare in shock at Joe.

'Can you come in at around ten? We can discuss it then.'

'Yes. Okay. Thank you.'

I hang up the phone and go to Joe. He cries hard into my shoulder, clutching my body as his tears dampen my T-shirt. I hold him as tightly as I can, crying too. Dyson meant the world to him. He loved him so much. He was his escape from reality, his only ally in a horrible home. He won't know what to do with himself now that Dyson's gone.

*

The bill is the next hurdle we have to face. Joe stares down at the white sheet of paper, his hands shaking as he reads the total. I take it from him and almost have a heart attack. My eyes dart up to his. For the first time in my life I consider doing a runner, but Joe reaches into his pocket and pulls out the wad of hard-earned cash that he asked me to retrieve earlier. He swallows, trying to keep his tears at bay.

'Maybe my parents could help,' I say.

'No.' He shakes his head.

'But that's for your car.'

He doesn't answer. The bill is even higher than it would have been because the vet had to open after hours. Even now, on Sunday morning, they would not normally have to deal with customers. But it's all money for nothing. Dyson died anyway.

'Would you like him cremated?' the vet's wife asks as she relieves Joe of a large chunk of his earnings.

'How much does that cost?' I interject before Joe has time to think about it.

She tells us. We both fall silent for a moment. Joe speaks first. His voice is practically a whisper.

'What will you do with him if I can't pay?'

'We'll dispose of him,' she replies sympathetically.

I put my hand on Joe's arm.

'Would you like a moment?' she asks.

'Yes, please.' I reply for both of us. As soon as she's gone, I turn to Joe. 'Maybe we could bury him? In one of the fields that he loved running around in.'

'He's too heavy. We wouldn't be able to carry him. And, anyway, I'm sure it's not allowed.'

'What about ...' I imagine conducting a serious funeral

ceremony at the edge of a cliff, before dramatically easing Dyson's weighted body into the water far below, but, again, we wouldn't be able to get him there.

'I'll have to leave him,' Joe says dully.

'No, you can't . . .'

He nods abruptly, and knocks on the counter. The woman returns. He informs her of his decision and then walks out of the door. I bolt after him.

'Don't you want to say goodbye?' I call after him. 'We could ask to see him!'

He spins around, his face wracked with pain. 'He's gone!' he cries. 'Last night is the memory I'm left with. I don't want to see him dead too.'

I rush to him and hold him in my arms as sobs ricochet through his body.

Chapter 17

'What's the time?' Joe asks flatly when we're in the car.

'Ten forty-five,' I reply.

Silence.

And then he sighs. 'I need to go home.'

'No way.' I shake my head vehemently.

'Alice . . .' He reaches over and puts his hand on my knee. I concentrate on driving. 'It's not to stay. But I want to get my things. It's a good time,' he adds. 'The pub doesn't open until twelve thirty – my parents will still be in bed. They get absolutely wasted after closing time on Saturday nights and they're usually out cold until close to noon.'

'In that case I'm coming with you,' I tell him.

'You can stay in the car,' he replies. 'I'd appreciate the lift.'

'No. I'm coming with you.'

'Even if they do wake up I don't suppose they'll do anything to you after Ryan landed me in hospital,' he muses. 'They'll know your parents will get them locked up . . . Okay,' he decides.

*

The pub is dark and quiet. His parents must still be asleep, but I'm acutely on edge as I follow him up the stairs to the poky bedroom overlooking the car park. The door to the bedroom on the other side of the corridor is open. I can see the view across the fields to the ocean. That must be his old room. The bed is empty, I note with a shudder. Which means Ryan is still missing. I turn back to Joe. He's frenziedly stuffing his belongings into plastic bags.

'Are you going to tell your parents you're leaving?' I ask quietly.

'No,' he mutters. 'They didn't give a shit about me while I was here, so they should be happy once I'm gone. Give them more time to devote to their precious favourite son,' he spits.

'They'll miss you behind the bar . . .'

He snorts. 'Yes, they fucking will. No more slave labour.'

He angrily dumps another bag on the carpet near my feet and reaches for a fourth to fill.

'I'll take these down to the car,' I tell him. He nods and gets on with the job at hand.

I return to the pub afterwards, still on edge in case his parents have woken up. I push through the doors and head to the stairs, before freezing in my tracks. Cigarette smoke. Almost in slow motion, I turn to look at the dark lounge area, curtains still closed against the sunlight. There, in a corner booth, is Ryan, lazily smoking a cigarette.

'Hello, beautiful,' he drawls.

My eyes dart towards the stairs, but he's on his feet and over to me more quickly than I would have ever imagined possible, given the bulk of his frame. Fear fills every part of me. He grips me round the waist, the smoke from the cigarette trailing up his fingers and into my nostrils. It's suffocating.

'You smell . . .' he whispers sinisterly into my ear, 'of *sex* . . .'

His breath reeks of stale cigarette smoke and alcohol. I can't move. My feet are glued to the spot. Where's Joe? God, where's Joe? I want him here with me, but I also want him as far away as possible.

Ryan throws his cigarette onto the stone floor and stamps on it without moving away from me, not even an inch. The next thing I know, his hand is up my skirt and groping me.

SMASH! I hear the sound of breaking glass, and at the same time the weight of him is thrown away from me. I clutch my hands to my head and stare at the scene before me. Joe, his face ripped with anger, is gripping the jagged end of a broken liquor bottle ... Ryan's unconscious body is sprawled out on the floor, blood oozing out of the back of his head. Joe and I meet each other's eyes at the same moment and then two things happen: one, his dad shouts something from upstairs and we hear his footsteps stumbling across the floor above our heads, and two, Joe grabs my hand and pulls me out of there. Then we run, run, run, as fast as we can to the car.

His hands shake violently on the steering wheel. I want to put my hand on his knee to calm him, but when I try I find I can't move. My whole body is juddering in shock and fear. Joe glances across at me and screeches to a stop – just in time for me to open the door and throw up on the grassy verge. I retch and retch until there's nothing left inside me except bile, but even then I can't stop. Joe rubs my back gently while tears, brought on by the incessant retching, stream down my cheeks. Finally I'm done. Joe opens the glove box in front of me and pulls out some tissues. I clean myself up, without looking at him. When I do eventually face him his appearance is pale and he's staring straight ahead, but his hands have stopped shaking.

I reach across and touch his knee, able to do this now that I've cleansed myself, but he doesn't move.

'Joe?' My voice sounds croaky.

Slowly, he turns his head, but his eyes won't meet mine.

'I'm sorry,' I whisper.

Then his eyes sear into me and I almost reel backwards at the rage I see in them.

'*You're* sorry?' he spits. '*YOU'RE* sorry?'

'Joe,' I say worriedly, stroking his leg.

He bats me away, violently. I stare at him in shock.

'What the *fuck*?' he screeches, staring out through the front windscreen again. 'What the *FUCK*! What the *fuck* just happened?'

'Joe,' I soothe. 'It's okay. *I'm* okay.'

His head whips back around to me. 'Did I *kill* him?'

'No!' I exclaim. 'No, I'm sure you didn't.'

'How can you be sure?'

I realise he's terrified, utterly terrified. 'Do you want to go back to check?'

He hesitates for a long moment, before nodding. 'Put your seatbelt on,' he instructs me.

I do as he says, then tell him to do the same. He ignores me, doing a manic five-point turn in the middle of a country lane. We speed back the way we came.

He pulls up at the bottom of the hill and we look at the pub. There's no sign of life inside.

'Maybe your dad called an ambulance,' I say.

He reaches for the door handle.

'NO!' I shout, pulling him back.

He looks across at me, regretfully. 'I've got to check.'

'You're not going up there! There's NO WAY you're going up there!'

Why did I suggest coming back? I thought we'd see something from the outside, some proof that Ryan is alive and . . .

No, I don't want him to be well. I want him to be gone for good, but not dead. The thought of Joe going to jail for manslaughter – or, worse: murder. The thought is too awful to contemplate.

'I'll be quick.'

'NO!'

'I won't go inside. I just need to get a bit closer.'

'No . . .'

'Alice, I'm going.'

'Joe! No!'

But I can't stop him. I know that he needs this, but I feel like I'm going to throw up again. I put my hand on my door handle. I don't know what I'll do if Ryan goes for him again. I can't protect him. But I want to be able to get out of the car quickly if I need to. If something bad is going to happen to him I have to be there, even if the bad thing happens to me too.

I can't stand this. I shove the car door open and fall out onto the road. Joe hears my footsteps as I run, but it's too late.

'ALICE!' he shouts. And at that moment, the pub door opens and Ryan stumbles out, fury contorting his features.

He lunges at Joe, wrapping his arm around his neck and dragging him backwards. Then, suddenly, Joe's dad appears.

He tears his eldest son away and nails him against the pub wall. Joe's mum runs out of the door.

'WHAT THE HELL ARE YOU DOING?'

It takes a moment for me to realise that she's screaming this question at her husband. She turns to Ryan, yanking her husband's crushing arm away from her son's chest. She caresses Ryan's blood-splattered face, calming him down, quietening him. Then Joe's dad turns on Joe.

'WHAT ARE YOU DOING BACK HERE, YOU LITTLE RUNT?'

'I . . . I . . . I wanted to check he was okay,' Joe stammers.

'Well, he's not okay, is he? You hit him over the fucking head with a bottle.' Yes – just like Ryan did to Joe!

'You CU—' Ryan's angry words are cut off by his father.

'SHUT IT!' Joe's dad points his finger at Ryan as his wife shushes him soothingly. 'Take him inside,' he directs her.

She walks Ryan to the door. His blond hair is matted with blood from behind, but he looks over his shoulder and smiles at Joe. A chilling smile. An evil smile. '*I'm gonna get you*,' he says in a sing-song voice. And then he looks at me and my blood runs cold. '*I'm gonna get you too*.'

'Shush!' Joe's mum snaps at him as she leads him inside.

'Get out of here!' Joe's dad pushes at Joe's chest. 'Go on, scat! I never want to see you again, you good-for-nothing little shit. You've always been a wuss. A fucking pansy with your long hair and your earring. You'll never be a real man like your brother. And if I hear you've gone to the police about him –' he looks at me, then looks back at Joe, meaningfully – 'I won't stop him.'

Joe backs away, then turns and hurries towards me. He takes my arm and ushers me to the car, waiting until I'm safely inside before going to the driver's side. He pauses before climbing in, and I turn to look at what he's seeing up there by the pub: his dad's departing back as he walks through the door. And then Joe is in the car, beside me, his hands shaking violently once more as he turns the key in the ignition.

We only get a mile down the road before he pulls over, and this time it's *him* throwing up outside the car while I rub *his* back. But his tears are not brought on by the vomiting. His sobs are real and heart-wrenching, and they make me cry too.

In an odd way it occurs to me that he'll despise himself in the future. He'll think of things that he could have said to his father, clever things, cool things, cutting things, but he said nothing. He'll never get that moment back. And I know that he'll regret it for the rest of his life.

Chapter 18

'You have to leave,' Joe says when he's calmed down a bit. 'You have to leave, today. You can't stay here.'

'I'm not leaving you,' I say.

'I'm not staying, either,' he replies.

'Where are you going?'

'London.'

'But your car! Your money!'

'I'll catch the train. I have to go now, Alice. And so do you. I won't be able to relax until I know you're safe.'

'I'm not going without you!'

'Stop it! Give it a fucking rest, would you?'

My mouth falls open.

'I'm sorry,' he snaps, not sounding it. 'But I have to go. I have to go to London.'

'What about Cambridge?'

'I'M NOT COMING TO CAMBRIDGE!' he shouts at me. I'm lost for words. Totally and utterly lost for words. 'I can't, alright?' Now he sounds frustrated. 'I can't. Not yet. Not until I've got myself sorted. I have to go to London.' He sounds adamant.

'But why?' I ask hopelessly. 'Why London?'

'It has to be London!' he shouts.

'But *why*?' I plead with him.

'It's my plan! It's my fucking plan! I've got to get something right. Stop going on at me!'

I stare at him as he puts his hands to his head. He looks almost shocked when he feels bandages there instead of hair, and then he's trying to rip the bandages off.

'Stop it!' I cry, reaching across to him. He knocks me away roughly.

'You have to go,' he says in a low, serious voice. 'You have to go today. Tell your parents what happened. Tell them to take you away.'

'No! I won't!'

'Then I will.' He tears away from the kerb.

'Joe, stop it!' I scream at him.

He screeches around the corner onto the dirt track leading to the cottage.

'Slow down!' I yell. But he doesn't. He slams on the brakes outside the cottage and my head jerks forward painfully. He's out of the car before I can even register.

'No!' I cry. I don't want him to tell my parents. He'll get his wish. They'll take me away. They'll take me as far away from his family – from him – as possible.

I run after him, but he's already banging on the door.

'Please!' I beg.

He pushes open the door and storms inside.

'What? What is it?'

I arrive just in time to see my mum asking these questions as she comes into the kitchen.

'Where's Alice?' my dad asks from behind her.

'I'm here!' I shout back. 'Joe, STOP!'

'You have to take her away!' he urges my parents. 'Get her as far away from here as possible!'

'Why?' my dad demands to know.

'It's my brother. He hurt her.' My mum gasps. 'Not . . . *seriously*. But he'll hurt her worse next time.' Joe meets my eyes, and his face is full of pain and regret. 'He's a serial rapist.'

My jaw hits the floor. He told me his brother was a bank robber.

'I'm sorry,' he whispers to me.

'I'm calling the police!' my dad erupts.

'PLEASE!' Joe shouts. 'Please,' he begs. 'Please, *just leave*. Just get away from here. As far away from here as possible. He'll find you. He'll find Alice. He won't forget. If you call the police he'll never forget even if he's locked up again for years. PLEASE!' he begs again.

My dad hesitates, then turns to my mum. 'Marie, get your things,' he tells her firmly, then to me: 'Go and pack.'

'No . . .'

'ALICE!' he shouts. 'Go and pack!'

'Go,' Joe urges me, nodding at the stairs. 'Go.'

'Come upstairs with me.'

'I'll wait here,' he tells me.

I glance at my dad, who I know was about to object to my request. He gives Joe a hard stare, then turns his eyes on me. 'Be quick,' he says. I notice his bag is already packed and by the door. He was about to leave for London himself.

'Wait!' The thought suddenly enters my head and hope fills every part of me. 'We're going to London tonight. You can come with us.'

'Just go and pack,' Joe says gruffly.

'But you can! Can't he, Dad? We can give him a lift?'

My dad doesn't reply.

'DAD!' I shout.

'Go and pack!' he snaps at me.

I glance at Joe. 'I'll wait here,' he tells me.

I regard him warily.

'Go,' he urges once more.

I take a couple of steps towards the stairs, then turn back to look at him. He smiles a small smile. His eyes are sad: shining, not sparkling.

He's gone by the time I return downstairs.

Six Months Later

Chapter 19

I'm sitting in my room in Nightingale Hall, staring out of the window. I can see treetops, church spires and the roof of the Fitzwilliam Museum from here. I sit here a lot, just staring. I go to most lectures – the ones I can face – and I do enough work to get by. The rest of the time you'll find me here. Staring. Wondering. Wishing. And trying to read the many, many, *many* books I need to get through in order to acquire my English Lit degree.

When I first came here some well-meaning students tried to coax me out of my room and down to the pub. They asked, often at first, for me to join them on nights out. They thought I had a shell that could be broken. They didn't realise that *I* was the broken one; my shell had nothing to do with it.

Now they leave me alone. The girl who keeps to herself. The *shy* girl.

To give them credit, they tried. But how could they know? I wasn't shy. I was heartbroken. I'm *still* heartbroken. It's a permanent state of being.

I hate it when my parents come to visit, which, thankfully,

isn't often. I have to pretend that I'm fine, otherwise they'll worry. It's the same when they ring me. I've stopped charging my mobile phone now. It's in a drawer in my bedroom, the battery permanently flat. I can't bear putting up the pretence on a regular basis.

At least no one knows me here. No one knows what I used to be like. Before Joe. Before love. Before loss.

At first, my room was my refuge. But as time has gone on it's felt like my prison. It's been a bitterly cold winter, but today the sun is shining. Something stirs inside me. Something I haven't felt for such a long time that I'm not sure if I recognise it. Could it be . . . happiness? No. Hope? Maybe.

I have a sudden urge to get out, so before the deep sadness sets in again I turn and hurry out of the door, grabbing my bag as I go. I jog down the four flights of stairs to the ground floor, keeping my head down so that I don't have to speak to anyone, and then I'm outside in the bright sunshine. The positive feeling inside me grows stronger, and I desperately don't want it to dissolve. So I walk, fast, towards the main road. On autopilot, my fingers curl under and I press my nails into my palms, causing me to wince. I flex my hands and try to stop myself from doing it. Pain has become so natural to me, but I don't want it, not today.

The Fitzwilliam Museum is straight ahead, the two stone lion sentries guarding the neo-classical building with its row of Corinthian columns. I turn left, away from the city centre. I take a right onto Fen Causeway, but the traffic is too noisy so I step off the pavement and cautiously climb over the cattle grid into the marshy parkland beside the river. I choose the grass path instead of the asphalt one, preferring the feel of its spongy softness under my feet. It reminds me of walking on the cliffs at Dancing Ledge, and then I'm transported back there with Joe.

I love you . . . I love you . . . I love you . . .

I halt in my steps as the pain debilitates me. I squeeze my eyes shut and try to push out the memory of him.

It turns out that my instincts were correct. I knew that he would hurt me. I just didn't know how.

When I came downstairs that day to find him gone I bolted, running out of the door and down to the road. I thought he might be waiting at the bus stop, but he was nowhere to be seen. In a panic, I tore back to the cottage and snatched Mum's car keys, but my dad stood in front of her car, blocking me from leaving. I screamed at him to move, but he wouldn't. Eventually my mum climbed into the car beside me and attempted to calm me down. I begged her to let me go to the train station, but she tried to convince me that Joe could be anywhere by now. I sobbed my heart out the whole way home. I still can't speak about Joe to my dad. I know that he was only trying to protect me, but I don't feel that I will ever be able to forgive him.

I spent every day of the next two weeks searching fruitlessly on the streets of London, knowing that my chances of seeing Joe were next to nothing. I never did find him. Never did see any trace of him or sense that I was on the right path. Now any reunion is in his hands.

He still hasn't come for me. And I'm still waiting.

I force my eyes open and the blurry yellow shape of a daffodil comes into focus. I concentrate on the flower, and slowly the pain dispels. I look around and see that I'm surrounded by the first flowers of spring. Winter has gone, and I've only just noticed. I wipe the hot tears from my eyes and then I straighten up and keep walking.

I come out onto a road that leads to Silver Street Bridge and one of the main punting stations on the River Cam. I look down at the rows and rows of long, narrow wooden boats chained to each other. I still haven't been punting. But as usual I put my head down to avoid being accosted by any of the scouts touting for business. I don't know why. I should take a tour. Maybe I will. One day.

I cross over the bridge, again heading away from the city, and then I follow the path that runs adjacent to Queens Road, with the backs of the colleges – known simply as the Backs – on my right-hand side. The sun is warm on my body and I'm hot from walking so fast, so I take off my black cardigan and tie it around my waist, before forcibly concentrating on slowing my pace to a wander.

In my six months here, I have been looking, but not really seeing. Now I take in my surroundings. Small green buds have formed on the trees, and some are drenched with blossom. A female jogger in purple shorts and a matching vest heads in my direction. I automatically avert my gaze as she passes. Up ahead a man walks his dog. I try not to look away and, sure enough, he nods and smiles at me. Feeling strange, I nod and smile back.

That's it, Alice. That's the way forward.

The next time someone passes I even go so far as to say good morning. The corresponding friendliness of these strangers feels oddly like a reward instead of a punishment, and soon I'm smiling for real.

King's College Chapel with its grand spires comes into view and I pause for a moment to admire the view. Mottled brown cows graze in the meadow in front of me and I can see punters gliding through the water beyond it, with King's as a backdrop. They're visible only from the chest up as they lift their poles and drop them down again. For the first time I'm genuinely struck by how breathtakingly beautiful it is here. Until now I've felt too deadened inside to appreciate it. I walk a little further before it occurs to me that I haven't yet used my Student ID pass that allows me free access through the colleges, regardless of the fact that I don't go to the university. On a whim, I turn into the black wrought-iron gates belonging to Clare College, stopping when I reach the bridge. I stand on the cobbled pathway and lean on the stone wall, small circular patches of yellow lichen rough underneath my arms.

Lizzy hasn't come to visit yet I haven't encouraged her to, because I haven't felt up for visitors, nor for visiting her in Edinburgh. Her mum is in remission, thankfully. I'm so relieved for my friend and her family. I can't imagine what it has been like for all of them. I tried not to let Lizzy witness the extent of my pain after Dorset, but it wasn't always possible. I still remember the look on her face when she saw me on one particularly inconsolable afternoon before we set off for university. She couldn't understand it. It was as if I was a stranger to her. As with my parents, I have to pretend that I'm fine when I speak to her now. Christmas was hell, putting on an act when we were face to face, and I'm dreading going home for Easter. I can't bear to witness Lizzy's disappointment in me on top of everything else. But back to the present ...

The sunlight reflecting on the river is almost blinding and it hurts to look at King's College Chapel now, which is there in front of me behind a perfectly manicured lawn. A cloud momentarily passes over the sun and the water ripples beneath a cool breeze. The gate to the manicured Fellows Gardens to my left is closed, although I can see striking red and yellow flowers decorating the banks.

I turn to see a lone punter drawing nearer. He looks to be in his late teens or early twenties and is wearing a black T-shirt and black trousers. The only colour on him comes from his hair, which is jaw-length and dark red. He's standing on a square wooden platform at the back of the punt, lifting his long pole clear of the water, before letting it slide between his hands until it hits the riverbed. He pushes down and away so the boat glides effortlessly through the water. I continue to watch as he punts towards the bridge that I'm standing on, oddly unable to tear my eyes away. And then he looks right at me. I try to avert my gaze, but I can't. He grins and salutes me, and I find myself smiling and saluting him back. His boat starts to pass under the bridge, but he's still looking up at me. I gasp with shock as his head hits the underside of the bridge, causing him to cry out in pain. I run to the other side.

'Are you okay?' I call out with horror.

The punt appears from under the bridge and thankfully he's still on it. He glances up at me and grins. I realise then that he was having me on.

'You bastard!' I shout to the sound of him laughing.

I hear a young woman's voice and curiously drag my eyes away to see a much larger punt full of tourists appear from behind me. She's wearing navy-blue shorts and a waistcoat over a white shirt. I eavesdrop as she approaches.

'Clare College was founded in 1326, making it the second-oldest surviving college in Cambridge,' the tour guide says. 'Clare Bridge is the oldest bridge in the city,' she continues. 'You'll notice that one of the stone balls adorning it has a missing wedge.'

A few of the tourists murmur their acknowledgement and I look around and find that the ball in question is right in front of me. It resembles Edam cheese with a slice cut out of it.

'Nobody quite knows why,' she says, 'but one theory is that the original builder of the bridge was not paid the full amount, so he cut out the segment to balance the difference in payment.'

The punter ducks her head and disappears under the bridge, appearing on the other side soon afterwards. I notice a novice in one of the smaller, slimmer punts heading upriver and coming straight towards the tour punt. Everyone gasps as the novice tries to correct himself, while one of his pals at the front of his boat madly paddles in the wrong direction. The experienced punter on the tour boat calmly punts herself and her boat full of chattering tourists away from the mayhem.

I assumed all the punters would be male. Clearly not. I can't help but feel a little in awe of her as she and her boat disappear from sight.

I cross the bridge and pass through the tall stone arch into Clare College. An army-green bicycle with an old-fashioned wicker basket is propped up against the wall. Then I find myself in a courtyard surrounded by a magnificent stone building. I walk along the grass-lined path and come out onto a narrow street to see that King's College Chapel, to my right, is open. My feet carry me in that direction and the sound of the organ fills the chapel as I queue to go inside. I wander through the doors and gaze upwards to see the masonry of the fan-vaulted ceiling. It's almost too stunning to contemplate, as are the enormous stained-glass windows towering overhead. I make my way up the aisle and under the intricately carved dark oak screen which houses the organ and its golden pipes. The leaflet in my hand reveals that it was a gift from King Henry VIII and his Queen Anne Boleyn during the three years of their marriage, before he had her executed. I shiver. The history surrounding me is mind-blowing.

This is my city now. And for the first time I'm starting to realise how incredibly lucky I am to be here.

Chapter 20

I return to the river the following day, strangely addicted to it now after my winter of discontent. This time, armed with a takeaway coffee and a brand-new tourist leaflet, I use my student card to gain access to St John's College. I try not to gawp as I pass through the awe-inspiring Great Gate into what the leaflet tells me is First Court. I cross over Kitchen Bridge to the expansive lawns on the other side, pausing to admire the pretty, enclosed bridge on my right. I take a left and wander beside the river before sitting on the grassy bank with the vast neo-Gothic 'wedding cake' building of New Court behind me. A willow tree on the bend in the river elegantly dips its branches close to the water.

I open my bag and pull out Virginia Woolf's *Orlando*, with the intention of reading it. I take a sip of my coffee. It tastes good. *I* feel good. It's been a while. I lean forward on my elbows with the book in my hands and just let myself *be* for a while. I finally feel like I'm making the most of this city, making the most of the sunshine, making the most of my life. Maybe it's not too late. It had felt like it was.

It's even sunnier than yesterday and it seems like the whole of

Cambridge is competing for space on the water. I smile to myself as I witness punts resemble bumper cars, crashing into each other as novices unsuccessfully attempt to navigate the river.

A tour punt comes along and I forgo my reading for a minute and listen with interest to the guide, a tall, broad, blond guy in his early twenties, who's dressed in a uniform of white shirt, cream-coloured shorts and canvas boat shoes, minus socks.

'St John's was founded by Lady Margaret Beaufort, the grand-mother of Henry VIII, on the site of a twelfth-century hospital. Up ahead you can see the Bridge of Sighs, which bears little resemblance to its namesake in Venice, aside from the fact that they are both enclosed. Some say that it's called the Bridge of Sighs because the students have to pass over it to go from their halls of residence to their examinations . . .'

Another tour punt comes along and it takes only a moment for me to recognise the guide, the red-headed guy from yesterday who pretended to bang his head on the bridge. This time he's manning one of the larger punts and has a boat full of Asian tourists.

'You again!' he calls out cheerfully, thrusting his pole into the riverbed and coming to a steady stop. He nods at the unread book in my right hand and then behind me at New Court. 'Do you go to John's?' That's how the locals refer to it; John's not St John's.

'No,' I reply as several sets of eyes regard me from on board his punt. 'I'm at Anglia Ruskin.'

'Nice.'

'What about you?' I ask, awkwardly aware of his boat full of tourists, but not wanting to seem rude and uninterested. 'Are you studying here?'

'Hell, no. Not bright enough for that. Where are you from?'

I glance at his passengers again. He looks down at them and

shrugs. 'They can wait. It's not like they can understand a word of what I'm saying. So where are you from?'

'London.'

'No, I mean, where originally?'

'London,' I reply with a smirk. I know what he's getting at. He gives me a wry look. 'My grandmother was Chinese,' I explain.

'Can you speak any Chinese?' he asks eagerly, jabbing his thumb in the direction of his passengers.

A pang goes through me. Joe suggested I take Mandarin as a language module if the university offered it. It turns out that they do, but I felt too raw to follow through with it, so I chose Introduction to Imaginary Writing instead.

'I'm afraid not,' I reply.

'Never mind. Hey, do you want to hop on?'

I'm taken aback. 'Really? I just told you I won't be able to translate for you.'

'Come and keep me company, anyway.' He holds out his hand, but sees me hesitating. 'What have you got to lose? I'm hardly going to commit first-degree murder in front of all these people.'

I don't know what it is about him, but I'm drawn to him. I'm aware of how strange that sounds, because I'm in no way attracted to him, but he seems so affable, so unthreatening, and I know that this isn't a come-on. Impulsively I stand up and gather my things. 'As long as you don't push me overboard.'

'Can you swim?'

'Yes.'

'There goes that idea.'

He grins and I take his hand, cautiously stepping onto the end of the punt.

'You won't tip it over,' he assures me. 'It's got a flat bottom.'

'Oh. Okay.'

'Budge up,' he barks at the man and woman seated below him. They seem to understand that command, at least, as they swiftly move over for me. I smile apologetically at the other passengers and sit down as he punts away from the bank.

'Have you been doing this job for long?' I ask.

'A few years. It started off as a school-holiday gig and became a profession.'

'You must enjoy it.'

'Not in the middle of winter. But that's okay, because I go snowboarding then.'

I smile up at him. 'Sounds like a pretty good life.'

He shrugs. 'I like it.'

It's been a while since I've conversed so easily with anyone. I stare out of the boat at the jaw-droppingly beautiful buildings lining the river.

'What's that?' I ask curiously.

'The Wren Library,' he replies.

'Wren as in Christopher Wren?'

'I didn't invite you aboard so I'd have to work,' he jokes, before adding in a sing-song voice: 'Designed by Sir Christopher Wren and completed in 1695, the Wren Library houses many special collections, including over a thousand medieval manuscripts, early Shakespeare plays, books from Sir Isaac Newton's own library and –' he pauses for dramatic effect – 'A.A. Milne's manuscripts of *Winnie-the-Pooh*.'

'Wow,' I say in awe. He looks unfazed. 'Don't you find it interesting?' I ask.

'I did the first ten times.'

'How many tours do you do in a day?'

'Depends on how busy it is. Once I did twelve.'

'Twelve?'

'That was in the height of summer, though. It'll be a while before it gets that busy.'

We continue to chat amiably until we reach Clare Bridge.

'I'd better let you off here,' he says, punting close to the bank. He digs his pole in to anchor the boat. 'I don't want my boss to give me a grilling for inviting a non-paying passenger aboard.'

'Sure, of course. Thanks for the ride,' I say with a smile as he helps me onto the grassy bank. I quickly look to check that the gate leading to Clare Bridge is open so I'll be able to get out.

'You're welcome,' he replies. 'Same time tomorrow?'

'Really?' I hesitate. 'Isn't it supposed to be tipping it down?'

'Aah, see, I'm here whatever the weather.'

'You're committed.'

He rubs his thumb and middle finger together. 'No, I'm broke.' He pushes off from the bank. 'See you later, China Girl.'

I grin. 'It's Alice.'

'Don't care. China Girl sounds better.'

'What's your name?' I call after him.

'You decide!' he calls back, as his boat starts to go under the bridge.

'Watch your head!' I shout, and sure enough he pretends to bash it, to the shock of his passengers. They may not speak English, but they certainly get the joke because I can hear their raucous laughter travelling down the river towards me for ages afterwards.

It's only when their laughter dies that I realise I haven't thought of Joe for the last twenty minutes. That's a new record.

Chapter 21

I do return to the river at the same time the next day. The rain has held off, although the sky is grey and miserable and drizzle threatens.

'You came!' he shouts.

'You have an empty boat!' I shout back.

'It's a bit quiet,' he says, holding out his hand to me.

'Are you sure this is okay?' I warily step aboard. 'You're not going to get into trouble, are you?'

'Nah. It's not like I've got anything else to do. As long as I'm back at the Magdalene Bridge station in time for my next tour in forty-five minutes, no one will give a monkey's.'

I sit down and look up at him. 'Are you going to tell me your name today?'

'Haven't you come up with one?'

I smile, feeling oddly relaxed with this flame-haired stranger. 'I'm thinking . . . Ron.'

'Ron?'

'After Ron Weasley.'

'Ron *Weasley*!' he exclaims.

'From *Harry Potter*.'

'Yes, I know who Ron Weasley is,' he snaps. 'I assume you mean the actor who plays him?'

I shrug. 'I don't know his name.'

The first movie only came out last year.

He looks disgruntled. 'I think you'll find it's Rupert Grint. And he's about twelve.'

'Well, you look like an older and more jaded version, then. How he'll look in ten years' time.'

'I'm nineteen!'

'Seven years' time, then.'

He looks mortally offended and I can't help but laugh. 'You asked for it.'

'Bollocks to that. My name is Jessie.'

I giggle. 'Too late. I'm sticking with Ron.'

He rolls his eyes. 'I suppose it's preferable to Weasley.'

My eyes widen with delight.

He moans. 'Oh, shit, now I've done it, haven't I?'

'Yes, you bloody well have. Weasley it is.'

'Fuck.'

We grin at each other.

'So are you a Fresher?' he asks.

'Yes.'

'What are you studying?'

'English Lit.'

'Like it?'

'It's not bad.'

'That doesn't sound too promising.'

'No, I do like it . . .' I try to convince him because I don't want to explain about Joe.

'Chuck it in and come punting instead,' he suggests offhandedly.

'Is it hard?' I ask with curiosity, remembering the girl punter I saw a couple of days ago.

'Dead easy once you get to grips with it.'

'How did you learn?'

'On one of the self-hire punts. Spent a few hours teaching myself.' He hesitates. 'Do you want to try it?'

'Um . . .' I'm weirdly tempted, but . . . 'No, I don't think so.'

'What shoes are you wearing?'

'Stilettos,' I joke, lifting up my trainer-encased feet.

He smiles. 'Go on,' he encourages me.

I look around, contemplating his offer. There's hardly anyone on the river today, so I won't humiliate myself too much. 'Okay,' I agree before I can change my mind.

'Swap,' he says.

I step up onto the wooden platform and he hands me the pole. It's much heavier than I thought it would be. He steps down into the seat bay.

'Wait!' I say, panicked. 'Aren't you going to help me?'

'Just drop the pole in and push the boat along,' he says, collapsing onto the bench seat below me and stretching his legs out. 'But let go if it gets stuck in the mud, otherwise you'll fall in.'

'Great,' I mutter sarcastically.

'What's wrong?' he asks, casually putting his hands behind his head. 'All of the other first-timers get thrown in at the deep end,' he adds.

'I'm not sure I appreciate your choice of words,' I say primly.

'Okay,' he concedes. 'Stand sideways to the edge of the punt, looking forwards.'

I do as he says.

'Now, lift the pole clear of the water, keeping it alongside the boat, then let it slip through your hands until it hits the bottom. Push away.'

Sounds easy enough ... But, ARGH! The boat is heading towards the bank. 'I can't do this!' I squeal.

'Let the pole float up and use it as a rudder to correct your position,' he advises calmly.

I'm a nervous wreck as I try to do what he says. Slowly but surely the boat steers away from the bank.

'That's it,' he says. 'Now lift the pole clear of the water again and angle it slightly backwards.'

'It's heavy,' I gasp as the water runs down the pole and up my arm, soaking my jumper.

'The metal ones are lighter than the wooden ones,' he says. 'But you get used to it,' he assures me.

'I doubt it. I don't think I'll be doing this again anytime soon.'

'You never know. You might surprise yourself.'

Chapter 22

It turns out that Jessie was right.

'Henry VIII founded Trinity College in 1546, generously endowing it with property seized from the monasteries.'

My passengers murmur with interest.

Yes, you read that right. My passengers . . .

After that first time, never in a million years did I think I'd become good at punting, and never in a *zillion* years did I think I'd become skilled enough to actually work as a punter, yet here I am, with a tour boat full of people, punting down the Backs, regaling them with stories of the kings and queens who built these colleges and studied here.

'When Prince Charles studied at Trinity he was treated like any other student, with the exception that he was allowed to have a telephone in his room. He was so annoyed at the no-car policy for all Cambridge students that one day he decided to bring his helicopter to college.'

Several of my passengers chuckle with amusement. This story has been passed on from punter to punter and the last part is probably not even true, but it makes for a more entertaining tour.

A familiar red-headed punter looms up ahead. I dig into the rocky bottom with determination and pick up my pace.

'Afternoon,' I say chirpily as my boat glides past.

'Oi!' he calls after me, his brow furrowed because I've overtaken him.

'Taking a nap?' I call over my shoulder.

'Preparation for tonight. You up for a drink at the Anchor after work?'

That's one of the local pubs on the river we all hang out in.

'Absolutely.'

'Watch your head!' he jokes as I duck under the bridge. I know this river like the back of my hand now. Sometimes I think I could punt blindfolded.

It's a sweltering afternoon and I breathe a sigh of relief as I glide up to the jetty with my last tour boat. A couple of tourists tip me generously as they disembark and I say a grateful thank you. That'll buy the first round. I wipe my arm across my brow. If it's this hot in May, I can't imagine what next month will be like. I've tied my hair up into a bun, but I can feel perspiration at the nape of my neck. A sudden burst of cool wind gives me some relief, but it's stifling again all too quickly. I'm glad I'm wearing a dress today: a white sundress. It's kind of become my uniform. Jessie, on the other hand, still punts all in black, even in the heatwave.

I step straight off the boat and walk up to the pub. Tables and chairs butt up against the ropes on the pavement overlooking the river. Jessie is already inside at the bar. He turns and flashes me a grin, before handing over what has now become my regular: a pint of lager. I never thought I'd be a lager girl, I can tell you that much.

'Here you go, China.'

'Cheers, Weasley.'

Our nicknames have stuck. We chink glasses and each glug down a few mouthfuls. The bitter-tasting liquid hits the back of my throat and instantly cools me down from the inside out.

'Pretty full-on day, hey?' Jessie comments.

'Just a bit.'

'How many did you do?' He's referring to tours.

'Five.'

'Pansy,' he teases.

'Yeah, yeah, I know I still haven't come close to touching your twelve, but I'm getting there.'

He nudges me affectionately. 'You don't do half bad, considering you're a little one.'

A stool comes free at the bar. He passes it to me, then leans up against the wooden bar top. We always seem to find ourselves standing up here until our pals arrive, and then more often than not we relocate to a table – outside if we can find one.

'Thanks,' I say for the stool. I'm desperate to sit down. 'How's your student search coming along?' I ask.

Last year, Jessie's parents left the UK to go abroad for two and a half years. His dad is a lawyer at a top firm and they wanted him to work in their Washington office for a while, so Jessie's parents left him to look after the house with permission to rent out two of the bedrooms to students. It worked well, but as both students were third years he needs to find a couple of new ones for September.

'Why don't you move in?' he asks casually, taking a sip of his lager and regarding me over the brim of his pint glass.

'You're serious? You wouldn't want to live with me,' I say dismissively.

'Sure I would.'

'You work with me. You want to live with me too?'

'Why not? We could walk to work together.'

'Commute together, as well? Why don't we get married and have two kids while we're at it?'

He looks disgusted. 'Christ, what a thought.'

'How rude!' I try to act outraged, but I can't keep a straight face. He grins and wraps his arm around my neck, before pressing his lips to the top of my head.

We have a very tactile relationship, Jessie and I, but there's absolutely no sexual chemistry between us whatsoever. I couldn't have been friends with him if there were. I know he doesn't fancy me in the slightest. And that's important to me. I still love Joe. I still miss Joe. But Jessie has been my saviour. He resuscitated me. I don't know what I would have done without him.

'You're not going to get anywhere with Blondie if you keep doing that in front of her,' I chastise him gently before looking over his shoulder at the girl behind the bar. He's been making eyes at her for weeks. He grins and chinks my glass again. I notice the blonde behind the bar glance our way and her brow furrows slightly. Maybe she does have the hots for Jessie after all. Me being here is not going to help his cause, but I can't leave. I need him too much. I literally shudder at the thought of losing him.

'You're not coming down with anything, are you?' he asks with concern, pressing the back of his hand to my forehead.

'No, I'm fine,' I change the subject. 'Shall we see if the others are here?'

'Sure.' He looks over at the bar girl, but now she's steadily averting her gaze. I can't help but feel guilty as he follows me out through the pub.

*

'No!' Jessie shouts at Chris, a tall, blond, good-looking guy who's also a fellow punter. 'She doesn't need another one.'

'Who are you, her father?' Chris shouts back from the doorway. 'Alice? What are you having?'

I wave him away and point to Jessie, who's sitting to my left on a long bench seat. 'No . . . He's right,' I slur. 'I should probably call it a night.'

'Party-pooper,' Chris mutters, turning to go inside.

We left the Anchor a couple of hours ago and relocated to the Pickerel Inn on the other side of the city, near our Magdalene Bridge punting station. We're sitting at a bench table in the courtyard.

'Aren't you coming clubbing?' Sammy asks with disappointment from across the table.

Sammy works at the kiosk selling tour tickets. She's pretty, a little taller than me, with shoulder-length brown hair and blue eyes.

'It's Thursday night,' she moans at Jessie, who's usually her most dependable drinking buddy.

'No, I'd better get China home,' Jessie says, sliding out from the bench seat.

'I can manage.' I try to stand up, but wobble dramatically. Jessie puts his hands on my waist and lifts me clear over the top of Mike – another punter pal – who's sitting on the other side of me.

'Whoa!' He ducks his head.

'Sorry,' I mumble a drunken apology.

'See you tomorrow,' Jessie calls to our mates, still half carrying me. He steers me through the old, narrow pub with its dark wooden beams and low ceilings to the street exit.

'Bye,' I say to Jessie, who lives in the other direction.

'You're not walking home alone in this state,' he snaps, pulling me back. 'I think you'd better stay at mine.'

'Again?' I groan. 'Everyone already thinks you're my boyfriend.'

'Not bloody likely.'

I crash over at his all the time. I've never been able to bond with the students at my hall of residence, maybe because I was so broken when I went to live there. But even though I'm, well, I wouldn't say fixed, but certainly in a state of repair, I don't feel like I can suddenly fit in. Jessie has been here for me through this transformation – or reformation, if you like. My fellow students put this down to him – down to love. It doesn't matter enough to me to convince them that he's just a friend. I tried once, but the girls teased me and didn't believe a word of it. They seem to want me to have found someone. I don't want to disappoint them. They can believe what they want to believe as long as it keeps them happy.

Bacon and eggs. Mmm. Now, that's a good enough reason for crashing over if ever I needed one. I sleepily open my eyes the next morning to see that, as predicted, Jessie is nowhere to be seen. Which means he's downstairs in the kitchen whipping up breakfast for us both.

I'm in Jessie's room at the front of the house. He's been staying in the master since his parents left, and their super-king-sized bed is more than big enough to comfortably house both of us.

I climb out of bed and drag on one of his T-shirts, which comes almost to my knees as he's about a foot taller than me, and make my way downstairs.

'Good morning,' he says chirpily.

I collapse on a chair at the kitchen table. 'I don't know how you do it,' I say.

'Do what?'

'How can you drink the amount you drink and still wake up feeling cheery the next morning?'

'What can I say? It's a talent.' He pours me a cup of coffee.

'One of many.'

'You're too kind.' He smiles at me and dishes up two plates of bacon and eggs. 'What are your plans for today?'

'I have a lecture this afternoon,' I reply.

'Ooh, exciting,' he says, although he's being completely sarcastic. He cannot for the life of him understand the attraction of my degree. 'I can punt you back up to Silver Street, if you like?'

'No, I'd better hightail it on foot. But thanks. I really need to get back to do some reading,' I tell him.

'I don't know why you don't bring your books with you when you stay over.'

'Are you kidding me? You've seen *The Norton Anthology*, right? It's like a small child.'

The Norton Anthology comes in two enormous volumes and surveys English Literature from the Middle Ages to the twenty-first century. It's been doing my back in for months; one girl I know pulls it around in a wheelie bag.

'Anyway, I didn't know I was staying over, remember?'

'Yeah, yeah. You should know by now.'

I smile at him sadly. 'I'm going to miss you this summer.'

His lips turn down. 'Me too. I hate it when you lot bugger off for the holidays.'

Some of our friends – Sammy, Mike and Chris – are also

students at Anglia Ruskin. They'll also be going home for the summer.

'I'm not looking forward to leaving, either,' I reply. 'I don't know what I'm going to do with myself for three months …' Being away from Jessie, away from my studies, which I do enjoy, away from the river … Having to live at home with my parents after almost a year of independence …

The truth is that I know exactly what I'll end up doing. I'll end up looking for Joe again. London is where he is. Where he said he would be. I know I'll spend long, heartbreaking days going on a wild-goose chase, and I honestly don't know if I'm strong enough to endure the pain when I don't find him.

'You know, you don't *have* to go home …' Jessie says thoughtfully.

'What do you mean?'

'You could stay here.'

'Are you still banging on about me living with you?' I tease. 'Just because you can't be arsed to advertise …'

'You wouldn't even have to pay rent,' he continues.

'Of course I would pay rent!' I exclaim.

'Not for the summer. I wouldn't be getting rent from anyone else until September.'

'My parents wouldn't be too impressed if I didn't go home …' It's a tempting thought, though, considering how upset I still am with Dad for letting Joe leave.

'Think about it,' Jessie says simply.

'Okay. I will.'

Chapter 23

I leave Jessie's and walk quickly towards the city centre, dodging to avoid zillions of cyclists shooting past on the roads and tourists consulting maps in the middle of the pavement. My white sundress from yesterday is grubby after a day's work, and I seriously need to have a shower and wash my hair. But it's another warm and sunny day, plus it's Friday and I'm looking forward to the weekend. Even the backstreets near the colleges are busier than usual and I consider heading over the river and walking along the Backs where it's quieter. It's a little out of my way, but King's Parade will be heaving. Yes, I think I'll do that.

I cut right, straight into the path of an oncoming cyclist.

'WATCH OUT!' he shouts.

Too late.

'OW!' I cry as he crashes into me and comes off his bike.

'WHAT THE HELL ARE YOU DOING?' he screams, stumbling to his feet. 'Watch where you're going, you fucking tourist!'

I'm about to scream back that I'm *not* a fucking tourist, but suddenly there's a man right in front of me, blocking my view.

'HEY!' he shouts over his shoulder at the cyclist as I angrily rub my sore arm. I'm about to hurl abuse at the cyclist when the stranger puts his hands on my arms. I look up at him in surprise.

He turns his head to the cyclist and says in a calm, foreign-accented voice: 'You were going too fast. *You* should watch where *you're* going.'

'Piss off, you wanker!' the cyclist snaps, mounting his bike and pedalling away from us.

'Juvenile delinquent,' the stranger mutters under his breath. 'Are you alright?' he asks me. His hands are still on my arms and he's too close, way too close.

'Yes, yes, I'm fine. Thank you.' I take a step backwards, out of his grasp. His hands fall to his sides. He's young – early twenties, I think – and well turned out in a smart grey jacket and white shirt. His hair is short and dark blond. He has very blue eyes.

'You're going to have quite a bruise, I think.' He studies the mottled red patch on my arm. 'You should put a cold compress on it.'

He sounds German, but he doesn't look it. At least, he doesn't look like the German students that Lizzy and I used to giggle at in Trafalgar Square, with their brightly coloured parkas, blue denim jeans and backpacks.

'Do you have one?' he asks.

I shake my head slightly with confusion. 'Sorry, do I have what?'

'A cold compress.'

'A cold compress?' What's he going on about?

'Yes. For your arm,' he says. 'To stop the swelling.'

'Oh, no, it's fine. I'll be fine,' I say again. Weirdo. What does he think I've got, an ice pack in my handbag?

'I can get you one, if you like. My room is only around the corner.'

I can't help it: I start to snort with laughter.

His brow furrows. 'What's so funny?'

'Sorry, no, thank you, I'm fine. Bye, bye!' I hurry away from him before I completely lose it. Who the hell has a cold compress in their room? And why is he calling it a 'cold compress' and not just 'ice'?

It occurs to me that maybe he's a doctor or a medical student and then I feel a bit mean, but I still make a mental note to tell Jessie about him later.

I arrive back at halls and climb the stairs to the 100s on the top floor. The rooms to the left and the right of the landing as you come up the stairs are named after decades: the 30s – i.e. Room 31, Room 32, etc., and then the 40s, 50s, 60s, etc., all the way up to the 100s. Since I've been here there have been at least three decade-themed parties. Last night there was a 70s party, judging by the Afro wig and the bright pink feathers from a feather boa strewn halfway down the stairs.

I walk to the end of the corridor and unlock the last door on the left. My room is cast in a murky orange glow, courtesy of Nightingale's infamous crappy curtains, so the first thing I do is draw them back and then open up the window to let in some fresh air. One of my fellow students is having a jokey slanging match with the residents of the neighbouring King's College Hostel. We can shout 'Toffs!' and 'Commoners!' at each other for ages. It passes the time. Time that I don't have today. With great effort I pick up Volume One of the 'small child' and delve into its three thousand pages. My shower will have to wait.

*

'What did you do to your arm?' Jessie asks with concern later down by the Silver Street punting station. Sometimes we start our tours from here, the rest of the time from Magdalene. It's so busy that I've been roped in to help out after my lecture.

'Bloody cyclist crashed into me,' I explain. 'Oh, it was funny . . .'

I start to tell him about the foreign stranger, but guilt appears out of the blue and pricks me. My voice trails off.

'Go on,' Jessie urges.

I shake my head dismissively. 'He was only trying to help.'

'What's so funny about that?' He looks confused.

'Nothing. It wasn't at all, actually. I don't know why I thought it was.'

'Freak.'

'That's me.' I look past him to see Sammy beckoning me. My next tour is about to start. 'See you later.'

'Bye.' He gives my arm a squeeze and I wince.

'Ouch!'

My arm continues to feel tender as I navigate a punt full of people away from the punting station. There's a young family seated directly below me: a man, a woman, a little boy and a baby girl. They live in Cambridge, from what I can gather, but it's hard to concentrate on giving the tour because their young son has the patience of a gnat and is climbing all over the place.

'If you could just keep his arms out of the water and inside the boat,' I suggest at one point on the approach to Trinity Bridge. The bruise on my arm would pale in comparison to the bruise their son would get if he got sandwiched between two punts.

'This is the Wren Library,' I start to say before I'm swiftly interrupted.

'Me and Daddy have willies, don't we?'

'Yes, yes,' the little boy's mother replies quietly, her face turning red as the ears of my other passengers prick up.

'And you and baby Molly have got chinas.'

China? *Vagina?* Jessie's *nickname* for me? Everyone laughs, and then – BANG! – I crack my head on the underside of the bridge. I cry out in pain and instinctively clutch my hands to my head, accidentally letting go of my pole as we continue to drift. My passengers stare up at me, some in shock, some with smiles on their faces because they've witnessed my joker colleagues do this. But there's no joking today. My head is throbbing like crazy.

'*Are you alright?*'

I recognise that voice. I look back at the people standing on the offending bridge and instantly spot the foreigner from earlier. A kind man on a self-hire punt comes to my aid and guides my boat towards the bank with help from his wife or girlfriend, who pushes the front end of the punt in with her oar. And then he's there – the foreigner – holding down his hand to me and motioning for me to climb off the boat. I'm utterly mortified and I wave him away.

'You should sit down,' he insists. My passengers murmur their agreement.

I notice yet another self-hire punter with a boat full of people attempting to retrieve my pole. I'm surrounded by concerned strangers and I'm so embarrassed I could die.

'Come,' he urges again, his hand still outstretched. I take it, not really knowing what else to do because I'm hemmed in without a pole, so I can hardly punt away from here. But I have feet. Maybe I could do a runner?

'Sit down,' a voice says firmly.

I give in and collapse on the bank, while he studies my head.

'You're going to have quite a bump,' he tells me.

'To add to my bruise from earlier.'

'How's your arm?' A small smile has formed on his lips.

'Better than my head,' I reply, and then I can't help myself: 'I could really do with a cold compress right about now.'

'Are you making fun of me?' he asks quietly.

I immediately feel bad and turn to murmur an apology, but then I notice that the smile hasn't left his lips. My eyes meet his, and, to my surprise, I feel my face heat up. His right eyebrow rises with amusement and I quickly get to my feet.

'Whoa!' He steadies me when I wobble.

'I feel a little faint.'

'Sit back down,' he commands, then, to my passengers: 'Ladies and gentlemen, I'm afraid the tour is over.' A couple of people groan and the little boy whinges that he's bored, but most of my passengers amiably accept their fate. The foreigner calls out to a young man crossing the bridge in the direction of Trinity. 'Kevin! Can you take these people through the college?'

Kevin hesitates, warily looking over at the scene, and then he nods abruptly and comes our way.

'That should keep them happy,' the foreigner says as an aside to me, stepping forward to help my now perky passengers off the boat. A free tour of Trinity – that wasn't in the package.

When they've been ushered up onto the bridge to join Kevin the foreigner turns back to me and nods at the self-hire punter who has been hemming me in.

'We'll moor it here for the time being.'

'Are you sure?' the man asks. 'It says "no mooring".'

'I think the Fellows will accept that we have extenuating circumstances,' the foreigner replies, climbing down the slope to secure the chain to the bank.

How does he even know a phrase like 'extenuating circumstances'? He clearly speaks fluent English. Perhaps he was brought up bilingual?

'Where are you from?' I ask, unable to contain my curiosity, because I can't keep calling him the Foreigner forever.

'Southern Germany,' he replies over his shoulder. 'Upper Bavaria.'

I was right! Well, about the Germany part. I didn't ask him to be specific.

'Thank you,' he says to the self-hire punter.

'No problem,' the man replies.

The forei— I mean, *German*, turns around and comes back to join me. 'How are you feeling?' he asks.

'My head hurts,' I reply honestly.

'You know, you really *could* do with a cold compress,' he says with a smile.

'You and your frigging . . . Go on, then,' I snap with a trace of humour.

He grins. 'I'll be back shortly.'

What a character. My eyes follow him as he jogs across the bridge towards Trinity. He must go to the college. Maybe my 'medical student' theory is correct.

'CHINA!'

My head whips around – and painfully throbs in response – to see Jessie punting towards me with a tour boat. 'What happened?' he asks with a frown.

I point to my head and then at the bridge.

'You didn't!' he gasps, his mouth falling open.

I nod wryly as his punt glides up to the bank. He anchors the boat with his pole.

'Hop on. I'll give you a lift back.'

'Oh, I . . .' I glance towards the college.

'Come on,' Jessie says impatiently. 'I'll send someone back for your boat.'

'I was just waiting . . .' My voice trails off.

'What?' Several of his passengers shuffle in their seats.

I feel bad about running off, but, really, what's going to happen if I stay? A German stranger is going to press something cold to my head and then set me on my way. He's not going to carry me over his shoulder, and nor would I want him to, but I could really do without walking right now.

I stand up. Jessie's tourists make room for me. We punt under the bridge and I stare back at Trinity with a twinge of regret. I do feel guilty. I should say thank you. But it's too late now.

Chapter 24

'I can't believe you bumped your head on the bridge!'

I'm sitting outside the Anchor with Jessie and a few others, nursing a lemonade. I daren't drink in case it makes my head feel worse than it already does.

'I won't be the first person to have done it,' I reply defensively as they all guffaw.

'Yeah, but you're always going on about how you could punt blindfolded,' Jessie teases.

'I've said that *once*!' I exclaim and he cracks up laughing.

'Aah, China, you're too funny,' he chuckles.

Suddenly it all comes flooding back: the reason why I took my eyes off the bridge in the first place. The little boy! China! Vagina! Argh!

'Maybe you should start calling me Alice,' I suggest offhandedly.

'What? Why?' He looks offended.

'It sounds a bit . . .' Dare I play the racism card? No, that's mean. 'Juvenile,' I decide, as déjà vu strikes me.

'*Juvenile delinquent* . . .'

The German stranger muttered that under his breath about the cyclist. Yet another phrase that you wouldn't expect to come out of the mouth of a foreigner. He *must* be bilingual. Again I feel a pang of guilt for leaving before he came back with the cold compress.

'*Juvenile*,' Jessie snorts with disgust. 'You'll have to do better than that.'

I'm tempted to tell him about the little boy, just so we can all have a laugh about it . . .

BIG mistake, I realise a few minutes later, when the whole table is chanting for the newly-christened Vagina – that's me, folks – to get the next round in.

'Oh, bugger off, the lot of you!' I snap jokily, before heading inside to the bar.

Jessie joins me. 'Thought you might need a hand,' he says with a grin.

'What can I get you?' I turn to see the blonde he has the hots for leaning towards him across the bar. He motions to me, so I relay the order. She doesn't look quite so happy to be serving me. I give Jessie a look and discreetly nod in her direction.

'Can you take these to the others? I'm going to nip to the loo.'

'Sure.'

'Talk to her!' I whisper as I walk past.

He's still at the bar when I return. She's laughing at something he said. 'Do you want me to take them?' I gesture to the pint glasses on the bar.

'Yeah. I'll be there in a minute.'

In the end, it's more like ten minutes, and when he does

re-emerge it's with a big grin on his face. 'Got her number,' he says, jiggling his mobile.

Chris and Mike whoop. Hurray, something to take everyone's minds off the China fiasco. But inside I feel a touch sombre. I want the best for my friend, but I don't want to lose him. I call it a night soon afterwards.

Chapter 25

It's the middle of June before Lizzy comes to visit and we're on a high because we've both finished all of our exams. I've half moved into Jessie's by the time my friend arrives.

'Happy belated birthday.' She chinks my glass. I turned nineteen in May, but we decided to wait until now to celebrate.

'Thanks!' I grin as she hands over a gift, which turns out to be some delicious-smelling bath goodies from the Sanctuary. 'Mmm, lovely.'

She tops up my glass. We're drinking white wine for a change.

'I can't believe you're not coming home this summer,' she moans.

'You can see why.' I motion around me.

Jessie lives in a Gothic terrace on Mount Pleasant, a hill. From the outside the house is dark and mysterious, but inside the walls are white and the floorboards sanded – the result of a renovation project by his parents before they went abroad.

'It's an amazing house,' she concedes. 'Incredible location. I had no idea Cambridge was as pretty as it is.'

'You haven't seen anything yet. Wait until I take you for a tour along the Backs.'

'Are we going punting?' she asks excitedly.

'Absolutely,' I reply. 'But not until tomorrow. Tonight we're going out on the town.'

She grins at me. 'It's so good to see you.'

'You too,' I say with a smile. 'How's your mum?'

Her face lights up. 'She's brilliant. Honestly, she's doing so well. Even her hair has almost grown back.'

'Oh, that's great!' I say. 'And your sister?' At sixteen, Tessa still lives at home.

'She's good. I think she misses me more than she thought she would.'

'I bet she does. Do you miss her too?'

'Yes. And I've really missed *you*,' she says a little sadly.

'Me too.'

We smile at each other across the table.

'Let's have a good time tonight!' I say cheerfully.

I know she wants to ask me about Joe, but I'd rather she didn't. I don't want to go back to that dark place.

I've still got half of my stuff in halls, but I'm slowly shifting it across. One of Jessie's third-year tenants – Gerard – has already moved out, so I've taken his room, which is the second largest of the three and looks out over the back garden. I'm excited about making it mine. I never did put my stamp on my room in Nightingale. It was a great location, but it took me too long to feel settled there. It didn't really seem worth it to put up posters and decorate for the sake of a few months. I feel much more committed about starting afresh in Jessie's pad.

Jessie's hooked up a few times with Blondie from the pub, but it hasn't turned into anything serious, yet. Her name is Darcy, but Jessie calls her Blondie, so if it's good enough for him . . . Not that she speaks to me much. I think she still feels threatened by me, which is crazy.

'Where's Jessie?' Lizzy asks.

'He's going out straight from the river,' I tell her.

'I can't wait to meet him,' she gushes.

'I can't believe you haven't, actually,' I say, pulling a face. It's terrible that this is the first time I've seen Lizzy aside from our holidays at home. With my work and studies, I just haven't had time to visit her in Edinburgh. And I haven't exactly pressed for her to visit me until more recently. I haven't felt myself enough, and I knew she wouldn't understand that I was pining for Joe.

I suddenly see him, crystal clear inside my mind. My heart automatically thuds more dully. I'm *still* pining for him. But I stifle my thoughts. I've become more proficient at doing this.

It didn't take much for Jessie to convince me to move in. In the end, I chose happiness over heartbreak, and I feel quite proud of myself for making that decision. I know, deep down, that London is not a good place for me to be. I want to move on from my pain, even if I can't. Not yet, anyway. Not fully.

I don't know why he hasn't come for me . . .

Stop.

'Let's go and get ready!' I suggest brightly.

'Ooh, check out the hottie at eleven o'clock . . .' Lizzy says a few hours later. We've ended up in a nightclub. I'm wearing skinny black jeans and a silvery grey top. My long, dark hair is down and Lizzy succeeded in getting me to wear eye-shadow: silvery-grey, this time. Her chocolate-brown hair has grown a little since I last saw her. Tonight it's wavy.

I look over her shoulder, but can't see the hottie in question.

Unless her taste has dramatically altered and she's now interested in women.

'Not eleven o'clock *your* time,' she says with a roll of her eyes. 'My eleven o'clock.'

I'm vaguely curious, but not interested in the slightest, if that makes sense, so I look left and scan the bar.

'That's three o'clock, you moron.'

'Jesus Christ, you don't half make this hard,' I chastise, looking in the opposite direction.

'Don't make it too obvious!' she screeches. 'He's looking this way!' I quickly avert my gaze. 'Did you see him?' she asks.

'No.'

'Dur!'

'You told me not to make it obvious!' I cry.

'Look now,' she commands.

I tentatively turn around. 'Where?'

'There. With those guys, there. There!'

'You've had way too much to drink.'

'Not him. Him!' This time she points. So much for not making it obvious.

'Oh, I see who you mean.' Luckily he's not looking.

Yes, he is quite cute, I concede in a detached manner. He's wearing dark-blue denim jeans and a grey T-shirt, with short hair and a graze of stubble on his jaw. Luckily, he's looking down. Scrap that, he's just looked right at me. Oh, my God, it's the German!

I quickly spin around to Lizzy.

I've thought about him a lot since that day a month ago, but I haven't seen him again. I'm sure my guilt is to blame, but I've found myself walking past Trinity's Great Gate more often than I've needed to.

'Has he looked away?' I ask nervously.

She shifts her position and sneakily glances over my shoulder. 'Yes. Wait, no.'

I can't resist. I look around. He meets my gaze momentarily before leaning in to listen to something his friend is saying. His normally neatly combed hair has fallen down across his forehead. I turn back, feeling a bit silly.

I feel compelled to say sorry, but I don't want to go over to him with all his friends there. And I certainly don't want him to think that I fancy him.

'I think I know him.' I fill Lizzy in.

'Oh, you *should* say sorry!' she exclaims. She's been making me feel increasingly worse since I began my story. For a start, she couldn't see what was funny about 'cold compress'. Apparently her mum uses the phrase all the time.

'Do you think so?'

'Definitely! He sounds lovely!' She looks over my shoulder again. 'Oh.'

'What?'

'He's gone.'

I spin around in time to see the last of his friends' backs winding out through the tables. The disappointment feels strange and unfamiliar.

'What a shame,' Lizzy says with dismay. 'Maybe he's pissed off with you.'

I shrug, trying not to let it bother me. 'Maybe. Or maybe he didn't recognise me,' I suggest hopefully.

I barely recognised him without his jacket on, plus it's dark in here.

'Maybe,' she says. 'Oh, well, plenty more fish in the sea, I suppose.'

I nudge her good-naturedly. 'What about Chris? He couldn't keep his eyes off you earlier.'

'Not for me, you idiot,' she scoffs. 'For you!'

'What?' I splutter. 'No! I'm not interested in anyone else!'

'Anyone else?' she asks wryly. 'Anyone else apart from *whom*?'

'Joe,' I reply with a frown.

'Thought so,' she says, unimpressed.

'Why are you saying it like that?' I'm feeling a bit annoyed now.

'I don't get it.' She shakes her head. 'You barely knew him.'

'I *did* know him,' I say fervently. 'I knew him better than I ever knew anyone.'

She pulls a face. 'How can that be? It was only a few weeks.'

She doesn't understand.

Luckily, Jessie intervenes. 'VAGINA!' He grabs me from behind and lifts me up.

I wriggle out of his grasp and hit him on his chest, before brandishing my forefinger in his face. 'I told you to stop calling me that!'

He grins and grabs me again, plonking a big wet kiss on my cheek.

'Gross! You're all sweaty!' I push him away and he hoots with laughter – literally hoots.

He's been on the dance floor with Chris, Mike and Sammy. Blondie is still at work, but will no doubt be joining us later. Jessie proceeds to rave dance overenthusiastically in the middle of our gathering. Everyone cracks up laughing, including me. Lizzy and I smile at each other, peace thankfully restored. We won't be talking about Joe again anytime soon.

Chapter 26

A week later I wake up early in the morning. I've now moved fully into Jessie's house where the curtains are blissfully white instead of murky orange, and I open them up to see that dawn has broken. There's a fine mist drifting across the city's rooftops. It will be beautiful on the Backs. The river beckons.

I throw on some jeans and a sweatshirt and set off to the Magdalene Bridge punting station. No one will be there now, but I have a key and I can unlock one of the punts.

Soon, the only thing I can hear is the occasional sleepy duck quacking and the sound of the water as my pole dips in and out of it. I was right. It's breathtaking on the river this morning. The Bridge of Sighs looms up ahead and I go slowly, trying to drink everything in. I breathe in deeply and feel calm.

I pass under St John's two bridges and look back to see the mist drifting across the lawn in front of New Court on the western bank. It will be a while before it burns off in today's predicted sunshine. I slow down in the middle of the river, making the most of the fact that it's deserted and that I'm not in anyone's way. I wish I had my camera, but at the same time I know that no lens could do justice to this sight. I jolt at the sound of someone clearing their throat up ahead. I pass under Trinity Bridge to see a man perching on the bridge wall to my right. I don't bloody believe it.

'Good morning,' he says.

The German.

'Hello.'

'Here we are again,' he adds with a raised eyebrow.

'Indeed.' I smile drily and drop my pole onto the riverbed to anchor my boat.

'You mean, you're *staying*?' he says with surprise. Is that sarcasm? Big words *and* sarcasm – impressive.

'I'm sorry I ran off that time. It's just that my friend came along and offered to give me a ride back to the punting station and then he made sure I got back to my halls of residence okay because I didn't really feel up to walking after all of that . . .' I know I'm rambling. He regards me with amusement.

'That's quite alright.'

'I did put ice on it,' I feel compelled to add.

He grins and looks down and my insides feel funny. Lizzy is right. He is good-looking.

'Are you a student here?' I nod to Trinity on the other side of the river.

'Yes.'

'What are you studying?'

'Physics.' There goes my theory about him being a medical student. 'What about you?' he asks.

'English Literature.' I usually just say English Lit, but something about him makes me feel more formal. 'Not here,' I add hastily. 'At Anglia Ruskin.'

He nods. He's not surprised. Students from the revered university are not supposed to work during term time. All their spare time is supposed to be spent on their studies. Where's the fun in that? I shift on my feet. The boat wobbles slightly underneath me.

'Well, then,' I say, nodding upriver and giving my pole a sharp twist to release it from the riverbed.

'What's your name?' he asks.

'Alice,' I reply, hesitantly pushing my pole back into the mud. 'Yours?'

'Lukas.'

Lukas. That sounds better than 'the German'.

'What are you doing out here at this time?' I ask him.

'I couldn't sleep. I sometimes come out here to read.' I notice a textbook in his hands. Something to do with electrodynamics, whatever that is.

'It's weird bumping into you again,' I comment.

'Cambridge is a small city.'

'True.' I gaze around me and back at him. He's wearing jeans and a black jumper. 'It's pretty here this morning, isn't it?'

'Yes.' His stare is unnerving. It strikes me that he's extremely confident.

I shift on my feet again. I feel oddly uneasy in his company. 'Were you . . . Was that you at that nightclub last week?'

He purses his lips and looks away. 'Yes, that was me.'

'Good night?' I ask feebly.

'I've had better,' he replies.

Talk about a stilted conversation. I wrack my brain for something to say. Of course, I could just leave, but something is keeping me here and I don't know what.

'Have you broken up yet?' I ask. 'From university, I mean?'

'I know what you mean,' he says. 'I've finished my exams, yes.'

'How do you think you did?'

'I'll find out today.'

'Aah, so that's why you can't sleep?'

'Part of it.'

Intriguing. 'What year are you in?'

'Two.'

'Only one more to go, then.'

'I'm doing a four-year course.'

'Oh, okay. How old are you?' I'm curious.

'Twenty.'

Hello? Help me with the conversation, here! Nope, he says nothing.

I try again. 'Are you going to the May Ball on Monday?'

'Yes. Yourself?'

'Not likely.' The tickets are like gold dust. 'No, I'll be working.' I indicate the punt.

'Aah, yes,' he says knowingly.

The description 'May Ball' is misleading, because the end-of-term balls actually take place in late June. I thought the students here were supposed to be bright – unless they named it the May Ball to confuse the rest of us. Anyway, each college has its own shindig, with Trinity, St John's and Clare all being renowned for their spectacular fireworks display. So much so that we offer punting tours on the nights of the balls, so those of us not invited – i.e. practically everyone alive – can still get a taste of the action, so to speak.

I suspect, from Lukas's tone, that he doesn't really approve of the gatecrashers. But the river belongs to us all.

'Do you have a problem with us commoners being there, then?' I ask a little shirtily.

He shrugs. 'Not at all. It all adds to the ambience.'

'Are you bilingual?' I'm distracted by his use of language and consequently overlook the fact that he accepted the term 'commoner' as a description for me.

'No,' he replies.

'Your English is very good.'

'Thank you,' he says. I get the feeling he finds me entertaining.

Silence. A man in a suit crosses the bridge up ahead. More silence. That's it. I can't do this anymore.

'I'd better get off,' I say, pointing back the way I came. 'My flatmate will think I've been kidnapped if he wakes up and finds me gone.'

'Flatmate? I thought you said you lived in halls of residence.'

He picked that up from my earlier ramble, then.

'I did. Until last week. Now I've moved in with a friend.'

'You're not going home for the summer?'

'No. I thought I'd stay here. What about you?'

'I leave after the ball.' He leans forward and rests his elbow on his knee.

'Back to Southern Germany?'

'That's right.' He smiles. 'You didn't get concussion, then.'

'Sorry?'

'When you hit your head. You remember me telling you where I was from.'

'Oh. Right. Yes. I still can't believe I did that. It was mortifying.'

'It's nothing to be ashamed about.'

'Yes, it is.' I give him a wry smile. 'My workmates gave me a major amount of grief for it.'

'I'm sure it happens all the time.'

'That's what I keep telling them.' Although I've never actually seen anyone else doing it . . .

'I thought you did well to stay aboard,' he says.

'Er, thanks,' I mumble. More silence. Another city worker crosses the bridge up ahead. 'I guess I'd better go,' I say again. This time he lets me.

'It was nice talking to you, Alice.'

'You too,' I reply. 'Maybe I'll see you around.'

He nods at my punt and then at Trinity. 'Next week, perhaps.' I gather he's talking about the night of the ball.

'If you're not too drunk to recognise me,' I tease.

'I doubt it,' he replies.

'Okay, then. Well, bye.' I give my pole a sharp twist and pull upwards to release it from the riverbed. 'Good luck with your exam results today.'

'Thank you.'

'Hope you get some sleep tonight.'

'You too.' He smiles and gets to his feet.

By the time I've turned the punt around and gone back under the bridge he's already inside Trinity's gates.

Chapter 27

I have a boat full of people – twelve in total. They're friends who have clubbed together to hire a punt on the night of the ball. They've been steadily making their way through several bottles of champagne, laughing, chatting and soaking up the atmosphere for the last three and a half hours. It's almost eleven o'clock and the fireworks are due to start soon. I've anchored my boat with my pole in the usual way, right outside the Wren Library. I wasn't here for the balls last year, and they're a sight to behold. Trinity's south paddock, in front of me to my left, has a fairground and there are marquees set up for food and attractions like a comedy club and a hog roast. There's a champagne bar situated under the cloisters of the Wren Library, and we can hear music coming from the main stage beyond that. Supergrass are one of the acts playing tonight and I'm gutted I can't go and watch them.

Jessie is on the boat next to mine, and our passengers have been plying us with champagne, so we're in high spirits. There are so many punts hemmed in on this part of the river that you could step from boat to boat all the way to the banks and back. Shame about the level of security: it's practically impossible to gatecrash.

Trinity Bridge is heaving with people, and I only wish Lizzy were here so we could dissect the vast array of ball gowns that we see in front of us, from the sublime to the extreme.

One of my merry passengers tops up my champagne and Jessie and I raise another glass to each other.

Then, once more, I scan the crowd for Lukas.

I wish I could stop myself from doing this, but I can't. I've been doing it all night. I keep telling myself that it's because he's the only person I know who goes to Trinity, so of course I'd feel compelled to look out for familiar faces. But that's not it. There's something else. He intrigues me, and I'm a little freaked out by how much.

The fireworks kick off and they're spectacular – but I'm distracted, and when it's all over and I still haven't seen Lukas I punt back to the station feeling quite deflated.

That night in bed I let myself think about Joe for the first time in a long while. I've become good at closing off my mind from him, protecting myself from the pain that comes with thinking those thoughts, but tonight I need to remember . . .

There's a full moon, and the air is unnervingly still. We lie together in a grassy field. He moves on top of me and I pull him in closer as his tongue explores my mouth. I want him desperately – we haven't yet made love – but Dyson distracts us.

I smile to myself as Joe berates him, and then my mind is flooded with the image of his beloved dog sprawled out and damaged, his fur matted with blood. Oh, Dyson . . . I can't believe he's dead.

Suddenly Ryan is groping me and I jolt and furiously shake my head to push out that memory. I stare ahead in the darkness.

Where are you, Joe?

What if something has happened to him? What if Ryan found him? A cold sweat washes over me. Why have I never wondered this before? What if Ryan hurt him? What if that's the reason for him not coming for me? How can I find out? I should be in London. I shouldn't be here, having fun on the river and being distracted by a good-looking foreign man. I shouldn't even be using the description good-looking in relation to Lukas! My fingers curl under and press themselves into the palms of my hands and the pain is a welcome distraction from the pain in my chest.

Tomorrow I'm going to London.

Having made this decision, I can't get back to sleep. Eventually I get up and start to pack, my heart hammering with adrenalin as I pull my suitcase out from the top of my wardrobe. I can't think straight. I don't know what I'll need. I rummage through my drawers, trying to get my head together. I hear a muffled knock and look sharply at the wall. Jessie. Am I being too noisy? Cautiously I return his knock. Moments later he stumbles through and climbs into my empty bed.

'What are you doing?' he mumbles, still half asleep.

'Packing,' I tell him. 'I've got to go home.'

'What? Why? Has something happened?'

'No, nothing. But I have to go.'

'*Why?*'

I take a deep breath and stare at him. I never told him about Joe. I didn't need to. Jessie – being Jessie – made me smile again. I didn't want to cloud our relationship by bringing sadness into the equation.

He sits up, trying to focus. I perch on the end of the bed.

'Last year . . . last summer . . . I met a boy. It was in Dorset. I was on holiday with my parents.'

No reaction. He waits for me to go on.

'I fell in love with him. And it wasn't just a holiday romance . . . It was real love. I know it was.' It's important to me that he understands this.

He nods at me. 'I believe you.' After that, I tell him everything.

'God,' he says, staring ahead when I've finished. 'But why now? What's making you think that you'll find him now, after almost a year?'

'Nothing. I haven't heard a thing from him.'

'So *why*?'

Lukas. But I'm not going to admit to that. Lukas is why I let myself dream about Joe. I wasn't expecting my memory to lead me to Ryan and the thought that he might have hurt Joe.

'It's only now occurred to me that something might have happened to him,' I explain. 'I need to find out.'

'But how will going to London help? Why don't you call the pub his parents worked at and ask them if they've heard anything from him?'

It's as if a brick has landed on my head. Why didn't I think of that?

'Or better yet, I could do it,' Jessie suggests. 'I could pretend to be an old friend. They might hang up if they realise it's you.'

All I need now is to get through the next few hours until it's pub opening time.

'Hi there, I'm trying to get hold of Joe. I'm a friend of his from Cornwall.'

I chew my fingernails nervously and study Jessie with intent. I can't hear what the person on the other end of the line is saying.

'Oh, right. Do you know where he's gone?' Pause. 'So you haven't heard from him at all?' Pause. 'Is Ryan there, by any chance?'

My heart leaps up into my throat. This was a last resort.

'Oh. Sorry to hear that. Do you mind if I ask what happened?'

Blah blah *whatthehellaretheysaying*?

'Damn. When was this?' Pause. 'Okay, then, thanks for your help.'

He hangs up and my interrogation begins.

'*What?* What did they say?'

'It was his dad, I think, and he doesn't know where Joe is and Ryan is back in jail.'

'No! *Why?*'

'Pub brawl, apparently. Back in October. Good news, hey?'

No. No, it's not good news. I'm still no closer to finding out about Joe. Jessie sees my expression.

'What are you going to do now?' he asks.

'I'm going to go to London.'

'What about work?'

'They'll have to make do without me.'

'Are you sure, Alice?'

'Yes. Why are you looking at me like that?'

He averts his gaze. He seems uncomfortable.

'Tell me,' I persist.

'Are you sure about him? About Joe?'

'What do you mean?' The bad feeling that had dulled now intensifies.

'It's just that . . . Maybe how you felt is not the same as . . .' His voice trails off. When he sees my expression he hurriedly speaks again. 'Don't get angry ... I'm just saying ... Him not coming here clearly doesn't have anything to do with Ryan. Ryan was back in jail in October – that's not long after Joe left, right? The chances of Ryan finding him in that time ...'

'It's still possible,' I say, although I don't really believe it any-more.

'Mmm, maybe.'

I don't want him to continue, but he does. Gently, this time.

'Perhaps he's moved on, you know?'

'No,' I say firmly, and then a lump lodges itself in my throat and my second 'no', comes out sounding gargled. My eyes fill with tears and a choked sob comes out of my mouth. Then I'm crying for real. Jessie edges closer and wraps his arms around me. I cry into his shoulder.

I can't bear to accept it, but Jessie could be right. It's been almost a year. If Joe cared about me, he would have come for me by now, surely?

Chapter 28

September rolls around far too quickly and soon I'm back at college for my second year. I've spent the summer punting and reading, mostly Shakespeare and Volume 2 of the 'small child' on Parker's Piece – the large expanse of parkland between the city and my campus – and I feel much more prepared than I did a year ago.

I finally invested in a bicycle, bought with the money that I've made from punting, and after a very shaky start, when I almost took out a couple of pedestrians and a bus almost took *me* out, I am relatively proficient at cycling. It's certainly going to make my journey to campus quicker, if a bit more precarious.

Jessie found a second student to move in – another girl to balance out his two male students from last year. Her name is Emily and she has medium-length black hair and a nose ring. She wears a lot of dark eye make-up and black clothes, even when it's hot. She has that in common with Jessie, but otherwise she's quiet and tends to stay in her room. Sometimes we forget that she's living with us at all.

We have a big night out in the middle of the month when Sammy, Mike and Chris return to Cambridge after spending the summer with their families in Brighton, Northampton and York, respectively. It's good to have the old crowd back together again, although we're having to spend more nights at the Pickerel and fewer at the Anchor because Jessie has been avoiding Blondie. He dumped her and now she's got another boyfriend, who gives Jessie evils whenever he's in the vicinity. It doesn't make for very happy evenings on the river.

I never did go to London.

That day – the day that I told Jessie about Joe – passed by without me going. The next day too. And the next. Eventually my need to go fizzled out. My parents were disgruntled that I didn't spend part of my holidays at home. They decided to come here for a long weekend, but it was awkward. I took them punting, which they didn't seem to appreciate, and then I spent the rest of the time trying to convince them that I needed to stay in Cambridge for the summer if I wanted to keep my job.

There's no denying that I don't feel as close to them as I once did. I can't help but feel regretful that my heart was not the only thing that was broken that summer in Dorset: my relationship with my parents suffered too. I know that it must have been difficult for them to witness what happened with Joe – and his family. All they wanted was to protect me, but I just can't get past the fact that my dad let Joe leave that night, without him even saying goodbye.

Sometimes, in the middle of the night, I wake up fully alert. I stare out at the darkness and I wonder if Joe still loves me. I know that it was real – nobody will convince me otherwise – but maybe time has made him forget. Maybe he *has* moved on. Maybe Jessie is right.

The more strongly this idea takes hold, the less sad I feel. And then a strange thing happens one day when I'm taking a tour boat full of people down the river.

I'm punting along as usual, regaling them with the history of Queens' College and the two queens who founded it, when suddenly I feel angry.

Why hasn't he come? He knows where I am. He knows how to find me. He promised me that he would. I was fucking distraught! I was fucking heartbroken! I need to fucking concentrate.

'The college was *re*-founded in 1465 by Elizabeth Woodville, who was the wife of King Henry IV and the mother of the two princes who were later murdered in the Tower of London.'

But, seriously! What a bastard! He took my virginity and buggered off to London! He didn't even think to check that I was alright.

I drop my pole into the water and furiously press it against the rocky bottom.

I have been crying my effing heart out for a year! A YEAR!

'Sorry, *what*?' I snap at a middle-aged, balding American man who has asked me a question. I try to force my features to relax, because I clearly have quite a glare on me as he's looking alarmed.

He clears his throat and speaks humbly. 'You said King Henry IV?'

'Yes? And?'

'I'm confused. I thought you said King Henry *VI* was married to the first queen who founded it.'

'Margaret of Anjou, yes, that's right,' I say impatiently. 'She founded it in 1448 and was married to King Henry VI.'

I know my history, you idiot. I've done this tour enough times.

'So . . .' His brow furrows. 'How can the *fourth* King Henry come after the *sixth* King Henry?'

Oh, I see what he's getting at. Whoops!

'Sorry, I meant King *Edward* IV. He was the one who was married to Elizabeth Woodville.'

'Aah, yes. I thought so.' He looks smug.

Bloody Joe. On top of everything else, now he's making me look like a moron.

Fucking wanker.

I'm still in a foul mood an hour later when I return to the house for lunch. Jessie is doing a tour, so the place is empty. I slam the front door behind me.

'ARGH!' I want to tear my hair out I'm so angry. 'FUCKING BASTARD!' I scream, storming into the living room and slamming that door too.

A very shocked, very pale-faced Emily looks up at me from the sofa.

'Oh,' I say, coming down to earth with a bump. 'I didn't know you were in.'

'Are you okay?' she practically whispers.

'Yes. I'm FINE.'

Clearly she doesn't believe me.

'FUCKING MEN!' I scream dramatically, unable to help myself. Her eyebrows go up and she presses her lips together as though trying to stop herself from smiling. I collapse on the sofa next to her and cover my face with my hands. There's movement on the cushions beside me and I almost expect her to be gone by the time I peek out from between my fingers, but she's still there, regarding me intently. She quickly looks away, and then curiously back at me.

'They're all bastards,' she agrees in a tiny, conspiratorial voice.

I stare at her in surprise and then we both start to giggle.

'It *is* weird,' my new best friend Emily concedes with a frown.

We've been to hell and back, Em and I. Now we're sitting at the kitchen table, drinking tea and making our way through a packet of malted milks. It's amazing how much bonding can be done in an hour.

'I know!' I exclaim. 'He knew I was studying English Lit at Anglia Ruskin. All he had to do was ask someone when the lectures were taking place and wait outside the door! You don't have to be a brainiac to work that out.'

Brainiac. That was the term he used for me.

Fuck that. Don't go all sentimental on me now.

Emily looks ahead, deep in thought. 'Maybe he believes *you've* moved on,' she suggests after a while in her gentle Scottish lilt. 'Maybe he wanted to get his shit together first and it took him longer than he thought it would. Maybe he *still* hasn't got his shit together.'

'Well, he'd better get it together soon, because if he doesn't, I *might* move on.'

I unexpectedly think of Lukas. I violently shake my head to unthink him, but it doesn't work.

'Cold compress . . .'

That does it.

I look at Emily to see her looking perplexed at my odd behaviour.

'Right, your turn,' I say. 'Why do you think all men are bastards?'

If she were a clam, she would have knocked herself out with the force of her shutdown.

'Oh, they just are,' she replies dismissively.

'I can't believe I'm hearing this!'

Emily and I jump at the sound of Jessie's voice. We turn to see him standing at the doorway.

'I leave you two alone for two minutes and you're calling me a bastard! Now I remember why I took in male students last year.'

'We're not talking about *you*,' I say.

'Oh, so now I'm not even a man? Thanks a lot.'

I smirk at him. I know he's joking.

'I'd better get on,' Emily murmurs, hopping up from the table and quietly leaving the room.

Jessie gives me a weird look. 'She speaks, then?'

I nod, still quite surprised by this fact myself. He pulls up a chair and delves into the biscuit packet. 'What did she say?'

'We were talking about Joe.'

'Oh.'

'Yeah.'

The room is filled with the sound of silent munching (him) and tea-slurping (me).

'Hang on,' he says abruptly. 'You told her about Joe?'

I shrug. 'Yeah.'

'You didn't tell me about Joe for bloody ages!' he exclaims with indignation. 'And now a mouse moves into our house and you blurt it all out over the course of one lunch break?'

I try to suppress a giggle. 'I don't know what came over me.'

He humphs in disgust.

It's funny how it's so much easier to talk about Joe now. It hurt intensely just to think about him before, but after verbalising the whole sorry saga to Jessie I feel like I've been anaesthetised. Plus, I'm still angry at the wanker. I update Jessie on my current state of mind.

'I've never heard you swear so much in all my life,' he comments with surprise. 'Can't say I think it's a bad thing,' he adds.

'What, the swearing or the fact that I'm angry with the fuckwit?'

'Both.'

'Good to hear it.' We grin at each other.

'We'll have to get plastered tonight,' he decides.

'Any reason for this?'

'We need to celebrate.'

'What are we celebrating?'

'The fact that you're well on your way through the seven stages of grief.'

'Am I?'

'Yep.'

'Are there really seven stages of grief?' I ask curiously.

'So I've heard.'

'What are they?'

'Fuck knows, but any excuse to get hammered, right?'

Chapter 29

'What a load of bollocks.'

'This one says "shock" is the first stage and "denial" is the second.'

'But that other website said "shock and denial" were both stage one.'

'But they're two things.'

'And it says stage three is "anger" *and* "bargaining".'

'Again, two things. That other website had "anger" down as stage five, and "bargaining" down as stage three. What the hell is "bargaining", anyway?'

Emily leans forward and reads from the computer screen. 'You may try to bargain with the powers-that-be for a way out of your despair. For example, "I will never eat chocolate again if you just bring him back".'

'Fuck that.'

Emily, Jessie and I are huddled around my laptop. A few days have passed since I told Emily about Joe. I'm still angry, and I'm still swearing a lot.

'I think this really only applies to people who have actually lost someone,' Emily says, scrolling down. 'As in, the person they've lost has died.'

'Are you trivialising my seven stages?' I demand to know. 'Because I've got a right to feel –' I peer closely at my laptop screen – 'guilty, just like anyone else.'

Jessie screws up his nose. 'What have you got to feel guilty about?'

My brow furrows. 'Good point.' I peer in closely. 'Depressed, then.'

'Agh, no, you don't want to do depression!' Emily exclaims. 'God, no, that's no fun at all.'

'You say it like you know?'

'You don't have to have had depression to understand that it's not a barrel of laughs,' she says. I'm not sure I buy it, but she clearly doesn't want to elaborate.

'Fuck it,' I decide. 'I'm sticking with anger.'

'Good job.' Jessie pushes out his chair and stands up, stretching his arms over his head so his T-shirt rides up over his navel. Emily quickly averts her gaze. I don't blame you, chick. Hang on, has her face turned red? No way!

'I like this one.' Emily recovers and reads from the computer screen. 'The seventh stage on this website is the return to the willingness to love.'

'You old softie,' Jessie says, ruffling her hair.

'Get off!' She bats him away.

I watch closely and, yes, there it is: the blush.

It's Jessie's fault that we got onto this. He keeps mentioning the seven stages of grief when we're out and about, but we never remember to look it up by the time we get home. Tonight, though, Emily is insistent that we clear things up once and for all. Unfortunately, though, we're now more confused than ever.

'Is confusion a stage?' I ask.

'I'm going to bed,' Jessie interrupts. 'Night, night, China. Night, Emily.'

'I'm too drunk to sleep,' Emily admits once he's gone.

'Me too. Let's crack open the malted milks.'

'Lukas!'

A few days later I'm walking past Trinity on my way into town to do some shopping in the mid-season sales. I peer into the vast courtyard and see him walking through Great Gate with his head down.

He glances over his shoulder. 'Oh, hi.' He waves back at me as he heads towards an old wooden door in the building opposite.

'How are you?' I ask with an enormous smile as he turns to face me.

'Good.' He nods curtly, glancing left and right. 'Are you well?'

'Yes, thank you.' I look down with confusion at his feet. They seem to be backing away from me. 'How was your summer?' I ask.

'Fine.' He points over his shoulder. 'I'm in a bit of a rush, sorry.'

And then his feet take him inside the door and out of sight.

That was a bit rude . . . I think with a frown, then: Fucking bastard!

I can't believe I acted so happy to see him! I can't believe it wasn't an act! I *was* happy to see him. I'm as angry at myself as I am at him. More angry, even.

I'm still fuming early that evening when I'm taking my third and final tour of the day. Lo and behold, there he is on the grassy bank of Trinity's south paddock.

'Alice!' he calls with a smile, standing up. He has a book in his hand.

I nod unhappily in his direction and return my attention to my passengers. Like I'm going to give *him* any of my time when he was so impolite this morning. *And* I didn't even manage to buy anything decent at the shops – what a waste of a half-day off. 'Trinity is the wealthiest Cambridge college . . .' Through gritted teeth I tell my boat full of tourists the usual spiel. 'It has been said by some that it is possible to walk all the way to Oxford on land owned by Trinity.'

I glance over at Lukas and notice a smile playing around his lips.

What's so funny? I remain stony-faced and continue with my tour, not looking back once.

'Thank you. Thank you very much.'

God only knows why my passengers are tipping me after the terrible mood I've been in on their tour, but I accept their money with a genuine smile in the hope that I'm making up for some of my bad behaviour. When the last of them has disembarked I fold up the notes and stuff them, together with a few pound coins, into the pocket of my skinny jeans. I've had to retire my white sundress – it's too cool to wear it now. I step back into the punt and pile up the cushions and blankets so they can be locked up for the night, then I wrap my arms around the whole lot and turn to see two black shoes standing on the jetty in front of me. My eyes dart upwards to find Lukas smiling down at me.

'Can I take these?' He extracts the cushions and blankets from my arms. I recover quickly and, with a roll of my eyes, I climb out of the boat.

'This way,' I say bluntly.

All men are bastards.

He follows me to the shed, where Sammy is folding up the blankets from other boats. She glances at Lukas and then grins at me before looking back at him.

'Hel-*lo*,' she says in an unusually camp manner, taking the bundle from him and placing it on a bench, without once taking her eyes off him. I give her a wry look – it's not what she's thinking.

'Sammy, this is Lukas. Lukas, this is Sammy.'

'I haven't seen you around,' she comments with a smile as she leans up against the doorframe and folds her arms.

'No, well, I've yet to go punting,' he replies with slight discomfort.

'See you tomorrow,' I say to Sammy before turning away.

'Are you not coming for a drink?' she calls after us, sounding disappointed.

'No,' I reply. 'Not tonight.'

I walk away from the punts and turn right onto Magdalene Street.

'Where are you going?' Lukas asks, struggling to keep step with me as I cross the bridge. Diners sit out on the balcony of a restaurant overlooking the river. The autumn leaves have started to fall and they look like little brown boats floating on the water. It's busy this evening; ever since the students returned Cambridge has come back to life. At times, in the summer, it felt like a ghost town.

'Home,' I reply. 'Where are *you* going?'

'I . . . I wondered if I might take you for a drink?' he stammers as we pass the Pickerel Inn. I glance through the wrought-iron gates to the courtyard at the side. It's already heaving with people.

'Why?'

'Because I . . . I thought it might be nice. I'd like to know how your summer was, what you got up to.'

'You could have asked me that earlier.'

'I'm sorry. I lost track of time talking to my tutor and then I realised I was late for an important phone call.'

I shake my head and scoff: 'What *student* has important phone calls?' I intentionally place the emphasis on 'student' – who does he think he is?

'If you *must* know . . .'

Ooh, have I annoyed him? Don't care.

'. . . my mother was calling me from hospital. My brother's wife has just had a baby who is premature. We weren't sure if he was going to make it through the night.'

I stop in my tracks. 'Oh.' How bad do I feel? 'Is he okay? The baby?'

'Yes.' He nods. 'He's still having some difficulty breathing on his own, but they think he'll survive.'

'That's good.' I smile awkwardly with relief.

'So, can I take you for a drink?' He regards me intently with those very blue eyes of his.

'Like I'm going to say no now.' I laugh uneasily.

'Good.' He starts to walk again. I hurry to catch up.

'Where do you want to go?' I glance sideways at him.

'There's a pub around the corner . . .' He points up ahead. 'The Punter. I believe it's quite nice inside.'

'It is.' Jessie and I stop there occasionally on our way home.

We reach the pub and Lukas opens the door for me.

'What would you like to drink?' he asks.

For some reason I think twice about ordering a pint of lager. I don't really want to drink it in front of Lukas, but I'm damned if I'm going to change for him.

'A pint of lager, please,' I stubbornly reply.

He doesn't comment. He heads to the bar, while I go off to find us a table. I sit down and wait. I'm surprisingly on edge.

'Here you are,' he says a short while later, placing a pint glass on the table in front of me. It looks so large and uncouth. Suddenly I really wish it were a glass of white wine instead.

He pulls up a chair and sits down. I'm relieved to see that he's also drinking lager.

'So,' he says with a smile, 'how was your summer?'

'Fab.'

'What did you do?'

'A lot of reading, and a lot of punting.'

'Did you make it home at all?'

'No.'

'Really?' He sounds intrigued. 'Where *is* home?'

'London. That's where my parents live.'

'You didn't make it back there to see them at all?'

'They came here for a long weekend.'

'You're not close?'

I shift in my seat and look down at the table. That's a bit personal. Not as much as we used to be, if truth be told.

He notices my reaction. 'I'm sorry, I don't mean to pry.'

'That's okay.' I take a sip of my pint and don't enjoy it. 'What about you? Oh, hey!' I remember something. 'How were your exam results?'

'Good.'

'What did you get?'

'A First.'

'Brilliant, well done.' I'm impressed. 'And did you spend your summer in Germany?'

He nods and smiles. 'I did. Part of it.'

'Where else did you go?'

'We also had a few weeks in Monaco.'

'Monaco? That's nice.' I process this information. Hang on … He said 'we'. Does he have a girlfriend? 'Who did you go with?'

'My family.'

I feel a strange sense of relief. But I'd better double-check: 'As in, your mother …'

'… my father, my sister, my brother and his wife.'

'The ones who've just had a baby?'

'Correct.'

I smile at him. 'What's his name? The baby.'

'Maximilian. I'm hoping we'll be able to shorten it to Max.'

'Maximilian!' I call in a light-hearted tone, pretending to be his mother; then, in a deep, cross voice, wagging my finger at an imaginary child as I say it: 'Maximilian! Don't be so naughty.' Then, clutching my face with horror: 'Maximilian! Come away from the edge!'

Lukas laughs. 'It has to be Max.'

'I don't know. Maximilian has a nice ring to it.'

'My grandfather was called Maximilian. No one ever referred to him as Max.'

'Not even "dear old Max"?'

'No, never. It was always Maximilian or, more commonly, Herr Heuber.'

'Is that your surname?' I ask.

'Yes.'

'Lukas Heuber.' I don't know why, but I put on a gruff German accent as I say it.

He grins. 'What's your surname?'

'Simmons.'

'Alice Simmons.'

Déjà vu. I've had this conversation before with . . . Joe. Argh! Out! Out! All men are bastards, remember? I turn my attention back to the one currently seated across from me.

Chapter 30

I find myself agreeing to let Lukas take me out for an early dinner the following Friday night. Jessie and my other punter pals were a bit put out when I told them I couldn't punt with them that evening. We're all working overtime on the Halloween Ghost tours that start now and continue until the end of October, and there's even more camaraderie than usual on the river.

I didn't tell them I was going on a date until the very last minute. I didn't want to have to endure the teasing that I knew would come. Not that I'm thinking of it like that. A date, I mean. Lukas is just a friend. Sort of.

He arrives at six o'clock on the dot. I knew he'd be on time, so I made sure I was. My hair comes halfway down my back and I'm wearing a black dress with white horizontal stripes and a black cardie. Initially I wondered whether this outfit was too dressed-up, but I suspected he would make an effort. Again, I was right.

He's about six foot two and he's wearing a white shirt and a navy-blue wool jacket with black leather piping. He's pushed his dark blond hair back off his forehead. He looks cool – like he's stepped off the pages of a Hugo Boss campaign.

'Ready?' he asks with a raised eyebrow.

As I'll ever be ... 'Yes.' I grab my bag from the hallstand and follow him out.

He hasn't commented on Jessie's house, but I guess he's seen more than enough impressive architecture in his time at Cambridge for it to not fully register. He turns left out of the gate.

'It's quicker this way,' I point right, trying to put on my coat and walk at the same time.

'We're not going into town,' he says over his shoulder.

'Oh, really?' I hurry to keep up. 'Where are we going?'

'You'll see.'

With curiosity I follow him down some steps to the road. We cross over it, his hand making my lower back tingle as he lightly guides me. He leads me to a slick black Porsche, which beeps and flashes as he unlocks it. I stare at him, confused, as he opens the passenger door for me and indicates for me to climb in.

'Is this yours?' I ask with incredulity.

'One would hope so.'

He owns a *Porsche*? 'I thought students weren't allowed to keep cars within the city perimeters?'

'They're not,' he replies with amusement. 'But I don't keep it *within* the city perimeters.' He again motions for me to get into the car, so I do, the smell of new leather instantly filling my nostrils. A moment later he's in the driver's seat and starting the ignition.

'Where are we going?' I repeat, a little flustered.

He shakes his head.

'I don't like surprises,' I add.

'You'll like this one.'

He seems incredibly confident about that fact.

He drives us west, away from the city. We hop onto an A road for a short while and then wind our way along country roads and through a couple of tiny villages with thatched cottages. Barely fifteen minutes go by before he's pulling into a long gravel driveway. An enormous, modern-looking house looms up ahead. It's three storeys high, square, with a flat roof, white walls and a lot of windows. The lights are off inside and it appears dark and unlived-in.

'Whose house is this?'

'A family friend's,' he tells me. 'They're not here.'

'Where are they?'

'The south of France.'

'On holiday?'

'No, this is their holiday house.'

Some holiday house . . .

'One of them, anyway,' he adds flippantly.

Oh. Glad we got that straight.

He climbs out of the car and opens my door, helping me out. I look around. The house is surrounded by tall trees with auburn leaves, many of which have fallen and crunch under my heels as I walk towards the front door.

'We're not going inside,' Lukas calls. He points to the stairs at the side of the house. I follow him with increasing interest.

We climb the two flights to the roof, and there, on an enormous, flat terrace, is a table for two, set within dozens of flickering candles in large glass vases. Then I notice the view. It stretches across the orange, red and yellow treetops to the gently undulating fields beyond. The sun is just dipping below the horizon, its orange glow spreading across the dark-blue sky. Wow. Lukas hands me a flute full to the brim with sparkling champagne. I stare down at it, bemused. Where did he get this from? And then I turn to see that dinner is already laid out on the table underneath silver domes, together with a champagne bottle, chilling on ice.

'How did you do all this?' I ask with amazement.

'I had some help,' he admits, gently chinking my glass with his own. He takes a sip but doesn't elaborate. I don't want to spoil the mystique so I don't ask him to. The bubbles tingle as they hit the back of my throat. Lukas motions towards the table.

'Shall we?'

He pulls my chair out for me, pushing it back in again as I sit down. I feel a little like a princess. I feel a little overawed, if truth be told. Warmth emanates from the outside heaters standing nearby.

I follow Lukas's lead and lift off the silver dome in front of me to see a smoked-salmon starter on my plate. It melts in my mouth. I look out to the west to see that the sunset has intensified.

'We're lucky with the weather,' I comment, then want to kick myself for not finding something more interesting to say.

'Yes.' He smiles. I take a large gulp of champagne, which goes straight to my head.

'I was going to say I feel overdressed for a picnic, but this isn't your ordinary picnic, is it?'

'You look incredible,' he says, and I blush at his unexpected compliment. 'And I don't do ordinary,' he adds.

'I can see that.'

He refills my glass and clears our plates. He opens a silver chafing dish on a nearby table and the smell of something delicious wafts out. He serves up and I look down to see a large, rosy-red lobster tail, drizzled with warm garlic butter. I help myself to new potatoes and vegetables.

'This is amazing,' I say.

'I'm glad you like it.'

'You knew that I would.' I remember his earlier confidence.

'I was slightly apprehensive about the seafood,' he admits with a smile. 'It can be a risk.'

Aha! So he *is* human. I laugh. 'True. Did you have an alternative?'

'Take-away.'

We smile at each other.

'And dessert,' he adds.

'Ooh, what's for dessert?' I ask, unable to help myself.

'Patience,' he chides.

By the time dessert comes around, the sun has long since set and there's a clear, cloudless night sky above us, twinkling with stars.

Our last course is indeed worth waiting for: a chocolate fondant, oozing chocolate from the middle, with cream. Lukas tops up my glass once more. I notice that he's barely drinking, which is good, because he has to drive me home.

'I can't believe I've drunk over half a bottle of champagne,' I say with a giggle. I'm feeling very tipsy now. 'I'm sorry you've had to drive.'

'I don't mind in the slightest,' he says. 'Let's take our coffees over there.'

He nods at a pile of oversized comfy cushions near the low wall at the back of the terrace. Hang on a minute. I hope he doesn't think I'm going to put out on the first date. A flurry of nerves passes through me, but I follow his suggestion while he goes to pour our coffees. He brings over two cups, and a small dish full of exquisite-looking truffles. I sit down on the soft cushions. It's cooler away from the warmth of the outdoor heaters, even with my coat on. He passes me a blanket.

'You've come amazingly well prepared,' I say a little drily, draping it over my knees.

'I can't take all the credit,' he admits.

'Why not?'

'I didn't think of the blankets myself.'

'Aah, your friend.' I remember him saying he had some help.

'Not strictly a *friend* . . .'

'Oh. Who helped you, then?'

'The same person who brought my car into the city tonight.'

'You're being very vague.' Then it dawns on me. 'An employee?'

He doesn't deny it as he takes a sip of his coffee.

'Are you very, very rich?' I blurt out.

He laughs and looks at me, his eyes shining under the flames of the candles surrounding us. Many have gone out, but just as many are still alight. 'It's not something I usually talk about.'

'Sorry.'

'You don't need to apologise.'

'So is your employee –' the word feels strange on my tongue – 'responsible for all of this?' I indicate the setting around us, feeling a small stab of disappointment.

'Physically, yes,' Lukas reveals. 'Theoretically, no.' He smiles at me. 'It was my idea.'

'All of it?'

He nods.

'The menu?'

'Yes.'

'The candles?'

He shrugs. 'Yes.'

'The cushions?'

'Yes.' Pause. 'But not the blankets.'

I grin at him. 'I'm glad we cleared that up.'

'Me too.'

It's grown darker, and I realise that a few more candles have gone out. The sky above is bursting with stars. Lukas rests his head back on the cushions and I do the same, gazing upwards.

He turns to face me and reaches over to take my hand.

I freeze. This is it. He's going to make his move now. What am I going to do? I think of Joe and feel overwhelmed with sadness. I try to conjure up rage instead, but it doesn't work. My head feels cloudy and confused. I have no idea how I'll react if he kisses me.

But he doesn't. Not yet, anyway. His hand is warm. He lets go and starts to trace circles on my palm. I turn to look at him and suddenly feel dizzy. I wrack my brain for something to say, something to stave off the inevitable, but my mind is blank. I look at his lips and back to his eyes, before my gaze once more falls on his lips. And at that moment I *do* want him to kiss me.

Abruptly, he sits up. I regard his broad back with bewilderment.

'I should take you home,' he mumbles, getting to his feet.

What?

He holds his hand down to me. Flustered, I come to my senses and stand up without taking it. I feel humiliated. He must have known what I wanted. Notice the use of the past tense here.

'Shouldn't we clear up?' I call after him as he stalks across the terrace to the stairs.

'Klaus will do it.'

Who's Klaus? Oh, the employee.

Lukas drives way too fast on the return journey, slamming the car through its gear changes as he navigates the country roads. I have no idea what the hell has got into him, but I clutch the armrest with terror, neither of us speaking. Then he's pulling up outside Jessie's house. He glares out through the windscreen, then he yanks open his door. I quickly open mine and climb out before he can reach me.

'I'm sorry,' he blurts.

'Don't be,' I snap. He puts his hand on my arm, but I shrug him off. I'm beyond perplexed now. I'm back to being angry again. All men, right?

'Alice, wait!' he calls as I hurry across the road. He runs after me. 'I said I was sorry.'

I spin around to face him. 'What are you sorry for, exactly?'

He looks away, then directly at me. 'For driving too fast.'

I shake my head and start to walk off.

'I want to see you again!' he calls. My footsteps slow to a standstill. I sigh. Yes, it was an amazing evening, but I ended up feeling humiliated and then confused. I could really do without these two emotions in my life right now.

'Thank you for dinner,' I say over my shoulder. 'I'm sure I'll see you around.'

He nods curtly and then stuffs his hands into his jacket pockets before determinedly setting off in the direction of the city.

Chapter 31

'How was your hot date?' Jessie teases the next day at breakfast. Regardless of the fact that I heard him stumble in at one o'clock this morning, he's in the kitchen at nine, rustling up pancakes.

'It wasn't a date. He's just a friend,' I say pedantically, although in truth I'm not even sure he's that.

I looked out of the living-room window first thing this morning to see that Lukas's Porsche had vanished, collected by the mysterious Klaus, no doubt. I hope the poor man wasn't up too late cleaning away after us.

'Morning.' Emily appears. 'I'm starving. What are we having?'

'Pancakes,' Jessie replies.

'Mmm, my favourite!'

'*That's* the reaction I was expecting.' He gives me a pointed look.

'I'm sorry, I'm not hungry.'

'What did you have for dinner last night?' Emily enquires.

By the time I've finished telling them, their mouths have dropped open.

'Who the hell is this guy?' Jessie exclaims. 'Prince fucking William?'

I smirk. 'Not likely.'

'You didn't have a good time?' Emily asks.

'I did, but . . .'

'What?' they both ask eagerly in unison.

'It ended a bit strangely.'

'What do you mean?' That was Emily.

'I . . . I don't know. I don't really want to talk about it.'

'Did he do anything?' Jessie demands to know. From his tone of voice, he means 'anything bad'.

'No, he didn't do anything.'

And, although I hate to admit it, therein lies the problem.

The next few days pass with no sign of Lukas. In fact, it's not until Saturday, a week later, that I see him at all. I'm halfway through a late-morning tour when I spot him up ahead, perching on the stone wall at the end of Trinity Bridge with yet another textbook. I decide the most professional thing to do is to press on with my tour and ignore him. Then it occurs to me that he might ignore *me* and I feel slightly sick. But for all my attempts to avoid eye contact, we end up looking straight at each other. He manages a shaky smile. I carry on regardless, regaling my passengers with tales about Trinity. He stands up as I approach the bridge, and by the time my boat has passed through to the other side he's standing in the middle of the bridge.

'Alice,' he calls.

'Yep?'

'I need to talk to you.'

'I'm a bit busy right now.'

The next thing I know, he's walking on the grass outside the Wren Library, a few metres away, keeping pace with my boat.

'Have lunch with me,' he says.

'I can't,' I reply, too distracted to tell my passengers about A.A. Milne's manuscripts of *Winnie-the-Pooh.* I think they're finding my conversation with this gorgeous undergraduate far more exciting. Did I say gorgeous? I didn't mean to.

'Please,' he persists.

I shake my head, trying to ignore the eager stares of twelve sets of eyes. And then I'm rounding the bend in the river.

He reaches Magdalene Bridge before I do, but thankfully he waits until all my passengers have disembarked before making his presence known.

'You know,' he says with a raised eyebrow as I step onto the jetty, 'it's not actually true what you told your passengers about Trinity.'

This statement makes me feel even more cross with him than I already was. But curiosity gets the better of me. 'Which part?'

'One can't walk all the way from Cambridge to Oxford on land owned by Trinity.'

'I don't tell them that it's true, I tell them: "it has been said by some . . ."'

'But it's nonsense,' he says.

'It's not nonsense,' I snap, even though I know that it probably is. 'Anyway, it makes for a more interesting tour.'

'I think there are plenty of other fascinating facts that aren't based in fiction.'

'Do you, now?' I fold my arms across my chest. 'Like what?'

'Like the fact that Lord Byron kept a pet bear when he was a student at Trinity.'

'I've heard that one,' I say with a roll of my eyes. 'He allegedly did it to spite the no-dog rule. *That* sounds like nonsense to me.'

'It's not. He wrote it in a letter to Elizabeth Pigot in 1807.'

'Who the hell is Elizabeth Pigot?'

'Come for lunch with me,' he pleads again. 'I'll tell you all about her,' he adds with a grin.

'Ooh, that sounds like an invitation I can't refuse,' I say sarcastically.

He grabs my arm and spins me around so I'm looking at him.

'Please, Alice.' His smile has vanished. Now he looks so sincere that I hesitate. 'I owe you an explanation.'

I regard him for a long moment and then I nod.

The restaurants we pass are heaving, so Lukas suggests we eat at Trinity.

'Isn't it really formal?' I ask worriedly. 'Don't you all wear gowns and dine in a big hall?'

He smiles. 'Students only wear gowns if they wish to go to Formal Hall, later at night. Lunchtimes and the early dinner sitting are casual.'

Formal Hall. It all sounds so unfamiliar. In truth, I'm intrigued.

Great Hall is already bustling with students sitting at four long tables spanning almost the entire length of the enormous room. I feel like I'm at Hogwarts as I survey my surroundings. The walls are clad in dark wood, the ceiling beams are gilded and there are stained-glass windows towering overhead.

'That's the High Table,' Lukas explains as we walk past some smaller tables on a raised platform. 'That's where the members of the Fellowship sit.'

'*No way?*' I gasp. 'Frodo sits there?'

He chuckles at my joke. 'Trinity came before Tolkien,' he replies.

I take a seat opposite him. It's like another world, here. An exclusive, elite world that I can't imagine ever being a part of. I have to admit I'm envious. To study within the walls of this college . . .

'Lukas!' Someone calls his name and I look up to see a tall, but slight, young man approaching. He has dark, dishevelled hair and round glasses. He's attractive, if a little nerdy, and he's wearing a tweed blazer and a checked shirt that hasn't seen an iron in who knows how long.

'Hello, Harry, take a seat,' Lukas says amiably, pulling one out for him.

'I've got the Mallard!' he tells Lukas in a conspiratorial whisper, opening up his backpack to reveal a wooden duck inside. What the hell? All of a sudden, Harry notices me. 'Hello, hello!' His accent is terribly posh.

Lukas introduces us.

'What's this about?' I ask.

'The Mallard fell down,' he says with excitement.

Is he barmy?

Lukas leans forward to explain. He points to the eaves above our heads. 'There's usually a duck up in the rafters. Don't ask me why. It's one of Trinity's traditions.'

'I've heard about it!' I suddenly recall a vague memory.

'Not "it": "them". A veritable flock have fallen down over the years,' Lukas reveals. 'Harry wants to put the next one up.'

'How will you do that?' I ask with curiosity. It's a very high ceiling.

He taps the side of his nose.

'Well, be careful,' I say, a little worried about this strange, er, stranger.

'Aw, she's concerned about me,' he tells Lukas with delight, before turning back to me. 'I haven't seen you around. Are you a first year?'

'No, second.'

'Alice doesn't go to Trinity,' Lukas explains.

'Don't tell me you go to John's,' Harry teases. 'Boo! Hiss!'

The two colleges have an age-old rivalry, although it's mostly good-natured.

'No.' I smile. 'I go to Anglia Ruskin.'

'Aah ... O-*kay*,' Harry says knowingly.

Why is he saying it like that? Is he being rude?

'Now it all makes sense,' he continues. 'I thought I must need new glasses.'

I stare at him, confused.

'He clearly thinks you're as beautiful as I do,' Lukas interjects, instantly making me blush.

'I was sure I would have noticed you before,' Harry adds.

'I'm surprised you haven't seen Alice on the river,' Lukas says to him. 'She works as a tour guide on the punts.'

'Argh, no!' Harry exclaims with mock horror, sitting back in his chair and throwing his hands up in the air. A few students sitting further along the table turn to look at us. 'I hope you're not one of the ones spewing ridiculous stories.'

Lukas tries to keep a straight face.

Harry continues in a silly voice. 'Trinity has a fortune of over two billion pounds; you can walk all the way to Oxford ... or *York* ... or *London* ... on land owned by Trinity ... What a load of tosh.'

'Er—' I start.

'Just ignore him,' Lukas interrupts, nodding at Harry. 'He's a mathematician.'

My brow furrows. 'Meaning?'

'They're usually either very introverted, or very extroverted, like Harry, here.'

Harry lunges forward in his seat, making me jump. 'So is that how you two met, then? Did you spy Alice on the river?' he asks Lukas.

'Yes,' he replies.

'Well, it wasn't quite like that,' I start to correct him. 'You saved me from the wrath of a cyclist, first.'

'I had seen you on the river several times before that,' he reveals, calmly meeting my gaze.

'Really?' I ask with surprise. I'd never noticed him. Then again, I don't suppose I'd been looking.

'What are you reading?' Harry drags my attention away from Lukas.

'Um, *Heart of Darkness* at the moment,' I reply. Harry looks perplexed.

'He means, "What are you studying?"' Lukas clarifies.

'Oh!' I forgot they say 'reading' instead of 'studying'. Another difference between their world and mine. 'English Literature,' I tell him.

He nods, regarding me intently. I shift in my seat. His stare is making me uncomfortable. Lukas seems to notice. He turns to Harry.

'Don't you need to speak to Terence about something?'

'Oh! Yes!' Harry jumps to his feet, almost knocking over his chair. He runs after a student who is on his way out of the hall. Lukas turns back to me.

'Sorry about Harry.'

'He's funny,' I say, and I mean it, even if I didn't feel overly relaxed in his company. 'Albeit a little eccentric,' I add.

'A little?' Lukas queries.

'Okay, a lot.'

He leans across the table and takes my hand. I look at him with surprise. 'I'm sorry about the way I acted last week,' he says earnestly. 'I was confused.'

'About what?' I want to understand.

He hesitates, but doesn't take his eyes from mine. 'About the way I feel about you.'

My blush returns in force. I can't keep eye contact with him so I look away.

'I would like to see more of you,' he says, squeezing my hand gently and bringing my focus back to him. 'What are you doing on Monday?'

'I'm supposed to be on the river.'

'You don't have any lectures?'

'No.'

'Can you take some time off?'

'Um . . .' I suppose I could ask one of the others to cover for me. Mike was looking for more work. 'Possibly.'

'Good.' He smiles and lets go of my hand. 'I'll pick you up at eleven.'

I nod. 'Okay.'

Harry returns and collapses down in his chair. 'I hate eating cold curry!' he exclaims in disgust.

Lukas and I smile small smiles across the table at each other and tuck into our food.

Chapter 32

At eleven o'clock on Monday, Lukas rings the doorbell.

'Where's Klaus?' I ask, spying the Porsche parked across the road.

'He's gone shopping,' he replies, taking my hand and swinging it as he leads me across the road.

'You're in a good mood,' I comment.

'I am.' He beams at me and my heart unexpectedly flips.

He's wearing a dark-grey sports jacket with tailored trousers and a light-blue shirt. His shirts always look so pristine and perfect. I wonder who does his ironing.

'Where are we going?' I ask when I'm safely buckled in. I hope he doesn't drive as fast as he did the last time.

'I thought I'd take you to Wimpole Hall.'

'What's that?'

'It's owned by the National Trust. It's quite a pretty house, I believe. I thought you might like to see something outside the city, for a change.'

'Yes, I would,' I reply. 'May as well make the most of your car, right?'

'Exactly.'

'Where does Klaus live?' I ask as he drives off.

'Girton. Just up the road from here,' he replies. 'It's outside the city perimeters,' he tells me with a grin.

'Glad to hear it,' I reply. 'Wouldn't want you getting into trouble, now, would we?'

'Absolutely not.'

He reaches across and squeezes my hand. He does this a lot. I can't say I don't like it.

'Quite a pretty house' are not the words I'd use to describe what turns out to be the largest country house in Cambridgeshire. Wimpole Hall, built of red brick and stone, is set within three thousand acres of parkland and farmland, and its landscaped gardens are beautiful.

We wander side by side along the gravel paths. It's a cold day today, but the skies are clear and blue. Some of the trees have been sculpted and look unreal, like something out of *Alice in Wonderland*. Lukas and I sit down on a bench facing the back of the house.

'It's lovely here,' I breathe, moving in closer to him to keep warm.

'It is nice,' he concedes.

The miniature hedges in the formal gardens form shapes like circles and triangles, and they're inset with pink and purple flowers. The lawn is perfectly manicured and its edges perfectly straight.

'I wonder how they get those grass edges to be so straight,' I muse aloud.

'Our gardeners do ours with scissors,' Lukas answers casually.

'*Scissors?*'

'It's the most effective way. My mother is very fussy,' he adds.

'But that must take forever!'

He shrugs. 'Not really.'

'How many gardeners do you have?' I remember he used the plural.

'Four or five.'

My mouth drops open. 'You have five gardeners?'

'Four or five,' he corrects me.

'How big is your house?' I exclaim.

'It's quite big,' he replies modestly, which probably means it's enormous.

'What do your parents do?'

'My father runs the family business, manufacturing car components.'

'Sounds interesting.'

'It's not, I assure you. At least, it has no interest to me.'

'What about your mother?' He didn't mention her.

'She runs the household.'

'Oh, right.'

A peacock ambles past and I'm distracted by a memory of being at Brownsea Island with Joe.

'If a peacock is a male and a peahen is a female, what's the generic term for them?' I remember Joe asking. 'Pea?'

I smile to myself. 'I wonder what the generic term is for peacock.'

'Peafowl,' Lukas answers without a moment's hesitation.

He didn't even need me to explain what I meant.

'How can you know that?' I cry. 'You're not even English!'

He laughs. 'My siblings and I had a very good language tutor.'

'Bloody hell,' I say, regretting my language immediately. Swear words sound wrong in front of Lukas.

'How many brothers and sisters do you have?' I ask him, moving on.

'I have one brother and one sister,' he replies. 'They're both older than me.'

'What are their names?'

'Markus and Frieda.'

'I love the name Frieda,' I coo. 'Markus is Maximilian's father, right?'

'Correct.'

'How is the baby doing?'

'Very well. They expect he'll be able to go home next week.'

'That's fantastic!' I enthuse, feeling guilty for not thinking to ask after him before.

'What about you?' he asks. 'Any brothers or sisters?'

'No. It's just me.'

'I bet your parents miss you.'

I stare ahead. 'Probably.'

'Why aren't you close to them?' he asks gently, leaning forward on the bench and resting his elbows on his knees.

I sigh. 'I used to be.' Pause. 'We had a falling out last summer. I still haven't fully forgiven them.'

'Do you mind if I ask what happened?'

'No, but do *you* mind if I don't want to talk about it?' I laugh slightly with embarrassment.

'Of course not.' He looks at me searchingly. 'I hope you'll open up to me someday.'

'Maybe.'

Or maybe not. Lukas is a whole different kettle of fish to Jessie and Emily. I have no desire to talk to him about Joe. My eyes fall to the ground and I suddenly feel full of melancholy.

'Let's go for a walk,' Lukas suggests.

I gladly agree.

Chapter 33

On Friday night, I'm halfway through my second pint of lager at the Pickerel with Emily, Jessie and co., when Lukas texts to ask me what I'm doing. I haven't seen him since Monday as he's been busy at the lab, but I've thought of him often. I write back to say that I'm at the pub, and I'm about to press Send, when I think to ask him what he's up to. His response comes quickly. He says he's at Trinity's college bar. I don't really know what he expects me to do with this information, but then another text comes in from him asking me to join him. An afterthought? Or indecision?

'Who are you texting?' Jessie asks nosily.

'Lukas,' I reply distractedly.

'What's he saying?'

'He's wondering if I want to go for a drink with him.'

'Do you?'

Yes . . .

'I'll finish my lager first,' I say. 'Hey, do you know what the generic term is for peacock?'

'What are you on about?'

'You know, a peacock is a male, a peahen is a female. Any idea what you'd call them jointly?'

'Fuck, no. They're all just called peacocks, aren't they?'

'Apparently not.'

'What is it, then?'

'Peafowl,' I tell him with a knowing look.

He snorts with laughter and I giggle and down my drink.

Butterflies fill my stomach as I wait outside Trinity. Lukas appears within a minute in a T-shirt and jeans.

'Aren't you cold?' I ask with a smile.

'I ran,' he replies, slightly out of breath as he bends down to kiss me on the cheek. The scent of his aftershave lingers and my pulse quickens. It's a little bit of a shock to discover how much I fancy him.

'The beautiful Alice!' Harry cries from across the room the moment we walk into the bar. I can tell from this distance that he's already had a few. I glance at Lukas and wonder how much he's had to drink. It's hard to tell; he's always so composed.

Harry jumps up and drags a heavy chair over for me. Lukas sits down on the leather sofa to my left, next to a guy who looks to be in his early twenties and is wearing a pale-pink shirt unbuttoned at the top. He's tanned with light blond hair, and is extremely good-looking. I've been quite taken aback by how many perfect specimens of guys and girls there are in Cambridge, actually. Tall, broad or beautiful and highly intelligent . . . A James Bond villain would have a field day here if he wanted to snaffle up a bunch of them to start a new race. Wasn't there a movie about that sort of thing? *Moonraker*, that's it.

'Alice, this is Matthew.'

'Hi,' he says with a raised eyebrow.

'Hi.'

Lukas jumps back up. 'What would you like to drink?' he asks me. I glance at the table: in front of him is what looks like neat whisky. Matthew is also drinking whisky and Harry has a pint glass in his hand.

'A vodka, lemonade and lime, please,' I reply. He heads off to the bar and I turn to Harry. 'So, does Great Hall have a new duck in residence?'

He looks embarrassed and Matthew play-punches him on the arm. 'Someone else beat him to it, didn't they?'

'Oh dear,' I empathise. 'On the plus side, you're still alive.'

'I'll put the next one up,' Harry mutters determinedly.

'Sure you will,' Matthew teases.

I smile and look around. Not your average college bar, I'd guess, although I haven't been to any, other than my own. But there *is* table football and . . . Yes! A pool table!

'Do you play?' Matthew asks, leaning forward to talk to me.

I turn back to him. 'Table football, no. Pool, yes.'

'Really?' Harry asks with interest.

'Well, yeah, a little.' My dad taught me to play at our local pub when I was about ten. We went there almost every Sunday for years. I became quite good.

'Do you want a game?' Matthew asks.

'Um . . . Could do.'

'Come on,' Harry urges. 'Doubles!'

Lukas returns with my drink.

'Game of pool?' Matthew asks him, indicating me. 'Alice is up for it.'

'Sure,' Lukas replies.

'Quick, it's free,' Harry says.

'You against us?' Matthew asks, nodding at Lukas and me as he gets a coin out of his pocket. Harry chalks up a cue.

'Yes.' Lukas puts our drinks down on a nearby windowsill and unexpectedly places his hands on my hips from behind. My stomach goes all jittery.

'Heads or tails?' Matthew asks us, glancing down at Lukas's hands.

'Heads,' Lukas decides.

He flips the coin. 'Heads it is.' Harry hands over the cue and chooses another one for himself.

'Do you want to break?' Lukas asks me.

'No, you go ahead.' I'm nervous now. I hope I don't make a fool out of myself.

Lukas breaks and three balls go straight into the pockets: two 'stripes' and one 'spot'. I watch him with glee as he pots a third stripe, but he accidentally snookers himself so he has to shoot the cue ball off a corner. It hits a stripe and sends it in the direction of a corner pocket, but the ball falls short and doesn't go in.

'Unlucky,' Matthew says, lining up his cue. He pots a spot and moves onto another.

'You're really good!' I whisper into Lukas's ear when he hands over the cue to me.

'We have a snooker table at home,' he whispers back with a smile, but he doesn't take his eyes off the action on the table.

'Leave some for me,' Harry complains, as Matthew attempts another pot.

He misses and glares at Harry. 'You put me off.'

And now it's my turn. I hope that my hands don't shake. I take a large sip of my drink, then I study the table. I could go for the easy pot – the stripe that Lukas lined up in his last shot – but I kind of fancy the one down the other end of the table. I lean across the table and line up my cue. The ball goes straight in.

'Whoa!' Matthew and Harry exclaim in unison. I line up my next shot: I plan to pot a ball on the other side of the table into a different corner pocket. Again it goes in.

'We've been had,' Harry jokes, nudging Matthew, who's regarding me with admiration. Lukas raises his eyebrows at me. I pot another stripe, but the cue ball follows in after it.

'Oh, no,' I groan.

'Bad luck!' Harry exclaims delightedly, chalking up his cue.

'Not bad for a girl,' Lukas teases in my ear, putting his hands back on my hips and making me feel jittery again.

'Oi.' I slap Lukas's thigh and he laughs under his breath. My thoughts suddenly jump to Joe and my smile falters.

No. I will not think about him now. Not tonight. Not ever. He couldn't even be bothered to try to track me down. Damn him.

Yes, I'm still angry, although my anger is waning. I think I might be moving onto acceptance, and then . . .

The return to the willingness to love.

I unwittingly snort with laughter as I recall Emily reading that out. 'What are you giggling about?' Matthew asks from beside me.

'Nothing,' I reply chirpily.

Suddenly it's Lukas's turn again and there is only one stripe left: the one that he set up earlier. It's an easy shot, and then he's onto the black ball. It's right up against the edge and it's practically impossible to pot from this angle. He gives it a good go, though, hopefully making my job next time slightly easier.

Matthew pots the rest of the spots, and it looks like he'll pot the black, but he misses it completely.

'Argh!' He buries his head in his hands. Harry theatrically screams 'No!' and Lukas with a smile hands over the cue to me. I line it up and barely feel any pressure, thanks to the relaxing qualities of my good friend Smirnoff. I pot the black and the game is ours.

Harry pretends to sob over the table. Then he looks up and brightly says: 'Another game?'

'Alice?' Lukas asks me.

'Why not?' I reply with a smile, holding up my empty glass. 'I might need another one of these, though . . .'

By the time Lukas and I win three out of five games, I'm feeling extremely tipsy. He's been drinking double whiskies, and must be a bit drunk by now, although you'd hardly know it.

'We're going to sit this one out,' he firmly tells a disappointed Harry and Matthew, before leading me to a sofa underneath the window. He slumps down onto it, and it's the least composed thing I've ever seen him do, so I figure I'm probably right about the drink thing. I sit down next to him and he wraps his arm around my neck and sighs. He's been very tactile tonight, and it's nice because we haven't even kissed. In my insecure moments, I've wondered if he just likes me as a friend. I turn to look at him. He's very close and he meets my gaze with those intensely blue eyes of his. We stare at each other for what feels like a long time, so much so that my heart starts to cartwheel.

'Do you want to come back to mine?' he asks quietly.

'A coffee might be a good idea,' I reply, not wanting to appear overly keen. I still feel a little bruised after the rooftop incident.

He nods and we stand up. 'See you later, guys,' he calls at Harry and Matthew as we pass.

'You're not leaving!' Harry exclaims.

'Bye,' Matthew replies with a half wave.

'See you in the morning,' Lukas tells Harry.

'Okay,' he says sorrowfully. 'Bye, beautiful Alice!'

I giggle and follow Lukas out.

Chapter 34

'Where do you live?' I ask Lukas as we hurry towards the main gate. He must be absolutely freezing.

'Just across the road.'

'Why didn't you bring a coat?' I ask with astonishment.

'I really am just across the road.' He glances down at me.

We pass through the gate and walk across the road to the wooden door I once saw him go into. He pushes it open and leads me right, up some stairs, then right again at the top. He nods at the small terraced houses in front of us.

'This is home.'

'No way.'

He unlocks the door and pushes it open for me, then goes to the third door we come to, unlocking that too.

He lives in a student bedsit above a bookshop on Trinity Street. His room is a lot larger than the one I had in Nightingale Hall in my first year, and there's a single bed, a desk and a couple of comfy chairs in front of a gas fire. Out of the windows I can see Great Gate opposite.

'I thought *I* lived centrally!' I exclaim.

'It's too noisy here,' he brushes me off, bending down to turn on the fire.

'It's amazing!'

'Your house is nicer.'

That's the first complimentary thing he's said about Jessie's house, which surprises me because it is pretty damn incredible.

'Come on, then,' I say, looking around. 'Where do you keep it?'

'What?' he asks with a frown, standing back up again.

'It's got to be here somewhere.' I go to his wardrobe and pull open the doors. His clothes are neatly lined up in front of me and the smell of his aftershave wafts out. 'Nope.' I open the cupboard to my left. 'Where is this cold compress that you keep?'

He laughs and shakes his head.

'Aha!' I say jubilantly, spying a small fridge. I open the fridge door, but can see nothing resembling a cold compress. 'Oh,' I act disappointed, and then spin around to find him right behind me.

'Is this cold enough for you?' He presses his hand to my head. He's so close – and I desperately, urgently, want him to kiss me. This time, thankfully, he does.

His lips are warm and soft and I can taste whisky on his tongue. I touch my hands to his toned waist and feel light-headed as his kiss deepens. He gently breaks away and then regards me seriously for a moment, before closing the curtains. He undresses me deftly, without taking his lips from mine, and when I'm standing in nothing other than my underwear he tugs his T-shirt over his head. He's perfect: broad and fit. I place my hands on his chest and he guides them down to his jeans. I don't feel experienced or confident enough to undress him and he seems to realise this, because he takes over, removing his jeans and pulling me down to the bed. He kisses me long and languidly and even if I hadn't had anything to drink I know I would still feel drunk. He pushes my hair away from the nape of my neck and kisses me there. I gasp and arch my back. And then he easily unhooks the clasps of my bra and moves his lips to my breasts.

This is a man who knows what he is doing.

And if that thought might have bothered me before, right now I just want to bask under his blissful touch.

I come to, feeling groggy. Daylight is already spilling underneath the curtains. I'm lying on my side facing the room, and Lukas's arms are around my waist. This bed is too small for us to be anything other than intertwined. Lukas kisses my back from behind.

'Good morning,' he murmurs.

'Hi.' I smile over my shoulder at him, feeling shy. 'Have you been awake long?' I ask.

'I didn't want to rouse you,' he replies, avoiding the question.

'You should have,' I tell him. 'Have you got any lectures today?'

'It's Saturday,' he replies.

'Oh, yeah.' A beat. 'Shit!' I bolt upright and my head pounds painfully in response. 'What time is it?' I clutch the covers around my now-exposed naked upper half.

'Nine thirty,' he replies calmly, tracing his fingertips down my spine and making me shiver. 'Have you got somewhere you need to be?'

'I'm supposed to be on the river.'

'It's early November. If there *are* dozens of tourists desperate to go punting on a cold winter's morning I'm sure one of your colleagues can take them.'

Hmm. I guess that's true. He reaches up and sweeps my hair back from my face before pulling me down on top of him. His stubble has grown overnight and he's unbelievably sexy. He kisses me passionately and then expertly flips me so that I'm underneath him. It becomes instantly clear that he's been waiting for me to wake up for quite a while . . .

It's ten thirty by the time I finally drag myself out of bed.

'I really do need to go,' I say regretfully.

'When can I see you again?' he asks.

'When do you want to?'

'Tonight?'

I nod, before remembering something. 'Oh, I can't. I'm going to the movies tonight with Jessie.' We go regularly. It's our 'thing'.

'Who's Jessie?'

I don't know why I haven't referred to him by his name before now.

'My flatmate. One of them,' I reply.

'Tomorrow, then?' he asks.

'Sounds good.'

'I'll call you.'

There's a strange atmosphere when I walk into the house. I thought Jessie would already be at work, but I can hear him talking to Emily in the kitchen. They fall silent as I close the front door behind me and walk down the corridor.

'Hello,' I say cheerfully.

'Nice of you to let us know you were staying out all night,' Jessie says grumpily.

'Oh. Sorry.'

He doesn't look at me. Emily flashes me an awkward smile. 'He was worried about you,' she explains apologetically.

'I was with Lukas,' I say.

'We gathered that,' Jessie comments wryly, standing up to clear the breakfast plates. I notice there's a third plate on the table, for me.

'Sorry,' I say again. 'I wasn't thinking.'

'Did you have a nice time?' Emily asks kindly.

'Yes, thank you.' Pause. 'Did you?'

'Oh, you know, same as usual.'

'I've got to get ready for work,' Jessie mutters, leaving the room.

'I thought he'd already *be* at work,' I say to Emily once he's gone. The afterglow I'd been experiencing disappeared the moment I walked in through the door and now I sit down at the table feeling glum.

'He overslept,' she says.

'Really? That's unusual for him.'

'Mmm.'

'Big night?'

'Oh, no bigger than usual,' she replies offhandedly. 'But tell me about your night! You stayed at Lukas's?' She props her elbows on the table and leans in closer.

'Yes.' I shift in my seat, but can't keep the smile from my face.

Her eyes widen. 'Did you do the dirty deed?'

'What a thing to call it!' I exclaim.

'You did!' she cries. 'What was he like?'

I smile.

'He was good, wasn't he?' she asks eagerly.

I shrug.

'Come on, you have to kiss and tell!' she squawks.

'Alice, are you coming to work or not?' Jessie demands to know from the doorway.

I jump to my feet. 'Yes. Give me five minutes to change.'

He humphs, but I know he'll wait.

'Talk to you later,' I say to Emily. She hunches over with disappointment and I rush upstairs to throw on some fresh clothes. A shower will have to wait until later.

Chapter 35

'So . . .' Jessie says on the walk to the Magdalene Bridge punting station. (When I lived in halls I used to start tours near Silver Street Bridge, on the other side of town, but now Magdalene is much closer.) 'You stayed over at *Lukas's*,' he continues, saying 'Lukas' in a sardonic way.

'Yes,' I reply crossly. 'Have you got a problem with that, *Jessie*?' I'm too annoyed to address him by his nickname.

'Well, it would have been nice of you to tell us.'

'I've already apologised for not calling. But, seriously, you're starting to act like my dad.'

Strangely enough, this comment does not bring him any closer to forgiving me.

'I won't bother worrying about you in the future, then!' he snaps.

'Please don't!' I bite back.

We don't speak to each other for the rest of the walk. In fact, we both continue to hold a grudge until later that afternoon when we see each other up ahead on the river. We're going in opposite directions, and I glare at him as he gets closer, just as I've done on the last two tours I've taken today. Suddenly he punts straight into me.

'Argh!' I manage to keep my balance and am about to hurl abuse at him, when I see his expression.

'Alright, China?' he asks casually.

My face breaks into a smile. 'Bugger off,' I say jokily, digging my pole into the mud to punt away from him.

'What time are we going to the movies tonight?' he asks as I glide past.

'Are we still going, then?'

'Unless you've got other plans with *Lukas* . . .' he replies in that same sardonic tone, completely disregarding the fact that both sets of passengers are listening.

'No, I told him I was going to the movies with you.'

'That was good of you.'

I glare over my shoulder at him, but he's grinning.

'Speak later.' I return my attention to my tour as Trinity Bridge comes into view. I've been totally and utterly distracted today. I can't think about last night – and this morning – without blushing. I really want to see Lukas again and I keep hoping he'll be there on the bank each time I pass Trinity, but he never is. And once more I have to go past feeling deflated.

Going to the movies turns out to be a total waste of time and money because in the darkness of the cinema all I can think about is Lukas. His eyes . . . his lips . . . his body . . . what he did to me . . . I'm so turned on I can barely breathe. I'm not sure I can wait until tomorrow to see him again. I desperately want to drop by his room later, but I don't know if I should play it cool. He wasn't there on the bridge today. Didn't he want to see me? Out of the blue I feel uneasy and anxious.

I never felt like that with Joe . . .

At this thought, my desire is replaced with a deep and aching sadness. Where is Joe? Why didn't he come to find me, like he promised? My bottom lip starts to wobble dangerously and I have an overwhelming urge to go home and cry into my pillow.

What if he *does* still love me? What if he intends to come for me? What if I've just . . . What if I've just *cheated* on him? I feel sick at the thought. Yet it's been well over a year . . . Surely he can't expect me to wait forever? What if *he's* found someone else? Pain shoots through my chest. The thought of him with another girl . . . Stop it, Alice! Stop thinking about this!

I try to concentrate on the movie, but it's hard.

Emily is still up when we get home. She comes out of the living room looking remarkably bright-eyed and bushy-tailed for this hour of the night.

'Do you want a cuppa?' she asks us hopefully.

'No, I'm shattered,' Jessie mutters, heading for the stairs. 'See you in the morning.'

'Oh, okay.' She watches him go, a hurt expression clouding her face.

I wanted to go to bed myself, but now I feel bad.

'I'll have one,' I offer, but she continues to look disheartened as I follow her into the kitchen. 'How was your evening?' I ask.

'Not bad.'

'Not bad? That doesn't sound too good.'

'No, it was alright. It's just my friend. She talks a lot about herself.'

'What was she talking about?' I ask.

'Oh, just everything.' The kettle boils and she sets about making us tea. I get the feeling she's devoted more than enough attention to her friend tonight without talking about her to me as well. 'How was your film?' she asks, passing me a mug as we wander through to the living room.

'Not bad.'

'That doesn't sound too good, either.'

'No, it was good,' I reply. 'Weasley liked it. I was just a bit distracted,' I add.

'What with? Lukas?'

'Mmm. And Joe,' I admit, as the melancholy returns.

'You do fancy Lukas, though, right?' she asks.

I nod, but I can't look at her. 'I just feel so disloyal to Joe,' I admit, my bottom lip starting to go again. I glance up at her sympathetic face and hot tears prick my eyes.

'Alice,' Emily chides. 'Where *is* Joe? He's not here. You'll probably never even see him again.'

She says it in such a blasé fashion, yet her words cut me like a knife. I clutch my hands to my stomach.

'Are you okay?' she asks worriedly.

'It really hurt when you said that,' I whimper. She sits next to me, worry etched on her face.

'When I said what?' she asks.

'About me never seeing him again.' I can hardly speak.

'But you probably won't,' she says gently.

'Stop!' I gasp, making her reel backwards.

I know my behaviour is freaking her out, but I can't help it.

'Alice . . .' She touches her hand to my arm. 'Alice,' she says more firmly, trying to bring me round.

'I think I should go to bed,' I whisper.

'No,' she says in a commanding voice. 'Stop this, Alice. Snap out of it.'

I open my eyes abruptly and stare at her, taken aback. She grasps my hand. 'You're a strong lassie,' she says. 'I know you are. So start acting like one.'

What's happened to the meek little mouse who moved in with us? Calm washes over me. Her words somehow do the trick.

'Okay?' she asks.

I find my voice. 'Yes.'

'Good.'

She squeezes my hand and forces a smile. 'Come on, then; tell me about Lukas. Was he a tiger in bed?'

I smile at her, but shake my head. 'I don't think I want to talk about it.'

'Yes, you do. Does he have a fit body?'

I giggle. She has me laughing again by the time we call it a night.

Chapter 36

'Am I calling too early?'

My heart lifts when I hear Lukas's voice. Last night's insecurities had carried over to this morning.

'Not at all,' I reply with a smile. He sounds weird on the phone. We've only ever texted until now.

'How was your movie?'

'It was good. Did you go out with Harry and Matthew again?'

'No. I stayed in my room and re-read Newton's *Principia*.'

'Wow. Fascinating,' I tease, absent-mindedly twirling my hair around my fingers.

'It was, actually.' I can tell he's smiling and all my worries fade away.

'I suppose you'll be too busy reading to see me today, then?' I ask.

'I might be able to squeeze you in.'

'Sounds like fun,' I joke. 'What time?'

'How long do you need to get ready?'

'I can be ready as soon as you like,' I reply.

'Shall we go somewhere for breakfast?'

'Um . . .' I can hear the sound of an electric beater coming from the kitchen. I can't ditch Jessie two days in a row. 'Jessie is making pancakes. Why don't you come over for a bit? We can go out afterwards.'

I go downstairs to fill in my flatmates.

'Ooh, exciting!' Emily enthuses. 'At last we're going to meet the mysterious Lukas!'

'Woo-hoo,' Jessie says sarcastically.

'Oi,' I warn. 'You'd better be nice to him.'

'Oh, I'll be nice,' he says in a tone that doesn't instil much confidence. 'I'm looking forward to checking him out.'

I roll my eyes, but don't bother to comment.

'I'm going to get ready.'

Luckily I waste no time, because Lukas arrives within fifteen minutes.

'That was quick,' I say as I open the door. I feel all weird and shy again.

'I was already dressed,' he replies, stepping over the threshold. He squeezes my waist and looks around the hall. The smell of pancakes is coming from the kitchen. He glances down at me and suddenly seems to remember something. 'Hello,' he says with a grin, cupping my face and kissing me gently on the lips. Some of my shyness dissipates. I smile up at him.

'Come and meet my flatmates.' I take his hand and lead him to the kitchen. Emily has clearly been watching the door with eager eyes and she smiles brightly when we appear. Jessie acts far less interested.

'Jessie, Emily, this is Lukas.'

Lukas steps forward and offers his hand to Jessie. 'Jessie?' He sounds confused.

'Yep. And she's Emily.' Jessie points at the table.

Lukas quickly recovers and shakes Emily's hand too. He surveys the kitchen and I can't help but see it through his eyes: it's an absolute tip.

'Sorry about the mess,' I mumble.

'Jessie's been whipping up a storm,' Emily explains. 'Have a seat. Tuck in.'

'Thank you.' Lukas pulls up a chair and sits down.

I place my hand on his shoulder. 'Do you want a tea or coffee?'

'Coffee. Please.'

'We only have instant,' Jessie interjects.

'That's fine.' Lukas nods awkwardly.

I glare at Jessie and hope Lukas doesn't notice. 'Be nice!' I mouth. The little shit sniggers at me.

'So ... Alice says you're studying Physics at Trinity?' Emily asks.

Reading, not studying, I can't help but silently correct her.

'That's right,' he replies.

'Wow. That sounds interesting,' Emily says.

He smiles politely. 'Are you at Anglia Ruskin?'

'Yep. Sociology,' she tells him before he can ask.

'Emily is from Scotland,' I say, passing Lukas his coffee and pulling up a chair.

Jessie grumpily plonks a fresh plate of pancakes on the table and scrapes a chair across the wooden floor before sitting down on it.

'Milk? Sugar?' I ask Lukas.

'White, no sugar,' he replies, glancing at Jessie with a frown. Gone is his polite smile. And why should it stick around when Jessie is being so rude?

I squeeze Lukas's knee under the table. I'll apologise to him later.

'I'm sorry about Jessie,' I say as we walk down the garden path and turn towards town. Breakfast did not improve with time and we left as soon as we could.

'Mmm,' he replies wryly. His tone does little to alleviate my unease. 'What was his problem?'

'I don't know,' I reply. 'He's probably still annoyed with me for staying out on Friday night.'

'Is he your keeper?'

'Of course not.' I squeeze his hand and try to make amends. 'He was only worried about me. Anyway, let's forget about it. Shall we go for a walk along the Backs?'

'If you like,' he replies moodily. We walk in silence for a while. Finally he speaks. 'When you said you were going to the movies with Jessie I thought you were referring to your *female* flatmate.'

'Oh.' Does that bother him? 'Well, the name Jessie is ... What's the word? Both male and female.'

'Androgynous,' he replies.

Bloody hell, he speaks better English than I do. I glance up at him. 'I was going to say "unisex".'

He grins and steps in front of me, taking my hands and kissing me gently on the lips. I tilt my face up to his and then he lifts me in his arms so that my legs are wrapped around his waist. He stifles my giggles with his kisses. I'm aware of people walking by and I feel self-conscious as his lips move to my neck.

'Shall we go back to mine?' he murmurs in my ear.

I nod quickly. 'Mmm.' My heart is all aflutter as he puts me down.

Chapter 37

'I can't believe I'm not going to see you at Christmas,' I say sadly, resting my cheek on Lukas's bare chest. He presses his lips to the top of my head. We're lying in his bed, staring out of the window. It's late afternoon and it's already dark outside, but the Christmas lights on Trinity Street cast the room in a warm glow. He leaves to go back to Germany early tomorrow morning.

'It will be good for you to go home too,' he says. 'How is your father?'

I had a shock a few days ago when Mum told me Dad hasn't been feeling too well. She said he's been under a lot of pressure at work and she wants me to come home for the duration of the Christmas holidays. Maybe part of it is emotional blackmail, but it's worked.

'No change,' I reply to Lukas's question about Dad. 'I think he just needs to rest.'

He runs his fingers through my hair.

'I'm going to miss you,' I say quietly.

'Me too,' he replies, drawing me up to kiss his lips. A bolt of desire shoots through me. I haven't seen much of him recently because he's been snowed under with a research project and I've had assignments to hand in. He takes his studies rather more seriously than I take mine.

He slowly pulls away from me. 'Do you want your Christmas present now or do you want to save it for Christmas Day?'

'Depends what it is,' I murmur, kissing him again.

'Stop.' He laughs under his breath.

I don't know what's got into me. I can't get enough of him at the moment.

'If you're not going to give me what I *really* want,' I pretend to be sulky, 'then I'll have it now.'

He reaches over to tug the curtains closed before walking, naked, to his wardrobe. My eyes follow him as he returns with a small, flat parcel wrapped in white satin paper with a red ribbon tied around it.

I sit up in bed. 'What is it?' I ask with a grin. It feels squashy when I press it.

'Open it,' he replies, sitting next to me.

I crack up laughing. It's a Mr Bump cold compress.

'You idiot,' I say, thumping his chest.

'Ouch,' he says. 'You're going to have to use that on me now.'

'Or I could just kiss you better, instead . . .'

This time, he lets me.

When I get back to Jessie's that night, after we've said our goodbyes, I find in my handbag a slightly larger present tied in the same red ribbon. I stare at it, bemused. And then curiosity gets the better of me. I can't wait until Christmas.

I open up the white satin paper to find a black velvet jewellery box inside. I gingerly lift the lid and there before me is a white-gold necklace with a diamond pendant hanging from it. I lean my back against the wall and slide down to the floor. The pendant sparkles under the bedroom light. I touch my fingers to the diamond and almost expect it to disappear in a puff of smoke. The cashmere scarf I got him is just not going to cut it compared to this. I can't possibly keep it. It's too much.

Jessie knocks on my door. 'Can I come in?' he asks, his eyes immediately falling to the box in my hand. 'What's that?'

'My Christmas present from Lukas,' I reply with disbelieving eyes.

He kneels on the floor to get a closer look. 'Is it real?' he asks with a frown.

I nod, looking back down at it.

'How do you know?' he asks. 'Maybe it's cubic – what's it called?'

'Cubic zirconia,' I reply. 'No. Lukas would never settle for anything less than the best.'

He humphs. 'It's alright for some.'

I don't know what his problem is with Lukas. I think he must feel threatened, man to man. It would be hard not to feel insecure around Lukas, with his looks, wealth, intellect . . . I could go on. Luckily they've met only a few times, because Lukas and I tend to do our own thing. Emily once commented that Jessie is jealous, but that's crazy and I told her as much. He's protective of me, true, but not jealous. Not in that way.

'Why don't you put it on?' Jessie asks grumpily.

'I'd be too scared of losing it,' I reply, looking down at the box in my hands. I don't want to admit that I'm thinking about giving it back. That would involve too much explanation.

'You won't lose it.' He gets up and waggles his hand for me to pass over the box. 'You'd be more likely to lose it in this tip of a bedroom,' he adds wryly.

I reluctantly hand over the box. 'I promise to tidy up before you get back.'

He lifts the necklace out of the box and drapes it around my neck, securing it from behind. It won't hurt to see what it looks like on.

Emily appears at the door. 'Hello!' Her eyes flick between us with confusion, then she spies the diamond and her face falls. 'What's going on?'

'My Christmas present from Lukas.'

'There you go.' Jessie pats my back and steps away from me.

'Oh, wow.' Emily's eyes widen and she comes closer to scrutinise it. 'Oh, my God, it's beautiful!'

'Right!' Jessie interrupts. 'Who's for one last Christmas tipple before I bugger off to the snow?'

'Me!' Emily and I both say in unison.

'Wait a sec,' I add, retrieving two Christmas presents from my wardrobe: a bottle of Baileys for Emily – she loves the stuff – and a bottle of Advocaat for Jessie. He recently told me that he and his parents always drank Advocaat at Christmas, and as they're not here . . .

He laughs when he unwraps it. 'Woo-hoo! Let's get this party started . . .'

'I'll be right with you,' I tell them. First I need to call Lukas.

When he answers the phone I know instantly that he expects me to be gracious about his gift, and anything less he'd find discourteous and possibly even offensive. So, in the end, I don't tell him I can't accept the necklace. But I don't feel entirely at ease about keeping it.

I turn in early that night – earlier than Jessie and Emily. I go to the mirror and stare at my reflection. My eyes fall to the glinting diamond, but my thoughts are of Joe, not of Lukas. I undo the necklace and put it away in its box, gently closing the lid. I rest my hand on the black velvet and close my eyes, and then I'm transported back to Dorset. I gasp for air and put the box on the bed before brushing away my tears. I can't deny that I fancy Lukas, but I can't honestly say that I love him, not like I loved Joe. Like I still love Joe. I suddenly miss him so much that my heart aches.

In the middle of the night I wake up and can't work out why. I lie there for a moment, listening, but I can't hear anything. I get up and go to the window, pulling back the curtains and staring out into the darkness. Then I hear a creak on the floorboards outside my bedroom. I tiptoe to the door and peek out, just in time to see Emily – wearing nothing more than an oversized black T-shirt – creeping into her room and gently closing the door.

What the . . .?

Emily and Jessie? *Noooooo!* I feel a strange mix of emotions. Since when has this been going on? Has it only just begun? Have they been hiding it from me for a while?

My mind continues to tick over, and even though at one point it occurs to me to wonder if this might mean true love and everlasting happiness for them both, my negativity won't let me dwell on that thought. I can't get back to sleep for a long time afterwards, and when I finally wake up again at ten o'clock in the morning, Emily's shell has clamped shut, and Jessie has already left for the airport. As for me, I have other things on my mind. It's time for me to go back to London.

Chapter 38

My mum is wearing a Santa hat when she comes to collect me from King's Cross. 'HO HO HO!' she shouts and I nearly jump out of my skin, before guffawing loudly.

I'm so relieved that I don't have to pack up all my belongings and bring them home again for the holidays, like I had to do when I lived in halls. Today I have only a small suitcase with me, but Dad has brought the car instead of making me catch the tube.

'Hi, Dad,' I say warmly as I climb in the back.

'Hello!' He beams with delight and reaches around to pat my knee with great affection.

'Come on, love,' Mum urges him.

He faces forward and pulls away from the kerb. I study the side of his face. He looks weary. He looks older.

'How was your journey?' he asks perkily.

'Great! It flew by. How are you? How are you feeling?'

'I'm fine,' he replies, brushing me off. 'I don't know what all the fuss is about.'

My mum says nothing.

She knocks on my bedroom door later. 'I'm so pleased you're home,' she says, coming in and sitting on the bed next to me.

'Me too.' And it's not even a lie. It's good to be back, albeit strange. My room seems unfamiliar, yet familiar too. It's exactly as I left it, apart from the small vase of fresh holly that Mum picked for me from the garden.

'Have you got any plans for tonight?' she asks.

'No, but I want to catch up with Lizzy soon.'

'She was due to arrive yesterday,' Mum tells me. 'I bumped into Susan in the street a couple of days ago.'

'How is she?'

'She looked well.'

'That's great.' But my smile quickly fades. 'How's Dad?'

She looks down. 'He's okay.'

'Tell me the truth.'

She sighs. 'His blood pressure is way up. He needs to take it easy.'

'Has he got much time off over Christmas?' I ask.

'A month.'

'A month!' I exclaim. 'Well, that's great!'

'Mmm.'

'What?'

'The doctor signed him off,' she reveals.

'Oh.' That's pretty serious.

'It'll help having you home,' she tells me with a smile.

My guilt intensifies. I've been so unforgiving – and why? He was only trying to protect me. I silently vow to make it up to him.

Mum has cooked a roast chicken for dinner and it's blissful sitting there around the table, just the three of us. It feels like old times, before . . . *Dorset* – I don't want to say his name.

Later Dad builds a fire and we sit in the living room: them with a sherry each and me with a Baileys on ice.

I hear my phone bleeping from my bag hanging on the coat stand. I go out into the hall to retrieve it and discover a message from Lukas, telling me he's arrived home safely. I text him back as I walk into the living room.

'Any news?' Mum asks.

'Um . . .' I glance up at them and smile weakly. 'A boy.'

'A boy!' Dad sits up straighter in his seat. 'Anyone we know?'

'No.' I shake my head and self-consciously study my phone. 'He's at Trinity College.'

'Ooh,' Mum says. They probably remember the college from the punting tour I took them on.

'Where's he from?' Dad asks.

'Southern Germany,' I reply.

'Germany!' Mum exclaims. I'm sure they were both expecting me to tell them where in England he was from.

'He's *German*?' Dad clarifies.

'Yes.' I nod, shifting in my seat. 'He's nice.'

'How old is he?' Dad pries.

'Twenty-one.'

'Where's he spending Christmas?' Mum asks, eager for details – or at least the ones I'm willing to share.

'He's gone home.'

'What's his name?'

'Twenty questions!' I erupt, only half joking.

'Sorry,' she says with a smile.

'His name is Lukas,' I reply.

'When can we—'

'You can meet him next time you come to visit,' I interrupt my

Dad's question and feel slightly nervous at the thought. Who would ever enjoy introducing their parents to their boyfriend?

'Good.' He seems satisfied. I try to recover from the inquisition, but it's not over yet. 'You look well,' Dad continues. 'He must be doing something right.'

I know he's comparing my appearance to last Christmas. I was a walking ghost, an empty shell, utterly distraught.

'You do look well,' Mum says warmly, patting my hand.

I smile a shaky smile, but don't meet her eyes.

'Susan looked *very* well when I saw her the other day,' she tells Dad.

'That's great,' he replies.

'She's made a fantastic recovery,' she adds. 'We should have them over for Christmas drinks, perhaps?'

'That would be nice,' he agrees.

She pats my hand again and I know that she realises I'm grateful for the change of subject.

Lizzy and I catch up the next day. We go to our local – the Bald-Faced Stag – for a pub lunch.

'I'm so glad you're back!' she squeals excitedly. 'Summer was such a bore without you.'

I laugh. 'It's good to be home.'

'What have you been up to? How's Jessie?'

'Jessie's great. He's gone off to the Alps to teach snowboarding for a couple of months.'

'Wow. That's wicked.'

'He's a talented chap,' I say casually.

'Still don't fancy him, though?'

I laughingly shake my head and then tell her about Emily.

'*Really?*' she asks, keen for the gossip. She hasn't met Emily yet. 'How long do you think that has been going on?'

'I have no idea,' I reply offhandedly.

'Does it bother you?' she pries.

'Um . . .'

'It does!'

'*Not* because I fancy him,' I'm keen to point out. 'But because I'm not sure how it's all going to pan out. I really love living there with those two. What if it all becomes horribly messy?'

'Yeah,' she says thoughtfully. 'And if it doesn't, it could be a bit "three's a crowd".'

I stare straight ahead. That's occurred to me too.

'You'll have to find *yourself* a man,' she says, taking a sip of her drink.

'Erm . . .'

'What?' She leans across the table. 'Have you met someone?'

'Might have done.'

'When were you going to tell me?' she demands to know.

I laugh. 'Now.'

'Who? What? When? How long?'

'Actually . . .' I grin at her. 'Do you remember that night in the club when you came to visit?'

She nods expectantly. 'Yeah.'

'Do you remember the "hottie"?'

'No!' she exclaims, but of course she means 'yes'. 'You're going out with *him*?'

'Mmmhmm.'

'But I thought you didn't like him?'

'Turns out I do.'

'No!'

'Yes.'

I grin at her reaction.

Her brow furrows as she recalls something. 'Wait, isn't he the cold-compress guy?'

I laughingly tell her about the Mr Bump present he gave me for Christmas.

She giggles. 'What a cheapskate.'

I hesitate before pulling out the diamond necklace from under my shirt. I've consciously been choosing outfits that wouldn't bring too much attention to it. I didn't want to have to explain about Lukas to my parents – or my friend – the moment I walked through the door. 'He also gave me this.'

She stares closely at it. 'Whoa.' She glances up at me. 'Is it real?'

I nod.

'Whoa,' she says again. She lets it go, then sits back in her chair and regards me. 'It's serious, then?' There's something a little accusatory about her tone.

I nod again. 'Yes. Pretty damn serious,' I reply a touch flippantly.

'Have you . . .?' Her voice trails off.

I purse my lips together.

'No way!' She leans forward. 'Are you blushing?' she exclaims, plonking her glass down on the table.

'What? No!'

'Yes, you are.'

'Okay, then, I am a little bit, but, you know . . .'

She raises her glass. 'Cheers. Here's to you.'

'Stop it.' I laugh and wave her away. 'How about you? Anyone on the scene?'

'Might be.'

'Tell me!' I squeal. 'Have you—'

'No,' she cuts me off. 'Not yet. But we've come close,' she admits self-consciously.

'What's his name?'

'Callum. He's Scottish,' she adds before I can ask.

'Is he at university with you?'

'He is, indeed. Studying politics.' She pulls a face. 'But he's well fit so I'll forgive him for it. What does . . . what's his name?'

'Lukas.'

'Cool name. What does Lukas study?'

'He *reads*' – I say this playfully – 'Physics at the University of Cambridge.'

'Ooh, get him!' she cries. 'What does that involve?'

'I wouldn't have the foggiest. All goes way over my head.'

She laughs. 'When can I meet him?'

Join the queue . . . 'The next time you come to visit.'

'You seem so much better,' she says, and instantly I feel anything but because I know what's coming. 'You're over Joe, then?'

I can't speak for a moment, but then I reply.

'No.' I swirl my drink around in my glass. 'No, I'll never get over him.'

'Yes, you will,' she brushes me off.

'No, I won't.' I meet her gaze seriously. 'I know I won't.'

She shrugs. She doesn't believe me, but there's no such thing as 'time heals everything' in this situation. Time will prove her wrong, that's what time will do. I'll always love him. I'm just trying not to think about him for the foreseeable future.

Chapter 39

My intentions remain stable until somewhere between Christmas and New Year, when I'm watching telly with my parents and a programme about Dorset comes on. I want to get up and leave the room, but my backside is glued to the sofa. I stare at the television screen and that night I can't sleep for the images going over and over in my mind.

Finally I allow myself to daydream about my time with Joe from beginning to end. I try to remember everything . . . the first time I saw him at the pub . . . the way I felt: the POW feeling when he looked up and met my eyes . . . how I was unable to get him out of my mind that evening when I went for a walk to Dancing Ledge, and how I bumped into him and helped him with his quiz questions. I'm full of butterflies as I recall that first kiss on Dancing Ledge . . . the fireworks going off in my stomach . . . sitting with him late at night on the bench outside the cottage . . . wanting to be with him every minute of every day, not caring about sleep . . . making love to him for the first time, and the next time, and the next . . . My heart flips again and again as I remember, and I don't even feel sad. I feel determined. I want to find him.

Early the next morning I get up and walk on autopilot down the high street to the tube station. I spend hours – I don't even know how many – wandering through the streets of central London looking for him. With every hour that passes I feel more lost – not physically, but emotionally.

My feet somehow take me home again, but I am broken. I tell my parents I'm not feeling well, then I climb into bed and stay there until the next morning, when I wake up to find my mum pressing her hand to my forehead. Her face is etched with worry, and I know that I can't allow her and Dad to go through this again. I find the resolve to put on an act – an act I hoped I'd never have to put on again – and somehow manage to make it through the next few days until it's time for me to return to Cambridge. Lukas rings me once during this time, but I divert his call. He texts to apologise for not calling me more; he's been busy with family commitments. I force myself to reply with a text that says pretty much the same thing, then I turn off my phone. I want to tell him it's over. But that will have to wait. At the very least, I owe it to him to say it to his face.

On the return train my feelings begin to feel quite surreal. The closer I get to Cambridge, the more the darkness inside me fades. By the time I walk through the front door into Jessie's house I feel oddly okay. The house is empty – Emily is in Scotland until tomorrow and Jessie is in Austria for another six weeks – but still I feel lighter than I did in London. I sit down on the sofa in a daze and stare ahead. What the hell is wrong with me? Why am I such a headcase?

I put my hand to my collarbone, but the necklace Lukas gave me is absent. I stopped wearing it the day I went to find Joe.

He's flying back into Stansted tonight. Lukas. Here and now I'm not sure how I feel about seeing him again.

I don't have to wait long to find out. I'm upstairs unpacking when I hear the front doorbell ring. I go downstairs with idle curiosity, wondering who it might be. It doesn't occur to me to wonder if it's Lukas, because his flight isn't due until tonight. I open the door and stare at him with surprise.

'Hello,' he says gently. He steps over the threshold, but I'm frozen, staring up at him. He's wearing the scarf that I gave him. It suits him. But I barely recognise him. He's like a stranger to me. We've been apart for only a fortnight, but it feels like a lifetime. He wraps his arms around me and I'm tense under his touch.

It's the scent of his aftershave that does it. I breathe it in and instantly soften. I hold him tightly as I squeeze my eyes shut.

Lukas. My boyfriend. I'm such a fucking idiot.

'Surprise,' he says quietly, pulling away and looking down at me.

'I . . . I didn't think you were getting back until tonight?' I stammer.

'I caught an earlier flight. That was a long two weeks.'

I smile weakly. 'It was.'

'Are you okay?' he asks. 'I tried to call you from the airport, but your phone went straight through to voicemail.'

'I need to charge it up,' I say dismissively, looking away. He tilts my chin up towards him and then he kisses me.

For a split second Joe passes through my mind, and then I shut him out. That's enough now. This is my reality and I should be happy with it.

Not 'should'. 'Am'.

'Hold on a moment,' he says, breaking away and going to the

door. He stalks down the path and lifts his hand to wave goodbye to someone down on the street, then he returns to the house.

'Klaus,' he explains. 'He's going to drop my bags to my room.'

'Nice,' I tease. 'Did he pick you up from the airport too?'

'Yes.'

'You should have introduced me,' I say.

'Why?' he asks with a frown.

'What do you mean, "why"?' I mirror his expression.

He shrugs and seems genuinely perplexed.

'He's . . . I don't know, he's a part of your life,' I explain. 'I feel bad that I haven't even met him.'

'Don't feel bad. He works for my family. It's not necessary for you to meet him solely for the reason of being polite.'

He pulls me back into his arms.

'I missed you,' he murmurs into my hair. He kisses me passionately and shivers tingle up and down my spine. Soon afterwards we relocate to my bedroom.

The feeling of surrealism returns later when I'm lying in his arms, but this time it's my trip to London that feels surreal. I can't actually believe that I acted like that. I really am a nutcase. Maybe I should see someone.

Lukas shifts beside me. I look down at him. 'Are you okay?'

'I'm good,' he replies, stretching. 'I like your bed,' he says with a grin.

'It's certainly bigger than yours,' I reply, propping myself up on his chest.

'When does Jessie return?'

'Not for another month and a half,' I tell him. 'But Emily gets back tomorrow.'

'Shame,' he muses, staring up at the ceiling. 'It would be nice to have our own house.'

'Steady on,' I joke.

He doesn't smile. 'I really did miss you.'

I don't reply. I stroke his jaw with my thumb – it's smooth to the touch. I gaze into his blue, blue eyes, and then he's kissing me again.

'How was your Christmas?' I ask him the next morning over breakfast. Cereal, no pancakes, sadly.

'Good,' he replies with an abrupt nod.

'How were your parents?'

'Fine.'

'Brother? Sister?'

'Good.'

'Baby Max?'

'Great.'

'Come on, tell me all about it,' I urge.

'It was fine. Everything was fine.'

This is a bit weird. A thought occurs to me. 'Did you tell your parents about me?'

'Um . . .'

'You didn't!'

'No, it's not like that . . .' He puts his spoon back into his bowl. For the first time ever, Lukas looks awkward.

'What is it, then?' I put my spoon down too.

'I . . . They . . . They want me to concentrate on my studies.'

'*Right* . . .' I say sarcastically.

He regards me coolly. 'Did you tell your parents about me?'

'Yes, I did, actually.'

'Why aren't you wearing your necklace?' he asks, not taking his eyes from mine.

'I . . . I don't sleep in it, do I?'

'You weren't wearing it yesterday when I got here.'

'I took it off to keep it safe,' I lie, averting my gaze. I can tell that he doesn't believe me. But for some reason he doesn't push it. I'm relieved enough to not press him further about his parents. It's only later that I wonder whether he knew that his own course of questioning would have this desired effect, but I hope he's not that manipulative.

Chapter 40

'Have you heard from Jessie?' is one of the first questions Emily asks when she arrives later that day.

'No,' I reply. 'Have you?'

'Nope.' A bit blunt. 'But he's hardly likely to contact me instead of you, is he?'

I wasn't planning on saying anything, but this comment gets to me. I don't want our friendship to be soured by secrets – and it will be, because I'll know they're both lying to me and I won't be able to *not* take offence.

'I know,' I say.

'You know what?' she asks.

'I know about you and Jessie.'

If I thought her face was pale before, it's practically reflective now.

'What? Did he tell you?' Her voice is barely more than a whisper.

'No. I saw you coming out of his room.'

'Oh.'

I think back to the time she came home after seeing her

friend – she seemed a bit down when Jessie went upstairs instead of joining us for a cuppa. Perhaps he is what Emily wanted to speak to her friend about, but she couldn't get a word in edgeways.

'You can talk to me about this, you know,' I say gently.

She sighs.

'I won't take sides,' I add, in case that's what she's worried about.

She doesn't say anything for a while, just stares at the kitchen cupboards in silence. I really don't know if she's going to open up to me and I'm trying not to feel too hurt.

'Has it been going on for long?' I ask tentatively.

'We'd only snogged a couple of times before that night,' she reveals.

I nod encouragingly, almost holding my breath so as not to scare her away.

'Drunken snogs,' she adds with a roll of her eyes. She still won't look at me.

'You've liked him for a while, though, right?' I remember spotting a few early blushes when Jessie was around. Speaking of which, she's now turned as pink as a prawn.

'Was it very obvious?' She looks mortified.

'Not really,' I fib.

'*You* don't fancy him, do you?' she asks.

'God, no!' I exclaim. How can this not be blindingly obvious to everyone? Whoops. She looks offended. 'I don't mean . . .' I quickly try to make up for my blunder. 'I don't mean I think he's *unfanciable*,' I say. 'It's just that he and I . . . God, no. Sorry.'

She grins. 'Okay.'

'So you'd had a couple of drunken snogs . . .' I will her to go on.

'Yeah. And it was always awkward the next morning,' she

explains. 'Neither of us knew how to act around the other. And then …' She breathes in deeply and exhales loudly. 'That night before he went away …'

The night they slept together. 'Yes?' I prompt.

'We carried on drinking after you went to bed and things kind of got out of hand.' She blushes again with embarrassment.

'How was he with you the next day?' I feel like I'm on *Trisha*.

She screws up her nose. 'It was really awkward. Like, *really* awkward. He barely spoke to me.'

'Oh.' Now I feel a bit sick for her.

'Well, I barely spoke to him, either.'

'Well, in that case …' I try to make her feel better.

'I should think he's shagging all and sundry now.' Her tone is bitter.

I shake my head. 'Jessie's not like that.'

'Isn't he? I mean, look at me.' She points to her face. 'I'm hardly Blondie, am I?'

'That didn't exactly pan out well, though, did it?' I say reasonably. 'And he wouldn't keep snogging you – or go to bed with you – if he didn't fancy you.'

'Beer goggles,' she says simply.

'No.' I brush her off.

'He hasn't even texted me.' Her eyes fill up. Uh-oh.

'Well, then, he's a shit,' I say crossly, hoping to snap her out of it. 'All men are bastards, right?'

She nods, but doesn't smile. Bloody Jessie. There goes our happy household.

'Mind you, have you tried to contact him?' I ask.

'No,' she admits.

'Maybe you should?'

'No,' she replies resolutely. 'No.'

Not much I can say about that.

The days and weeks tick by. I'm conscious about not leaving Emily out, so Lukas and I don't hole ourselves up in my bedroom as much as we'd like to. She continues to refuse to contact Jessie, so finally I do, mainly because I've grown worried about him. I needn't have been. He sends a jovial text back a whole two days later saying he's having a whale of a time. No mention of Emily. I'm so not impressed with him.

She's a bag of nerves the night before he returns home. We sit in the living room, just the two of us, and have a few drinks to take her mind off things.

'I'll have to move out,' she says simply at one point.

'No, you won't,' I reply with dismay. 'It will be fine.'

'How could it possibly be fine?' she asks flippantly, buoyed by the alcohol she's consumed. 'This is a no-win situation.'

'Don't say that. Do you still like him?'

She stares straight ahead and doesn't reply. I'll take that as a yes, then.

'I can't believe he never contacted you. I didn't class Weasley as a proper bastard.'

'Me neither. Should have learned my lesson by now.' She downs her drink in one.

I know she's been hurt badly before, but she's never spoken about it. 'I'm guessing you've known a few bastards in your lifetime,' I say.

She hesitates. 'One in particular was worse than the others.'

'Who was he?' I pick up a half-full can of lager on the table and empty it into her glass.

'A guy I used to know in Irvine.' That's where she's from in Scotland.

'What was his name?'

'Anthony. He's in his early thirties now.'

'Really?' I ask with surprise. Hang on . . . 'How long ago—'

'I was fourteen,' she interrupts.

My mouth drops open.

'He was twenty-eight,' she continues. 'Nice, eh?' She downs the rest of her lager.

I'm lost for words. Eventually I discover my tongue.

'Were you together long?' I ask.

'Long enough,' she replies bitterly. 'He wasn't a very nice man.'

I gather this is an understatement.

'Was it serious?'

She knows what I'm trying to ask her.

'Oh, yeah,' she replies sardonically. 'And he was quite persistent.' She folds her arms across her chest.

'Shit.' I exhale loudly. 'He should be in jail!'

'He's far too clever for that. When he's with you he makes you feel like the luckiest girl in the world. He told me that he loved me, that he wanted to marry me, but he'd get into trouble if anyone found out, so it had to be our little secret. He cried when he broke it off with me. Said he was heartbroken, but that he had to do the right thing by me. I was crushed. I felt like Juliet.' She laughs cynically. 'Later I found out he'd done the same thing to another girl from my school. God knows how many other girls there were.'

'You should go to the police!' I cry.

'No. I have no proof.'

'I bet there are other girls you could track down.'

'I can't.' She shakes her head fervently. 'I can't go through that again.'

'Did he rape you?' I whisper.

'No.' She pauses. 'But he didn't exactly ask me, either.'

'So it *was* rape!'

'Well, it was in the eyes of the law, anyway, because I was a minor. I don't want to talk about him anymore,' she says suddenly. 'And he wasn't the only bastard on the block – there were plenty more. I seem to attract them.'

'Jesus,' I say with sympathy, and then I feel angry. Angry with Jessie. 'Fucking Weasley!' I blurt out.

I'm still fuming the next day when he gets back. He sweeps in, all full of himself.

'CHINA!' he shouts with glee.

'Hello,' I say drily. I don't get up from the kitchen table.

'What's up?' He looks confused. 'Where's Emily?'

'Upstairs. Probably hiding from you.'

He drops his bags on the floor – they land with a thump. 'What? Why?'

'How could you?' I say crossly. 'Why didn't you bloody well ring her?'

'I texted you,' he says shiftily, then in a slightly accusatory tone: 'Did she tell you?'

'No. I saw her coming out of your room.'

'Oh.'

'Why do you have to be such a bastard?'

'Hang on,' he says, coming into the room. 'It's not like she rang me, either.'

'She thinks you've been shagging your way around Austria.'

'I haven't,' he replies firmly. 'But she only ever lets herself go when she's had a few and then she's always weird with me the next morning. I never know how to act or what to think.'

'She's shy!' I exclaim. 'And she doesn't trust guys easily.'

Jessie frowns. 'Why not?'

'You'll have to ask her that.'

He glances out through the door in the direction of the stairs.

'Just be honest with her,' I say gently. 'If you don't fancy her, don't lead her on.'

'Who said I don't fancy her?'

'Do you?' My heart lifts. 'Go and speak to her,' I plead.

He nods solemnly and walks out of the room.

They're upstairs for almost an hour.

'Where's Weasley?' I ask when Emily comes downstairs alone.

'He's having a shower.' She tries to keep a straight face.

'Everything okay?' I ask, grinning at her.

'Yes.' She nods determinedly. 'Yeah. Everything's fine.'

Chapter 41

It doesn't take long for Emily and Jessie's relationship to blossom, and I'm right there in the thick of it, a witness to the developments. At first they seemed shy and tentative around each other, without the freeing qualities of alcohol to get them by, but they've moved on from that stage, and now I can't walk into the living room without seeing them there on the sofa, their arms and legs intertwined as they watch telly. I'm happy for them – so very happy – but I have taken to spending more of my time at Trinity with Lukas.

Usually I go home at night because his bed is too small for both of us to sleep comfortably, but one Sunday morning I wake up to find myself in his room. We went to the college bar last night with Harry and Matthew, drank a bit too much and ended up stumbling back here. I open my eyes and realise he's not beside me. I roll over to see him wide awake and sitting in one of his armchairs, watching me. He smiles a small smile.

'Are you okay?' I ask. He has a strange expression on his face that I haven't seen before.

He nods and comes over to the bed, kneeling down on the

floor in front of me. He makes eye contact for a long moment. I'm about to ask him what's wrong, but he speaks first.

'I love you,' he says quietly.

It's the first time that either of us has said it.

Our lovemaking that morning is more intense than ever before.

'I don't want to go back home for Easter,' he tells me afterwards in a pained voice. 'I want to stay with you.' He sounds a touch desperate. 'Could we go away? Just the two of us?'

I think for a moment. My parents would like me to go home, but I'm wary after what happened at Christmas, with the way my feelings for Joe intensified and spiralled out of control. My dad went back to work at the end of January and Mum says he's been a lot better. They came to visit me last month and finally met Lukas – it went well, I think. He's so polite and respectful that it would be hard for it to go wrong.

'We could do,' I say hesitantly. 'But I should speak to my parents first.'

He nods and pulls me back into his arms.

In the end, we compromise. I go home for a few days without Lukas while he gets his head into his revision for his forthcoming exams. He does insist on driving me to London himself, and he promises to collect me again on Bank Holiday Monday before we go away together. But when my mum finds out he has no one to spend Easter Sunday with, she insists on him coming a day early. Dad pretends to be cool with the fact that my boyfriend is staying over, and I can't help but wonder what Lukas thinks of my parents' humble abode. I don't ask, but I think we're all a little relieved when it's time for us to go.

Lukas takes me to a country house and spa, and we have an incredible few days walking in the nearby forest, swimming in the heated outdoor pool, drinking hot chocolate in front of the log fire and then falling into our super-king-sized bed at night. I've never experienced such luxury and they're almost the best days I've ever had. Almost, but not quite.

After Easter, our studies hitch up a notch, so I see less of Lukas than I would like to. Lizzy takes a break from her exam revision and comes to stay for a weekend in May to celebrate my birthday. We go shopping for ball gowns – she's going to her university ball soon and, excitingly, Lukas is taking me to the Trinity one next month.

'How's it all going with Lukas?' Lizzy asks me over a coffee. We figure we need caffeine before we get down to the serious business of shopping.

'Brilliantly,' I say.

'You're still wearing your necklace, then.' She nods to said piece of jewellery.

'Yep. Every day.' I smile.

'It's beautiful. I'm not surprised.'

I automatically fiddle with the chain.

'How's Callum?' I ask. They're still seeing each other – and, yes, it is now officially 'serious'.

She beams. 'Really good. He's gutted I'm away this weekend.'

'Aah. Softy.'

I met him in March when I finally made it up to Edinburgh for a weekend visit. He's cute, with light-brown curly hair and blue eyes. They look a bit alike.

'Did I tell you we're going to Tenerife together this summer?'

'No! Wow. That's so grown-up!'

She laughs. 'Isn't it? His mate's got a holiday house down there – well, it belongs to his parents – and he invited us along, so we're going for two weeks.'

'That will be great! Who else is going?'

'There are eight of us in total. All couples, though, so it should be good fun. One of his mates' girlfriends is really lovely. We go out quite a bit as a foursome, and I'm looking forward to spending some more time with her.'

'Great,' I say. I can't help but feel a bit jealous, even though I know it's wrong and uncalled for. 'You'll have a great time,' I add.

'What about you and Lukas?' Lizzy asks. 'Are you going away this summer?'

'No,' I reply regretfully. 'He's going back to Germany for the duration.'

'Really? How long is that?'

'It's supposed to be three months, but—'

'Three months!' she interrupts, aghast.

'I think he'll go for just two.'

'Two!' She's still shocked. 'And you're not going to see him for any of it?'

'No.' I shake my head sadly.

She frowns. 'Can't you go to Germany too?'

'He hasn't invited me.' I feel embarrassed as I admit this and she doesn't seem to know how to react.

'Oh, right.'

'I think I'll just stay here and work,' I tell her. 'I'll go home, but not for too long. I might see if Mum and Dad can come and stay with me for a while.' The other day Emily offered me the use of her room. She said she'll stay in Jessie's room when she's not in Scotland. She does most of the time, anyway.

'Bummer,' she says.

I finish the last of my coffee. 'Shall we make a move?'

'Absolutely.' She stands up and grabs her things, then says: 'Let's find ourselves the most beautiful ball gowns in Cambridge so our images are etched on their memories for evermore.'

I drop by Lukas's room later to show him my purchase: a pretty black dress with lace around the shoulders and hemline, which falls to just below the knee. I also bought some heels to go with it. I'm making good use of my tour savings and the birthday money Mum and Dad gave me.

He smiles. He's sitting at his desk. 'Nice.'

'Do you want to see it on?' I ask eagerly.

'I'd rather see it off,' he replies with a grin, hooking his forefinger through the belt loop of my jeans and pulling me towards him.

'I thought you had work to do?' I say, as he lifts me onto his lap and kisses my neck.

'I can take a break.'

Lizzy is at Jessie's, putting her feet up. 'I should probably get back to see Lizzy,' I say as he slides his hands up inside my T-shirt.

'We'll be quick,' he murmurs into my mouth before kissing me passionately.

Trinity's May Ball takes place every year on a Monday evening towards the end of June, and on the Monday morning Lukas comes to the house with what he says is a surprise for me. He's more animated than I usually see him and I can tell he's excited. He ushers me upstairs to my room and closes the door, before handing me a black plastic bag.

'What is it?' I ask.

'Open it,' he replies.

I peek inside to see a white box. I pull it out and lift up the lid to discover another package wrapped in white tissue paper – as though a shop assistant at a nice shop has wrapped up a purchase. But this tissue paper is crumpled and the package has already been opened once. Lukas is almost jumping on the spot. I've never seen him like this. Curiously, I peel back the paper to find a fold of shimmering greeny-gold fabric. I pull it out and realise it's a dress.

'What . . . How?' I'm a bit lost for words.

'Try it on,' he says.

'What's it for?' I ask, perplexed. When am I ever going to get a chance to wear something like this?

'For the ball,' he says simply.

'But I already have a ball dress.' I'm bewildered. He knows this. I showed it to him.

'I thought you could do better.' He reaches forward to start unbuttoning my shirt. I push his hand away. He freezes and stares at me.

'Hang on,' I say, wanting to clear this up. 'Where did you get it from?'

'I had it made.'

'You had it *made*?'

'Yes.' He nods. 'I had it made in Paris. It arrived this morning.'

'You had it made in Paris?' I say the words slowly.

'Yes,' he replies, regarding me with a deadpan expression.

What student has a dress made for her, let alone in Paris?

'Don't you like it?'

'No, I *do*,' I say, putting the emphasis carefully on 'do', 'but I'm just a little confused.'

'Try it on,' he says again.

I hesitate and then do as he suggests, out of interest more than anything else.

It fits like a glove and skims the floor. I need heels.

'You need heels,' he says before I can go to the wardrobe.

'I know,' I reply bluntly. I don't understand why I'm annoyed with him – he bought me a dress, no, he had a dress *made* for me – but still I feel a bit put out.

I slide my feet into some black heels and then open the wardrobe door further to reveal the hanging mirror inside. I regard my reflection with surprise. It is the most stunning dress I've ever seen. The colour is sublime. Lukas appears in the reflection behind me.

'What do you think?' he asks quietly, wrapping his arms around my waist from behind and resting his chin on my shoulder.

I nod. I'm lost for words for the second time that morning.

'You look beautiful,' he says seriously, turning me to face him.

'What about my other dress?' I ask, aware of it hanging on the rail beside me. It's as if I'm going to hurt its feelings.

'You can still wear it,' he says. 'Out to dinner, sometime.'

'Didn't you like it?' Now *my* feelings are hurt.

'Yes.' He shrugs. 'But it isn't special. This –' he spins me around again to face the mirror – 'is special. There's no other dress like it.'

He's right, of course. I debated with Lizzy about whether or not someone else might wear the same black dress as me – always a concern.

'I'll pick you up at six,' he says, pecking me on the cheek.

'You don't need to,' I reply, struggling to tear my eyes away from the girl in the mirror. 'I'll come to you.'

'No,' he says firmly. 'I'm not letting you out of my sight for a minute when you look like this.'

Chapter 42

Lukas gives me flowers – cream-coloured roses to match the one in his buttonhole.

'Should I bring them?' I ask hesitantly. I remember last year seeing some girls walking around with small bunches of flowers, but I'm not sure what Lukas expects of me.

'Put them in a vase.' He nods to the kitchen. I do as he says, then return to him. He looks dashing – that's the word I'd use to describe him – in a well-fitted black suit and white bow tie.

'Where are your shoes?' he asks, glancing at the bottom of my dress. The hem is dragging on the floor.

'Here.' I grab my heels from under the hallstand and lift them up, then grin as I kick my legs out to show him my flip-flops. 'If we're walking now, I won't be able to last in them all night.' Trinity isn't far, but it would feel like it in heels.

'I brought the car,' he says.

'Really?' I crane my neck, but I can't see the road over the wall at the end of the front garden.

'Yes,' he says, and then he nods meaningfully at my shoes.

'Okay, then.' I hold onto his arm and wobble on one foot as I replace my flip-flops.

'Where are you going to leave it?' I ask of the car. There's nowhere to park near college – not for students, anyway.

'Klaus is waiting to take it from me.'

'Klaus?' I ask, then, excitedly: 'Am I going to meet him?'

He nods abruptly. 'If you wish.'

'Woo-hoo!' I giggle with glee. He raises one eyebrow at me.

We drive as far into town as we can go before the roads become pedestrianised or only navigable by bus, taxi or bicycle.

Lukas pulls up around the corner from Trinity. A slight blond man, who I can only assume to be Klaus, rushes to the driver's door and opens it. He's so much younger than I expected him to be. Mid-twenties, perhaps? For some reason I thought he'd be an old codger, like the butler who works for Batman.

Lukas snaps something in German and nods in my direction. Klaus looks almost as mortified as I do as he rushes around to my door. He gives me a curt bow as I climb out.

'Thank you,' I say as warmly as I can muster, embarrassed by Lukas's behaviour. I hold out my hand. 'I'm Alice,' I say. He looks alarmed for a moment before dutifully shaking it.

Lukas gets out of the car and says something else in German. It's strange hearing him talk in his own language. I don't know what he's saying, but his tone is sharp. Klaus replies in German – I hear the words 'Herr Heuber' – and the next thing I know he's in the driver's seat and pulling away swiftly from the kerb. Lukas smiles at me, his expression softening. He offers me his arm.

'Shall we?'

I nod, but I don't smile back. I feel oddly uneasy. We set off towards Trinity, but I can't let it lie.

'Did you have a go at him for not opening my door first?' I ask.

'Yes. He should know better,' he replies gravely.

I don't know what to say. I haven't seen this side of him before. I let go of his arm.

'What is it?' he asks, sensing the atmosphere.

'I don't know . . . I mean, he's just a man. I'm not used to hearing you speak to people like that.'

'Like what?'

'Like . . . Like he's *below* you.'

'You're being naive,' he says, which I find immensely patronising. I'm about to tell him as much, when he reaches for my hand. 'Hey,' he says gently. 'I'm sorry. Don't let it ruin tonight.' He squeezes my hand, but I don't squeeze his back.

All around us, students are dressed up to the nines, on their way to one ball or another. Clare and Jesus Colleges also host their balls tonight, and Cambridge is buzzing even more than usual. We approach Great Gate and stand in line with our tickets. The queue is much longer than I expected, wrapping around the perimeter of Great Court, but the atmosphere and anticipation are electric and I soon forget about Lukas's behaviour regarding Klaus. We finally reach the front and hand over our tickets, then we head straight to the champagne bar under the cloisters of the Wren Library before wandering to the bridge. The fairground and catering marquees are on the south paddock, on the other side of the river.

'Wait,' I say to Lukas as we cross the bridge. 'I want to see if I can spot Jessie.'

He reluctantly joins me in scanning the water. I go to the other side of the bridge and he follows half-heartedly.

I got a whole lot of grief from my punter pals for coming to the ball tonight. Good-natured grief, but grief none the less. 'Ooh, look at her, hasn't she gone up in the world!' 'She'll be too posh to talk to us commoners now.' That sort of thing. Lukas starts shifting his feet. The river is already crowded with punts, but I can't see anyone I know.

'It's a bit early for the tours, actually,' I say with mild disappointment. 'I'll look out for him later.'

He nods brusquely and puts his hand on my back to guide me across the bridge. I'm quite sure he's not relishing that thought. He still has a problem with Jessie. I don't think he's ever forgiven him for his attitude early on in our relationship. Luckily they don't see each other very often.

'LUKAS!' We turn to see Harry and Matthew crossing the bridge behind us.

'Hello!' he says, grinning. I'm glad *they've* cheered him up. They slap each other on the back and then Harry turns to me. He looks me up and down and then stumbles backwards, pretending to be struck dumb by my appearance. Matthew picks him up and whacks his arm.

'You idiot,' he jokes, then smiles at me. 'You look beautiful, Alice.'

'Oi!' Harry exclaims. 'I was going to say that!'

'Too late,' Matthew replies, not taking his eyes from mine. Lukas puts his arm around my waist.

'You both look very smart,' I say, smiling at them, then my eyes widen with shock. 'Harry!' I gasp. His face freezes. 'You've ironed your shirt!'

He puffs out his chest like a peacock, before prancing about. 'I bought it at the weekend.'

I laugh. 'That explains it.'

'You two coming on the dodgems?' Matthew asks us.

'Ooh, yeah, I love the dodgems!' I cry.

Lukas shakes his head. 'No. But we'll walk there with you.'

Oh. 'Really?' I ask with surprise as we set off.

The corners of his lips turn down and he shrugs.

'Why don't you like the dodgems?' I ask under my breath.

'I just don't,' he replies abruptly.

We stand and watch as Harry and Matthew rush onto the track and climb into separate cars. They laugh as they collide with each other. I hop on the spot, desperate to join in the fun. Matthew glides to a halt in front of us.

'Want to jump in?' he calls in my direction.

I glance at Lukas. 'Can I?'

He nods, but doesn't smile. Where's his sense of fun? He's starting to annoy me.

Harry comes along and crashes into the back of Matthew, whose head jerks forward.

'You moron!' Matthew yells at him.

Harry beckons desperately at me. 'Get into mine!'

Bugger it. 'I don't trust you!' I shout at Harry as I clamber ungraciously into Matthew's car. He zooms off. I'm laughing as he attempts to take out Harry's back end. I glance over at Lukas on the sidelines, wanting to see him smile at us, but he's nowhere to be seen. I scan the crowd with a bad feeling in my stomach. The ride comes to an end.

'Stay on,' Matthew urges, briefly touching my leg.

'No, I'd better go.' I hurry across the track and carefully climb down the steps, searching the crowds. I can't see him anywhere. I search for several minutes before returning to the dodgems. Surely he'll come and find me here. I hope so. Harry spots me and waves. I smile a shaky smile back and turn to look behind me. No sign. I wait with an uncomfortable feeling. Someone touches my back. I spin around to see him.

'Where did you go?' I demand to know.

'For a wander.' His eyes follow Matthew as he races around the track.

'I couldn't find you! I was worried!' Am I overreacting?

'I'm back now.' Finally he meets my gaze. His expression is cool. 'Let's go.'

He sets off and I follow him. 'What's wrong with you tonight?' I ask.

'What makes you think something's wrong with me?' he replies over his shoulder as I hurry after him in my heels.

'Come on, Lukas,' I snap, catching up with him. 'Don't play games.'

'He likes you, you know.' He looks across at me. His tone is dry.

'Who likes me?'

'You know who I'm talking about.'

'Harry?' I ask. Of course, I know he means Matthew. Harry is no threat to Lukas.

He regards me wryly. I look away.

'No, he doesn't,' I brush him off. It's clear we're now talking about Matthew. It became apparent quite early on that he and I have a bit in common – he's also studying English Lit – and we often find ourselves talking about all things literature, while Lukas and Harry rattle on about astrophysics and God knows what else. Also, Matthew has given me a few too many meaningful looks since that first time I met him at the college bar. A few too many to ignore. I've suspected for a while that he's attracted to me.

'Anyway, what does it matter?' I continue. 'I'm with you. He knows I'm with you.'

'You're right,' he says, leading me away. 'It doesn't matter. I just wanted you to admit it.'

I feel slighted, and I don't know why. Neither of us has done anything wrong.

'I heard you discussing with him recently that you're thinking of taking a language module next term,' he comments offhandedly.

'Yes, that's right. Mandarin.'

It's been two years since Joe suggested I learn my grandmother's language at university. Two years that I've wasted. I mentioned my regrets to Matthew recently and he insisted it wasn't too late – I could still learn some of the basics in my third year.

'Yet you've never attempted to learn a word of German,' Lukas adds.

His comment strikes me dumb.

'Let's go to the comedy club,' he says.

I don't feel much like smiling. I hope the comedians are good. Harry and Matthew join us in the marquee. I make a point of putting my hand on Lukas's leg and cuddling up to him more than I usually do. He doesn't respond, but he does seem to relax more after that.

The comedy does the trick, and later, much later, we return to the champagne bar, just the two of us. I've been trying to pace myself, but I feel decidedly tipsy. I don't know how I'll make it through to six a.m., when the ball ends. Lukas passes me a glass of champagne and puts his arm around my waist.

'Cheers.'

'Cheers.' We chink glasses.

'Are you having fun?' he asks.

'Yes.' I smile. 'I love seeing it from the inside. Thank you for inviting me tonight.'

'Who else would I ask?' he replies with amusement.

A thought occurs to me. 'Did you bring anyone last year?'

He shrugs. 'No.'

'I remember looking for you.'

'Looking for me?'

'Yes. I was down on the river.' I suddenly remember Jessie. 'Hey, let's see if we can spot my punting pals!'

I drag him towards the bridge. The fireworks are due to start soon, so it's even more crowded than before. I manage to squeeze between a couple of people leaning on the stone wall. The punts are well and truly crammed in now. I spot Chris leaning on his pole at the back of a boat.

'CHRIS!'

He doesn't hear me.

'CHRIS!' I shout louder. And then I see Jessie. I wave with delight.

He puts his hands to his mouth and shouts with glee at the top of his voice: 'VAGINA!' My mouth falls open. Little shit! I'm aghast. I quickly recover and am about to give him the finger when Lukas roughly drags me back from the wall.

'What the hell is he thinking?' he hisses, angrier than I've ever seen him.

'He's only joking!' I exclaim, horrified by his reaction. I rub at my arm – it feels tender from where he grabbed me.

'He's pathetic!'

Right, that's it. The night is under definite threat of ruination. People around us turn to stare. Lukas gives me a look that makes my blood run cold and then storms off through the crowd, shoving past people as he goes. I'm absolutely mortified. I hurry after him, not knowing what else to do. Fireworks start to go off behind me, but I'm far too distracted to pay them any attention.

'Lukas!' I shout, my eyes on his departing back. We're pushing against the crowd because everyone is coming this way to watch the fireworks. 'LUKAS!' I shout again, but his pace doesn't slow. Eventually there's a break in the crowd and I manage to totter after him in my heels. 'STOP!' I shout, reaching for his hand and tugging it, hard. He spins around.

'Stop it!' I gasp. 'Where are you going?'

'Home,' he spits.

'What? *Why?*' He doesn't answer. 'Because of Jessie?'

'I've had enough,' he says, glaring at me.

'Enough of what? *Me?*'

He shakes his head and keeps walking.

'Wait!' I call after him desperately. He pauses in his tracks, and then turns around to face me.

'I'm going back to Germany on Friday,' he says over the sound of the explosions. The sky above our heads is glowing with colour.

'I didn't think you were leaving for two more weeks?'

'I'm going on Friday,' he reiterates.

'Why?'

His expression softens, but only slightly. 'There's so much . . .' His voice trails off.

'What is it?' I ask. 'What's wrong?'

He takes a deep breath, but won't look at me.

'Lukas,' I say gently, taking his hand and willing him to open up to me. 'What is it? Is it your parents?'

A long moment goes by before he nods. 'But not just them.'

'What else? *Who* else?'

He meets my eyes. 'We should go back to my room,' he says solemnly.

I follow him out of the gate, feeling sick to the pit of my stomach.

We get up to his room and he indicates one of his armchairs, sitting down in the other. The firework sounds are muted, but still present in the background.

'I need to tell you something,' he says. 'About a girl I know in Germany.'

My nausea steps up a notch.

'Her name is Rosalinde,' he explains grimly. 'I've known her all my life. She's from a very good family.'

Why is he telling me this?

'It has always been assumed that I'll marry her.'

I put my hand to my mouth. He regards me with compassion.

'I don't want to marry her,' he adds, 'but it's complicated.'

'I don't understand. You have an *arranged* marriage?'

'Not exactly.'

So he doesn't live in the Dark Ages.

He continues. 'But my parents expect certain things of me. It's how I was raised. To break off my engagement to Rosalinde—'

'You're engaged?' I ask sharply.

'It's not like that. I have never proposed to her, but we have always had an understanding.'

'Have you slept with her?'

Please say no, please say no, please say no . . .

'Yes.'

'Oh. So she's your girlfriend?' What does that make me?

'No, she's not. As I said, it's complicated.'

'Why didn't you tell me about her before?' I whisper.

'I was going to. That day I invited you to lunch after our first date. But Harry came along and we seemed able to move on without me going into ... *details*. I didn't know how things would pan out between us.' He motions to the two of us.

I stare at him. 'And how have things panned out, exactly?'

'Alice ...' He gets up and comes to me, kneeling on the floor and gazing up at me earnestly. 'I love you. You know I love you. I want to be with you. I don't want to be with Rosalinde.'

'Could you stop saying her name?' I wince. I know it's just a name, but I already have a picture of her in my mind and she's perfect and beautiful.

He takes my hand. Mine is shaking, but he seems very calm. Freakishly calm, considering.

'We have never talked about our previous relationships,' he says seriously.

It's true. I've been curious about his past – it's clear from our lovemaking that he has vastly more experience than me – but I don't want to open up this particular can of worms, because talking about his past would inevitably mean talking about mine.

'But perhaps that was a mistake.'

I take a deep breath. I don't want to speak to him about Joe, but this is serious. If any time calls for complete honesty, it's now.

'Rosalinde—'

'Stop!' I hold up my hand.

'How do you want me to refer to her?' he asks gently.

Good point. 'Okay.'

'She was my first,' he continues.

God, this hurts. I'm slightly taken aback by how much, actually.

'We grew up together, we played together as children; she was my friend. Our parents used to tease us about being boyfriend and girlfriend, but it wasn't until we turned sixteen that things grew *serious* . . .'

He gives me a meaningful look and the pain is intense. I didn't think I cared about him to this extent.

'We both went back to boarding school after the summer, and the next time I saw her something had changed. I don't know if she'd met someone else, but it was another year before we became friends again. Perhaps it was the pressure from our parents, but we made a pact that, if we got married, it would be our choice. And first we agreed we needed to live a little.'

Wait. 'Is that what you're doing with me? Living a little?' A lump forms in my throat.

'No.' He shakes his head resolutely. 'You're different to anyone else I've ever known.'

Tears trek down my cheeks. The fireworks have ended and now we can hear the music from the main stage. I think Mark Owen is playing.

'Have you told your parents about me?'

'I'm going to tell them when I go home. I'm going to tell *everyone*.'

I hadn't felt too bad about not seeing him this summer. Now I feel nauseous at the thought of him going back to Germany. No wonder he never asked me to go with him.

'Come here,' he says, pulling me out of my chair.

We don't make love that night. We don't even get undressed. We lie on the bed, him holding me from behind as I listen to the sound of the college balls still going strong by the river. He didn't even ask me about my past. I didn't have to talk about Joe. But that doesn't mean he's not on my mind. Early the next morning when I walk home, I look like any other female student who has stayed up all night – one of the six o'clock survivors still wearing her ball gown. But inside I feel more dead than alive.

Chapter 43

It eats me up that summer. It infests me. Lukas rarely rings – he sends the occasional text, and if I try to call him, his mobile diverts straight to voicemail. I return to my dark place. I lose myself in it for weeks, until Jessie and Emily intervene, but not before I've gone to London. Searching, never finding.

At the end of August, Lukas flies back to England. He's like a stranger to me. It feels like *Groundhog Day*.

'Did you tell her?' I ask him across the kitchen table. He seems to have expected the coolness of my behaviour, but he's going with it. He has no other option.

'You know that I did,' he replies reasonably, reaching forward to take my hand.

'That's right. One of your *texts*,' I say sarcastically, snatching it away.

He sighs and slumps back in his chair, but doesn't take his eyes from mine. 'It was hard to talk.'

'Clearly.'

'But we can talk now.'

'Maybe I'm not in the mood to talk now.'

'Don't say anything, then. Just listen.'

I'm not in the mood to listen, either, but I can't be bothered to get up and leave the room.

'My parents already knew.'

What? 'How did they know?'

'Klaus.' He gives me a hard stare. 'I suspected he'd squeal.'

'That's a horrible thing to say.'

'It doesn't mean it's not true.' He taps his fingers on the table. 'Of course, I knew he'd tell them about you after the ball, but I had already decided to confess by then.'

Am I supposed to feel comforted by that thought?

'In fact, I believe he revealed your existence after our first date. No wonder my mother gave me such a trying time about not going home for Easter,' he muses, staring out of the window. 'She must have known my plans involved you; that our relationship was serious.' He looks back at me.

I shift in my seat. 'Are they really that unhappy about us?'

'They're not pleased.' He shrugs. He seems different – more aloof, or harder, somehow. 'Anyway,' he says, resting his elbows on the table, 'Klaus has gone back to Germany now, so we won't be bothered by him. It is a shame about my car, though. It's ridiculous that I'm not allowed to keep it here,' he snaps petulantly.

'Bloody hell, Lukas, I think we've got bigger things to worry about than your car,' I say crossly.

He regards me with irritation. His eyes fall to my collarbone, where his necklace is absent. 'It seems that every time I go away from you, your affections for me diminish.'

I cast my eyes heavenwards. 'Can you blame me? For all I knew, you weren't coming back!'

'When did I ever give you that impression?' His tone is icy.

He has a point. I'm comparing him to Joe. I look away, guiltily.

'How did Rosalinde take it?' I finally find my voice.

'It's hard to tell with her.'

I bet she's cool, calm and collected. Or perhaps she's just cold and efficient. I hope it's the latter.

'She'll move on,' he adds, gazing out of the window again. 'She probably already has.'

'When was the last time you slept with her?' I ask, a horrible feeling settling over me.

He frowns. 'Why is that important?'

Talk about deflecting the question!

'Are you going to answer me?'

'When was the last time *you* slept with someone?' he asks nastily.

'Before I met *you*!' I exclaim. 'Can you say the same thing?'

'No, as it happens.'

The blood drains from my face. Suddenly he looks sympathetic. He reaches across to touch me, but I shove my hands under the table.

'It was before we were together,' he says gently, holding eye contact. 'The summer after I first met you, before we had the rooftop picnic.'

'Is that why you acted like you did? You didn't kiss me; you drove too fast; you seemed angry . . . Were you thinking of her?'

He hesitates before nodding. 'Yes.'

I can barely speak. 'What about at Christmas?'

'No,' he says abruptly. 'Nothing happened then.'

I so want to believe him . . . My eyes fill up with tears.

'Alice,' he says softly, holding his hands out to me. I slowly take mine from underneath the table and he grips them tightly.

I hear the front door slam and turn to see Jessie appear from the hall.

'Are you okay?' he asks me directly, his stare accusatory as it darts towards Lukas and back again.

'Yes,' I answer. Lukas lets go of my hands and sits back in his chair.

And so, after a shaky start, our relationship returns to normal, although 'normal' has changed somewhat. Lukas no longer lives in his bedsit on Trinity Street. Now he's moved closer to his campus, to Burrell's Field. It's on the western side of the river, further away from town. Unfortunately, he still has a single bed, so I don't stay over very often. And, thanks to Jessie's cold shoulder, he doesn't stay at mine very much, either.

Two weeks before I'm due to start my third and final year at Anglia Ruskin, I bump into one of my tutors in town. Mitch Turville is my favourite tutor, and I've always done my best in his classes. Even when I was practically catatonic in my first year he managed to coax an A out of me.

'Alice!' he says. 'How are you?'

'Good!' I reply. 'How's your summer?'

'Excellent, excellent. Spent a lovely couple of weeks in Spain with the family. You?'

Mitch is in his late forties and has thinning brown hair and glasses. Sometimes he has a beard, sometimes not. Today he appears to be at the halfway stage.

'Actually, I'm glad I bumped into you,' he says after I've responded to his question. 'Did you ever put any thought into becoming a member of the literary society?'

Before we broke up for summer he asked me if I'd like to be involved, but I never got back to him. Between punting, reading zillions of books and seeing Lukas, I don't have much spare time.

'Sorry,' I say. 'I wasn't sure if—'

'Because we could really do with someone like you to get involved,' he interrupts, sensing my reluctance and refusing to accept it. 'Victoria, Rachel and Kelly are keen for another person to help out during Freshers' Week. Can I tempt you?'

And so it is that I find myself dressing up as Alice from *Alice in Wonderland* during Freshers' Week and helping to rope in new recruits. Victoria, Rachel and Kelly have been friends with each other since the first year. They've always been nice to me and I like them a lot. I haven't actually lived a proper student life in the respect of having a group of fellow students for friends, and it's something that I've suspected I'll regret. It was with this in mind that I agreed to Mitch's request.

Victoria is dressed up as Dorothy, Rachel as the White Witch and Kelly as Little Red Riding Hood. We manage to sign up an impressive forty-three undergraduates thanks to our enthusiasm, and the day is much more fun than I expected it to be. When our work is done we decide we'll stay in character for a laugh and head to the pub to celebrate. I text Lukas to let him know that I probably won't be able to see him tonight after all, and then set about helping the other three to clear up. It's not until we're walking towards the main entrance that I think to check my phone and see that I have seven missed calls from him. No voicemails, though. How odd. I'm about to call him back to ask him what's wrong, when I hear the sound of several car horns beeping.

'Who on earth is that?' Victoria asks, but my face has already flushed with embarrassment because *that*, my new friend, is Lukas.

He has pulled up on the double yellow lines on the main road outside college – in his Porsche, no less – and is being persistently tooted at by cars trying to get past him. I want to bury my head in a sandpit.

'God, sorry,' I say to the girls. 'That's my boyfriend. I have no idea what he's doing here, but I'd better go.'

'Can you join us later?' Kelly asks hopefully.

'I'll try,' I say, running towards the car. Lukas leans across the passenger seat and pushes open my door.

'What are you doing?' I hiss, climbing in because I have no other choice. The people in the cars behind are getting increasingly angry and right now I want to be as far away from here as possible. Lukas screeches away from the kerb and goes straight through an amber light.

'Why didn't you answer your phone?' he snaps, putting his foot down.

'I didn't hear it!' I reply indignantly. 'I was about to call you.'

'Too late. I had to resort to this.' He glances across at me with a look of distaste. 'What the hell are you wearing?'

Anger rushes through me. 'I told you about this! Alice from *Alice in Wonderland*? Children's Literature is one of the modules of my degree.'

'That's right,' he sneers. 'I remember thinking how ridiculous that sounded.'

'What would you know?' I demand. 'You've never been in the slightest bit interested in any of my studies!'

'Oh, and you've been interested in mine?'

I ignore that comment and continue with my rant. 'Or my work!'

'Work?'

'Punting!'

'You call that work? You wouldn't know what work is.'

'Oh, and you would? Poor little rich boy!'

He slams on the brakes.

'Good! I wanted to get out, anyway!' I reach for the door handle, but he grabs my elbow and roughly pulls me back.

'That hurt!' I scream, hitting him on his arm.

'STOP!' he shouts, grabbing my wrist.

'WHAT THE HELL IS WRONG WITH YOU?' I'm feeling a bit hysterical now.

'MY MOTHER IS HERE!' he shouts back.

That stuns me into silence. He lets go of me. Suddenly he looks crushed.

'What's your mother doing here?' I ask.

'She wants to meet you,' he replies, white as a sheet. 'You'll need to get changed.'

Chapter 44

Frau Heuber – that sounds scarily austere – is currently in a limousine on her way to Burrell's Field. I get changed quickly into my smartest skirt and a white blouse, while Lukas waits outside in his Porsche. I haven't even asked him where he got the car from – I thought he gave it up after Klaus left.

His mother called Lukas en route to let him know she was on her way. I have no idea why she thought it was a matter of such urgency that she couldn't give us more than an hour's notice, but perhaps she wants to catch us out. Perhaps we should be grateful that she decided to call at all.

We go back to Lukas's room and wait apprehensively. I sit on the bed and fidget, before thinking it might look better if I relocate to a chair – I don't want to appear too comfortable. Eventually Lukas can stand the suspense no longer so we both go downstairs to keep an eye out for her. She arrives ten minutes later in an enormous, shiny black limo. The driver – wearing a navy suit and a proper chauffeur's hat – gets out to open the door for her. I don't know what I expected. A grand woman in a fox's fur, or something similar, flouncing out and pretending that I don't exist . . . I wasn't expecting this.

Lukas's mother is short and, for want of another word, fat. She's wearing a large brown and pink floral dress and she looks like she should be in a kitchen baking apple pies and other yummy, heart-warming things to eat. I can't for the life of me work out why he seemed frightened of her – until she looks at me.

Ice. That's the word I would use to describe her eyes. Cold, blue ice, and now my stomach feels full of the stuff.

Lukas steps forward to greet her and kisses her hand. Not her cheek. Her hand. I can't imagine what she'd do if I gave her a hug – probably keel over. Now, there's a thought . . .

'Mother, this is Alice,' he says in English, turning to look at me. I've never seen him so nervous.

'Hello,' I say, my smile wavering. She doesn't offer me her hand, which is a relief, because I'm not sure if she'd expect me to kiss it too.

She redirects her gaze to Lukas without responding, and says something in German.

'Not yet,' he replies with an awkward smile in my direction. 'I believe she starts her course next week.'

I think she's asking if I can speak German. I haven't decided for sure, but I've been thinking of switching from Mandarin to German. Lukas's comment at the ball got to me.

A lot of tutting commences when we go inside. From what I can gather, she doesn't approve of Lukas's room.

Lukas asks her a question with an uncomfortable glance at me, and after that she converses in perfect English.

'I was telling my son that his room is too small,' she says with a look of disgust on her features. 'How can you bear to stay here?' Her question appears to be directed at me.

'Well,' I glance at Lukas self-consciously. 'I live in a house with two friends.'

'You must think I'm naive,' she snorts.

'What? No!' I exclaim. 'I mean, I do stay here, just not very often.'

'Humph.' She turns away from me.

God, this is awful! First Joe and now Lukas! Why can't I be like Lizzy and have a nice potential mother-in-law? She recently joked that Callum's mum is her second-best friend. After me, I hope.

Lukas gently intervenes. 'Perhaps we should go out?'

'You can accompany me to my hotel.'

It doesn't sound like it's up for discussion.

She's staying at a super-swish hotel in Cambridge. Her chauffeur drops us off at the door and hurries to get her bags out of the boot. A doorman takes them from him and we're ushered inside to the lobby.

'I will call you tomorrow,' she says to her chauffeur, before turning to Lukas. 'He's an excellent driver. You can have him, if you like. I'll arrange it.'

'Thank you, Mother,' Lukas says, caught off guard by her generosity. 'But I still have my car.'

'I thought you sold it.'

I'm glad someone is clearing this up.

'Not yet,' he replies.

She signs in at reception and Lukas takes the key. We go to the lift and press the button for the sixth floor.

'Your father wants Klaus to return,' she muses as the lift starts to climb.

'No,' he says firmly. 'I can make do without him.'

She humphs again. 'We'll see.'

Frau Heuber is in the penthouse and it's spectacular – panoramic floor-to-ceiling windows look out over the river and rooftops of Cambridge. The sun is just beginning to set. I notice that Lukas, not his mother, tips the doorman when he arrives with the bags.

'Wow!' I enthuse, peering out of the window at the rows of boats lined up at the Magdalene Bridge punting station.

'I suppose it's only for two days,' she says snootily.

How can this not be good enough for her?

'It was very kind of you to come,' Lukas says, not asking the question that's certainly been plaguing *my* mind: *why* did she come?

She joins me at the window and looks down.

'I should like to go on a punt,' she says.

'I can take you,' I offer uneasily.

She regards me with alarm.

'Alice is a punter,' Lukas interjects with an anxious glance at his mother.

'A punter?' she snorts.

'Yes, I work as a tour guide.'

'You work as a *tour guide?*'

Sorry, is there something wrong with her hearing?

'Alice has been able to pay her own way through university,' Lukas says calmly.

'Well, my parents have helped too,' I add quickly.

'But you pay your own rent,' he says.

'That's true.'

'How very interesting,' she says flatly, turning away from the window. 'My son, I have run out of indigestion tablets. Could you go downstairs and ask the receptionist to get me some?'

'Er, why don't I ask on the way to dinner?' he suggests.

'No, I think I should like them to get some for me now,' she replies with an air of finality.

He glances at me apprehensively and then gives a little nod, before leaving the two of us alone. Her icy gaze falls on me.

'Perhaps we would be more comfortable through here.'

I follow her nervously to a small, but stylish living-room area. She indicates the sofa for me, before settling herself in a chair.

'You have been seeing my son for some time,' she says.

I nod carefully. 'Almost a year.'

'You know of his situation?'

'I'm not sure what you're referring—'

'He was to be engaged to Rosalinde Pfeifer by the end of the year.'

I jolt at the sound of her name. 'I knew he was set to marry her at some point. By definition, I thought that meant they were already engaged.' I try to keep my cool, but my heart is hammering inside my chest.

'No announcement had been made. It was not official. Not yet.'

I don't know what she expects me to say. Eventually she continues.

'Lukas is not my husband's heir. He will not inherit the house. That right falls to my eldest son and, his son after him.' Markus and Maximilian, I presume.

'I'm not after him for his money, if that's what you mean.' I find my courage. 'I just really like him.' Her eyes narrow. '*Love* him,' I correct myself.

'Then surely you want what's best for him?'

'Of course.' I shrug, feigning nonchalance. 'But he's amazingly bright, you know. I think he's capable of choosing that for himself.'

She regards me for a long moment. I don't know how I manage it, but I don't break eye contact, and neither does she. Finally she nods.

'So be it.'

So be what?

I never get an answer to that question because Lukas returns.

'Rosalinde has met someone else,' he tells me later that night as he walks me back to Jessie's.

'Oh.' I frown. 'When did you discover this?'

'When you went to the bathroom during dinner.'

'And how do you feel about it?'

'It's for the best.'

'Does your mother agree?'

'What do you think?' He gives me a sidelong glance. 'She can't force me to do anything.'

'Did she try to convince you to leave me?' I ask in a small voice.

He nods abruptly. 'Yes. She insisted I act quickly before it's too late, but it's already too late.'

'You mean, Rosalinde wouldn't take you back now?' I'm not sure I would in her position. She must feel humiliated.

'No,' he says, coming to a stop in the middle of the pavement and spinning around to face me. 'It's too late because I want you, Alice. They can't make me give you up.'

I don't know why I think of Joe at that point, but I do. Lukas turns and keeps walking.

'You are going to learn German, aren't you?' he asks tersely.

'Yes.' It's the least I can do.

Chapter 45

'Argh!'

I wake up with a jolt at the sound of Lukas exploding. 'What's wrong?' I ask him. It's the middle of a cold and frosty night in January and I'm in his room at Burrell's Field.

'I can't sleep!' He pounds the mattress. 'My mother was right. This room is too small.'

'You've managed in a room this size for over three years,' I say reasonably. He once told me he enjoyed experiencing student life like any other student. But he's been living it up at home for weeks. Maybe that's the problem.

'I've had enough. I can't stand this bed. It's ridiculous!'

I sit up. 'I'll go back to Jessie's, then.'

'Don't be stupid,' he snaps, pulling me back down. 'But I need to sleep. I have a lecture tomorrow and I won't be able to concentrate.'

'Why did you insist on me coming here tonight, then?' I'm annoyed now. I met up with the literary society girls earlier at the pub to talk about a Dickens quiz we're organising for next month.

I declined Lukas's offer to collect me, but he turned up, anyway. In his Porsche. He's got to stop doing that.

'I missed you,' he laments.

Christmas passed by without any hitches. I went home and Lukas returned to Germany, but this time he called me every couple of days so I didn't lose my head like the last few times.

'Well, I've also got a big year ahead of me, so I could do with a decent night's kip too, you know.'

'Do you have to write another essay on *Harry Potter*?' he asks in a derogatory tone.

'Children's Literature still involves work, you know!' I exclaim. 'Bugger this, I'm off.'

He grabs my arm. 'Don't go. I'm sorry.' He caresses my face with his hands and gazes at me in the darkness.

'I know you think my work pales in comparison to yours, and it probably does, but it still means a lot to me,' I say earnestly. 'I have to think about my career options and . . . God, I'm too tired for this.'

My eyes are stinging and my body feels like it's weighted down.

'I'm sorry,' he says again. 'I'm sorry.' He presses his lips to mine and I feel him twitch beneath me as his kiss deepens.

'Not now,' I groan.

'It will help you relax . . .' he murmurs, moving against me.

It will help *you* relax, you mean. I push him away and hold him at arm's length.

'No, Lukas, I need to get some sleep.'

He curses in German. I haven't learned all the swear words yet, but I'm guessing this is one of them.

'What is *wrong* with you tonight?' I ask crossly. 'First you drag me away from my meeting—'

'Meeting about a *pub* quiz!' he interjects.

'*So?* It's still an event and I'm helping to organise it so I don't appreciate you turning up in that bloody Porsche again and embarrassing me!'

'I'm sorry if you find my Porsche so embarrassing.' He's not sorry in the slightest.

'It's not the car, it's you!' I get out of bed and start to drag on my clothes. I've had enough of this. 'You can't control me; you can't make me do what you want me to do. I'm my own person. I haven't made many friends here and—'

'Rosalinde is engaged.'

His interruption is firm, but his tone is flat.

I instantly stop what I'm doing. 'What?'

'Rosalinde is engaged.' He stares up at the ceiling.

'She's *engaged*? Who to?'

'Frederick Schulz.' Before I can ask who that is, Lukas says: 'He's from a very good family.'

'What is it with you and very good families?'

'He's far too old for her,' he continues, ignoring me. 'He's thirty-three and he's a banker. *Extremely successful.*' He elongates these last two words, almost as though he's drunk.

'How do you know all this?' I ask with confusion.

'My mother told me.'

'When? In Germany?'

'No. On the phone tonight.'

I should have guessed as much.

'What does your mother expect you to do, run home and woo this girl back into your arms?' I can't help the bitterness of my tone.

'No. She told me to *spite* me.' He's a competitor in the bitterness stakes.

'Oh.' I sit down on the bed, dejectedly. 'Do you regret how things have turned out?' I don't want to ask the question, but I feel compelled to.

He doesn't answer for a moment, which is unlike him. 'No,' he says bluntly. 'If she can do this, then it proves she isn't the right woman for me.'

As if proof were needed?

He reaches over to take my hand and turns to look at me. 'We should get a house.'

'What?'

'We could move in together.'

'Steady on, I'm only twenty.'

'I could ask my parents—'

'No!' I interrupt.

'Why not?'

'Lukas, if your parents buy you a house—'

'Not buy, rent,' he says.

'If your parents *rent* you a house I won't live in it with you.'

'Why on earth not?'

'Because it's not right! Aside from the fact that I'm far too young to be moving in with my boyfriend . . .'

'Don't you love me?' he asks sharply.

'Yes! But that's not the point!'

'I can't cope with this bedsit for much longer, Alice. I hardly get to see you – you're always too busy with punting and this *literary* society.'

'It's you who's always too busy with your studies!' I say indignantly. When we see each other it's always more on his terms than mine.

'But if we lived together we could see each other every night . . .' He tries to persuade me, but I'm resolute.

'No.' I let go of his hand. 'I don't want your parents' help. There is *no way* I'll move in with you if you ask them.'

I probably should have been more specific.

He turns up at Jessie's a few weeks later with a brand-new, shiny silver bicycle. It's a refreshingly bright and crisp February morning.

'You bought a bike!' I exclaim. 'At long bloody last.'

'Come for a ride with me,' he urges with excitement. 'I have a surprise for you.'

I'm perplexed as he pushes past me to grab my coat and scarf from the hallstand. 'Isn't the bike a surprise enough?'

'It doesn't compare,' he says with a grin, helping me into my coat.

'Where are you taking me?' I think I might burst from the curiosity as we ride away from town.

'You'll see,' he replies with amusement, turning right onto Conduit Head Road. I follow him along a gravel road until he comes to a stop outside a picturesque thatched cottage. 'What do you think?'

I give him a quizzical look. 'About the house?'

'Yes.'

'It's lovely, but . . .'

'Welcome home, honey.' He says it in a comical voice, but I have a feeling he's not joking.

'You didn't?' I gasp.

He nods. 'I did.'

My face falls. 'But I told you . . .'

'I didn't ask my parents for help,' he says swiftly.

'Then how . . .'

'I sold my Porsche.'

I stare at him, gobsmacked.

'It's too late if you don't like it,' he adds flippantly, climbing off his bike. 'I've already paid up front for the rent. Come and see inside.'

I'm too dumbfounded to comment. I follow him in a daze.

It's quaint and cosy, full of antiques and Cath Kidston-style furnishings. There's a small garden behind the house and a sun-drenched field beyond that.

He leads me up the wooden staircase. The first room is small and poky, the second is slightly larger, but the third has a king-sized four-poster bed and a view out onto the field. The excitement builds inside my stomach. Is that wrong?

'What do you think?' he asks eagerly.

'It's . . . beautiful,' I reply. 'But—'

'Don't say anything else,' he interrupts, kissing me quickly on the nose.

'But Lukas!' I exclaim.

'What?' he exclaims back.

'I can't live here with you!'

'Why not?' he asks. 'You have to move out of Jessie's house soon – his parents are returning.'

'Not until Easter.'

'That's next month!'

'They said I could continue to live there.'

'In Emily's tiny bedroom?' He tries to reason with me. 'We'd have even less room there than we have in mine.'

I can't disagree. Jessie's parents are due back soon, and while they very kindly agreed to let Emily and me continue to live in their house, it means me moving into Emily's single room, and

Emily shacking up with Jessie in my double, so that he can surrender the master. Emily went with Jessie to see them at Christmas and they got on well, so the new arrangement will suit her; and it seems futile for me to find somewhere else to live for the sake of a few months until term finishes.

Lukas senses me wavering, but I'm brought back to reality with a bump when I remember one very important point. 'What would my parents say?'

'You're an adult,' he reasons. 'What you do is up to you.'

'*If* I want to endure their wrath . . .'

He sighs. 'Look, I'm going to live here, anyway. Keep your room at Jessie's and stay here with me whenever you wish. It doesn't have to be a big issue.'

I look out at the field and then back at the enormous bed. Lukas and I grin at each other.

'Shall we christen it?' I say.

'I thought you'd never ask.'

Chapter 46

It's not long before I'm living entirely with Lukas. I never thought that I'd move in with a boyfriend so speedily, but I can't say that I don't like it. Our relationship has been fast-tracked. Not just in terms of moving in together, but how we feel about each other. I've got to know him so much more quickly than I would have done in a normal student-relationship set-up, and being with him is strangely easy. We spend most of our days apart, but make up for it in the evenings. It means I don't see as much of my punting pals as I used to, and I haven't helped out with the literary society as often as I would have liked, either, but they don't feel like big sacrifices to make. Not usually, anyway.

Jessie had a go at me yesterday because I had to cancel our movie night. Our cinema outings have become less and less regular, but I wish he were more forgiving. I would understand if his commitments with Emily stole him away from me.

Anyway, I needed last night to prepare because Lizzy is coming to stay. Not just Lizzy. Harry and Matthew are coming too, but she's the one I'm most excited about. She broke up with Callum last week and is pretty cut up about it, so it feels insensitive to say I'm excited, but I'm determined to cheer her up.

I haven't seen Matthew since the night of the ball back in June. Harry stayed on to do a Ph.D. and we catch up with him often, but Matthew returned home to Buckinghamshire and I believe he's now working for a newspaper in London. I don't like to ask about him.

Having agreed to cook for everyone, I spent last night uncharacteristically burning mince and chopping up my fingers instead of the onions. Eventually I gave up and went out to buy a lasagne. I think I can manage a salad. I should have gone to the movies with Jessie, after all.

Lizzy's train is three and a half hours delayed, so she doesn't arrive until four o'clock on Saturday afternoon. I hear her taxi pull up and go outside to greet her.

'Hello!' I call as she climbs out. I go to help her with her bags.

She gazes up at the cottage. 'This is a bit nice, isn't it?'

Inside, she heads straight to the living-room window. It's late April and our garden is full of colour.

'Wow! Look at that view!' she says of the field.

'It's alright,' I kid.

'Where's Lukas?' she asks, spinning around.

'He's at the lab.'

'On a Saturday?'

'Oh, he's there all the time. He's revising for his exams at the moment, but he's promised to take a break tonight. He should be back soon. How's your mum?' I ask on the walk upstairs to her room.

'She's fine! She said to give you her love.'

'Aah, give her mine back.'

I've put her in the double – Matthew can have the single. Harry will no doubt go back to his bedsit in Burrell's Field – if he doesn't crash out on the sofa, that is.

'Let me see your room,' she says. We wander through. 'I bet that gets some use,' she jokes, nodding to the bed. I smirk at her and then go to close the wardrobe.

'What's that?' she asks curiously, her eyes spying a flash of glinting greeny-gold in my wardrobe.

'Oh, that's my ball gown,' I reply carelessly, pulling it out.

'It's beautiful!' she cries with surprise. 'Gosh, you're organised this year.'

'Oh, no,' I brush her off. She misunderstood. 'This is last year's.'

'What do you mean?' she asks, perplexed.

I never told her about Lukas having a dress made for me. I'm not sure why – I think I might have been either slightly embarrassed, or worried that she might take offence.

I shrug, trying to play it down. 'Lukas had it made for me.'

'*What!*' Her mouth falls open. 'What was wrong with the dress we bought together?'

It appears I was right about the latter reason.

'Nothing,' I say quickly. 'It was lovely. It's just that ... Well, he thought I could do ...' My voice trails off, but she finishes my sentence.

'*Better?*'

I glance at the dress and run my fingers down the material. 'Somebody else might have had the same one,' I say.

'Welcome to the world,' she says sardonically. 'Well, I'm sure you looked amazing.'

I close the wardrobe doors.

'What the hell happened to your fingers?' she asks with horror as she spies the plasters.

'Cooking casualty,' I explain. 'Lukas wanted me to cook ... Well, I wanted to, as well. But I gave up in the end.'

'Who else is coming tonight?' she asks, sitting down on the end of the bed and bouncing up and down.

'A couple of Lukas's friends: Harry and Matthew. It's not exactly the girls' weekend you might have hoped for ...'

'No, it's fine!' she exclaims, her shoulders slumping as she stops bouncing. 'Any distraction will help.'

'Can you tell me what happened?' I ask.

'Is four o'clock too early to start drinking?' she bats back, getting to her feet. I can tell that she's fighting back tears.

'God, no. Just don't let me forget to put dinner in the oven!'

Back in the kitchen, I pull a bottle of Veuve Clicquot out of the fridge.

'Is that real champagne?' she asks with widened eyes, peering at the label.

'Yeah.' I shrug. 'Lukas buys it.'

'Bloody hell. Handmade ball gowns ... champagne ... a thatched cottage all to himself ... He's not your average student, is he?'

I give her a wry look. 'Not exactly.' I lift up the bottle. 'Want some?'

'Go on, then. If you're sure he won't mind.'

'No, he got it in for tonight.' I peel off the foil at the top.

'How are things going with him?' she asks as she lifts herself up onto the countertop. She met him only briefly that time she came to stay with me last year to go shopping for ball gowns.

'Excuse me,' I say, and she ducks her head so I can open the cupboard behind her to get out a couple of champagne glasses. 'Really well,' I reply to her question.

'I bet you stay over here all the time, don't you?' she says with a knowing look.

'Oh, totally,' I reply casually. 'I moved the last of my stuff out of Jessie's a few weeks ago.'

'You moved out of Jessie's?'

'Yeah.' I'm instantly uneasy at the look on her face. 'His parents came back from the States,' I explain.

'So you're living with Lukas.' It's more of a statement than a question.

'Yes.'

'You're living with your boyfriend.' She seems a bit dumbfounded.

'Yes.'

'Bloody hell, Alice!'

'What?' Now I'm feeling put out.

'That was a bit fast, wasn't it?'

I don't say anything as I pour the champagne.

'I don't mean to have a go,' she says hurriedly. 'I just wasn't expecting it.'

'Why not?' My lips are set in a straight line. 'I don't see what the big deal is.'

'What did your dad say?'

'I haven't . . . He doesn't . . .'

'You haven't told them?' she gasps.

'It's not like that,' I reply firmly. 'It's not that big a deal.'

'It's a huge responsibility.'

'Jesus, Lizzy! When did you turn into my mother?'

She frowns at me and then looks away, hurt.

'Sorry,' I say, although I'm not really sure why I'm the one apologising.

'Don't worry about it,' she replies, not meeting my eyes. 'I'm just a bit surprised, that's all.'

'I don't know why,' I snap. 'It's not like we're getting married or anything.'

'I should hope not!'

I hand her a glass.

'*Would* you marry him?' she asks with narrowed eyes.

'I don't know.' I shrug.

'Do you love him?'

'Yes, of course.'

'More than you loved Joe?'

'What sort of a question is that?' I take a deep breath and exhale loudly.

This time she's the one to apologise. 'Sorry,' she says, hopping down from the countertop. 'I'm being a cow. I've had a shitty week and I'm taking it out on you.'

'It's okay.' I indicate the door to the living room. She leads the way through. 'So what happened with Callum?'

'Oh . . .' She slumps down onto one of the sofas and almost spills her drink. 'Whoa!'

'Sorry. You can get lost in those cushions.'

Suddenly she snorts with laughter and I can't help but join in, relieved to have my friend back.

'Cheers,' she says between giggles. At least the tears have been kept at bay. 'I don't want to go into it too much, but he was being a bit of a shit and I'd had enough.'

'A shit in what way?' I ask.

'I hardly got to see him – he was always out playing football at weekends – and the last straw was him telling me he wants to go to Ibiza this summer with his mates instead of going away again with me.'

'That sucks,' I empathise.

'You don't see much of Lukas, though, do you?'

'Not during the day, but that's the bonus about living together – I see him every night.'

'Fair point. But he goes home to Germany all the time without you?'

'Not all the time,' I say dismissively. 'And it's not like he's going away with his mates; he's going home.'

'To see that girl.'

What the hell? 'He doesn't *see* Rosalinde!' I exclaim. 'He sees his parents! And his nephew and his brother and sister! Anyway, she's engaged,' I feel compelled to add.

'Is she?' she asks with interest.

'Yes. She's marrying some banker.'

'Will you be invited to the wedding?'

'I don't know, Lizzy!'

'I don't mean to be annoying,' she says suddenly. I'm feeling slightly less excited about having her here at the moment.

'Don't worry about it.' I try to calm down. 'Anyway, you were saying about Callum . . .'

'Oh, I don't know. Maybe I'm expecting too much.'

'No, it does sound a bit crap about him wanting to go off on holiday with his mates.'

'Yeah, but they all finish university this year and have been talking about having one last lads' holiday before they all have to grow up and get jobs.'

Is she talking herself into asking him back? I don't know, but I'm staying well out of it.

I hear Lukas's key turn in the lock and I get up to greet him.

'Hello,' I say warmly, giving him a kiss on his lips.

'Champagne!' he exclaims with a look at my glass.

'You don't mind, do you?' I ask with alarm.

'No, no, of course not. It's early, that's all.'

'Don't worry – I've warned Lizzy not to let me forget to cook dinner.'

'You only have to put it in the oven,' he teases. I follow him through to the living room. 'Hello.' He waves at Lizzy.

'Hi!' she replies brightly.

'How was your journey?' he asks.

I go to the kitchen while they make small talk. I should probably get on with the salad.

Harry arrives before Matthew. 'My beautiful Alice,' he says when I answer the door. He brandishes a bottle of red wine in my face, then wraps his arms around me for a hug. I laugh into his shoulder as he squeezes me hard.

'Would you get your filthy hands off my girlfriend,' Lukas jokes as he relieves him of his bottle. They shake hands.

'Come and meet my friend Lizzy,' I say, taking him through and making the introductions.

'It's very nice to meet you,' he says politely to her.

'How did your revision go today?' Lukas asks.

'Frightful,' he replies. 'Symmetry and particle physics.' Blah blah blah, something about mesons, baryons and quark structure. It's like another language to me.

'Have a glass of champagne?' I interrupt.

'I wouldn't say no,' he replies.

Matthew arrives soon afterwards. I see his taxi pull up outside the kitchen window and go to let him in. He hands me an exquisite bouquet of green and white flowers.

'They're beautiful.' I kiss him on his cheek.

'It's been far too long,' he says intently, his hand on my waist. I can't help but think about my conversation with Lukas at the ball. 'How are you?'

'Great! You?'

'Hello, there!' Lukas appears in the hall. I back away into the living room.

Lizzy's eyes widen when she sees Matthew. She tries to sit up straighter on the sofa when he shakes her hand, and then blushes furiously when he collapses down next to her. I smile to myself as I go into the kitchen to put the flowers in a vase. Lukas follows me.

'You okay?' I ask him.

'Why wouldn't I be?' he replies frostily, staring at me for a long moment before going back through to the living room. I shiver inadvertently. For the first time since I met him, his eyes reminded me of his mother's.

Matthew is telling Lizzy about his job when I re-emerge. 'The *Guardian*,' he answers her question about which newspaper he works for.

'Cool!' she enthuses.

'I'm not sure that's the word I'd use to describe it,' he replies good-naturedly.

She giggles. 'No, it's not exactly the *Daily Mirror*, is it?'

'The *Daily Mirror* is "cool"?' Matthew asks her with a raised eyebrow.

She giggles again. 'Okay, maybe not cool, but definitely fun.'

'When will dinner be ready?' Lukas asks me.

'In about five minutes,' I tell him. 'We can sit at the table now, if you like.'

'I'm not sure I'll be able to stand,' Lizzy says, her glass of champagne wobbling precariously as she tries to sit up.

'That sofa has almost swallowed you whole!' Harry laughs and takes the glass from her.

Matthew extricates himself from the cushions and then offers her his hands. She takes them and he pulls her to her feet. She blushes again.

'Let me help you in the kitchen?' she offers, mouthing, '*Phwoar!*' as the boys go through to the dining room.

I laugh under my breath. 'Thought you'd like him.'

'Seriously, *how hot*?' she exclaims when we're out of earshot. 'Does he have a girlfriend?'

'I don't think so,' I reply. I'm sure Lukas would have revealed that piece of information, if nothing else.

'This is delicious,' Matthew enthuses later, a few mouthfuls into his lasagne.

'I can't take any credit,' I reveal before anyone else does. 'I got it from the farm shop at Coton.'

'The fig and mozzarella salad was amazing too,' Lizzy adds.

'I only had to peel the figs,' I reply modestly.

'Well, you managed it triumphantly!' Harry exclaims, raising his glass. We've moved onto red wine. 'Here's to old friends – and new,' he adds with a pointed look at Lizzy.

We chink glasses. I notice my friend pursing her lips. She's done this occasionally throughout dinner, usually when Harry speaks. I don't think she gets him.

'Don't you like Harry?' I ask her later when she comes through to the kitchen to help me prepare dessert: farm-shop meringue nests with cream whipped by *moi* and berries, also washed by yours truly.

She pulls a face. 'It's like they're from another era. Matthew's a toff too, but he's a bit more normal.'

I pause for a moment as her comment sinks in. 'Are you saying Lukas is from another era too?'

She backtracks. 'He's just a bit different, isn't he? Quite proper. Not like Joe.'

The shooting pain is still there, but the alcohol has taken the edge off.

'I can't believe you've brought him up again.'

She looks mortified. 'I'm sorry,' she says quickly. 'I don't know what I'm saying. I've had too much to drink.'

'You hardly know Lukas,' I add bitterly. 'And Harry is lovely,' I say in his defence.

'I'm sorry. He is. He's very nice. And Lukas is too. I'm not really slagging him off.'

Actually, you are. But I let it lie.

'I think Alice will make a terrible teacher!' Harry exclaims when we walk back through with dessert.

'Why?' I reply, slightly affronted as I place a plate down in front of Lukas.

'Those boys won't be able to concentrate if you're in the room.'

'I'm going to be teaching six-year-olds, you idiot!' I thump him on his back. 'And I've had more than enough practice dealing with juveniles over the last two years.'

Matthew cracks up laughing.

'What's this?' Lizzy regards this exchange with confusion.

'I think I'm going to go into teaching,' I explain, sitting back down.

'Are you really?' she asks with surprise. 'In London?'

'No, in Cambridge.' I glance with pride at my boyfriend. 'Lukas has got a job with the university.'

Lukas will be a research associate. Something to do with astrophysics and extragalactic astronomy observational projects. Or something.

Harry pats him on the back. 'Well done, old chap.'

Old chap? Inadvertently my eyes go to Lizzy, but she manages to keep a straight face this time.

'I'm disappointed with your friend,' Lukas says later, when we're climbing into bed.

'What's that supposed to mean?' I keep my voice down so she can't overhear.

'I found her to be quite uncouth.'

'Uncouth? She's not uncouth!'

'Do you know, she actually rolled her eyes when Harry and I were conversing about Minkowski spacetime.' I refrain from commenting. 'And she was fawning all over Matthew,' he adds. 'It was embarrassing.'

'Lukas!' I hiss. 'Give her a break. She's just split up with her boyfr—'

'Exactly!' he interrupts loudly.

'Shh!'

'I would have thought she'd behave better,' he continues. 'She can't be that heartbroken.'

'A little flirting never hurt anyone,' I say reasonably.

'That's what you think, is it?' A chill goes through me at the iciness of his stare. I'm lost for words as he turns his back on me and switches off the light.

Seventeen Months Later

Chapter 47

A little under a year and a half later Rosalinde gets married. She wears a beautiful cream-coloured gown decorated with lace and a shower of Swarovski crystals, with a five-metre train. Her long, blonde hair is intricately twisted into a bun below a diamond tiara that has been handed down to her by her mother and her grandmother before that. Four hundred guests attend her wedding.

I am not one of them.

Lukas is. I think he wants to put some closure on their relationship. He said it would be inappropriate for me to go.

And so I read about it online. The wedding is a big deal in German high society, and I can understand the majority of what went on, thanks to the German lessons which I continue to take, even though I have long since graduated. I got a 2:1, just missing out on a First. Lukas blamed my spending too much time on the river, but I was happy with my result. Naturally he graduated with a First.

I'm currently working in a primary school in the city, after spending a year doing a Graduate Teacher Programme. I'm now fully qualified and I'm enjoying having a class of six- and seven-year-olds all to myself. Mind you, it's only been two weeks, but so far so good, as they say.

The phone rings. It's nine o'clock on a Sunday morning and I'm sitting on the bed, propped up with pillows. We're still in our little cottage on Conduit Head Road. It feels like home now. I reach across to my bedside table and pick up the hand-set.

'Hello?'

'It's me.' Lukas.

'Hi!' I put my laptop to one side and sit up properly. 'How was it?' He's still in Germany. The wedding was yesterday, but he didn't call me last night.

'It was fine.'

'She went through with it, then?' I say with a shaky laugh.

'There was never any doubt in my mind that she would.'

I'm glad he could be so certain. I spent yesterday on tenter-hooks, wondering if Lukas's parents would succeed in getting him to do a last-minute intervention. Maybe now we can all get on with our lives – I feel like I've been ever-so-slightly in limbo since she got engaged. Was that the longest engagement in the history of engagements? I guess not. It felt like it to me, though. And now that it's all over I'm surprised I'm not more relieved. I still feel numb, to be honest.

'I'm coming back on Tuesday,' Lukas says in a quiet voice.

'Are you?' He isn't supposed to return until Saturday. 'Why?'

'There's no point in me staying.'

'Are you okay?' I ask hesitantly.

He sighs. 'I'm fine. I'll speak to you when I get home.'

I feel uneasy and tell him as much.

'It's okay,' he tries to reassure me. 'It's nothing for you to worry about. I'm just exhausted, that's all.'

I'd like to blame his work and the hours he does, but I have a feeling this exhaustion is emotional. The tone of his voice reminds me of when he returned from Germany at the beginning of the year, after Christmas. He seemed mentally fatigued. I suspected his parents had put pressure on him to fix things up with Rosalinde. He didn't deny it when I brought it up. I still haven't met his father or the rest of his family. His mother hasn't come back to England and I haven't been invited to Germany. I should feel slighted – I do feel slighted – but I actually have no inclination to go there when I know the reception I'll receive. They don't – and probably never will – approve of me. Maybe now Rosalinde is out of the picture, Lukas will get some respite. A few months ago they tried to persuade him to return to Germany to live and work. His father had lined up an interview for a research position in the Faculty of Physics at Munich University. Lukas point-blank refused. I've never seen him so angry. He's usually so composed, but on this occasion he lost it. I still remember the sound of his mobile constantly ringing, and him refusing to answer it. He was so cross with them for trying to run his life and not accepting the choices that he had made.

He didn't even go back to Germany this summer. He only went to the wedding because he had a point to make. He wanted to show Rosalinde – and everyone else – that he was happy for her. That there were no regrets, no hard feelings. Like I said, maybe now we can all get on with our lives.

I call Jessie after speaking to Lukas.

'Are you up to anything tomorrow night?' I ask him hopefully.

'Twice in one week?' he exclaims. 'I've never felt so popular.'

'No,' I say awkwardly. 'It's just that Lukas is coming back on Tuesday . . .'

We were supposed to be going to the movies on Friday night, but with Lukas being back early . . .

'Oh,' he says flatly. 'Yeah, yeah, that's fine. We can go tomorrow night, instead.'

'What time do you want to go?' I ask. 'Seven? We could go to Wagamama first?'

'Good plan. See you downstairs.'

He's already there when I arrive. I notice him checking his watch.

'I'm only five minutes late,' I chide.

'I'm starving,' he says, leading the way inside and up the stairs. There are six people ahead of us in the queue.

'How's your job?' he asks.

'Oh, my God, I have been dying to tell you!'

'What?'

'Do you remember the china boy?'

He looks confused, then suddenly: 'Oh! From the punt?'

'Yes!' I'm referring to the boy who called vaginas 'chinas' and consequently made me lose my concentration and bump my head on the bridge.

He laughs. 'How could I forget? What about him?'

'He's in my class!'

'No way?'

'Yes way! He's a right little character. I couldn't work out why I recognised him, but it came to me this afternoon.'

'Hilarious. So you're enjoying it, then?'

'Definitely.'

'You don't miss punting?' He gives me a sideways glance.

'Yeah, of course.' He should know this. It actually feels strange to walk past the river now. My eyes kept welling up during my last tour. Jessie tried to convince me I could go back to work during the school holidays, but once I became a fully qualified teacher, in my heart I knew that that part of my life was over. 'I still miss everyone,' I add.

'It's not the same now that you guys have all left.' I presume he's talking about the other students, like Chris, who only finished his Masters in June. 'It's weird to think that none of you are coming back after this summer.'

'You'll have a fresh crop of students to torment before long.' I try to reassure him.

'Nah. Won't be the same.'

A couple of people in front of us are led away to be seated. We wander forwards in the queue.

'You seem a bit down.' I look up at him.

He doesn't meet my eyes. 'I am a bit.'

I turn to face him. 'Everything okay with Emily?'

'Yeah, yeah, she's great. Wish I got to see more of her.' He glances at me. 'We're talking about getting a flat together.'

'Really? That's great!'

He grins. 'Yeah.'

Emily moved out of Jessie's parents' house as soon as she graduated, but she didn't go back to Scotland. Instead, she went to London. I wondered if that would be the end of their relationship, but they've seen each other most weekends, either in London or in Cambridge. She's working for Social Services in the Child Welfare department.

'Hang on . . .' My mouth drops open. 'Are you moving to London?'

'I think so.' He shrugs. 'Alice,' he prompts, nodding behind me. I turn around to see the waitress standing there, ready to take us to our table.

He doesn't call me China anymore. I didn't notice at first. Now I try to avoid calling him by any name at all. It makes me feel sad to think that we've grown out of our nicknames. Not that I'd ever admit that. I don't know why he stopped. Perhaps we just don't see enough of each other to harness that familiarity.

The restaurant is busy, and there is another couple seated directly to my right and Jessie's left. The girl is chattering away ten to the dozen. Jessie rolls his eyes at me, but I can't smile.

'You alright?' he mouths.

I nod and look down at the menu. I can't believe he's moving to London. The waitress comes back and we place our order. The girl is now regaling her date with a story about something immensely boring that happened to her at work.

'Have you heard from Lukas?' Jessie asks.

'Yesterday,' I confirm.

'How did the wedding go?'

'He didn't really talk about it, but it went well, I think.'

'Why's he coming back early?'

I glance at the girl. I've never heard anyone talk so loudly. It's very off-putting.

'I don't know, exactly,' I reply. 'Your guess is as good as mine.'

The girl gets up to go to the toilet. I exhale loudly, glad of the peace and quiet.

'Do you ever think about Joe?' I'm instantly tense again.

'Of course I do,' I tell him.

'Do you ever consider trying to contact him?'

I shift in my seat. 'I wouldn't know how to start, anymore.'

'You don't want me to call the pub?'

I look up at him sharply. There's something in his expression.

'What is it?' I ask.

He looks uneasy and a terrible sinking feeling settles over me.

'I'm sorry,' he says, glancing up at me. Jessie rarely apologises for anything.

'What for?'

'I don't know why I did it . . . I guess I was just curious . . .'

'What?' I say again. The girl returns and strikes up another loud one-way conversation, but I'm barely aware of her.

'I called the pub a few months ago,' he admits.

My heart skips a beat and my insides fire up with hope. 'And?'

'His parents don't work there anymore.'

The flames in my stomach are instantly snuffed out. 'Where did they go?'

'Manchester, apparently.'

They were my last link to Joe. While I couldn't stand them, just knowing they were there gave me some comfort. Now I have none.

'What made you call?' I ask flatly.

He looks awkward. 'It was after that night of your birthday . . .'

A chill goes through me. We'd all gone out to a club, but Lukas didn't want to be there. I was drinking lager, which I know he hates. He considers it unfeminine, but it was my birthday and I was intent on doing as I pleased. Anyway, I got a bit too drunk and Lukas had to carry me home. The next day Jessie sniped that Lukas had 'dragged' me out of there. That was the way he put it. We had a huge argument – Jessie has always had it in for him, without anywhere near enough justification. I didn't speak to him for a week after that.

The waitress brings our food, but I've lost my appetite. I can tell Jessie regrets bringing Joe up.

'What do you want to see at the movies?' He tries to change the subject.

I feel numb. 'Don't care.'

'In that case, how about *Strike*? It's a documentary on kick-boxing,' he explains when I don't react.

Normally I'd make some sarky remark about how riveting that sounds, but now I just say: 'Whatever . . .'

In the end, we decide to see *The Last Kiss* because *Strike* doesn't start until Friday. But we could have gone to see anything, because my thoughts are elsewhere.

Chapter 48

I'm at work when Lukas returns from Germany. It's starting to drizzle so I cycle home as quickly as I can. He opens the door before I've even pushed my bike up the garden path.

'Hi!' I say. He comes outside and engulfs me in a hug. 'Are you okay?' My voice is muffled by his shoulder.

'I missed you,' he murmurs, stroking my hair.

I pull away and look at him. He seems anguished. 'What's wrong?' I ask.

'Nothing.' He shakes his head vehemently. 'Not now.'

I smile at him and glance down to see that he's in his socks. 'Your feet will be wet through!' I usher him back inside. He tries to hug me again, but I tentatively step out of his grasp.

'Why did you come back early?' I ask, searching his face. He presses his lips to mine. I resist for a moment, but as his kiss becomes more passionate I gently, but firmly, put my hands on his chest and push him away. His behaviour is freaking me out a bit. He's only been away five days. He stares at the carpet, looking crestfallen.

'Do you want me to make you a cup of tea?' I ask, because I

don't know what else to say or how to handle him. He hesitates, but then nods. I hurry into the kitchen.

He's in the living room when I return, sitting in an armchair and staring out of the window. I place a cup and saucer on the table next to him and sit on the sofa, facing him.

'Thanks,' he says.

'Are you alright?' I ask anxiously.

Then he looks up, right into my eyes, and there's an intensity there that I don't recognise. 'I want to marry you.'

'What?'

'I want to marry you,' he says, more fervently.

'What? When?' I splutter.

'Now. As soon as possible. I don't want to wait any longer.'

'But, Lukas . . .'

'Don't you love me?'

'Yes, but . . .' Joe.

'Then why not?'

'I'm only twenty-two!' Joe.

'It doesn't matter! It shouldn't matter!' He gets up and comes to sit beside me. 'I want a life with you. I don't want to wait any longer. I've had enough of my parents trying to control me!' His tone turns to anger. 'I don't want to wait any longer,' he says again.

Joe, Joe, Joe, Joe, Joe. It's like a chant repeating over and over in my mind.

'Say something,' he demands.

'I . . . I can't . . .' I shake my head, hopelessly, and my eyes fill with tears.

'You can't what? Can't speak or can't . . .'

'I can't marry you. Not now.'

'Why not?' He takes my hand, pleading with me. 'Why not?'

'I'm only twenty-two,' I say again in barely a whisper.

'We'll wait a year. We'll get married next summer.'

'I'll only be twenty-three!' I find my voice. 'I don't understand what the rush is.'

'I don't understand why you won't consider it,' he says coldly.

'It's not that I won't . . .' My voice trails off. 'I . . . I . . .'

'What?'

I take a deep breath and wait a moment before speaking. 'Rosalinde was your first love.'

'Well, yes.'

I feel shaky as I look out of the window. 'Joe was mine.'

'Who's Joe?' He's confused.

'A boy I met in Dorset, the summer before I came to university.' I meet his eyes. 'He was my first love. My first . . . everything.'

He stares at me, understanding. And then he returns to his armchair, resting his chin on his hand as he gravely regards me. 'Tell me about him,' he commands.

And so I do, fully aware that my words might drive him away. Accepting that fact, knowing that I might lose him, but unable to keep quiet any longer.

He listens without comment, calmly observing me as I tell him everything.

When I've finished he doesn't speak for some time. The silence is deafening.

'So let me get this straight,' he says eventually in a cold voice. 'You're still in love with a boy who broke his promise to you, who you've fruitlessly searched for, who you will likely never see again, and you're willing to lose *me*, all for the sake of a dream that will never come true?'

I stare at him, not speaking.

He speaks in a low voice. 'I have alienated my family, lost the woman *I* was meant to marry, committed to a life in this country . . . For what? For a girl who I thought loved me. A girl who I thought was mine. But you were never mine, were you?'

Out of the blue his eyes fill with tears, and it's so shocking to me because I've never seen Lukas cry.

'I'm sorry. I'm so sorry.' I scramble over to hold his hands as tears roll down his cheeks. 'I don't know what I'm doing. I don't know why he's still so much on my mind.'

'Don't say that!' His face contorts with pain and I feel distraught for hurting him.

'Please . . . I'm sorry.' My heart feels so full of love for him. Joe did break his promise to me. I must be insane for waiting around for him. It's been four years, for crying out loud! What is wrong with me?

He lets go of my hands and roughly brushes away his tears. I climb up onto his lap and press my face into his neck. A moment later he puts his arms around me and holds me tightly. We stay like that for a very long time.

Chapter 49

That Christmas, Lukas takes me to Germany to meet his family. His mother sends their chauffeur to collect us from the airport. I was kind of hoping it might be Klaus – I think any familiar face would help settle my stomach – but apparently he now works in Berlin.

'Don't be nervous,' Lukas says to me in German, squeezing my hand.

'I'm trying,' I reply, also in German. For the last two months we've attempted to converse in his language as much as possible. I'm not too bad. I wouldn't say I'm good, mind you, but at least I should be able to understand a little bit of what's going on.

Lukas's family live in a stately home on a lake south-west of Munich. By the time we reach it we have already driven through some of the loveliest countryside I've ever seen, past multi-turreted castles and tall pines capped with thick, fluffy snow. Now, in front of me, at the end of a long driveway, is a majestic cream-coloured mansion punctuated with row upon row of arched windows. Snow is melting on the roof and I can make out occasional flashes of red tiling underneath. The lawn and flowerbeds are covered with snow, but nonetheless, after our trip to Wimpole Hall all that time ago, I know that the lawn edges will be perfectly trimmed, with scissors.

'It's beautiful,' I murmur in awe.

'It's home,' he says drily.

The driver pulls up and comes around to open my door. I step onto the snow-crusted gravel and look up at the enormous house. I see movement at one of the windows, but when I look harder there's no one there. I shiver inadvertently. It's cold and I took my coat off for the journey. Lukas joins me at my side of the car and guides me towards the door. I've had my hair cut – although it still comes to well past my shoulders – and a hairdresser blow-dried it straight this morning before our flight. I'm wearing a long, chocolate-coloured woollen skirt, with brand-new brown leather boots that Lukas bought for me especially for this trip, along with a designer coat and scarf. He wants me to look my best, but I'm under no illusions that his family will fall for my charms.

The door opens before we reach it. A man in his forties, smartly dressed in a black suit, bows and welcomes home 'Herr Heuber' and his guest. We step into a grand, double-height hall. The ceiling glints with gold and I look up to see figures carved in stone around the edges. I feel like I'm dreaming.

Lukas speaks in German, but I understand that he's asking the whereabouts of his parents. From what I gather, they're joining us for tea later. We follow the butler – if that's who he is – up the sweeping staircase and along an opulent gilded corridor. He opens a door and I'm taken aback to see that my suitcase is already in the room. The driver must've taken a short cut through another part of the house. Lukas says something to the butler and he bows his way out of the room. I hurriedly thank him in German before he closes the door.

'Wow,' I say to Lukas, sinking down onto the bed. 'Where's *your* bag?' I ask with confusion.

'I'm in the family wing at the other side of the house.'

I instantly feel a pang of homesickness. I've been here only five minutes, but I already miss him.

'Are these the guest quarters?' I ask.

'Yes.'

'Are we not allowed to sleep in the same room, then?' This feels like a lonely place to be.

'No. Not until we're married,' he says poignantly.

Since that day, back in September, he hasn't spoken of marriage. At first it was a relief, then it just felt surreal, almost as though the conversation had never happened. He hasn't brought up Joe, either.

I walk to the window and look out. I'm bothered by the room revelation. His mother knew we'd been sleeping together when she came to visit almost two and a half years ago. She hasn't returned since, but surely she knows we've been living together for nearly two years. Things are obviously serious between us. I take a deep breath and try not to let it get to me. My room overlooks the back gardens. There's a rectangular, man-made lake directly behind the house, and beyond that is a natural lake that seems to reach for miles.

'We go waterskiing in the summer,' Lukas says and I jump at his voice because I didn't realise he was right behind me.

'Sounds fun.'

We're going skiing in a few days. I've never skied before and I'm slightly dreading it. I'm not sure I'd fare any better at waterskiing. I look back at the lake in the garden. It's frozen and there are swans walking on it.

'Hah!' I point. 'Look at those swans!'

He chuckles and pulls me away from the window.

'I'd better go and get changed,' he says. 'I'll come and get you before we go downstairs.'

'I'm scared,' I admit.

'Don't be,' he says gently, kissing me on my nose. I kiss him on his lips, not wanting him to leave. He slowly pulls away.

'Can I come with you?' I ask desperately.

He regards me with amusement.

'Do you really have to get changed?' I know I sound a bit manic. 'Am I supposed to get changed? I hope not, because this is my best outfit.'

'You look beautiful,' he says.

'You look fine too,' I tell him. 'You don't really need to change, do you?'

I kiss him and push him onto the bed. He starts to laugh and tries to get up again, but I keep pushing him backwards until finally he gives in and lies there, with me in his arms.

'Okay, I won't get changed,' he says.

'Phew.'

'But we should go downstairs soon.'

'Okay.' Not yet, though.

I hold Lukas's hand as we walk down the corridor together, going back the way we came. There's not a soul to be seen as we step down the sweeping staircase, and turn left at the bottom. Lukas drops my hand and I follow him to a large door. He pushes it open. I instantly hear voices and instinctively step behind him, before berating myself for trying to hide. He reaches out and takes my hand again, leading me into a huge room where the walls are dark red and hung with oil paintings. There are several unfamiliar people seated on antique gilded chairs and once more I feel like I'm in a dream, then, suddenly:

'LUKAS!' A dark-haired man in his late twenties shouts with joy and leaps to his feet, rushing over to swamp my boyfriend in a bear hug. They pat each other's back and slap each other's cheeks with delight as they chatter away in German. I am too on edge to concentrate on understanding, and before I know it the man has turned to me.

'You must be Alice,' he says affectionately, taking my hand. 'I'm Markus.' And all of a sudden we're surrounded by people. I meet Markus's wife, Eva, who is serene and beautiful, but seems nice. Their son, Max, is a cuddly toddler with blond hair and a cheeky grin, and Lukas's sister, Frieda, is warm and welcoming. I barely have a chance to speak to Lukas's matronly aunt, gruff uncle or two cousins, one of whom has a wife and a little girl of about five, because Frieda ushers me away to one of the antique sofas. She's taller than me by a couple of inches and is reasonably big-boned. She has light-blonde hair cut in a jaw-length bob, her eyes are green and her smile is blinding. She's two years older than Lukas, which makes her twenty-six.

'I'm so happy to finally meet you!' she exclaims as soon as we're seated. Lukas is in the midst of his extended family. 'I can't believe my little brother kept you from us for so long!' I laugh awkwardly and shrug. 'But you're here, now.' She pats my hand. 'Tell me everything about yourself!'

'Um . . .'

'Frieda, leave her be!' Markus exclaims as he and the rest of the family return to join us on the opulent chairs and sofas.

Frieda snaps something in German which I can't understand and Markus tuts. She quickly turns back to me.

'Ignore my brother. He's a bore.'

He seems nothing like a bore to me, but I think she's joking.

'We have so much to talk about!' she cries.

'You have four days,' Markus says in German, before apologising to me in English.

'It's okay, I understood,' I tell him. 'My German is not very good, but I'm trying to learn.'

'Aw!' Frieda rubs my arm with great affection. 'She's so sweet, Lukas!'

'Never mind,' Markus says. 'We will speak in English for the duration of your visit.'

I feel bad. 'You don't have to . . .'

'Absolutely we will!' Frieda exclaims. 'It gives us a chance to practise.'

'It doesn't sound like you need to practise,' I say. Their English appears perfect to me.

The door opens and everyone starts as Lukas's mother walks through, accompanied by a slight grey-haired man about ten years her senior. Along with everyone else, I quickly get to my feet. The atmosphere is wholly changed.

'Be seated, be seated,' Frau Heuber says in German, waving her hand to illustrate her words. Lukas nods at me to indicate that I should remain standing. I do so, trying not to fidget.

'Aah, Lukas,' she says, spying her younger son.

'Hello, Mother,' he replies. 'Father.' He goes to kiss her hand and shake his father's, before beckoning to me. I step out through the feet of his extended family, aware, as though in a dream, that even the children have fallen silent.

'Welcome to our home, Alice,' his mother says with an icy, penetrative stare.

'Thank you.' I find myself bowing slightly. What the hell?

'Father, this is Alice.' Lukas speaks in English. I hope they don't mind too much.

His father grunts an acknowledgement.

'Perhaps we should go through,' his mother says. It's not a question. Once more the others scramble to their feet. We wait patiently as Lukas's parents lead the way to the adjoining dining room, where a long mahogany table has been laid with china. His mother sits at one end of the table and his father at the other. Lukas sits beside me and squeezes my hand under the table.

Afternoon tea is a formal affair, and it's hard to enjoy the many delights that appear on the table because I feel too ill at ease. Frieda tries to make conversation with me, but whenever she gets too animated her father snaps at her in German. It's uncomfortable to see. Eventually his parents take their leave, along with the matronly aunt and gruff uncle, and the room visibly relaxes once only the twenty-somethings and children remain.

'Sometimes I think we live in the nineteenth century,' Frieda jokes, and I can't help but giggle, even though Markus frowns at her. I'm glad to have found a like-minded person. I think we're going to get on well.

Later I manage to escape with Lukas for a stroll around the garden. The light is quickly fading and it's cold, but there's no wind so it's not unbearable. We wander past the man-made lake to the lake at the end of the garden. There's a summerhouse there, lit with fairy lights; icicles hang from the eaves. We stand on the porch and Lukas pulls me close.

'It's beautiful here,' I say, permanently awestruck. 'I can't believe you grew up with all of this.'

He shrugs. 'I didn't know any different.'

'Don't you ever feel homesick?' I ask, studying his face.

'Sometimes,' he admits.

'I didn't know that.'

Why didn't I know that? Isn't that something I should know?

'I'll take you to the Christmas market in Munich tomorrow,' he says.

'That would be great.' Pause. 'Would you like to move back here?'

He thinks for a moment before answering. 'Yes.'

The thought sends a chill through me.

'But not yet,' he says.

'What does Markus do?' I ask suddenly. 'And Eva?'

'Markus works with my father.'

'Eva?'

'She's a lawyer, for now.'

'For now?'

'Once Markus inherits she'll run the house and the estate.'

'Why can't she be a lawyer too?'

'It wouldn't work.'

I give him a perplexed look.

He sighs. 'It's okay if you don't understand, but when she married Markus she took on certain responsibilities. *This* is her life now.'

'I *don't* understand,' I say firmly. 'But never mind. I don't suppose it matters if everyone's happy about it.'

'They are,' he says.

Four days later we drive to Ischgl in Austria to go skiing. Lukas's father lends him a black four-wheel-drive Mercedes G-Wagen, and I grip the armrest tightly as he navigates the Alps with a look of satisfaction on his face. I know he misses his Porsche. The money from its sale has long since been spent on our rent and living expenses, but it's only a matter of time before he'll buy another car.

The journey along the winding mountain roads is far from relaxing, yet with every mile I feel weight slide from my shoulders. We weren't with Lukas's parents for long, but it felt like forever. The pressure to perform was immense. I went there with the attitude that I would not be bowed by them – that they're no better than me – but I felt far less brave once I was there in that enormous mansion. Luckily Lukas's siblings, partners and children continued to make me feel welcome, even if I never felt comfortable enough to truly be myself.

We're staying at a modern five-star hotel with big windows looking out over the snow-covered mountains. There's an expensive bottle of champagne waiting on ice for us in our super-luxurious suite. I fall onto the bed and sigh with happiness as the last of the weight slips away.

'Happy?' he asks.

'Mmm.' My eyes are closed, but I feel the mattress move as he hovers above me. I open my eyes to look into his.

'You did really well,' he says earnestly.

'With your parents?' I ask.

'Yes. With everyone.'

I prop myself up on the pillows so I can converse with him more easily. 'The others were easy to get along with,' I say.

'I'm glad you liked them.'

'I did. I do,' I correct myself. 'I hope your parents don't disapprove of me too much,' I add with a smile.

'No.' He shakes his head and looks grave. 'They'll get used to you with time.'

What an odd thing to say. 'Let's hope so,' I say. He fails to spot the sarcasm. 'So what do you want to do now?' I ask. He's going to hit the pistes tomorrow, while I plan to take to the nursery slopes with a personal instructor. Lukas is keen for me to learn as quickly as I can so we can go skiing together – that won't be this trip, though. I hope I enjoy it – the spa and heated pool looked pretty damn enticing to me – but I reckon I could just about manage tobogganing if all goes wrong.

'I thought we'd take a ride up the mountains and watch the sunset,' he suggests.

'Sounds lovely.'

We manage to secure a cable car all to ourselves and it glides up, up, up the mountain to the very top, where the snow is the purest white and the sky is the bluest blue. Ischgl is a tiny dot far below. I notice Lukas watching with envy as skiers shoot off down the slopes. I bet he's a brilliant skier – he's good at everything else.

'Tomorrow,' I say with a grin, squeezing his thickly gloved hand. He turns to face me and his expression is a mix of emotions. 'What are you looking like that for?' I tease, but he doesn't smile.

'I love you,' he says.

'I love you too.'

'No, I *love* you, Alice.' I'm shocked to realise that he's close to tears. 'When you said Rosalinde was my first love . . . You were wrong.' He shakes his head fervently. '*You're* my first love. I love *you*. I've never loved anyone more.'

I swallow. I so want to be able to say the same about him. Out of the blue I feel like screaming with frustration. JOE IS GONE! He's in my past. Lukas is my future. He may not be perfect, he may be a bit aloof at times, but he's also smart, sexy and anything but ordinary, And... he's here. He's never left me. He's never deserted me. He has always come back to me when he's said he would. I know, without a shadow of a doubt, that he loves me. I want to slap myself around the face for not being able to accept that this is enough.

Suddenly Lukas pulls off his glove and delves into his coat pocket. He doesn't meet my eyes and it's like the world around us has come to a standstill as he kneels on the brittle snow and presents me with a diamond ring.

'Alice Simmons,' he says in a clear, precise voice. 'Will you marry me?'

He sounds so formal, so ... *nervous*, I realise with a flood of love for him. Finally he meets my eyes and I know that I can give him no other answer.

'Yes.'

Goodbye, Joe.

Chapter 50

'That is the most enormous fuck-off diamond I have ever seen.'

I smile at Lizzy and take my hand away.

'Seriously, how do you lift your arm?' she asks.

'Oh, stop it,' I chide.

'Husband. *Husband*,' she emphasises the word. 'Husband,' she repeats.

'Stop it!' I say again. 'He's not my husband yet.'

'It won't be long, though. You may as well get used to calling him it.'

'Stop going on and help me find a wedding dress.'

We're waiting in a bridal shop for an appointment I booked six weeks ago. I've gone to London for a weekend of shopping.

'Are you sure the Husband isn't going to have one made for you?' she asks wryly.

That's a really good point. 'He'd better not,' I say. 'This is one dress I'm choosing myself.'

'I hope he knows that,' she mutters.

'He does,' I say firmly, making a mental note to double-check later.

The sales assistant flourishes through and invites us into the hallowed boutique, where rows and rows of white and cream gowns are lined up on padded silk coat hangers.

'Whoa,' Lizzy says, looking around.

'Let's start over here,' I direct.

'You seem remarkably calm considering the wedding is only months away.'

'Why shouldn't I be calm?' I ask, not really wanting an answer.

'I still don't understand what the rush is,' she says.

'Lizzy, can we please not go there again?'

I've had this discussion before, both with Lizzy, and with my parents. Lukas's father turns sixty next summer, and apparently things are growing serious between Frieda and her boyfriend, who I didn't meet at Christmas. Lukas persuaded me that we should secure a date for this year before any other family commitments got in the way. And so we're getting married in August. This August. Five and a half months away.

AAAARRRRRRGGGGGGHHHHHHHH!!!! Deep breath.

'I can't believe you agreed to get married in Germany,' she says.

'Neither can I,' I admit. Lukas's mother insisted. I found out later that he asked his parents for their blessing – or permission, I'm not sure which – when we were at his house over Christmas. His mother agreed to the engagement on the condition that they hosted the wedding. My parents were a little put-out. I'm their only child and my mum, in particular, had always assumed she'd play a large part in organising my Big Day. I feel bad for hurting her feelings, but I hope she'll understand when she meets Lukas's family. Things have to be a certain way when you come from high society. Or whatever.

'Anyway, she's dealt with most of the arrangements so far, so I'm trying to go with the flow.'

'You're a better woman than I am,' Lizzy says. 'Ooh, this one's pretty.'

I turn to see the glittering gown she's extracted from the rail. I've been pulling out dress after dress and not really seeing any of them.

'Mmm, it is,' I agree.

'Can she try this one on?' Lizzy asks the sales assistant, who rushes over to take it from her. We continue looking.

'Are Jessie and Emily coming to the wedding?' she asks.

'I hope so.'

'I didn't think the Husband was too keen on them.'

He's not keen on you, either. I keep this revelation to myself.

'Can you stop calling him that? Anyway, it doesn't matter what he thinks. They're my friends and they're coming to my wedding.'

If they want to. I'm not entirely convinced that they will. News of my engagement went down like a lead balloon. At least Mum and Dad have come around to the idea. They may have expressed some concerns about us getting married so quickly – *and* in Germany – but they do like Lukas and they know he makes me happy.

'Did you have a nice time?' Lukas asks me later.

'Yes, thank you. Lukas, you do know that I want to choose my own wedding dress, don't you?'

He frowns. 'Do you honestly believe I would choose it for you?'

'No, not really . . .'

'Is this about your ball gowns?'

Note the use of the plural, here. I attended my second and final

Trinity ball in a dress that was once more chosen and paid for by Lukas. Lizzy doesn't even know about that one, but it didn't escape Jessie and Emily's attention. I seem to remember that was the first time Jessie called Lukas a control freak.

'That's completely different,' I say, brushing him off. 'But this is my wedding dress. If nothing else, that's the one thing I want to have my say on.'

'Of course,' he soothes, helping me out of my coat. I've barely got past the front door. 'And you will have. Did you find anything that you liked?' he asks casually as he hangs my coat on the hall-stand.

'Not really.' My shoulders slump. He takes my hands and looks down at me.

'Listen,' he says gently. 'I know you want to exert your authority, but don't cut off your nose to spite your face.'

'What's that supposed to mean?'

A week later I fly to Paris to meet with his family's dressmaker.

Chapter 51

It all spirals out of my control in the end. I don't know whose wedding I'm going to, but it doesn't feel like mine. I'm detached as I sit in my room at Lukas's house – yes, in the guest wing – and it still feels lonely, even though my parents are next door and Lizzy and Callum are across the hall. That relationship has been tempestuous, to say the least. But they're back on again at the moment and are even talking about moving in together. They both still live in Edinburgh, but I know Lizzy misses London.

There's a knock at my door. 'Come in!' I call.

Frieda pushes the door open. 'Rise and shine,' she says, proffering a tray laden with cups, a milk jug, a teapot and extra hot water.

I sit up in bed and smile at her. 'Where did you get that from?'

'I stole it from Mariella on the way up.'

Mariella is the family's longest-serving staff member.

'How are you feeling?' She places the tray on a table under one of the grand arched windows. There are four in my room alone.

'Okay,' I say.

'Did you sleep well?'

'No,' I admit. It's only six thirty now, but I've been awake since five.

'It's a big day.' Even though she's speaking quietly, I can hear the excitement in her voice. She's one of my bridesmaids. Lizzy is my chief bridesmaid, and I have three others, one of whom I met only yesterday. Like I said, I'm going with the flow.

Well, trying to. Lukas and I did have a bit of a row – if it's possible to have a *bit* of a row – about Emily. I said if I was going to have five bridesmaids then she should be one of them. But his family is bigger than I realised and there are so many politics . . . In the end I gave in, only because I had to concede that he's right: I do hardly see her these days.

'The hairdresser is already here,' Frieda tells me.

'Is she?' I ask with alarm, getting out of bed.

'Don't worry!' she exclaims. 'There's no rush.'

If my room was on the other side of the house I would have seen her arrive, but I face the lake.

Lizzy, Callum and my parents were all completely blown away by the house. The gardens are so lush and green at the moment, although they're not as pretty as they were back in April when Lukas and I came here for Easter. That trip was supposed to involve some serious wedding planning, but his mother had organised practically every last detail by then. Like I said, this doesn't really feel like my wedding. But that's not to say it won't be spectacular. You should see the size of the marquees that have been erected on the back lawn overlooking the lake. They're dripping with fairy lights and I know it will look beautiful. But right now everything feels very surreal. I hope I'll feel more connected to the proceedings when it comes to saying, 'I do.'

There's another knock at my door.

'Come in,' I call again.

Lizzy pushes open the door. My face falls when I see her expression, but then she spots Frieda and quickly recovers.

'Oh, hello!' she says.

'*Guten Morgen*,' Frieda says with a grin.

'What's wrong?' I ask her with concern.

'Nothing,' she replies dismissively, her eyes flitting towards Frieda.

'The hairdresser is already downstairs,' Frieda tells her. 'Would you like a quick cup of tea?'

'Sure.'

They try to make small talk, but I'm distracted. Her face . . . She looked . . . terrified.

The hours whizz past like minutes. The wedding is at one o'clock today, but there's so much to do, so much to think about. Not that I need to do or think about anything – it's all being done for me. I keep wishing I had five minutes to myself to collect my thoughts, but there are bridesmaids, make-up artists, hairdressers, dress designers and God knows who else permanently buzzing around my room. I feel so abstract and so disconnected from all of it – I'm craving time and space to get my head together, but neither is forthcoming. I keep catching Lizzy looking at me with a strange expression on her face, but if I ask her what's wrong she rearranges her features. Finally my hair and make-up are sorted and there's nothing left for me to do other than force down a light snack so I don't faint at the altar. I'll be buttoned into my dress after that – I'm currently still in my dressing gown. I take Lizzy to one side.

'You're going to have to tell me what's bothering you before I walk down the aisle,' I say gravely. She regards me with that expression again: fear.

'Can we go to my room?' she asks quietly, her eyes darting around at all the people.

I grab my mum and confide that I'm going to escape with Lizzy for some quiet time.

'I think I'll do the same with your father,' she tells me. 'I'll let everyone know not to bother you for a while.'

'Thanks, Mum.'

I give her a kiss and follow Lizzy out of my room. Callum is getting ready at the hotel where Jessie and Emily are staying, so as to keep out of the way. He and Lizzy had a few drinks with them after the rehearsal dinner last night, while I came back here to get an early night.

Lizzy gently closes the door behind me and I turn on her immediately.

'What is it?'

She takes a deep breath. Her expression has changed. Now it's . . . pity?

'It might not be him,' she starts.

I'm confused. 'Who?'

She walks to her dressing table and picks up a DVD case. She turns around and hands it to me. It's a movie called *Strike*. I vaguely remember hearing something about it. On the front there's a picture of a man's muscled back, partly cast in shadow.

'What's this?' I ask.

'It's a documentary about kick-boxing. Jessie lent it to Callum for us to watch last night.'

Now I remember. This is the film that Jessie wanted to see last autumn. It hadn't come out yet so we saw something else instead.

'What about it?' I have no idea what's going on.

'The guy in it . . . He looked like . . . Joe.'

I knew she was going to say his name a split second before she said it. I sink down onto the bed and stare at the DVD case.

'Put it on,' I say in a monotone.

She doesn't say another word; she just gets her laptop out of a drawer and places it on my lap. The DVD is still inside and the movie is halfway through, so all she has to do is press Play.

I recognise his voice instantly. He's talking about fighting, but I can't see his face. All I can see is a figure in a dark-grey hoodie punching a punch bag, while his commentary plays over the top. And then suddenly the hooded figure attacks the bag with a high, powerful kick and his hoodie flies back to reveal his face. I nearly knock the computer off my knees in shock. Lizzy swiftly takes it from me before I break it.

'It's Joe!' I gasp.

My friend's face is wracked with anxiety. 'I'm so sorry. I didn't know if I should show it to you . . .'

'It's Joe,' I say again. 'It's him.' I feel breathless and dizzy, like I'm going to faint.

'I'm so sorry, Alice.' She's fretful and worried.

'You'd better get Jessie,' I say.

She looks perplexed. 'Why?'

'You'd better get him.' I don't know why. I just need him here. I feel like I'm having an out-of-body experience. She calls him on her phone, but I don't take in what she's saying. I'm staring at the laptop on the dressing table. I daren't put the movie back on again.

She ends the call and comes to sit next to me. She takes my hand. Mine is limp.

'I thought I recognised him, but I wasn't one hundred per cent sure,' she says. 'He looks . . .'

'Different,' I interject. He's cut his hair – it's short and black – and his body is more muscular and toned. 'What happened to him?' I whisper.

'I don't know.' She shakes her head.

'Why didn't he come for me?' My eyes fill with tears.

She squeezes my hand. There's nothing she can say about that.

'I know this is all really big.' She waves her hands around her. 'But you don't have to go through with it. It's not too late. You could still track him down.' She picks up the DVD case. 'It says on the credits his name is Joseph Strike,' she tells me.

'Joseph Strike?' I ask with dulled surprise. 'Not Joe Strickwold?'

'No. Joseph Strike. I guess it sounds better. It's more showbiz.'

I don't know him anymore. It hits me like a ton of bricks. The Joe I knew wouldn't have changed his name. Maybe he's altered beyond all recognition. He won't be the boy I once knew. I *know* Lukas. I know where I stand with him. I'm not going to hurt him like Joe hurt me.

'Tell Jessie not to come,' I say in a flat voice.

'What? Why?'

'I need to get dressed.'

She looks startled as I calmly stand up. 'Alice,' she says.

'And you need to get dressed too,' I add. I can't meet her eyes.

'Don't you want to watch any more of it?' she asks in a gentle voice.

'No.' I shake my head. 'There's no point.'

*

I'm not me as I walk in a daze down that long, long aisle lined with over four hundred guests – most of whom I don't know. I see Jessie's red hair in my peripheral vision as I pass him, but I don't look his way; I don't want his sympathy. I hold my dad's slightly shaking arm tightly as he guides me towards married life with my new husband. My husband who is not and who will never be my first love, and that's got to be okay because I can't turn back now.

I see Lukas up at the end watching me solemnly as I approach and I remind myself that I love him. It doesn't matter that I don't feel it right now, right this second. At this very moment, I feel numb. I don't feel anything at all.

Twenty minutes later we're married.

Three and a Half Years Later

Chapter 52

It's like someone drugged me the day I got married. I wasn't me. I managed to shut out that DVD and barely think of Joe as I flittered around like a social bloody butterfly, making small talk in a foreign language and ignoring my friends because they knew way, way, *way* too much about the old Alice. That Alice was dead and buried. And I didn't even mourn her.

Not at first, anyway. And certainly not for the first four days of our honeymoon. Then reality started to set in. I had to nurse Lukas because he got 'food poisoning', which turned out to be a stomach bug. Naturally I caught it and consequently spent a miserable day throwing up my guts in our suite-on-stilts in the Maldives while he went on a full-day's dive trip. Sitting there in a cold sweat on our immaculate bathroom floor in front of a vomit-stained toilet was bizarrely the most human I had felt since weeks before our wedding. And it struck me – *finally* – that I was married.

And I had found Joe.

I threw up again.

When I was done being sick I gingerly went outside to sit on the porch overlooking the crystal clear ocean. I needed air to clear my head – even if the air was a bit muggy.

How did Joe end up filming a kick-boxing documentary? What happened to him after we both left Dorset? Did he fall into a black hole like I did? Or did he pick himself up and move on, never to look back? I knew one thing: I had to try to speak to him. Now more than ever I needed answers. Without them I didn't think I could give myself wholly to building a life with my new husband.

The thought of contacting Joe ate away at me over the course of our honeymoon, but it wasn't until we returned home that I decided to confide my intentions to Lukas. I thought honesty was the best policy – I didn't want our marriage to be founded on deceit – but as I told him about the DVD, his stare grew harder and colder until it chilled my bones.

'*If you* ever *try to contact him again, our marriage is over*.'

Those were the first words he said to me. I desperately tried to explain I wasn't seeking a reunion with Joe, just some answers so I could move on, but he was resolute.

A few days later I came home from town to find Lukas watching *Strike* on DVD. I've never seen him so jealous. When he saw my face he got to his feet and kicked the DVD player. Not the DVD, the actual player. He kicked it again and again, paying no attention to my screams as he picked it up and threw it across the room. When he'd finally stamped open the machine to find a still-intact disc he very coldly, very calmly, snapped it in two before demanding I give him my wedding ring.

'No,' I said.

'Give it to me.'

'No,' I said more strongly, backing away from him as he started to come towards me. I ran into the bathroom and locked the door until he'd calmed down.

That was three and a half years ago. So much has changed since then.

Lukas and I bought a house in Newnham, near the city centre. He got a promotion and I continue to work as a teacher in a local school. I adore my current class, a group of six- and seven-year-olds with so much character and energy that they keep me constantly on my toes. I love children, but I'm not ready to have one of my own just yet. Unlike Lukas. He's been talking about trying for a baby ever since Rosalinde had a son two years ago. Sometimes it feels like a competition.

My parents are great. My dad took early retirement and has never seemed better. Mum's latest art collection sold incredibly well and they've been talking about relocating to Brighton to open a B&B.

Sadly, I can't say the same of Lizzy's mother. Susan's cancer returned in force, and this time she lost her battle. Lizzy was devastated. She moved back to London to be with her father and sister in her mum's last few months. Callum wasn't very supportive and Lizzy finally called time on their relationship, but not before they had one last stint of make-up sex which got her pregnant. She gave birth eighteen months ago to a beautiful baby girl known as Eleanor Susan McCall, who has grown into a chubby-cheeked toddler called Ellie, with blue eyes and wavy brown curly hair like her mother's. I try to be there for my friend as much as I can. I can't imagine what it's like to have a child so soon after losing your mother. Just the thought of it makes a lump form in my throat. Lizzy currently lives with her father and sister at home, but is wondering if it might be time to stand on her own two feet.

As for Jessie and Emily, their relationship is going from strength to strength. They're in London now and I try to catch up with them when I can, which isn't as often as I'd like. Jessie tried to ring me a couple of times over Christmas, but I still haven't had a chance to return his calls.

Frieda did get married, and her wedding was even more spectacular than ours. I shouldn't admit it, but I enjoyed it more. I still don't feel at ease in Lukas's house, but it's better now that we're married. At least we're allowed to sleep in the same room. We went there for Christmas and Markus announced that Eva is pregnant with their third baby. This gave Lukas another excuse to pile on the pressure. But I'm not ready. Not yet.

'Be careful, Bennie.' I'm on playground duty and my class has returned to school after the Christmas holidays with even more energy than usual. I'm blaming all the sugar. It's had the opposite effect on me. It's a cold and dreary January and I feel lethargic and bloated after eating too much gingerbread in Germany. I've become oddly addicted to the stuff.

Bennie continues to karate-kick an imaginary villain near the climbing frame.

'POW! POW!' he shouts.

'You'll need a cold compress for your foot if you're not careful,' I warn him again. 'Cold compress' has been part of my everyday vocabulary since I became a teacher. Something which greatly amuses Lukas.

He continues to ignore me. He's one of my more challenging

pupils. Another child comes a bit too close so I hurry over to him. 'Bennie.'

'No!' he shouts. 'I'm Joseph Strike! POW! POW!' Kick! Kick!

That imaginary villain might as well be my stomach.

'Who did you say you were?' I feel like someone has just walked over my grave as I bend down to speak to him.

'Joseph Strike. POW! POW!'

I try to regain my composure and stand up. 'Go and play on the slide. Now!'

His shoulders slump dejectedly and he sulks off.

I don't know how I get through break time, but as soon as I'm in the staff room I make a beeline for a computer and type the name Joseph Strike into Google. I feel light-headed as a gazillion links come up. I click on one which takes me to the IMDb: the Internet Movie Database.

It's his actor page. My stomach cartwheels when I see his headshot. He's unbelievably good-looking, his jawline appearing more defined than it was at the age of eighteen, and there's a shadow of stubble across his tanned features. His hair is short, his eyes are as black as night, and he's looking past the camera, only half-smiling.

'Look at you, checking out pictures of Joseph Strike.'

I jolt at the sound of my colleague's voice. It's Roxy. She teaches the eight-year-olds.

'He's well hot, isn't he?'

'How . . . how do you know about him?' I stammer.

She laughs in disbelief. 'Where have you been for the last few weeks? Haven't you seen *Sky Rocket*?'

'We've just got back from Germany,' I say weakly.

'Don't they have cinemas over there, love?' She's teasing me, but I can't smile. Lukas's family aren't into film or watching TV. It's all about walking, skiing, reading and, when I'm lucky, playing snooker.

Sky Rocket does sound familiar. 'I have heard of it,' I murmur.

'I should think so. That movie has been an even bigger hit than Santa this Christmas. You've *got* to check it out,' she urges.

Roxy leans forward and nudges my hand off the mouse, scrolling down to reveal a film poster. There are five actors in the picture, but Joe is almost unrecognisable. He's wearing a futuristic outfit and is looking up, so I can't see his face properly. I vaguely remember seeing this image now, but I wouldn't have known this was him.

Roxy continues to scroll down to his filmography. There are seven movies listed.

'Wait!'

'What?' she asks.

How could I not have known about all of these films? *Strike* is at the very bottom. 'Have you seen all of them?' I feel like my throat is closing up.

'Half of them haven't come out yet,' she says, tutting good-naturedly at my stupidity. 'I saw *Strike* just last weekend. I bought it on Amazon straight after seeing *Sky Rocket*. *Phwoar!* And I did see *Hong Kong Kid* and *Capture* when they came out a year or so ago, but he only had small parts in them. Look –' she peers closely at the screen – '*Night Fox* is still in post-production. So is *Phoenix Seven*, and he's currently filming *Magnitude Mile*.'

My heart is pounding like a jackhammer.

'Can you go back to the top?' I ask. She does. It says he was born Joseph Strike, but that's not true; his name is Joe Strickwold.

His age is correct, though: he's two months older than me, which makes us both twenty-six.

'He's so hot,' she sighs, nodding at his headshot. 'Although that picture doesn't do him justice. Damn, I was devastated when Johnny Jefferson married that girl recently. Thank God there's some fresh eye candy on the scene ...'

But I'm not listening to her rant about a rock star. I've got other things on my mind.

I spend the rest of the day on autopilot. As soon as I can escape I go home and call Jessie.

'Jessie? It's me, Alice.'

'Hey,' he says gently. There's concern in his voice. 'Have you seen it?'

He knows exactly why I'm ringing. He tried to call me twice over Christmas – I assume, about this.

'No.' Pause. 'Have you?'

'Em and I caught it last weekend.'

'What's it like? What's *he* like?'

'He's ... good.' He sounds impressed. 'You can understand what all of the fuss is about. If you're a girl,' he adds nonchalantly.

I notice that my hands are shaking.

'What are you going to do?' he asks.

'Sorry?'

'Are you going to try to contact him?'

'Why would I do that?'

'I just thought—'

'No,' I interrupt. 'No, I'm not going to try to contact him. If I was going to do that I would have done it years ago.'

There's silence at the other end of the line. The phone beeps to let me know there's another call coming in. 'I'd better go,' I say, informing him of the other caller. We hang up and I answer the phone. This time it's Lizzy.

'Are you okay?' she asks, slightly breathless. It doesn't surprise me that she, also, belatedly found out about Joe in *Sky Rocket*. She doesn't make it to the movies much. In fact, she barely makes it out of the front door on some days.

'Yes,' I reply, taking a deep breath. 'I've been on the phone to Jessie.'

'Did he tell you?'

'No, a little boy in my class did. When did the name Joseph Strike become part of a six-year-old's vocabulary?'

'Bloody hell,' she says with disbelief. 'I couldn't believe it when I saw him being interviewed on a daytime chat show.'

'Where?' I ask quickly. 'In this country?'

'Yes. He's in London at the moment.'

'He's here?'

Suddenly it feels very real.

'You could try to contact him again, you know,' she says softly.

Again.

She's the only one who knows my darkest secret. Despite Lukas's threat that our marriage would be over if I ever tried to contact Joe, in my heart of hearts I couldn't let it lie. I felt sick and nervous and guilty and deceitful, but I managed to speak to someone in the film distribution company that had made *Strike*, and their press department informed me that Joe had moved to Los Angeles. They gave me his agent's details – a man called Nicky Braintree – and I rang and asked to speak to him. He couldn't take my call and I didn't want to leave a message. I almost gave up, but a few days later I managed to ring him again. This time he was on another call, but I held on and waited, telling the receptionist it was personal. Finally he came on the line . . .

'My name is Alice . . .' I didn't want to give him my married name, Heuber, but Simmons felt fraudulent.

'Yes?'

'I'm trying to get hold of Joe . . . Joseph Strike.'

'You and everyone else, sweetheart. What's it about?'

His comment threw me. I managed to stammer out a reply about how I used to know him.

'I'll tell him you called,' he said shortly. 'Give me your number and I'll—'

'Couldn't you give me his number?' I asked, already knowing the answer.

'I can't give out my client's details, darling,' he said in a patronising tone. 'Like I said, give me your number and I'll pass on the message.'

'No, I, er, I can't.'

I couldn't risk him calling with Lukas around.

He sighed and muttered something about time wasting, before hanging up on me.

I've never tried to contact him again. I also resisted Googling him. I tried to put him out of my mind once and for all for the sake of my husband.

'No,' I tell Lizzy. 'I can't risk my marriage.'

And, anyway, now I'm just some girl Joe shagged before he became famous.

The pain at this thought is crippling.

Chapter 53

I plan to tell Lukas about Joe's new-found fame before he finds out from someone else. I'm worried that he's going to hit the roof like last time, but that was three and a half years ago; a lot of water has passed under the bridge since then.

He doesn't usually get home from work until about six thirty, so I knock off my marking and my preparation for tomorrow's classes, and then I crack on with making him his favourite dinner: fillet steak with green peppercorn sauce and hand-cut chips. I'm hoping that this meal will soften the blow. He arrives home at quarter to seven and he looks exhausted.

'I hate this perpetual drizzle,' he says with a sigh as he takes off his coat. 'I was hoping we'd be able to go for a drive to the Norfolk coast this weekend, but the weather forecast is miserable.' I go into the hall and put my arms around his waist.

'Hey, you,' I say, gazing up at him.

He looks down at me and gives me a quick kiss. 'What's that cooking?'

I tell him, although I have yet to put the steaks on.

'Mmm. I'm starving. Shall I open a bottle of champagne?' He never calls it bubbly.

'Um . . .' I don't think this is going to feel like a celebration anytime soon, but whatever makes him happy. 'Sure.'

'How was your day?' he asks as we walk into the kitchen.

'Fine,' I reply breezily. This is my chance to tell him about Bennie, but I chicken out. 'How was yours?'

'Good. We made a breakthrough with the blah, blah, blah.' I have no idea what he's talking about. 'You haven't any idea what I'm talking about, have you?' he asks with a raised eyebrow.

'Not now, not ever,' I reply with a grin. 'You're the brainiac in this family.'

Ouch. With a short, sharp shock I'm reminded of Joe. There's no getting away from this.

'Something happened today,' I tell him softly.

His brow furrows as he unwraps foil from the top of the champagne bottle. 'What?'

'Wait,' I interrupt before he can go any further.

He hesitates, his thumb at the base of the cork. It feels wrong to say this to the sound of it gleefully popping.

'This shouldn't be a big deal. I don't want it to be a big deal. But I heard about . . . Joe again.'

His eyes bore into me. 'Go on.'

'He's in a film called *Sky Rocket*. One of the children in my class was talking about it. It's quite a big . . . deal . . .'

He looks down at the bottle in his hands. 'I know.'

'You know he's in it?' I ask with surprise.

'No, I know about the film. A colleague went to see it at the weekend.' He places the bottle on the countertop.

'I'm sorry,' I blurt out.

He meets my eyes for a moment before looking away again. He shakes his head. 'You don't have to be sorry,' he says quietly. 'It's not your fault.'

The relief is immense. He touches his fingertips to the champagne bottle and slowly pushes it across the countertop, away from him.

'I don't really feel like this anymore.'

'Should I get on with dinner?' I ask tentatively.

'No,' he says. 'I've lost my appetite.'

To my dismay, he walks out of the kitchen. I hear his footsteps on the stairs and then over my head as he goes into our bedroom and shuts the door. I switch off the hob warming the peppercorn sauce and go after him.

'Lukas,' I say gently, walking into the room. He's lying on the bed with his arms folded over his face. I sit down next to him and put my hand on his stomach. He flinches under my touch.

'Do you still love him?' he asks in a muffled voice.

'I don't even know who he is anymore,' I answer truthfully.

He takes his arms away from his face and looks at me. 'You're avoiding the question.'

'Of course I don't love him,' I snap. 'I knew him years ago. We were eighteen! I don't know anything about him now.'

'Do your parents know who he is?'

'No. Well, I doubt it. I'm sure they would have mentioned it if they recognised him.'

'Don't tell them,' he says fervently. 'I don't want anyone else to know.' He stares at the ceiling. 'I want to have children,' he says in a low, determined voice.

I look away from him. 'We will.'

'I want to have children *now*.'

'Is this about Rosalinde?' I can't help but ask.

He closes his eyes with frustration, but doesn't deny it. I take my hand away from his stomach and he sits up on the bed. 'Why won't you have children with me?'

'Jesus, Lukas, I'm only twenty-six!'

'Age is your excuse for everything! Twenty-six is a perfectly reasonable age to start a family.'

'Yes, but I want to have a career first.'

'You're a *teacher*.'

'What the hell is that supposed to mean?' I ask coldly as anger builds inside me.

'Nothing,' he replies quickly. 'You can always go back to teaching.'

'Do you still love Rosalinde?' I ask out of the blue.

He gets down from the bed and gives me a hard stare. 'Now you're being ridiculous.'

'When was the last time you saw her?'

His silence is unnerving.

'Lukas?' I prompt with worry mounting inside me.

He goes to his wardrobe and opens it, placing his shiny black shoes inside.

'I saw her at Christmas,' he reveals offhandedly.

'Christmas just gone? When I was there?' I don't understand. I still haven't met her, but sometimes I think that I should. She didn't come to our wedding, although she *was* invited.

'Yes. I bumped into her in Munich, that day we went to the Christmas market. She had Ferdinand with her.' That's her little boy.

'Why didn't you tell me?' We'd split up for an hour so I could go shopping.

He shakes his head. 'I don't know.'

'*Do* you still love her?' I ask anxiously.

'Of course not, Alice,' he says crossly.

'Does she still love you?'

'If she did she would never tell me.'

That doesn't sound like the most reassuring answer.

'Did she seem happy?'

'I think so. She's pregnant again.' Why doesn't this feel like good news? 'How did we get on to talking about Rosalinde?' he asks suddenly. 'I thought we were talking about *Joseph Strike*.' He says his name with mockery.

'There's nothing more to say,' I reply simply.

I know this isn't the end of our discussion. If Joe is as big a star as Roxy says, we haven't heard the last of him.

Chapter 54

That couldn't have been more of an understatement. In the summer, the second blockbuster in which Joe has a starring role hits the big screen and the furore around him reaches fever pitch. It's impossible to go anywhere without hearing or seeing something related to Tinseltown's latest flame. Much as Lukas and I try to conduct a normal life, we're constantly living in Joe's shadow.

My parents never did put two and two together – they're not really big cinema fans and, following Lukas's request, I kept quiet. But the fact that Lizzy, Jessie and Emily know about my history with Joe is another nail in their coffins. As far as Lukas is concerned, he feels more uncomfortable in their company than ever. To him it feels like they're judging us, comparing him to Joe, wondering if I regret our marriage. And they probably are.

Towards the end of August, Lizzy's little girl turns two and I go to London on my own for her birthday party. It's not worth forcing Lukas to come – it's easier to keep these two sides of my life apart. I decide to stay for the whole weekend – to help Lizzy out with the party on Saturday, and to catch up properly afterwards.

She moved into a flat in East Finchley a month ago so she could still be near her father and sister without everyone living in each other's pockets. She's hired out a space in a church hall and I barely have time to drop off my bags before we have to head over there to blow up balloons. My parents are on holiday in France at the moment so this weekend Lizzy and Ellie have me all to themselves.

Later, at the end of a long day, when Ellie is asleep and Lizzy and I have collapsed on the sofa in front of the telly with two very large glasses of wine, she tells me that I should have been a children's entertainer. I've been rounding up pre-schoolers all day to play games.

'I think there's more money in teaching,' I say wryly.

'And more respect.'

'Some teachers would disagree,' I say with a raised eyebrow. 'Although that shouldn't be the way it is.'

'It's definitely not in your case,' she says warmly. 'You're a great teacher.'

'You've never seen me in the classroom,' I comment with a smile, taking a sip of my wine.

'I can imagine. I know you're brilliant. I only wish Ellie could go to your school.'

'Move up to Cambridge!' I cry.

She grins and shakes her head. 'It's tempting. I have never seen a city with so many fit boys in it. Or girls, for that matter,' she muses. 'It's a shame the colleges aren't still single sex, that would sort out part of that problem.'

I laugh. She picks up the remote control and starts channel surfing.

'Wait!' I shout, sloshing some of my wine out of my glass onto my knees. She freezes, the remote paused.

Joe's face fills the screen.

'Turn it up,' I command.

He's being interviewed on a late-night American chat show, and he's so cool, so composed. He laughs and my heart flips because he's instantly recognisable and familiar, and then a woman's voice-over says: '*But the young Joseph Strike had to fight his way to the top . . .*' The programme cuts to an advert break. This appears to be a documentary about his road to fame. Lizzy looks over at me. There's compassion in her eyes.

'He's so . . . He's so . . .' I can't find the words.

'Haven't you ever seen him being interviewed?' she asks softly.

'No.' I swallow. 'Have you?'

She nods. 'Yes.'

'You never talk to me about him,' I say in a small voice.

'I didn't think you *wanted* me to talk to you about him. I thought you considered it too disloyal to Lukas.'

'I do. I don't want you to talk to me about him.' But that's a lie. Right now there's nothing I want more.

'Shall I change the chan—'

'NO!'

She gingerly places the remote control down on the sofa between us, and soon the programme comes back on. Now they're interviewing the director who made *Strike*, a grizzled-looking American man in his late fifties with wiry grey hair and horn-rimmed glasses.

'I knew the kid was a star from the moment I laid eyes on him. When I found him he was bruised and battered mentally. I could tell he'd been physically beaten too. You just knew it. It was in his eyes. No wonder he learned how to fight. No wonder he got so good. Of course,' he chuckles, 'I had to convince him to come back with me to Hollywood. He thought acting was a mug's game, but in the end he came around to the idea. The same went for changing his name.'

The interviewer asks a question off-screen. She sounds confused: 'Change his name? Isn't his name Joseph Strike?'

The director shakes his head with a wry grin. 'No, no, no. Joseph, yes. Strike, no.'

'What's his real name?' You can almost hear her salivating at this exclusive.

He laughs knowingly. 'I can't tell you. That was part of the deal. He didn't *want* to change it,' he says animatedly, sitting forward in his seat, 'but in the end I guess he was okay with the idea of leaving his identity behind and trying something new.' He looks thoughtful for a moment, and then the documentary cuts to a fight scene from *Strike*. Joe and another guy are pummelling each other with their fists and feet. Suddenly Joe knocks his opponent out. The camera cuts to Joe's face and it's full of fury, but it changes in a flash to remorse.

'Shit!' he shouts, dropping to his knees and trying to rouse his opponent.

We cut back to the grizzled director, who is shaking his head with amusement. 'He's not a fighter at heart. But that pain he feels?' His face grows serious. 'That pain he feels every day about God knows what?' He jabs his finger at the air to punctuate his point. 'That pain translates to the audience. He has the *control*, the *spirit*, the *drive*. It was only a matter of time before he became a superstar.'

I watch the rest of the documentary without being able to say a word. I keep feeling Lizzy's eyes on me, but mine are glued to the screen. I go through so many different emotions. One minute I can see the boy I knew, the vulnerable, beautiful boy I fell in love with, and my eyes fill with tears and my heart reaches out to him . . . The next he's being cast as a womaniser and a playboy, photographed out on the town with models and actresses hanging off his arm, and I barely recognise him at all.

'Are you okay?' Lizzy asks me when the credits start to roll.

'No,' I mumble. 'I'm so confused.'

She has to lean in to hear me because I'm speaking so quietly. 'What do you want to do?'

'I want to watch *Sky Rocket*,' I tell her in a daze. 'I don't suppose you've got it on DVD?'

'As a matter of fact . . .' She gets to her feet. 'I do.'

She's exhausted, but she manages to stay up with me while we watch *Sky Rocket*, and he's incredible in it – I'm completely and utterly enthralled. It's a sci-fi flick, but not a full-on action film. Lizzy tells me that *Hong Kong Kid* was a martial arts film and he had to master kung fu for the role, but he had only a small part in that. This is more of a futuristic drama set in space, with a fair few fight scenes thrown in for good measure. There's also a love scene in it which turns my stomach into a jittering mess. My heart thump, thump, thumps and I'm on the edge of my seat as I watch him take that evilly beautiful actress with raw desire. Jealousy courses through my veins, even though I know it's not real, it's only an act, but it's harder to tear my eyes away than it is to watch it.

'I can see what you saw in him,' Lizzy says when it's finished.

She has no idea how horrible her comment makes me feel. What I saw in him is very different to what she and the rest of the female population see in him now. Isn't it? Oh, God, maybe it's not.

'Are you okay?' she asks me when I don't answer.

'Do you still have that copy of *Strike*?'

I see her hesitate. I can see how tired she is. 'Yes . . .'

'You go to bed,' I say quickly. 'I know you're knackered.'

'It's just that Ellie will probably wake up in an hour and I'll be up half the night with her . . .'

'Of course, of course.' I feel bad for even asking. 'We'll chat in the morning.'

'You're going to watch it?' she asks. 'It's not the copy that Jessie lent us,' she adds hurriedly. 'That would have been a very long "rental" period.'

'Did you buy a copy for yourself?' I can't not ask.

'Yeah.' She tries to brush it off.

Thinking about it, *Sky Rocket* came out on DVD only a couple of weeks ago. The fact that she's also got a copy of that . . . The realisation that she's a fan of Joe's is surreal and makes me feel very strange.

I decide I'd rather not know any more.

'I'll get your bedding first,' she says, standing up. It's only a small two-bed flat so I'm sleeping in the living room. I walk over to the DVDs on the shelves and look through them until I come across *Strike*, then I go to the DVD player and put it in. Lizzy returns and helps me make up the sofa.

'Thanks,' I say.

She comes over and gives me a hug. 'Are you okay?' she asks again.

'I'll be fine,' I say dismissively. 'Get some sleep!'

'I will. We'll talk tomorrow.'

She squeezes my arm and leaves the room. I climb into my makeshift bed and press Play.

I don't sleep at all that night. *Strike* is gritty and real and I understand what the director says about Joe's pain translating to the audience, because it does; I feel it in my core and I'm one of very few people in the world who know why he's hurting so much.

After *Strike*, I surf the internet for interviews and articles, photographs and videos, until I feel like I've seen everything that there is to see.

Finally I can ignore the truth no longer. I have to admit that I still love Joe. I feel like I've cheated on Lukas, but I still love Joe. Along, it seems, with every other woman on the planet.

Chapter 55

I hear Ellie wake up at six o'clock in the morning. Lizzy goes to get her some milk from the kitchen. I call out to her on her way back.

'Sorry, did she wake you?' she asks, coming into the living room.

'I haven't been asleep,' I admit.

'You've been up all night?' She looks shocked, then she glances at her open laptop screen and it dawns on her. 'Ah.'

'Yeah,' I say sheepishly.

'You've caught the bug.' She looks amused.

I don't like that description. 'Do you want me to take Ellie so you can go back to sleep?' I change the subject.

'No, I'm awake now,' she says. 'Thanks, though. She didn't sleep too badly in the end.'

'She slept straight through, didn't she?'

'She woke up at one thirty,' Ellie tells me. 'You were still in the thralls of *Strike*,' she says teasingly.

I wish she'd stop making these comments. I'm not just another Strike Stalker. The press coined that term.

'You'll have to go and see *Night Fox* next,' she adds.

'I was thinking I might go today,' I tell her, feeling a prickle of guilt about Lukas and trying to stifle it.

'Ooh, yes!' she exclaims. 'I'd see it again!'

'Have you already seen it?'

'Twice.' She giggles. Bloody hell, she really must be a fan. 'I'll ask Dad if he can take Ellie.'

Speaking of whom . . .

'MUM-MUM-MUM-MUMMY!' The cry comes from the next room.

Lizzy lifts up the beaker of milk. 'Back in a tic.'

There's a ten o'clock screening of *Night Fox* at the nearby multiplex. 'Or we can see the 3-D version at eleven?' she asks.

'We'll just see the ordinary one, won't we?'

She shrugs. 'I don't mind. I've seen both. The 3-D is good, though.'

'I don't think I can wait the extra hour.' I don't know how I'm going to get through the next three and a half.

'I know how you feel!' She giggles again. Her behaviour is doing my head in.

Lukas calls me at nine thirty, when we're on our way to the cinema. I divert his call, before thinking better of it and ringing him back. I don't want to have to explain away a two-and-a-half-hour AWOL session while I'm in the cinema.

'What happened there?' he asks irritably.

'Sorry, I pressed the wrong button,' I fib.

'When are you coming home?' he demands to know.

'This afternoon.' Lizzy flashes me a wary glance from the driver's seat.

'I might come and pick you up,' he says.

'No, I've got a return train ticket for three o'clock,' I reply steadily. 'I'm catching up with Lizzy and Ellie today.'

'Didn't you do enough catching up yesterday?'

'I'll see you later, Lukas,' I say firmly.

Silence.

'Love you,' I add.

'Bye,' he says shortly, before hanging up. I switch off my phone and stuff it back into my bag as Lizzy turns into the car park.

'Are you going to tell him what you've been doing?' she asks.

I shake my head. 'No. He'd go mad.'

'He can't blame you for being curious,' she says reasonably as she pulls into a space.

'He can, and he does.'

'But that's unfair.'

'It's not really.' I look across at her. 'Put yourself in his shoes. Imagine if . . .' I can't say Callum anymore. '. . . your future husband's first love was, I don't know, Angelina Jolie. Wouldn't you feel threatened?'

She thinks about it for a moment, before grinning. 'Actually, yes.'

I shrug. 'Come on, let's go.'

Night Fox is even better than *Sky Rocket*. I'm on the edge of my seat and on an emotional roller coaster from start to finish. When Joe's character gets killed at the end I actually let out a full-on sob. Beside me, Lizzy laughs tearfully at my reaction and I look across to see her face streaming with tears. I can't help it: I let out another sob and start to cry properly.

'It's so sad, isn't it?' she says, crying and laughing at our behaviour at the same time.

I nod, but I can't speak. She delves into her bag and pulls out a handful of tissues. 'I knew you'd need these.'

I'm not ready to stop crying, but the lights have gone on in the cinema and, even though there's only a handful of other people in here at this time on a Sunday morning and they're all sniffling, I feel silly. I wish I were at home so I could cry in peace . . . Jesus, no! Imagine if Lukas could see me now!

'Now can you understand why I've been to see it three times?' she asks me pointedly.

I nod. It's not the same thing, mind you. It's different for me. Oh, God, maybe it's not different for me! Maybe I'm just the same as all the other self-confessed Strike Stalkers that I read about in the middle of the night. That magnetic pull that I felt when I first met him – that POW! moment when our eyes first met – maybe everyone gets that! I can't bear it.

I'm still red-eyed and a little tearful on the car journey back to Lizzy's flat. She's been enthusiastically discussing the film with me and I've been trying to compose myself and readjust to life as I now know it. I do still love Joe – that fact is beyond denial. But I can't be entirely sure how much of it is love for the Joe that I see on the big screen. That's got to be a big part of it.

We're walking towards Lizzy's block of flats from the car park when I hear the sound of a car door opening and closing.

'Alice!'

I turn around to see Lukas standing beside his silver Porsche, a wedding gift from father to son four years ago.

'What are you doing here?' I gasp.

'I went for a drive,' he replies. 'I thought you might like a lift after all.'

I glance at Lizzy, but she looks away. I can tell she's not at all impressed.

'I wasn't going to come home for another couple of hours,' I tell him pedantically.

'Do you want to come in for a cuppa, Lukas?' Lizzy asks coolly.

'No. Thank you,' he replies in an equally cool manner. 'If you're not ready I'll drive around for a bit until you are.'

I sigh heavily. There's no point arguing about it. He's here now. 'Give me half an hour,' I say.

He nods curtly and gets back into his car. Lizzy surreptitiously rolls her eyes as we make our way to the stairs. We can hear the sound of his Porsche engine ricocheting off the apartment block's walls as he roars onto the main road.

'Sorry about that,' I say, as we go inside.

'It's not your fault,' she replies. 'Why did he come?'

I shrug. 'I guess he missed me.'

She tuts. I know she also thinks he's a control freak, but she doesn't know him like I do.

She puts the kettle on.

'Shouldn't we go and get Ellie?' I ask.

'She'll be okay with Dad for another half an hour,' she replies.

I sit down at the kitchen table and she pulls up a chair opposite me.

'Why don't you stay here with me for a few days?' she suggests gently.

'What? Why would I do that?'

'It would give you some space from Lukas. Don't you think you need some time to sort out your head?'

'I could *definitely* do with some space to sort out my head, but I wouldn't not go home to Lukas. That would totally freak him out!' I exclaim.

'He'd get over it.'

'Lizzy, I know you're not a big fan of "the Husband" as you like to call him, but he *is* my husband. Contrary to popular belief, we have a lot of fun together.' I know she doesn't think we have much in common, but she's wrong.

'Doing what?' she asks.

I refrain from telling her the sex is good. I don't want to rub her nose in it when she's not getting any. 'I don't know,' I reply, 'going for daytrips to museums or to the seaside or to National Trust properties. Cuddling on the sofa at night.' I'm not sure this information is winning her over, but I respect Lukas for not being your Average, er, Joe. Wrong term to use. 'He's very sweet to me,' I add. 'I know how much he loves me. And I love him.'

'As much as you loved Joe?'

I don't reply.

'I didn't think so.'

'What do you think I'm going to do about it?'

'You could try to contact him again?'

'No,' I say resolutely. 'No. I tried that. And don't you ever tell anyone!'

'Of course I won't,' she scoffs. 'But you didn't try very hard.'

'What was I supposed to do? I couldn't leave my number – what if he rang me back when Lukas was around?'

'You could leave *my* number,' she suggests thoughtfully.

Hmm, bet she'd like that.

'He wouldn't call, anyway,' I say in a flat voice. 'His agent probably wouldn't even pass on my message,' I add. 'In fact, he definitely wouldn't. He'd think I was just another mental Strike Stalker.'

'But surely you still want answers. You still *need* answers.'

'Well, I'm not going to get them. Look at him! He's a huge Hollywood star!' He's even less tangible than he was before, I think despondently.

Lizzy's mobile starts to buzz. It's still on vibrate after our trip to the cinema. She picks it up and stares at the caller ID. 'It's Lukas.'

I'm taken aback. 'Is it?'

She answers the call. 'Hello?' Pause. 'Oh, okay.' Pause. 'I'll tell her.' She ends the call and looks at me. 'He's downstairs. He's been beeping his horn, he said. Your mobile is still switched off.'

'Oh, for pity's sake,' I snap, getting up and grabbing my things together.

'Tell him to wait!' she cries.

'No, I'd better go. I don't know what his problem is.'

I soon find out. The second I'm buckled in, he throws a tabloid newspaper on my lap.

'Have you seen this?' he asks stonily.

I unfold the paper and stare at the front page. There's a paparazzi shot of Joe looking miserable, with the headline:

EXCLUSIVE! MY RAPIST SHAME

Oh, no. They've found out about his past, about his brother. I scan the words and discover that Ryan is still in prison for rape, but soon he'll be up for parole.

'Have you seen it?' Lukas asks again.

'No. No, I haven't,' I reply quietly.

'At least you haven't been talking to Lizzy about it behind my back,' he mutters.

If only he knew . . .

A few days later there's another 'exclusive'. This time it's an interview with Joe's parents, who talk about how their son, little Joe Strickwold, shamefully disowned them when he became famous.

Lukas is scathing about the whole thing. 'You fell in love with that? Look at his family! Disgraceful.'

But all I can think is *poor, poor Joe*. He must be distraught. There's been no sign of him since the news broke, and I keep imagining him inside his sprawling mansion in the Hollywood hills feeling utterly alone because no one in his new life knows where he came from or what he's been through. The fact that his parents – his mother all dolled up with make-up and his father in a suit – are making out that he's the bad egg of the family . . . I'm disgusted to my very core. I want to go to the papers myself and tell the truth. I want to defend him, to slate them, to tell the story from Joe's point of view. But of course I can't.

Days pass and more pieces hit the headlines, but Joe is still in hiding. Journalists delve further into his past and manage to speak to his friends in Cornwall, including, to my distress, the girl he shared his first kiss with. I can't imagine how I'd feel if they ever came knocking on my door.

I'm utterly distracted with all of this, but I find the strength to reassure Lukas and somehow pretend that I'm taking it all in my stride, even though I'm not. Luckily he goes off to work each day, and because school doesn't start for another couple of weeks I'm able to scour the internet for news.

At the beginning of September, Lukas flies home for a long weekend and I go to stay with my parents. Rosalinde had a baby girl a couple of months ago, and I know he wants to catch up with her while he's in Germany, but I can't even summon the energy to care. I go over to Lizzy's on Saturday night after she's put Ellie to bed.

'How are you feeling?'

'Weary,' I confess.

'Did you know half the stuff they're going on about in the papers?'

'Yeah. All of it.'

'You knew it all?' She looks surprised.

'And quite a bit more.'

She gives me a strange look.

'What are you thinking?' I ask.

'You knew him for only a few weeks . . .' she replies with confusion.

'It felt like a lot longer,' I say with a rueful smile.

She looks thoughtful. 'I never could understand why you were so heartbroken after Dorset. I think I get it now.'

'Why, because you, like everyone else, can see what all the fuss is about?' I say this drily.

'That's part of it,' she admits. 'But I guess I didn't really believe you were properly in love with him. I thought it was just a holiday romance, a teenage crush, that sort of thing.'

'No. It was real. Well, it was for me, anyway,' I add sadly.

She regards me through narrowed eyes. 'Do you still love him?'

Every second of every minute of every hour of every day . . .

I look down at my hands. There's no point in denying it. 'Yes.'

'Bollocks,' she says with a sigh.

'That's one way of putting it.'

She sits up suddenly. 'What if he does still think about you? What if he still loves you? What if something went wrong and he tried to come for you, but he couldn't? What if he's been trying to find you for years?'

'No. Stop it. He could have found me – I wasn't hard to find – but he didn't. And why would he think of me now? Have you seen the women he goes around with? He's clearly not lacking in female attention. God, it's embarrassing even talking about this! It's over. I don't want to talk about him anymore.'

'But what if—'

'No,' I interrupt. 'No more. Talk about something else or I'm going back to Mum and Dad's.'

'Okay, okay!' she cries. 'Blimey.'

Adele's 'Someone Like You' comes on the radio.

'I love this song,' she says.

'It makes me sad,' I reply.

'Me too.' We sit there in silence, listening. 'Hey, it's like you and Joe!' she exclaims.

'What are you going on about?'

'It's like you and Joe! Except he's Adele. You're the one who's settled down and married now. I bet he'd cry if he knew.'

'You've had too much to drink.'

'Imagine that, though! Imagine if he did still love you and he found out you were married! He'd be so cut up!'

'I thought we were changing the subject.'

'Yeah, but, seriously!'

'Right, that's it. I'm going to my parents'.' I make to stand up.

'Don't go! I'm sorry. Let's talk about something else.'

Hesitantly I settle back down on the sofa.

'Did you see that *Phoenix Seven* is now coming out in early December?' I stare at her in disbelief. 'They must've brought the release date forward to capitalise on all the press,' she continues.

'Are you *seriously* talking about Joe's new film?' I ask with amazement. I can't even be cross about it.

'Sorry, sorry!'

More silence. She starts to say something and then stops.

'What?' I ask.

'Did you . . . Were you . . . Oh, never mind.'

'Spit it out!'

'Why did you marry Lukas when you were still in love with Joe?'

'Fucking hell, Lizzy!' I exclaim.

'Sorry, but I just don't understand!'

'I'm in love with Lukas too, you dimwit!' I snap, but I'm not really angry. Not properly.

'Yes, but . . . when you saw that DVD of *Strike*, didn't you even contemplate not going through with it?'

'With the wedding, you mean?'

'Yeah.' At least she has the grace to look awkward with this line of questioning.

I sigh. 'I was too freaked out to watch the whole movie. You said something about his name change and I wrote him off as a different person to the boy I fell in love with. And calling it off didn't seem like a viable option,' I add wryly.

'It *was* a bloody big wedding,' she concedes. 'But if you'd seen *Strike* when it came out at the cinema the year before, do you think it would have made a difference?'

I think back to a few weeks ago, when I finally gave in and allowed myself to watch *Strike* from start to finish, along with *Sky*

Rocket and all those interviews. That was when I realised he hadn't changed all that much.

'I almost did go to see *Strike* at the cinema,' I tell her, recalling how Jessie had wanted to see it but it wasn't out yet. And then it hits me with sudden realisation that Jessie and I were supposed to go to the movies on *Friday* – the day that *Strike* came out. We changed our date to Monday because Lukas came back earlier than planned from Rosalinde's wedding.

The colour drains from my face.

'Are you alright?' Lizzy asks. 'You look like you've seen a ghost.'

'I've just remembered something,' I say in a low voice.

'What?'

I tell her.

'So you would have seen it well before the wedding,' she says slowly.

'I would have seen it before Lukas had even proposed,' I reply.

'Would you have still said yes?' she dares to ask.

I don't dare to think about it.

Chapter 56

The next week, my period is late and I nearly have a heart attack. I'm pretty sure the ensuing sickness I feel is too early to be related to pregnancy, but I finally manage to get to a chemist to buy a pregnancy test. And of all the evenings for Lukas to come home early, this is the one he chooses.

'Alice?' he calls.

'Shit!' I mutter, stuffing the pregnancy test box into the bin. I snatch up the wand and stare at the result – willing something to appear before he does. I can hear his feet on the stairs. I open the bin, about to throw the test in regardless of its result, but something makes me hesitate. He knocks on the door.

'Alice?' he asks.

'I'm coming,' I say, flushing the toilet and hoping he doesn't enter.

Fat chance.

His eyes fall on the wand in my hand and then he's staring at my face in shock.

'Are you . . .'

I look down at the wand. What does one line mean? Shit! I've already binned the box. I delve back into the bin and pull it out, while Lukas waits with bated breath. Why didn't I go for one of those whizzy digital ones that just say pregnant or not pregnant? One line means . . .

Not pregnant.

'No.' I laugh with relief and glance up at him.

He looks crushed. My face falls.

'I'm sorry,' I say, feeling awkward.

'You're happy you're not?' he asks.

'Um . . .'

He stalks out of the bathroom. I hurriedly follow him downstairs to the living room. He opens the French doors and goes out into the garden. There's a bench at the end. He sits on it. I tentatively go to join him.

'Did you see Rosalinde while you were in Germany?' I ask.

'This isn't about Rosalinde!' he exclaims. 'This is about us! You and me. I want to have children!'

I take his hand. 'I know you do.'

'I feel like you can't commit to me,' he says quietly.

'I married you!'

'Yes, but you didn't want to, did you?'

'Of course I did!'

He sighs. 'I know you're still confused about . . .' He lets go of my hand. 'How did things end between you?' he asks, turning to face me. His stare is not cold or icy – his blue eyes are full of pain.

'Not well,' I admit. I haven't gone into all the details with Lukas. It wasn't necessary, and I don't like to remember.

'Can you tell me about it?'

Maybe he needs to understand. With reluctance I tell him

about that night, about how Ryan killed Joe's beloved dog and then tried to hurt me, how Joe's parents told him to leave and never come back. How my dad made me go and pack up my things, and how Joe was gone by the time I got back downstairs. I tell Lukas how I searched for him everywhere, how I continued to search for him for months, how I barely had a life at university for the first term and a half. Until I met Jessie and got a job on the river.

The ache inside my chest intensifies as I recall this last part. I barely see Jessie these days. It's not a lie to say that he saved me. I miss Emily too.

'You wanted answers,' Lukas says quietly. 'I wouldn't let you seek them after we were married.'

'I understand,' I tell him.

'Do you still need answers?' he asks.

I don't reply for a while.

'That's a yes.' He sounds hurt.

'It's not like I'm going to get them,' I say swiftly. 'He probably doesn't even remember me.'

'Of course he does,' Lukas says, and there's no bitterness in his voice. 'No one could forget you.'

A lump forms in my throat.

'I love you.' Tears fill his eyes.

'Please don't be upset,' I beg.

'You know,' he says, laughing sharply, 'I came home early to tell you that I've got a promotion.'

'You've got a promotion?' I sit up straight. 'But that's brilliant!'

'It's in Germany,' he says dully.

My stomach falls. 'But I don't want to live in Germany.' I shake my head violently.

He turns to face me. 'I've lived in the UK for almost a decade.'

'But we met here! You can't expect me to leave my friends and family and move to another country.'

'What friends?' he asks gently. 'You barely see them.'

'That's not my fault – you don't like them. It's hard for me to see them.' I feel desperate.

'What about *my* friends and family?'

'But you bought into a life in England when you met me!'

'Alice,' he chides, 'that's not strictly true, is it? We've never explored the possibility of living in German—'

'Exactly!' I interrupt. 'You can't bring it up now, that's not fair! What about my job?'

'I was hoping you'd have a baby . . .' He sees the look on my face. 'But you could get another job as a teacher. Your language skills are coming along well—'

'I didn't even WANT to learn to speak German!' I practically shout. 'I wanted to learn to speak Mandarin!'

He sighs and regards me. 'Perhaps now is not the right time to talk about this.'

'It will never be the right time to talk about it!'

'Calm down.'

'No!'

I get up and start pacing the lawn, feeling like a caged animal. I can't go to live in Germany. I can't. I won't!

I realise I'm acting like a spoilt brat, but I can't help it.

'It's a very good job,' Lukas says. 'It's with LMU Munich.' That's the university. Hold on a moment . . .

'But you told your father you refused to work there!' I exclaim.

'That was when *he* lined up the interview. This time it's on *my* terms. It's much more money,' he adds.

'I don't care about the money,' I snap.

'Couldn't we try it for a couple of years?'

Oh, God, is he really going to make me do this?

'When do you have to let them know?' I ask.

'I already have. I start in a month.'

Chapter 57

A week later one of Joe's mates from Cornwall goes on live television to defend his old friend. It was supposed to be a very gentle piece about how he was always a good guy growing up. No one expected him to come out with the revelation that Joe's brother had beaten him regularly as a child, while his parents did nothing to stop it.

After the programme airs, Joe's parents threaten to sue the TV station and the following outcry is enormous, but more witnesses come forward, including two people who were at the pub in Dorset the night that Ryan hit Joe over the back of his head with a bottle. Suddenly there are pictures everywhere of the back of Joe's head, cropped in to show that the scar is still there underneath his short black hair. Anyone who's ever had any sympathy for Joe's parents, loses it. The tide has well and truly turned.

Soon afterwards Joe goes on *Oprah* and his superstardom reaches new heights. He talks about his difficult upbringing, but doesn't slate his parents, saying only that they're not on speaking terms and haven't been ever since the bottle incident when he was eighteen. Roxy and I watch the interview in the staff room the moment it's loaded up onto You Tube.

It's a tiny screen and the quality is shocking, but both of us hang on every word. My heart goes out to him more than ever.

'I bet you're in his thoughts now,' Lizzy says on the phone that afternoon, when clips from the *Oprah* interview are shown on the news. 'I can't believe you were there when his brother smashed his head open.'

'Yes, but what a horrible thing to remember me by,' I reply. 'I bet he'd rather forget.'

'Not likely now, is it?'

'I can't really talk,' I tell her with a sigh. 'Lukas will be back soon.'

'When's he leaving for Germany?' she asks.

'Two weeks.'

It's not a permanent arrangement, but for now I'm staying in the UK. He understands that I need to give my work notice, and he also wants to find us a house and get settled in. We plan to rent our house in Newnham. I couldn't sell it – not yet. Not if he's promising we can return to the UK after two years.

'How do you feel about him going?'

'Awful,' I reply.

'You're still not coming around to the idea of moving yourself?'

'No. But I guess I will.'

'I'm amazed he didn't ask you about it before he accepted the job.'

'I'm not. He knew what I would say.'

*

A fortnight later I stand outside our house and say goodbye to my husband. He's driving back to Germany.

'Drive safely,' I say with tears welling up in my eyes.

'I will.'

He touches his hand to my face and I look up into his eyes. 'I can't believe you're going.'

He regards me sadly and takes me in his arms, pressing my cheek to his chest. 'I love you,' he whispers into my hair.

'I love you too.' I breathe in his aftershave and out of the blue I remember going to his bedsit on Trinity Street and opening his wardrobe, searching for a cold compress. I tilt my face up to him and he kisses my lips as hot tears sting my eyes. He releases me and climbs into the car. Then he starts the ignition, and I stand and watch with blurry vision as he drives away from me and the life we've built together.

Chapter 58

I sob my heart out that day, but as the weeks pass I get strangely used to being without him. Soon December rolls around and it will be only a couple of weeks before school breaks up and I'll head to Germany for Christmas. Well, New Year. I'm spending Christmas this year with my parents – for the last two in a row I've been with Lukas's family, so this year they made me promise. Lukas is working right up until Christmas Eve, and again the day after Boxing Day, so it's not worth him flying to the UK to be with us for just two days. I feel oddly detached about seeing him again. He sounds unfamiliar when he calls. I've always hated talking to him on the phone.

One night they show *Strike* on the telly and I watch it again, my heart in my mouth. There's one point when Joe looks straight into the camera and I feel like he's looking at *me*. It makes my heart flip.

Lizzy calls me during the advert break.

'Are you watching it?'

'Yep.'

She laughs. 'Thought so.'

I hate this. She makes me feel dirty. I know I should switch the telly off, but I can't. *Night Fox* comes out on DVD next week. I've already one-clicked it on Amazon.

'You know he's going to be in London next week for the *Phoenix Seven* premiere?'

Her comment is casual, but my heart doesn't take it as such.

She giggles. 'I was thinking we could go to Leicester Square and see if we can catch his eye!'

Her words are still ringing in my head a week later, when school breaks up for the holidays. I'm not due to go to my parents' until tomorrow, but Joe's premiere is tonight. I couldn't sleep last night for thinking about it.

I'm seriously thinking about going. Actually, that's not true. I *know* I'm going. I made up my mind in the middle of the night.

'I love you so much. I can't imagine ever loving anyone more . . .'

That's what Joe said to me. I remembered his words last night. I *have* to find out why he didn't come back for me. I have to know that he no longer loves me. I need closure before I can move on. And I know that Lukas would never forgive me – I know that – but if he ever finds out I'll have to make him understand. He has to if he wants me to move to Germany, to have a family with him, to *fully* commit to him . . . because he's right: I haven't.

I plug in my headphones, but I can still hear the train clunking down the tracks as the fields and farms flash past. I've booked myself into a hotel in Leicester Square on a last-minute deal. I need somewhere to drop off my bags because I don't want to see my parents first. I don't want to have to explain why I'm getting dressed up – or why I'm so on edge. I need space to collect my thoughts before I see him again. And if there's any chance – any chance at all – that he'll spot me and want to speak to me, then I need somewhere private where we can go.

One song finishes and another one starts. The gentle tap, tap, tapping of the drums is instantly familiar, followed by keyboards as the music builds up and then the bass and lyrics kick in. Kingmaker's 'You and I Will Never See Things Eye to Eye' fills my ears and then I'm there with Joe at Corfe Castle when we first talked about this song. He's wearing his Kingmaker T-shirt and looking at me across the table in the café, and we haven't even kissed yet, and Dyson is there at our feet, and I can't believe it was over nine years ago: he feels so real, so much more real than he feels when I see him on the big screen. I want my Joe back so much. So much that it hurts.

I'm full of nerves and anticipation as I get ready. Leicester Square is already bustling with Strike Stalkers desperate to catch a glimpse of their idol. I wish school had finished yesterday so I could have caught an earlier train, but I'll push my way to the front of the crowds if I have to.

I have a quick shower and then dry myself off, pulling my clothes out of my bag. I'm wearing the outfit that I wore the night that Lizzy and I went to see Joe at the pub: dark-blue jeans and the pink and red top that I dragged out of the bottom of my wardrobe on a recent clutter clear-out. I want to wear something he might recognise and it still fits me. I do my hair and make-up the same too. Well, as much as I can without Lizzy's vast Shu Uemura collection. My hair is shorter than it was back then, but it still comes to past my shoulders. I wonder if I've aged much? Urgh, what a thought.

I look over at my mobile on my bedside table and, on a whim, go and switch it off. I don't want to think about anyone other than Joe tonight. Sorry, Lukas. I squeeze my eyes shut and guilt prickles away at me. I need to do this! I'm doing it for him too.

I grab my bag and rush out of the room.

Leicester Square is heaving when I get downstairs, and the atmosphere is electric. The big screen above the cinema entrance keeps playing clips from the movie and every time Joe's face shows the screams get louder. I duck, dive and push my way through the crowds to get as close to the barriers as I'm able. I can't get right to the front – there are girls there holding banners and photographs and I can tell from the look in their eyes that they'd rather kill than budge. But he should be able to see me here. I hope. I can't believe I'm doing this.

Limousines pull up and stars begin to hit the red carpet. The screams go up a notch, but there's no sign of Joe. And then, out of the blue, the crowd ROARS. It's like nothing I've ever heard, and suddenly I see him. He's there on the red carpet ten metres away! People are pushing me from all angles. I'm not tall enough and I'm finding it hard to breathe as the crowd swamps me. I push back as hard as I can and manage to catch another glimpse of him. He's signing autographs.

Oh, God, the *SCREAMS*!

There are so many people here. So many people wanting him to notice them. All of a sudden I feel very, very silly.

'Joseph! Joseph! Joseph!'

What am I doing here?

'Joseph! Joseph! Joseph!'

The crowd parts again and I see him grinning at a young girl as he signs her poster. She starts to sob and he poses cheek to cheek with her while her mother takes a photo.

Oh, Joe. It's you. It's you.

Love rushes through me and I desperately want to hold him in my arms again, just one more time.

'JOE!'

It takes a moment for me to realise that this scream came out of my own mouth. I watch, stunned, as Joe seems to freeze. His eyes dart in my direction and my heart stops. I'm about to scream again, but a woman appears and moves him on. He smiles and waves and then he's gone.

No. Come back. No. 'JOE!'

I can't believe it's over. Two teenage girls look at me and giggle. The crowd swamps me again, but this time I let them. Here I am, a twenty-seven-year-old in an eighteen-year-old's clothes. I feel like a fool.

Chapter 59

I can't stay at the hotel. I feel too sick, too sad. So I go to stay at Lizzy's. She can't believe it when I confess to her where I've been.

'I feel so sad for you,' she murmurs, hugging me as I cry. 'I'm so sorry I wasn't there for you.'

'I should have told you I was going,' I manage to choke out.

'I know I laughed about it, but I didn't really think you would.'

I cry harder.

'Oh, Alice, what are you going to do?'

She already knows it's not a question that I have an answer for.

The next day I go to Mum and Dad's. They haven't yet seen through their dream of moving to Brighton and opening up a B&B, but they still talk about it. I unlock and open the door to find my mum trying on some fluffy reindeer ears in front of the hall mirror.

'You're early!' she cries. 'We were going to come to the train station to collect you!'

'I caught an earlier train,' I explain, keeping the rest of the facts to myself. 'Nice look,' I say with a giggle.

'I was going to surprise you.' She puts her hand to her festive headband. A moment later the reindeer ears start playing 'Rudolph the Red-nosed Reindeer'.

I snort. 'I think I had a lucky escape.'

She steps forward and gives me a hug.

'Where's Dad?' I ask.

'He's in the garden.'

I go outside to find him.

'Alice!' he shouts, hurrying down the garden path and throwing his arms around me. 'We weren't expecting you until later!'

'I know. Rudolph's already told me.'

'Come in out of the cold!' Mum shouts. 'I'll put the kettle on.'

I smile and follow Dad back into the house. It's good to be home. The thought of leaving my parents to move to Germany . . . I should call Lukas to check up on him. Later.

Evening comes around and the three of us find ourselves on the sofa in front of the telly drinking sherry (them) and Baileys on ice (me). My favourite Friday-night live chat show comes on, hosted by a raucous gay comedian called Andy Carl.

'I love this show,' I tell my parents enthusiastically. Dad shifts on the sofa. 'But we can watch something else, if you prefer?' I add reluctantly.

'You can watch it, if you like,' Mum says. 'Can't she, Jim?'

'Sure,' he says, reaching for his *Financial Times*.

'*And JOSEPH STRIKE IS GOING TO BE HERE!*'

I turn sharply to look at the television as Andy Carl grins goofily at the audience's over-the-top reaction.

'I always think that that Joseph Strike lad looks kind of familiar,' Dad comments, glancing up at the television.

This is ridiculous. I should be able to tell my own parents about him. But Lukas made me promise that I wouldn't.

Mind you, I've done quite a bit of promise-breaking lately . . .

And that's exactly why I shouldn't break this one, I think uncomfortably.

The first guest comes on and Dad turns back to his paper. I'm on the edge of my seat for the next horrendously long half an hour, until, finally, Andy Carl welcomes 'JOSEPH STRIKE, LADIES AND GENTLEMEN!'

Joe jogs down the winding staircase to rapturous applause and deafening screams. Andy engulfs him in a hug.

'Alright, mate? You well?' Joe asks him.

My mobile rings. I distractedly snatch it up, expecting it to be Lizzy, but it's Lukas. I ignore the call and turn my attention back to the telly.

My phone rings again. Dammit! I switch it off. Sorry, Lukas. I feel bad, but not bad enough.

The home phone starts to ring. My dad gets up to answer it and I lean in to try to hear what Andy is asking Joe.

'Alice!' Dad calls. 'It's Lukas.'

'Can I call him back?' I ask anxiously. Something about his new film . . .

'Can she call you back?' I hear Dad ask him. 'Oh, okay.' Dad calls through to me: 'He's going to bed shortly!'

ARGH! I'm missing half the interview!

'We can pause it,' Mum says, reaching for the control.

'Okay,' I say hurriedly, jumping up from my seat. Dad hands over the phone. 'Hi,' I say offhandedly.

'Hi!' he says.

'What's up?'

'Er, nothing. I haven't spoken to you for a few days.'

'All's good here,' I say, glancing at the door. Can I hear the telly?

'I found a house today. I think you'll like it.'

'Oh, right.'

'I put a deposit down in case.'

'In case of what?' Now I'm confused.

'In case you like it.'

'What sort of a deposit? This is a house to *rent*, isn't it?' I ask quickly.

'Yes, of course, Alice.'

'Phew. Sorry, stupid question. Right, then . . .'

'Aren't you going to ask me what it's like?'

I sigh. This conversation isn't going to end anytime soon.

Eventually we say our goodbyes and I hurry back down the hall towards the living room. The downstairs toilet flushes as I pass, and Mum comes out. To my horror, I find my dad watching a nature documentary. My stomach falls. 'Did you change the channel?' I demand to know.

'Sorry,' he says flippantly, throwing me the remote. 'I got fed up waiting.'

'But did you record it?' I ask anxiously. Please say you did, please say you did . . .

'No,' he replies.

'Bloody hell!' I cry, hurrying to change the channel back.

'It's only a television show, Alice,' Mum chides, settling herself back on the sofa.

I find the channel in time to see Joe laughing quietly. 'It's a deal,' he says.

'Thank you very much, Joseph Strike!' The audience roars and Andy Carl turns to camera. 'We'll be back after the break ...'

'For fuck's sake!' I exclaim.

'ALICE!' my dad berates me.

I never say 'fuck' in front of them. I rarely say it at all. I storm out of the room.

'What on earth is wrong with her?' I hear my mum ask as I run up the stairs, close to tears.

I'll have to look it up on the internet. I hurry into my dad's study and shut the door, then switch on his computer. It takes forever to start up, but finally I get going with my search. I'm not sure it's on iPlayer yet ... The phone rings again and I ignore it. I don't want to speak to anyone; my parents can get it. I realise I'm acting like a sulky teenager, but too bad.

'Alice!' Mum calls up the stairs. 'It's for you!'

For pity's sake, who is it now? If it's Lukas again I'll give him an earful.

I pick up the phone and snap into the receiver: 'Hello?'

'It's Lizzy.'

'Oh, hi,' I say with zero enthusiasm.

'Did you see it?'

'No, I bloody well didn't. My dad changed the channel.'

'I recorded it,' she says breathlessly. 'Can you come round?'

'Yes!'

I practically run all the way to her flat. She gleefully opens the door to me. 'Quick. It's ready to go.'

I hurry into the living room and sit on the sofa. She sits next to me and presses Play. We get past the introductions and the general chat about Joe's new film and then we come to the nitty-gritty.

'None of your relationships have lasted more than a few weeks,' Andy Carl says. 'What's with that? Don't you *like* women?'

The audience gasps with shock and delight at Andy's forthright interviewing style. Joe laughs.

'Because I might be able to help you out, if you don't,' Andy adds with a flirtatiously raised eyebrow.

Cue more outraged laughter.

'Thank you,' Joe says, joke-sincerely. 'But I *do* like women. I just haven't found the right one yet.'

'Aaaaahhhh.' The audience joins in, but quick as a flash Andy moves on. 'You're clearly *far* too picky.'

Joe laughs.

Andy leans forward with over-exaggerated interest. 'Or maybe you're *scarred* . . .'

Joe shrugs and Andy's eyes widen. I'm sitting on the edge of my seat.

'You *are*! Who was she?'

Joe looks awkward.

'Tell me! Was she the one that got away?'

'It wasn't like that.'

'What was it like, then? First love?'

'Well . . .'

Andy's eyes widen even further. They look like they could pop out of his head. 'You never got over your first love?'

'Does anyone?' Joe replies, trying to sound casual. My heart is in my throat.

'Well, yeah, if they're an utter shit like mine was,' Andy says. 'But we won't go into that. Tell me about *you*! Who *was* she? What was her *name*?'

'Aah . . .' He shifts in his seat.

'Julie?' Pause. 'Katherine?'

'No.'

'Sarah?'

'No.'

'Jennifer? I could go on . . .'

'I bet you could.' Joe raises one eyebrow. God, he's sexy.

'Kim? Gertrude? Annabel?' Pause. 'Just tell us!'

'Her name was Alice, if you must know.'

Oh, my God! I fall off the sofa and scramble over to sit right in front of the television.

'Alice! You never forgot about Alice. Aww! Where is she?'

'I don't know. We lost touch a long, long time ago.'

'But you still love her?'

'I've never stopped loving her.'

I nearly die, then and there.

The audience 'aah', and Andy clutches his hand to his chest and wipes away an imaginary tear. 'Maybe we can find her for you.' He turns to the audience before Joe can react. 'Does anyone know an Alice?'

A couple of people whoop. 'You do? Perhaps we need a little more to go on.' He turns back to Joe. 'Alice Who? What's her last name?'

Joe shifts uncomfortably and looks down. 'Oh . . . I don't think I should say. Maybe she doesn't want to know me now.'

'Of *course* she does! *Look* at you!' Straight to camera: 'Alright, then, Alice Whateveryournameis, you know who you are, you know where to find him. If you want to get in touch with this Love God all you have to do is call the studio.' He turns back to Joe. 'But you have to invite *me* to your wedding . . .'

Joe laughs softly. 'It's a deal.'

'Thank you very much, Joseph Strike!' The audience roars. 'We'll be back after the break with—'

Lizzy presses Pause and looks straight at me. My mouth is wide open. I shut it abruptly.

'Holy shit,' I whisper.

She looks like she's about to burst. 'Don't kill me,' she says.

'What?'

'I called the studio and gave them your mobile number.'

'You *didn't*!'

'I did.'

'Holy FUCK!' I dig my mobile out of my pocket and turn it back on. 'Holy fuck,' I say again.

'ARGHHH!' she screams with excitement.

'What if he doesn't call?' The thought is too horrendous to contemplate. Then again, what if he *does* call? My whole body shivers with nervous excitement. This could be the longest wait for a phone call that I've ever experienced in my life.

'I think we need a drink!' Lizzy exclaims.

'Yes!'

She rushes out of the room and I look at my mobile. My thoughts flit to Lukas and I instantly feel guilty. I relocate back to the sofa and put the phone down beside me.

Suddenly it starts to vibrate. I snatch it up and look at the screen: caller ID withheld. I can practically hear my heart thumping inside my chest as I press Answer and put it to my ear.

'Hello?' I ask tentatively.

'Alice?'

'Joe.'

'Alice?' he asks again.

'Yes. It's me.'

'Is it really you? Alice Simmons?' He sounds so heart-rendingly hopeful.

'Yes, Joe Strickwold, it's me.' I feel like every part of my body is smiling.

'I can't believe I've found you,' he says in a small voice.

Lizzy rushes back into the room with two glasses of wine. 'Right!' she says, then freezes on the spot when she sees me on the phone. 'Is it him?' she mouths, her eyes wider than a goldfish's.

'Hang on a minute, Joe.' I get up and go into the kitchen, closing the door behind me. Much as I know this will kill her, I need to have this conversation without feeling self-conscious about someone listening in. I pull up a chair and sit down.

'Are you there?' I ask.

'I'm here,' he replies quietly.

After all this time I don't know what to say.

'Can I see you?' He sounds choked up.

'Yes, of course.'

'When?'

'When is good for you?' That was a bit formal.

'Um, well, I . . . Where do you live?'

'I'm in north London at the moment with my parents. But usually Cambridge.'

'You still live in Cambridge?' he asks with a little surprise.

'I do.'

'Can you . . .' He hesitates. 'Can you meet me tomorrow morning?' He seems unsure of himself.

'Where?'

'You *can*? Good.' I hear the relief in his voice. 'Can you come to my hotel?'

'Yes, where are you staying?'

He gives me his address and room number. 'There will be . . . *security* outside the room.' He seems embarrassed. 'But I'll tell them you're coming.'

'Okay.'

'I'll see you tomorrow?'

'Oh, what time?'

'Oh, yeah.' He laughs nervously. 'How early can you come?'

'As early as you'd like.' I'd go there now if he asked me.

'Is . . .' Again, hesitant. 'Is eight o'clock too early? Or nine?'

'Eight o'clock is fine.'

'Great. Okay.' More relief. 'We can call room service. Breakfast,' he adds.

'Okay. I'll see you tomorrow, then.' I don't want to hang up, but this exchange hasn't exactly been lacking in awkwardness. I hope face to face will be better.

'Okay,' he says. 'See you tomorrow.'

'Bye.'

'Wait!' he shouts.

'Yes?'

'Alice?'

'Yes?'

'Let me give you my mobile number.'

'Oh, okay.'

'I don't want to lose touch again.'

I smile to myself as I jot it down.

'See you tomorrow,' I say.

'Bye.'

He hangs up.

How the hell am I going to get any sleep tonight?

Chapter 60

I set my alarm for six so I have plenty of time to disguise the bags under my eyes with make-up, although of course I don't need it. The alarm, I mean. The make-up I most certainly do.

I wear jeans with high-heeled boots and an emerald-green jumper, and I keep my hair down. I set off at seven a.m. so I have plenty of time, even though it should take only half an hour or so on the underground. He's staying at the W Hotel in Leicester Square – the penthouse suite, no less. I leave a note for my parents to say that I've gone over to Lizzy's for breakfast. They'll think it's strange, but she'll cover for me if they ever ask. Again, I feel as though I'm acting like a teenager.

I arrive ten minutes early, but I can't bear to wait any longer. The huge W outside the hotel glows in the early morning light and I walk straight into the dark lobby and go to the lift, hoping the doormen will think I look like I know what I'm doing. Inside the lift I press the button Joe told me to press for the penthouse, but nothing happens. Shit. I bet I need a key card to make it move. I press the button for reception instead and the lift takes me up one floor into a sumptuous area sparkling with mirror balls.

I daren't ask anyone to call Joe for me, so I get out my mobile and call him myself.

'Hello?' He sounds out of breath.

'It's Alice. I'm in reception. I can't get up to your room.'

'I'll send someone down for you,' he promises.

He'll send someone down for me? Now I feel like a right tit. I hate the idea of anyone knowing about us. It cheapens it, somehow. But then, I don't suppose he could come himself. His is one of the most recognisable faces in the world today.

Who is this man I'm about to meet? What's become of that boy from one summer, long ago in Dorset?

The lift doors whoosh open and a woman steps out. She's medium height, super-slim, and immaculately turned-out with blow-dried hair and perfect make-up. She looks around and then her eyes fall on me. I feel apprehensive until she smiles at me.

'Alice?' she asks.

I nod uneasily.

'I'm Melanie, Joseph's PA. Please come with me.'

We step back into the lift.

'He's been waiting for you,' she tells me with a raised eyebrow as the lift climbs upwards.

This morning or for the last nine years?

We come to a stop and the doors open. I swallow and follow her onto the landing. There's a big, burly man in a black suit standing outside a door further down the corridor. Joe's security guard, I presume. She leads me to him and turns around to smile at me. 'He's inside,' she says, indicating the door. 'Lewis!' Her tone is expectant as she cocks her head at the doorman.

The man nods curtly and follows her back down the corridor.

'Thank you!' I call after them. I'm relieved they're not going to be witnesses to our reunion. I hope there's nobody else inside. I wait until the lift doors have closed behind them before I knock.

The door opens and there in front of me is Joe. Not Joseph Strike, the actor, but Joe. *My* Joe.

We look at each other for a long, long moment, and my eyes well up with tears.

'Come in,' he says quickly.

I step inside and he shuts the door behind me, turning to face me. He's wearing casual black cargo pants and a black T-shirt.

'I can't believe it's you.' He lifts his hand as though he wants to touch me, but lets it drop again to his side. 'You're exactly the same as I remember you.'

'You're . . . different.' He's quite a bit broader – not the slim eighteen-year-old that I knew – and it's impossible not to notice his famous biceps protruding under his T-shirt. He no longer has a ring through his eyebrow – I realised that a year ago when *Sky Rocket* came out – but I can just make out the holes there from when it was pierced.

He smiles. 'I'm still the same inside.'

Are you?

'Come and take a seat.' I follow him into a living room, where there's a circular sofa underneath a huge mirror-ball sculpture.

'Cool room,' I say.

'It's . . .' He shrugs and his voice trails off.

What you're used to, I finish his sentence for him inside my head.

'So you saw . . . the interview?' I realise he's nervous.

'My friend did,' I explain, sitting down on the sofa. Then I remember that he knew her: 'Lizzy!'

'Lizzy? Wow.' He sits down next to me, his left knee resting on the sofa so that he's facing me. I turn to do the same to him.

'She called the studio.'

He shakes his head in amazement. He hasn't taken his dark eyes from mine.

'How . . . are . . . you?' he asks slowly.

'I'm okay.' I shrug. 'I'm good. You?'

He half laughs and looks around the room. 'I'm alright.' He meets my eyes again. 'So you still live in Cambridge?'

'I do indeed.' This feels so surreal. The small talk . . . But it's been over nine years. There's so much to say that we hardly know where to start. 'I'm a teacher,' I say with a little smile.

'You're a *teacher*?' His eyes widen. 'Wow,' he says again.

'Yeah, well . . .'

'I bet you're amazing.'

I laugh awkwardly and tuck my hair behind my ear. And then he spots my diamond. His face freezes. It's like the world is moving in slow motion as his eyes travel from my ring back to my face. 'You're . . .' His voice is a whisper.

'Married.' I nod sadly.

'Oh, God.' He puts his hand to his mouth and the blood drains from his usually tanned features. He's in shock. He can't look at me. He's staring at my ring which is glittering even more than usual under the reflection of the lights above the mirror ball.

'When?' he asks in a daze.

'Four and a half years ago.'

'Oh, God.'

His eyes fill up with tears.

I reach over and gently take his hand. It feels like the right thing to do. It's warm, but it doesn't respond when I squeeze it. It doesn't feel at all familiar.

'Are you happy?' he asks.

I hesitate. 'Most of the time.'

He looks up at me, almost hopefully. That wasn't a categorical yes. And then he holds my hand properly and the familiarity of him comes flooding back. A lump forms in my throat.

'I waited for you,' I whisper. 'Why didn't you come?'

'I did come!' he exclaims, suddenly animated. 'Not at first – I was royally *fucked* after what happened in Dorset. But when I came you had already moved in with your . . . *boyfriend*.' He says this bitterly.

'But that was *years* later!' I cry.

'No!' He denies this ardently. 'No, it was *months*! I came to your halls of residence and a girl told me you were staying in with some bloke called Jessie!'

I gasp with horror as understanding dawns on me. My fellow students used to think that Jessie was my boyfriend.

'He wasn't my boyfriend,' I say in a tiny voice. 'He was my friend.'

The shock on his face must surely mirror mine.

'You *came* for me?' I reiterate.

He nods. 'Yes.'

'I thought you didn't care. I thought something had happened to you!'

He shakes his head again. 'No.'

He lets me go and buries his face in his hands, his elbows resting on his knees. Tears start to trek down my cheeks.

'I can't believe you're married,' he whispers.

'What did you expect?' There are so many emotions running

around my body. 'It's been almost a decade! A *decade*! You haven't exactly waited for me, either,' I say dryly.

He glances up at me.

'I've seen you with all those women. It's not like you've been waiting around, yourself.' He'll be able to hear the jealousy in my voice, but I don't care.

'None of them meant anything to me,' he says passionately.

'Oh, come on.'

'They didn't! Fucking hell, Alice, it's not like I married any of them!' He gets to his feet and starts pacing the room. I watch him, miserably.

'What's his name?' he asks.

'Lukas.'

He half snorts. I realise he's riddled with jealousy himself.

'He's German.'

He snorts again.

'What does he do?' He's trying to sound casual, but his eyes flit to my really-quite-large diamond.

'He's a physicist.'

'Fucking hell.' He shakes his head, almost in disgust.

'What?'

'He's a brainiac too, is he?' He raises one eyebrow at me. 'I fucking knew you'd end up with a brainiac.'

'*Joe!*'

'You were never going to settle for a loser like me,' he adds sullenly.

'That's not true!' I exclaim, jumping to my feet. 'You're not a loser.'

He laughs sardonically and I know what he's thinking: he's not a loser, *now*.

'You were *never* a loser,' I clarify.

'Have you got any children?' he asks suddenly.

'No.'

He falls to his knees on the floor and looks utterly crushed. I kneel in front of him. He looks up at me.

'Why didn't you contact *me*?'

'I tried. I tried for a long time after you left – I would go into central London and search the streets for you. Jessie even pretended to be an old friend of yours and called the pub to speak to your parents to see if they'd heard from you. When I saw you in *Strike* I managed to get hold of your agent, but he wouldn't give me your number, and I was already with . . .'

'Lukas.'

Each of us regards the other with desolation. There's a knock at the door. Joe jumps to his feet – literally jumps from knees to feet with a catlike martial arts move – and goes to the door. I quickly get up. He peers through the peephole and opens the door to reveal Melanie standing there.

'Do you want me to order you some breakfast?' she asks hesitantly, glancing through at me.

'No,' he replies shortly. 'Not for me. Alice?' he calls.

'No, thank you,' I respond.

'Joe, you need to eat,' Melanie chides. She calls him Joe too, I realise with a start. Maybe all his friends do. I suppose they would.

'I'm not hungry,' he reiterates firmly. He starts to close the door on her.

'Don't forget about the interview!' she shouts as the door shuts in her face.

'You have an interview?' I ask.

'Fuck the interview,' he snaps. Suddenly he looks contrite. 'I shouldn't have been rude to her.'

'She's your PA, right?' I ask.

'Yeah. She's great.' He comes back towards me.

'You told her about me?'

'Well, a bit.' He shrugs and smiles with embarrassment as he looks at me. 'Not everything.'

I feel my face heat up. 'What time is your interview?' I try to sound nonchalant.

'Nine. I'm sorry, I didn't realise it was scheduled that early when I asked you to come this morning.'

'It's okay. Another exclusive, hey?' I ask knowingly.

'You saw that about my parents, did you?' His tone is wry.

'It was hard to miss. I'm sorry,' I add quietly. 'I thought about you a lot during that time.' Who am I kidding? I think about him *all* the time.

'I thought about you a lot too. Still do,' he half laughs. 'What are you doing for Christmas?' He changes the subject. I can't believe it's Christmas Eve.

'I'm staying with my parents.'

'Where's your . . .'

'He's in Germany.' I save him the trouble of saying his name.

'You're spending Christmas apart?' Again: hope.

'Yes.'

'Why?' His brow furrows and he comes closer.

'Lukas got a promotion and he moved back to Germany. I'm still working in Cambridge.'

'You're living apart?' The look on his face . . . I don't want to hurt him, but . . .

'For now. He wants me to move there as soon as I can. I'm going to Germany for the holidays.'

He falters a few steps away from me. There's another knock on the door.

'What is it now?' he mutters, returning to the door and wrenching it open.

'I'm sorry,' Melanie says. 'She's early.'

'Who?'

'The journalist.'

'Tell her to wait!' he bites, about to shut the door.

'It's Christmas Eve,' Melanie hastily tries to reason with him. 'She just wants to go home to her family.'

Joe scratches his eyebrow with frustration. He nods abruptly. 'Give me five minutes.'

Melanie flashes me an apologetic look as the door shuts once more in her face.

'I'll go,' I say, reaching for my bag and slinging it over my shoulder.

'No,' he says resolutely, shaking his head. 'You haven't even had breakfast.'

What a small thing to be worried about.

'I'm not hungry, anyway.'

'I don't want you to go,' he says.

'I have to, Joe. If the press find out about us . . .'

'Fuck!' he exclaims. Did he used to swear this much? I guess so. Lukas rarely uses bad language. I'm not used to it.

'When do you go back to America?' I ask.

'Next week, but . . .' He looks at me. 'When are you going to Germany?'

'Tuesday.'

'Please, Alice, this can't be it. We need more time ... Without all these interruptions.'

'What do you suggest?'

His eyes light up. 'We could go back to Dorset! To your cottage! I wonder if it's free?'

'I don't know.'

'Can you find out? Would you go with me?'

'Um, I ...'

'Please!'

'I don't know!'

'Please. *Please!* There's so much more we need to say. Please!'

What the hell am I doing? I take a deep breath. 'Okay.' I nod.

'Really?'

'Yes.'

'*Really?*' He can't quite believe it.

'I said yes!'

'When?'

'I'm not sure ... Boxing Day?'

'Yes! How will we get there?'

'Train?'

I can see his mind ticking over ten to the dozen. 'I can't travel with you. I'll have to meet you there. Melanie will sort it out. I trust her. It's better that no one else knows about you.'

'How long do you want to stay? If I can get the cottage ...' I add.

'A few days?'

That would mean rescheduling my trip to Germany. I'd have to come up with some excuse ... But this is something I need to do. 'I'll let you know when it's booked,' I say.

He grins and my stomach fills with butterflies.

Chapter 61

It's all very cloak and dagger. I have to ask my parents if they still have the rental details for the cottage in Dorset, and then I have to lie and tell them that I'm going to Germany early, while I tell Lukas that I want to stay with my parents a bit longer because he has to work until the weekend, anyway. No one is thrilled with this change of plan, but I don't feel like I have any other choice if I'm going to get closure.

Closure. I keep telling myself that this is what I'm after, but the very idea makes my blood run cold. The thought of never seeing Joe again after this week, the thought of only ever seeing him on the big screen and in the press . . . It's too awful to contemplate.

The cottage, thankfully, is empty, and the owners are happy to have a last-minute rental. They give me the code for the key safe and I text it to Joe in case he arrives first.

Lizzy is the only one who knows what I'm doing, and she's gobsmacked that it's come to this. I feel even more disloyal to Lukas for telling her but, in the grand scheme of things, Lizzy knowing is the least of his problems.

I'm determined not to cheat on him, though. This is all about moving on. I have to keep reminding myself.

I have never been less interested in Christmas Day, and I haven't lived off as little sleep since I was with Joe nearly ten years ago. Finally I step off the train at Wareham Station and climb into the taxi I called in advance. Gale-force winds are predicted for tomorrow, but today it's just cold and grey, a far cry from that summer long ago.

We drive past the red telephone box on the corner of the track that leads to the cottage and I remember standing in there when the vet's wife told us that Dyson hadn't lived through the night. I remember Joe's face – his heartbreak – and all of a sudden I feel like crying. A short while later the driver pulls up outside the cottage.

It's exactly the same as it looked years ago: the stone wall, the bench underneath the kitchen window. I pay the driver and climb out of the car. The lights are off: I've arrived first.

Out of the blue it hits me that he might not come, and I have to catch my breath before finding the key and letting myself in. I breathe in deeply. It smells the same. I go upstairs to my one-time bedroom and stare at the bed that we made love in. I remember those early days of lovemaking, how raw they were when it was the first time for both of us. I hear a car outside the window and walk over to see a blue hatchback pull up. That won't be him. He'll have a fancy car, for sure. I'm startled to see him climb out of the car and open the gate, before returning to the vehicle and parking it in the driveway. I guess he chose something inconspicuous. Smart.

I delve into my bag and rummage around until I find my mobile phone. I switch it off, then, my heart hammering inside my chest, I go downstairs to meet him. He comes inside before I reach the door.

'You're here.' He grins, and once more my heart somersaults. He's wearing a dark-grey hoodie and he seems so normal, so . . . like himself all those years ago, without the longer hair and the Emo eyebrow.

'I beat you,' I reply, smiling at him.

'Hardly surprising with that pile of junk.' He glances over his shoulder.

'All you wanted was a car,' I tease. 'And *that's* what you ended up with?' He gives me a wry look. Obviously I know he rented it. 'Trying to keep your cover?' I ask.

'Doing my bit.'

I know from my internet research that he's got a Ferrari back in LA.

'It seems to be working.' I go to the kitchen window and peer out. 'Nope, no hordes of screaming girls following you here.'

He chuckles. I turn to face him. He's looking around the kitchen. 'Still the same,' he says, going to the counter. 'This is where you made me a sandwich.'

'Ham and cheese.' It comes back to me:

'Ham and cheese? Peanut butter? What do you fancy?'

'You,' he said.

He smiles a small, regretful smile, as though he's remembering too.

'Do you want to go for a walk?' I feel like I could do with some air.

He nods. 'I'll just get my bags in from the car.'

He returns a short while later with two oversized leather gym bags.

'Which room am I in?' he asks.

'Mum and Dad's?' I suggest.

'Why don't you have their room? It's bigger.'

'I would have thought the Hollywood star is used to something grander than my little room.'

'Alice,' he chides with a frown, and as the butterflies make their way into my stomach I realise that I really do love hearing him say my name, even when he's telling me: 'Don't be ridiculous.'

For want of something better to do, I follow him up the stairs. He turns left to go into my room.

'I'm in here,' I say quickly.

'You have the bigger room,' he insists again, regarding the bed.

'No, I *want* this one,' I tell him firmly.

He flashes me a cheeky grin and my heart does that thing again. 'Do you remember?' he asks me softly.

I blush furiously. 'I am not even talking about this!' I exclaim, laughing with embarrassment as I turn and go out of the room. 'Put your bags in the other room,' I snap jokily, pointing back at the door.

'Later,' he replies with amusement as he follows me back downstairs.

There are so many butterflies inside me now that I feel like I could take off.

He goes to the table and picks up my coat, which I left there when I came in. He holds it open for me while I shrug it on.

'Where's yours?' I ask, trying to inject normality into my voice as his hands rest on my arms for a moment too long.

'In the car.'

'Come on, then.' I usher him out, locking the door behind me.

He pauses at the gate and glances back at the bench, before giving me a playful look. I roll my eyes and purse my lips. He's obviously remembering the hours we spent there, kissing like there was no tomorrow. He opens the gate for me and waits for me to pass through.

'Where shall we go?' I ask casually.

'You know where,' he scolds gently.

We walk down the path towards Dancing Ledge.

'Can I hold your hand?' he asks suddenly.

'Um . . .'

He reaches across for it, anyway, and I hesitantly let him take it.

This isn't real. It's not real. I'm in another lifetime. No one is here except for Joe and me. And, with that, I let myself go.

We pass the field that we lay in under a full moon. I stop in my tracks and stare at it. I jump with surprise as he wraps his arms around my waist from behind and rests his chin on my shoulder. 'Do you remember?'

I glance back at him. 'Joe, I haven't forgotten a thing.'

He stares at my lips and a bolt of electricity shoots through me. I haven't forgotten this feeling, either.

'Let's keep walking,' I say. He meets my eyes for a brief moment and then steps away from me. Feeling flustered, I set off down the lane, folding my arms across my chest so he can't hold my hand again.

'What happened to you after we left Dorset?' I ask, giving him a sidelong glance.

He shoves his hands into his pockets. 'I went to London, like I said I would. I slept rough for a bit, then I got a job working in a bar. One night there was a bar fight and I tried to break it up. I got hurt.'

'Were you okay?'

He grins at my concern. 'Yes, but a workmate of mine told me about these kick-boxing classes he was taking, and I thought it was probably about time I learned to defend myself, so I went along with him one day.' He glances at me. 'Did you see *Strike*?'

I nod. 'Not until after I was married.' Not properly, anyway.

He looks away. 'Well, then, you know about that chapter of my life.'

I know that he learned how to fight and that the director saw something in him and decided to make him a star.

'Did you film that documentary before or after you came to Cambridge to find me?' I ask.

'Oh, after. Much later. After Cambridge I was a bit fucked again.'

'Oh.'

'Mmm.'

I don't understand. My words come out in a flood. 'Why did you give up so easily? When you came back for me and thought I was with someone else, why didn't you try to find me, to speak to me, to, I don't know, *win* me back?'

'Alice . . .' His face is full of regret. 'I wasn't in a good place. When I found out you'd already moved on . . . I'd actually told myself that's what I should expect before I came looking for you. Why would you wait for *this*?' He indicates himself with his hands. 'But it still came as a total shock when I found out you'd met someone else. The thought of seeing you with another guy nearly killed me . . . I had to get away from there as quickly as possible. I . . . I . . . wasn't in a good place.' He uses that phrase again. 'I tried to forget about you after that, but there were times when the thought of you consumed me.'

'I know what you mean,' I say sadly. 'It was the same for me.'

'There were other times I tried to track you down. Every so often I'd look you up on Facebook, search through all the Alice Simmons I could find.'

'I'm not on Facebook. Lizzy was always trying to get me to join. I'll never hear the end of it when she discovers you did that.'

Lukas despises social networking sites. He considers them vulgar.

But certain things still need clarifying. 'Why did you leave Dorset so suddenly?' I ask. 'I went upstairs to pack and when I came downstairs you were gone.'

He sighs. 'Your dad told me I needed to sort myself out before I contacted you again.'

'*What?*'

'He was right,' he says hurriedly. 'Don't blame him. I didn't want to screw up your life at university. And what happened that night . . . with Ryan . . .' He shudders. 'It still gives me nightmares.'

'Me too.'

'Does it?' He looks distraught. 'I'm so sorry.'

'It's not your fault,' I say firmly.

'I should have told you the truth about him. I'm so sorry I lied to you.'

'I understood. I forgave you the second you told me.'

His face darkens as he stares ahead and picks up his pace. I have to hurry to keep up with him – but he seems oblivious. 'Sometimes I think about seeing him again,' he says in a low voice.

I pause before asking: 'What would you do?'

'I think I'd fucking kick his head in.'

I jolt at his language and he realises he might be freaking me out.

He looks apologetic. 'Sorry.'

I don't speak.

We reach the gorse walkway and scramble down the steep incline to the grassy hill. The sea is rough and grey. We stand there for a moment and stare at the view. It's the middle of winter and the place is deserted apart from a couple of lone dog walkers on the cliffs in the distance.

'Can we go to the ledge?' he asks me abruptly.

'Sure.'

'Let's run,' he says with a grin, taking off down the steep hill. I laugh and follow him, the momentum propelling my legs at such a fast pace that I don't know how I'll stop at the bottom. Somehow I do. I'm in stitches – literally – and I'm laughing hard too. I bend over and clutch my stomach until I can recover.

'You're not even out of breath!' I gasp up at him.

He laughs at my mock annoyance. He's too fit for his own good. This isn't fair.

'Do you want me to carry you?' he asks with amusement.

'You'd better bloody not,' I rebuke.

He comes towards me with a raised eyebrow. I hold up my hand. 'I'm warning you!'

He grins and grabs me. I scream as he throws me over his shoulder and starts to run towards the rocky steps that lead to Dancing Ledge.

'PUT ME DOWN!' I yell.

He laughingly does and I hit him on his chest. Flippin' heck it's hard.

'Ouch,' I joke, rubbing my hand. I lead the way to the steps.

'Don't slip,' he says. I think he's teasing me, but I realise he's not when he puts his hands protectively on my shoulders.

'Let me go first,' he says at the bottom of the steps, moving in front of me. He easily climbs down the rock face and waits for me at the bottom. 'Be careful,' he warns with concern. I navigate the rocks with far less grace and speed. He holds his arms out to me and steadies my fall as I jump down from the last foothold.

He takes my hand again as we walk along the ledge. The swimming pool is still there, carved out of the rock and full of water, reflecting the murky sky. I look ahead to the cave. I know that's where we're going and my stomach is a jittery mess. We walk into the dark space.

I take a deep breath and stare at the ground where we made love for the very first time. He's silent as he remembers too.

'I still love you,' he says suddenly, looking at me with anguish in his eyes.

'Joe . . .' I caution sadly.

He glances at my wedding ring and then turns and faces the cave entrance before sitting on the ground.

I cautiously sit down next to him.

Neither of us speaks for a very long time. The sound of the waves crashing on the rocks outside fills the small space. Eventually I huddle in closer to him and rest my cheek on his biceps. He puts his arm around me and draws me closer. This is unbearable.

'Do you still love me?' he asks after a while.

I hesitate before answering. 'Yes.'

I can feel him tense up. It's almost as though he's too afraid to speak.

'But I love Lukas too.' I have to tell him this. I have to be honest.

'Do you love him more?' His voice wavers as he glances down at me.

I look up into his eyes. Then I shake my head, ever so slightly.

'Alice . . .' He touches his hand to my face.

No. No, no, no, don't kiss me. I don't want to cheat on my husband.

But then his lips are on mine and the feeling is so blissful that I'm rendered powerless. I can't help but kiss him back.

This isn't real. It's not real. I'm in another lifetime . . .

Our kiss deepens and we fall back onto the hard cold stone. I want him so much. More than I've ever wanted anyone. More than I even wanted *him* all those years ago.

'I love you,' he murmurs into my mouth.

Lukas.

'Stop.'

Lukas.

'Stop it!' I push him away. 'I can't do this,' I say agitatedly, beginning to stand up. 'I'm married! I should go. I should go to my parents, or to Germany.'

'No! Please don't. Please don't,' he begs, looking up at me. 'I'm sorry. I won't touch you again.'

If I'm being honest that's the last thing I want to hear, but I nod slowly and focus on his chin. 'We should get back. It will be dark soon,' I say in a daze.

Once more he bounds to his feet and in a surreal way I'm reminded that he's Joseph Strike, martial arts expert and A-list actor. We walk back to the cottage, mostly in silence.

Near the house Joe stops suddenly and looks at the ground. I realise with a start that this is where we found Dyson. I go over to him and take his hand. We walk on.

'Did you ever think about getting another dog?' I ask quietly as we approach the gate.

He shakes his head quickly and lets go of my hand. 'It wouldn't be fair. I travel too much.' He opens the gate for me and holds it back for me to pass.

'Couldn't someone look after him while you're away?'

'That's not very "me", Alice.' He looks at me and smiles.

I take the keys out of my pocket and open the door. We go inside and take off our coats.

'Do you want a fire?' he asks.

'Yeah, that'd be great.'

'Cool.' He heads off to the living room.

'What do you want for dinner?' I call after him.

He pokes his head back through to the kitchen. 'Shit! I didn't think about bringing food.'

'Don't worry, I did.'

'Ever the planner,' he says with a smile. 'Anything would be great. You know what I like,' he adds.

'Are you sure you're not on some dodgy macrobiotic diet?' I ask wryly.

He grins at me. 'New Year's resolution?'

'What did you do for Christmas?' I ask curiously.

'Nothing. Spent it in my hotel. Just another day to me.'

I frown at him. He shrugs and returns to the living room. That's so sad. He has no one to spend Christmas with. I guess that's always been the way for him – ever since he was a teenager. He has no family. Pity engulfs me. I pause and then walk through to him. He's piling logs in the hearth. I sit on the sofa and watch him.

He glances up at me. 'What's up?'

'I'm sad that you have no one to spend Christmas with. I wish I could have invited you home to my parents' house.'

He looks amused. 'I'm sure that would have gone down very well. Here's that idiot bloke again, except *this* time he's screwing up our daughter's marriage instead of just her university experience.'

I give him a look, but don't say anything.

'I'm starving,' he says meaningfully.

'I'm going!' I jump up and head back to the kitchen.

He comes through after a little while. 'So what are we having?'

'Now don't get angry, but I've only got ready meals.'

He laughs. 'Why would I be angry?'

I shrug. 'I don't know.' Lukas hates ready meals. Even home-made lasagne from the farm shop. 'We're having Indian.'

'Brilliant!' he exclaims.

I laugh. 'Are you joking?'

'No! I bloody miss Indian. They don't do it at all well in the States.'

'I'm not sure this is going to be a very good substitute for the real thing.'

'We should go out to a restaurant one night!' he says excitedly before his face falls. 'Oh, we can't.'

'You might get recognised?'

He nods dejectedly. 'I . . .'

'What?'

'Sometimes I wish I wasn't famous.'

'No, you don't,' I chide.

He looks up at me sharply. 'I do. It's so fucking complicated . . . I wasn't expecting it.'

'But you're an amazing actor,' I say gently. 'You must enjoy it?'

He nods. 'I do. But . . .' He sighs. 'I don't know.'

'What? Go on.'

'Sometimes I wish I had a normal life like you, a normal job, living in a normal little house and . . . Well, I bet your house isn't little at all.'

'It's not that big,' I tell him. 'It's Lukas's parents who have the . . . Well, they're, you know, he's from a pretty good family.'

'I bet he is.' He looks thoroughly fed up.

'When I say "good", I don't mean "nice".'

'You don't like them very much?' He clearly wants everything *not* to be rosy.

'I like his brother and sister. But his parents, no, not really.'

'At least he and I have that in common.'

He comes over and hoiks himself up onto the countertop. He watches me as I prick the cellophane of the rice packet with a fork and swap it over with the now-cooked curries in the microwave. I look over at him. *This* is so normal, so domesticated. This is what our life *could* have been like.

My face crumbles. He looks horrified.

'What is it?' He jumps down from the counter and puts his hands on my arms, studying my face. I shake my head quickly, willing the tears away, but they don't comply. 'Come here.' He wraps his arms around me and pulls me in. I let out a sob into his chest and he holds me tightly while I cry.

'Shhhh, shhhh,' he says into my hair, kissing the top of my head over and over. 'It's going to be okay. It's going to be okay. I love you, Alice. I love you.'

But it's not going to be okay. There's nothing okay about this at all.

That night I take my wedding ring off.

Chapter 62

I come down in the morning to find him doing press-ups on the living-room carpet. I have no idea how many he's already done, but I stand on the last step and watch in awe as he does thirty more, the muscles on his back rippling. He bounces to his feet and then nearly jumps out of his skin when he sees me.

'Shit! You scared me.'

'Sorry.' I try to keep a straight face as I wander through to the kitchen and fill the kettle with water. I barely slept, but I don't feel tired.

He follows me through, slightly out of breath. I glance at his bare chest. It's hard not to.

'I can't actually believe you're Joseph Strike,' I say with a shake of my head as I switch the kettle on. 'Did it feel weird changing your name?'

'At first the thought of it did, yes. But when it came down to doing it, it was surprisingly easy to let it go.' He grins at me and says in a teasing voice: 'Anyway, Alice Strike sounds better than Alice Strickwold.'

A thrill goes through me. 'Oi. Enough of that.' I blush and change the subject. 'Do you still like Kingmaker?'

'Yeah, of course.' He hops up onto the countertop again and inadvertently I glance at his famous six-pack. I try to concentrate.

'You haven't thought about putting "You and I . . ." on one of your film soundtracks?'

He looks at me with disbelief. 'I'm working on it, actually.'

'Really?'

'Yeah.' He lightly kicks my leg with his foot. 'You know me so well.'

Feeling jittery, I turn my attention to the kettle. It's taking forever to boil.

'Hey, do you have the number for the people who own this cottage?' he asks casually.

'Er, sure. Why?'

'I'm going to ask them if I can buy it.'

'Seriously?'

'Yeah. Don't you think it's a good idea?'

'Well, yes. But can you really just buy a cottage?'

He looks amused.

'Okay, yes, I know you can afford it,' I say drily. 'But there's more to buying a house than handing over your credit card details.'

'Can you help me?' he asks. 'I mean, I could ask Melanie, but I'd rather keep it between us.'

There's something quite loveable about that.

'Of course I can help you,' I tell him warmly. 'Do you want me to call the owners and see what they say?'

'Actually, that would be great,' he says chirpily, jumping down from the counter. 'Hold off on my cuppa. I'm going to go and take a shower.'

My eyes follow him out of the room.

I go upstairs and dig out my mobile, feeling awful as I switch it on. I don't want to have to face reality yet. Maybe no one will have called. I look up the number of the cottage owners and ring them.

'Is everything okay?' the landlady asks with concern.

'Everything's fine,' I reassure her. I can hear my phone beeping to let me know that other messages are coming in, but I try to ignore them so I can concentrate on the business in hand.

A few minutes later I end the call, just as Joe comes out of the bathroom with a towel wrapped around his waist.

'They don't want to sell,' I call after him with disappointment.

'Oh.' He stops and comes back into my bedroom. 'Offer them more money, then.'

'They don't want to sell,' I say again, more firmly.

'Everyone has a price. Find theirs.'

'Yes, sir!' I say jauntily, saluting him.

He looks shamefaced. 'Sorry. Do you want me to speak to them?'

'No, it's alright. But if you're really serious you should pass this on to your solicitor. How much are you willing to pay, exactly?'

'As much as they want,' he replies offhandedly, tightening the towel. I try not to get distracted.

'But it's got to make financial sense. You can't just buy it if they ask way more than it's worth.'

'It's worth everything to me,' he says simply.

'Why do you want it so much?'

My phone starts to vibrate on the mattress beside me and I look down at it with alarm. Shit!

'It's Lukas,' I say, snatching it up. I glance at Joe.

He looks shaken as he backs out of the room and closes the door behind him.

Should I answer it? Suddenly the phone stops ringing.

I scarcely dare listen to my voicemail messages. In fact, I don't dare. I switch my phone back off and go downstairs. Joe joins me a short while later. He's wearing the black cargo pants and an indie-rock T-shirt.

'Did you speak to him?' He's trying to sound casual.

'No. He hung up,' I add.

He flicks the kettle back on and gets out a couple of mugs. 'Tea?' he asks.

'Sure.' I get on with breakfast.

'So what does a *physicist* do, then?' he asks sardonically.

'I wouldn't have a fucking clue,' I reply as I lift the lid off the bread box. He looks at me in surprise and then laughs.

'You never swear!' he exclaims.

'Ooh, you say that, but you should have heard me the year after you left. I was ANGRY . . .' I grab a bread knife and start to slice through the loaf.

'Were you?'

'Absolutely fucking furious.'

'Alice!' He's slightly outraged.

'I was taking a group of tourists on a punt—'

'You were what?' he interrupts.

'I worked as a punter.'

'You can punt? No way!' He looks amazed. 'I would *love* to go punting!'

'I'll take you.' I grin.

'Will you?'

'Yep.'

Reality check. *When* will I take him? In that other lifetime that I keep talking about?

I put my head down and slice another piece of bread, before popping four pieces into the toaster.

'I thought we'd go for a walk to the pub after breakfast,' he says, stirring sugar into his mug.

'The pub?' I'm taken aback. '*Your* pub?'

'Well, it's not my pub anymore.' He stares out of the window and takes a sip of his tea. 'But I'd like to see it again.'

I understand. This is about closure for him too. That word again. I can't bear it.

The wind has picked up properly today and my hair whips around my face as we traipse across the field to the pub. I wish I'd brought a hairband. I try to tuck my locks into my coat, but the wind keeps dragging them out again. Suddenly Joe grabs my hand.

'You're not wearing your rings,' he says with shock.

'Don't read anything into it,' I reply, shaking his hand free. I feel his eyes on me as I keep walking. The truth is that my fingers feel naked without them, yet it feels wrong to keep them on.

Finally we walk over the crest of the hill and the pub is there before us. Joe comes to a standstill.

'Are you okay?' I ask him.

'I've wanted to come back here for years,' he breathes, taking it all in. I reach over and squeeze his hand. 'You know I couldn't have come back with anyone other than you.' He looks across at me.

'Do you want to go in for a drink?' I ask him.

'I'd better not,' he replies, backing away. 'I'd like to go back to Brownsea Island too.'

At exactly the same time we glance at each other and say one word:

'Peafowl.'

Our mouths fall open in disbelief and then we fall about with hilarity.

'You knew what I was going to say!' I scream with laughter.

'You knew what *I* was going to say!' he laughs back.

He pulls me down on the rugged grass, both of us still in fits of giggles. He puts his hands on my hair and pushes it back off my face, and then suddenly we're not laughing anymore. His eyes are serious as he gazes at me, and then his lips are on mine and this time I have no willpower to stop.

I kiss him like there's no tomorrow, only today, the here and the now.

Somehow we make it back to the cottage and undress each other slowly in my bedroom, our lips barely parting. He's so careful with me – almost as though he thinks I'm going to break – or flee . . . But I'm going nowhere. Every part of me – my heart, my soul, my body – is here with him in this moment.

I love him like I've never loved anyone.

We're both overcome with emotion when it's over, and he stays on top of me for a long time as we both breathe heavily. Finally he lifts his head and gazes at me.

'This could be our place. Where we'd come to get away from it all.'

I close my eyes and gently push him away. My heart hurts, and it's not because his chest is pressing so hard into mine.

'What's wrong?' he asks me worriedly as he rolls off me.

My bottom lip wobbles and my eyes fill up with tears. 'This isn't real. It's not real.'

'What do you mean?' He looks pale.

'What do you think is going to happen? Do you think I'm going to leave my husband? Break the vow that I made to him?'

He looks uncomfortable. 'I hoped so.'

I sit up. 'You're living in la-la land! This isn't a Hollywood film!'

He climbs out of bed and starts dragging on his clothes. 'I know you're smarter than me, but do you have to be quite so patronising?'

'There is no future for us! How could there possibly be? You don't have a normal life. You will *never* have a normal life. Even if you chucked in fame and never made another movie, you'd still be recognised for years. And it would be wrong of me to even want you to give up your acting career when you're so damn good at it!'

'I would give up everything for you,' he says simply, giving me a poignant look before walking out of the room.

I fall back onto the bed and sigh loudly. And then I get up and get dressed. I go downstairs to find him on the sofa, staring at the wall. I climb onto the sofa and snuggle into him. He's tense and then he relaxes, putting his arms around me and pulling me in. I nuzzle into his neck, wanting to be close to him, not wanting to spoil the time we have together. We don't have much of it left.

'I love you,' he whispers.

'I love you too.'

'I want to be with you forever.'

I don't reply.

Chapter 63

The more time I spend with him, the more my sense of reality changes. Soon it's my other life that feels unreal, my other life with Lukas and my parents and Lizzy. I still haven't listened to my phone messages. I was supposed to fly to Germany yesterday and I know that I'm evil and that there's something wrong with me for sending a vague text about being delayed instead of calling to let Lukas know what's actually going on.

We're living in a bubble. A bubble that is all too soon going to pop. We spend half of our days and most of our nights making love, and it's so much more passionate than it used to be. Neither of us acknowledges how we got this extra confidence, this extra experience between the sheets, but we connect like we were meant to be together, like there could never be anyone else. I can't get enough of him. I don't want to ever leave his side. I'm in that other lifetime.

Finally we can't go any longer without food, so on New Year's Day I borrow Joe's car and take it to a nearby shop, stocking up on the bare basics: bread, milk, cheese, pasta, tinned food. My heart swells as I imagine him sitting on the countertop, watching me prepare dinner. I have no idea that my dream is about to become a nightmare.

I see the glint of silver up ahead, but I don't click until I'm further down the track. Then I realise with horror that Lukas's Porsche is parked outside the cottage.

I pull up behind his car and hurriedly undo my seatbelt, stumbling out of the car and running towards the cottage. Through the kitchen window I can see Lukas and Joe squaring up to each other.

'You don't want to fight me,' I hear Joe saying firmly through the open door.

'Are you telling me your fight scenes aren't all digitally enhanced?' Lukas snipes.

'You really don't want to find out, buddy.'

'Stop it!' I shout, falling into the kitchen.

'Alice!' Lukas exclaims, rushing towards me.

I take a step away from this stranger and glance at Joe. Lukas halts in his steps. He looks behind him at Joe and then back at me. Pain contorts his features. He takes another step towards me. I step backwards. 'How did you find me?' I ask.

'Your parents. You asked them about this cottage. We were all worried.'

'I'm sorry.'

I know there's nowhere near enough remorse in my voice to cover all of *this*.

'Alice?' Joe asks tentatively.

'Do you mind?' Lukas snaps. 'I'd like some time alone with my *wife*.'

I glance at Joe and nod. He turns and walks into the living room.

'What are you doing?' Lukas asks in not much more than a whisper.

'I'm not sure,' I tell him honestly.

'Perhaps it was wrong of me to stop you from seeking some sort of resolution years ago. Is that what this is about? Finding answers?'

I can hardly bear to look at him. I nod.

'Did you find them?' He sounds desperate.

'I don't know,' I say in a small voice. 'I'm so confused.'

He takes another step towards me. I can't go any further backwards – I'm pressed up against the kitchen counter.

He walks the rest of the way to me and puts his hand on my hip. 'I think you should come home with me now,' he says in a low voice.

I shake my head. 'I'm not ready. Not yet.'

He nods. Then, quick as a flash, he grabs my wrist and drags me out of there.

'NO!' I scream.

Joe appears before Lukas reaches the car.

'LET HER GO!'

I've never seen Joe so full of rage as he stands with his fists raised, ready to strike, *wanting* to strike.

Lukas flings my wrist away, and the look he gives me . . . I feel like a knife has pierced my heart. I know he will never, ever forgive me for this. And I'm sorry. I'm so sorry. I'll never forgive myself, either.

Joe steps in front of me and puts his hand on my stomach, gently pushing me behind him. But there's no need to protect me anymore. Lukas is already in his car. He flashes the two of us a venomous look before roaring away down the track, creating a dust cloud in his wake.

'That's kind of put a dampener on our secret little hideaway,' Joe says. I know he's trying to lighten the mood, but I'm in no mood for jokes. I run inside and up the stairs. He follows me.

'Are you okay?' he asks.

'*What have I done? What have I done?*' I yank open the top drawer of my bedside table and pull out my engagement and wedding rings.

Clear as day I see Lukas kneeling before me on the crisp white snow at the top of an Austrian mountain. '*When you said Rosalinde was my first love . . . You were wrong.*' His eyes brim with tears as he fervently promises me, 'You're *my first love. I love* you.'

Oh, Lukas. My husband. He may have his faults, but he doesn't deserve this. I stare down at the rings with despair. 'What have I done?'

Joe sits down on the bed beside me and takes my hand, closing my fist with my rings inside.

'You've made a decision.'

'I didn't make a decision! Lukas has made one for both of us.'

'No, Alice,' he says, calmly and firmly. 'You made the decision when you agreed to come here with me. You knew this would happen. In your heart, you knew.'

I look up at him and my eyes fill with tears. 'What now?'

'Now we start our new life together.' He gently opens each of my fingers and takes the rings from my palm, then he puts them back in the drawer and closes it. 'Do you think you can handle it?'

'I don't know.'

He tilts my chin up to look at him. 'I do.'

I pull away. 'No. No. This is all wrong.'

'It's not!' he exclaims.

'No. We can't start off like this. I have to go back. I have to sort things out.'

'No!'

'Yes. I have to. This isn't right. It's so wrong. We've been living in a dream world and I have to go back and face up to my responsibilities. I have to talk to Lukas. I owe it to him to explain, at the very least. I need to talk to my parents. And Lizzy's going to do her nut in . . .'

'No.' He shakes his head. 'No.'

'Joe, you have to let me go. You have to let me do this.'

'I can't. What if he takes you back?'

'He won't.'

'*I* would.'

'No, you wouldn't. Not after all of this.'

'I *would*.'

'I have to go.'

'No!'

'Yes. If this is meant to be, if we are meant to be together, then we will be.'

'We *are* meant to be together!' he shouts.

I sigh and look at him. He's overwrought with anxiety. He takes a deep breath, and then speaks: 'How long do you need?'

'I wish I knew.'

He wants to drive me back to my parents, but I'm worried someone will see us.

'I'd be thrilled if they did,' he says.

I give him a wry look.

'I'm not being sarcastic – I *want* people to see us.'

For the first time I think about the Andy Carl interview. This would be big news. I'm the 'Alice' Joseph Strike spoke about on live television.

'And then everyone would find out that the love of your life is an unfaithful bitch who cheated on her husband.' He flinches. 'You know we should do this properly,' I add.

He reluctantly agrees to drive me to the station instead. In the car he turns to face me. His expression is a mix of emotions.

'Alice, if he takes you back—'

'He won't!'

'If he does ... And if you choose to have a normal life with him instead of a crazy one with me, I'll still want you. Even if I can't have the whole of you.' He stares at me directly. 'Do you understand what I'm saying?'

I can't speak for the lump in my throat.

'This could still be *our* place ...' He grips my arm. 'I need to know you understand what I'm saying!' he adds heatedly.

I regard him warily and then, hesitantly, I nod.

He pulls me to him and kisses my lips once more before letting me go.

Epilogue

It's a hot and hazy summer's day. There's a naval ship out on the horizon and white gulls swoop across the cliffs and directly above my head. There's an indentation on my finger where my rings should be and it feels strange not to have them on.

I arrived early and left a note, but there was really no need. He'll know where I am. I wait for him on the yellow-green grass, under the sun and the blue, blue sky. I wait for him, full of anticipation and hope and love.

I sense him behind me, but don't turn around. A smile forms on my lips as his hands gently touch my shoulders, and then I look up into his brown eyes which still manage to sparkle even when it's dark. But today there's no darkness, no sadness, only light and love.

'You came,' he says, pulling me to my feet and touching his hands to my face.

'I told you I would.' I slide my hands around his neck and gaze up at him. 'I love you.'

'I love you more,' he says.

'Still?'

He smiles and my heart flips. 'Always.'

Acknowledgements

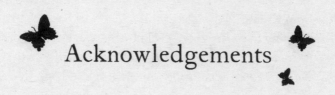

MASSIVE thanks to my readers, who continue to blow me away with their incredible messages of support, both on Facebook and now Twitter. Please keep them coming – you have no idea how much you make me smile.

Thank you to Nigel Stoneman, not only for letting my family and I stay in the beautiful Dorset cottage that inspired the story for *One Perfect Summer*, but also for saying, 'you should write a book', and twenty minutes later, passing on my idea for *Lucy in the Sky* to his Publishing Director, Suzanne Baboneau. One week later I had a two-book deal, and I still can't believe how lucky I am.

Thank you to the aforementioned Suzanne Baboneau, who is a brilliant editor and who I would trust with my life and not just my books. And thank you to the whole team at Simon & Schuster. For the last five books I've wanted to name names, but I have always been too worried I'd leave someone out. This time though, I really must thank the following people: Sarah Birdsey, for selling my translation rights to more countries than I can count (or at least, remember); Florence Partridge, for her ongoing hard work with publicity; Matt Johnson and Lewis Csizmazia, for the beautiful cover design; and Dawn Burnett, Ally Glynn, Sara-Jade Virtue, Maxine Hitchcock, Georgina Bouzova, Alice Murphy and copy-editor extraordinaire, Clare Parkinson.

Thank you also to my film agents, Charlotte Knight and Tanya Tillett from Knight Hall Agency.

This is going to be my longest acknowledgements ever, because I have so many people to thank for their help with writing this book. We moved to Cambridge in August 2011, at the exact point in the story that Alice goes to university there, and it was such a joy to research the city that had become our new home.

Thank you to Victoria Parrin, Rachel Kittow and Kelly Clarke from Anglia Ruskin University. I wish I could go back in time and study English Lit with you – I'd join your Literary Society in a flash. Thank you also to Dr Colette Paul for putting me in touch with these three fantastic students. (NB: when Alice went to Anglia Ruskin, it was still called APU, but I've used Anglia Ruskin to avoid confusion.)

Thank you to the very kind Geoff Morley for showing me around Bridget's and Nightingale Halls and for his brilliant recollections of student life there. I wish there had been room in the book for maintenance man Clive and his legendary spooky stories!

And immense gratitude to He Who Shall Not Be Named for his assistance with Lukas's research. You risked the mirth of your colleagues (I still giggle every time I remember you saying you'd 'never live it down'), but you helped me more than you know and I sincerely appreciate it.

Huge thanks to Katherine Reid for the proofreading – I will be roping you in for years to come, whether you like it or not.

Cheers to Sarah Bailey and Tim Snelle (from Cambridge

Chauffeur Punts) for their punting advice, and thank you to their son 'Baby Jack' for entertaining Idha when my deadline was looming. Thank you also to the punters at Scudamores, and to Mille Rytter and Annabel Diggle.

Thank you to my sister-in-law Gretta Ford for her teaching guidance, to Karl Molden for his physics feedback (and Matthew Ford for putting me in touch with him!), to *Heat*'s film editor, Charles Gant, for the agent-related advice, to fellow S&S author Ali Harris for her support, friendship and the many, *many* cups of tea, to Vickie Robertson for introducing me to kingmaker all those years ago, to Chenoa Powell for the idea about 'the brother', and also to Wendy, Becky and Sarah for keeping me topped up with tea while I've been beavering away at 'my' table in the corner.

Thanks also to my friend Lucy Branch and her son Finn for inspiring the 'China' punting story. (Oh, and you're quite right, Lucy, I do think the bronze in the Guildhall could do with a bit of a polish. . .!)

On a more sombre note, the character of Lizzy was originally called Katy, but I renamed her in memory of my friend Helen's sister Elizabeth 'Lizzy' Angell, who passed away tragically and unexpectedly at the end of 2011. My Lizzy bears no resemblance to Lizzy Angell – she was one in seven billion and I would never attempt to recreate her in print – but she liked my books and we think she would have appreciated the sentiment.

Thank you, always, to my parents, Vern and Jenny Schuppan, and my parents-in-law Ian and Helga Toon. It's been a full-on year, and I couldn't have met the earlier deadline for this book without your help, especially Mum's.

And, of course, thank you to my husband, Greg, my son, Indy and my daughter, Idha. I love you all to bits.

Please read on for a taster of Paige Toon's
wonderful summer read

Baby Be Mine

Chapter 1

'Happy birthday to you,
Happy birthday to you,
Happy birthday, dear Barney,
Happy birthday to you.'

I'm singing this very quietly so as not to wake him. He's had a busy day with his nanny, grandad and me, and now he's crashed out in his cot. He's going to grow out of it soon. I can't believe my baby has just turned one. It's frightening how time flies.

Bit of a bummer that his daddy wasn't here today. I say that flippantly, but inside I'm not happy. Not happy at all. Then, suddenly, I'm fine again. It's the guilt. It balances out the anger. I can't stay cross with Christian for long. That word: 'Daddy'. It's a lie. I'm a liar. And I hate myself for it.

I can hear my parents clattering away in the bathroom next door. They'll be in bed soon, and then I'll have the living room to myself. I'm getting the urge again. My head is prickling with the thought of it. It will be the first time I've done it in six months. The last time was when Christian and I had a big fight.

That was before I knew. Before I knew for sure. But I'd suspected it for a long time.

Oh, Christian . . . What have I done?

One year and nine months ago, I had sex with my boyfriend's best friend. It sounds horrendous when you say it like that. Don't get me wrong, it is horrendous. But there was a history there. I was in love with Johnny. I was in love with him first.

I look back once more to my sleeping baby, who is no longer a baby. I lean over his cot and kiss him softly on his forehead as tears fill my eyes.

I'm so sorry, my darling. I don't know what to do.

If I told Christian now and he threw us out, as of course he would, how would my son be affected? Would he remember the person who was his father for the first year of his life? Christian is away such a lot at the moment that we're almost getting used to life without him. Maybe it wouldn't be such an upheaval. Maybe it would be okay. Oh, who am I kidding?

I think my parents have finally retired to bed. I get up and quietly walk out of my bedroom into the living room. My laptop screen is dark, the screensaver having switched itself off hours ago. I take a seat on the sofa and pull the computer onto my lap. My head is prickling again. I shouldn't be doing this.

'I thought you were in bed?'

I almost jump out of my skin at the sound of my mum's voice.

'You frightened me!'

'Sorry, I wanted a glass of water.'

I quickly push down the laptop lid and put the computer back on the side-table, the urge momentarily quashed. 'I was just checking my emails,' I lie as I get up and join my mum in the kitchen.

'Can't you do that in the morning?' she asks, pulling a bottle of water out of the fridge. 'You've had a busy day,' she adds.

'I know, I know,' I brush her off, not enjoying being told what to do, especially now that I'm a responsible parent myself. Allegedly.

'Have you spoken to Christian?' she asks as she decants water into a tumbler.

'No, I haven't called him back yet,' I admit.

'Don't you think you should? I'm sure he'd like to know about Barney's birthday.'

I bite my tongue and take the bottle from her, pouring a drink for myself. 'I will,' I reply shortly.

'Good,' she says annoyingly.

I follow her out of the kitchen and switch off all the lights, taking one last look at my laptop sitting silently on the side-table in the living room.

You'll keep . . .

I follow my mum down the corridor to the bedrooms. She and Dad are sleeping in Barney's room to the left of the bathroom, while he and his cot have been temporarily relocated into my bedroom on the right.

'Night, night.' Mum turns back to give me a peck on the cheek.

'Night,' I reply, and go into my bedroom.

I shut the door and take a deep breath before exhaling as quietly as I can. My iPhone is charging on my bedside table. I see that there's another message from Christian:

Boarding now. Will ring when I land

I feel bad. I should have called him earlier. I'm surprised to discover I'm looking forward to seeing him.

Why am I surprised? He's my boyfriend. I love him.

I know why: it's the guilt. It's poisonous. And deep down I know that it's going to be the death of our little family.

Paige Toon

Lucy in the Sky

A lawyer. A surfer. A 24-hour flight. The frequent liar points are clocking up and Lucy's got choices to make . . .

It's been nine years since Lucy left Australia. Nine years since she's seen her best friend Molly, and Sam, the one-time love of her life. Now her two friends are getting married. To each other. And Lucy is on her way to Sydney for their wedding.

Life for Lucy has moved on. She's happily settled with James, her gorgeous lawyer boyfriend, with their flat in London and her glamorous job in PR. Surely there's no reason to expect this two-week holiday in the sun will be anything out of the ordinary?

But just before take-off, Lucy receives a text from James's mobile. She can't resist taking a look . . . and, in one push of a button, her world comes crashing down . . .

'I loved it – I couldn't put it down!' MARIAN KEYES

ISBN 978-1-84739-043-1
PRICE £7.99

Paige Toon

Johnny Be Good

Lots of girls fall for their bosses . . . but how many work for the hottest rock star on the planet?

I'm Meg Stiles. This is my leaving party. And that song we're making a mockery of? That's written by one of the biggest rock stars in the world. And I'm moving in with him tomorrow. Seriously! I am not even kidding you. Well, maybe I'm misleading you a little bit. You see, I haven't actually met him yet . . .

No, I'm not a stalker. I'm his new PA. His Personal Assistant. And I am off to La-la Land. Los Angeles. The City Of Angels – whatever you want to call it – and I can't bloody believe it!

Celebrity PA to wild boy of rock Johnny Jefferson, Meg's glam new life in sun-drenched LA is a whirlwind of showbiz parties and backstage passes. Cool, calm Christian, in town to write his famous friend's biography, helps keep Meg's feet firmly on the ground. But with Johnny's piercing green eyes and a body Brad Pitt would kill for, how long will it be before she's swept right off them again?

'Wonderful, addictive, sharp and sexy' COSMOPOLITAN

ISBN 978-1-84739-044-8

Paige Toon

Chasing Daisy

If you fall too fast . . . you might just crash.

'You don't have to worry about me. I have no intention of getting my heart broken again.'

Of course I'm lying. I feel like Will is chipping a little piece of it away, day by day. It's killing me . . .

Daisy Rogers is in love . . . and that's no good thing. It's not just that her very famous ex is neither out of sight *nor* out of mind, but that the man of her dreams, William Trust, has a girlfriend – a childhood sweetheart, no less – and as a Formula 1 racing driver, he puts his life at risk every day he goes to work.

From Melbourne to Monte Carlo, and São Paolo to Singapore, Daisy and her best friend Holly travel the world as hospitality girls on the Grand Prix scene. But with more secrets between them than Paris Hilton has shoes, life promises to be nothing short of a whirlwind.

'Laugh-out-loud funny and touchingly honest . . . This is summer's poolside reading sorted!' . . . *Company*

ISBN 978-1-84739-390-6

PRICE £6.99

Paige Toon

Pictures of Lily

'Will you marry me?'

I think of you, then. I think of you every day. But usually in the quietest part of the morning, or the darkest part of the night. Not when my boyfriend of two years has just proposed.

I look up at Richard with his hopeful eyes. 'Lily?' he prompts.

It's been ten years, but it feels like only yesterday that you left. How can I say yes to Richard with all my heart when most of it has always belonged to you?

I take a deep breath and will myself to speak . . .

Ten years ago when Lily was just sixteen, she fell in love with someone she *really* shouldn't have fallen in love with. Now, living in Sydney and engaged to another man, she can't forget the one that got away. Then her past comes back to haunt her, and she has to make a decision that will break her heart – and the heart of at least one of the men who love her.

ISBN 978-1-84739-391-3

PRICE £6.99

Paige Toon

Baby Be Mine

'He's not mine, is he?'

That's the question I fear the most.

You see, I have a secret. My son is not fathered by my boyfriend, but by one of the most famous rock stars that ever lived. And he doesn't even know it.

One-time celebrity personal assistant to wild boy of rock Johnny Jefferson, Meg Stiles is now settled and living in the south of France with her doting boyfriend Christian and their son Barney.

But they're living a lie – a lie that will turn their lives upside down and inside out – because as Barney reaches his first birthday, Meg can no longer deny that her son is growing to look more and more like his rock star father every day, and less and less like Christian, and sooner or later, the world is going to realise . . .

'Fun, summery, chick-lit with bite – if you want a bit of escapism, this is perfect poolside fodder.' Cosmopolitan

ISBN 978-1-84983-126-0

PRICE £6.99